THE RETURN OF THE RIPPER

THE SHERLOCK HOLMES
AND LUCY JAMES MYSTERIES

The Last Moriarty
The Wilhelm Conspiracy
Remember, Remember
The Crown Jewel Mystery
The Jubilee Problem
Death at the Diogenes Club

The series page at Amazon:
amzn.to/2s9U2jW

For a FREE copy of
THE CROWN JEWEL MYSTERY – the prequel to the series
please visit sherlockandlucy.com

OTHER TITLES BY ANNA ELLIOTT

The Pride and Prejudice Chronicles:
Georgiana Darcy's Diary
Pemberly to Waterloo
Kitty Bennet's Diary

Sense and Sensibility Mysteries:
Margaret Dashwood's Diary

The Twilight of Avalon Series:
Dawn of Avalon
The Witch Queen's Secret
Twilight of Avalon
Dark Moon of Avalon
Sunrise of Avalon

The Susanna and the Spy Series:
Susanna and the Spy
London Calling

OTHER TITLES BY CHARLES VELEY

Novels:
Play to Live
Night Whispers
Children of the Dark

Nonfiction:
Catching Up

THE RETURN OF THE RIPPER

OF THE

A SHERLOCK HOLMES | LUCY JAMES MYSTERY

BY ANNA ELLIOTT AND CHARLES VELEY

Typesetting by FormattingExperts.com
Cover design by Todd A. Johnson

ISBN: 978-0-9991191-4-3

PREFACE

Fear washed through me in a cold, slimy wave before I even opened my eyes. My head was throbbing, my whole body hurt, and a part of me wanted to just sink back into unconsciousness. That way, I wouldn't have to face whatever was going to confront me when I came fully awake and remembered—

Sometimes memories trickled back slowly. This one, though, hit me with the sharp precision of a knife sliding between my ribs.

Baker Street ... the window breaking ... chloroform ... Becky's scream ...

My eyes flew open, and I sat bolt upright—which made my head spin and my stomach twist, bile rising in my throat. I had to press my fingertips against my eyes to stop the world from tilting sideways.

Which was when I discovered the manacle and chain around my right wrist.

That moment occurred nearly three months ago. It is one I truly wish I could forget. But I cannot. I can only try to get outside it. To do that, I must set down in my journal many, many others—all those moments that came before and after.

Lucy James
London, 4 January, 1898

Lucy James has been kind enough to let me read her notes on a recent adventure we shared with Holmes late in the autumn of the past year. For a brief time, parts of the affair transfixed all of London. There were other aspects of which Lucy was not aware, however, so I have added my notes to hers. For obvious reasons, this account will not be published during this century nor the next.

John H. Watson, M.D.
London, 18 January, 1898

PART ONE

WATSON

1. A HARBINGER

My account begins on the morning of October 6, 1897, when Sherlock Holmes and I learned that a young woman had been murdered in Whitechapel.

I had overslept. The midnight chimes of the church clock had jarred me out of a distressing dream, and I tossed and turned and listened to the rain pelting down against my sleeping room window until the first gray light of dawn emerged between the curtains. Then, perversely, I fell into a heavy slumber, not waking until the sound of voices and breakfast dishes came from below my sleeping room at 221B Baker Street. I dressed hastily and shaved badly, and I was still groggy when I came down my stairs to our sitting room.

My first glance at our breakfast table showed me that Lucy James, Holmes's daughter and frequent investigative partner, had come and gone. Her plate and coffee cup and napkin were stacked tidily on a tray opposite Holmes's usual place. Breakfast had been prepared by Mrs. Hudson in her kitchen, of course. Lucy had taken the spare flat on the ground floor below ours, partly as a security precaution and partly because of the distressing memories associated with her former residence on Exeter Street. She had lately begun the practice of carrying up our meals on those occasions when she wanted to see Holmes. I was always glad to see her, particularly at breakfast, for that meant she had come home safely from the previous night's performance at the Savoy Theatre. Holmes and I both worried about her safety, though neither of us admitted it.

I was also gratified to see Holmes's napkin and utensils atop his own plate on his side of our table, which indicated that he had also breakfasted. He was now in his chair by the fireside, his face hidden behind an unfolded newspaper, wreathed in a blue-gray cloud of shag tobacco smoke. A stack of unread newspapers lay before him on the hassock, and more papers, those he had already perused, lay in an untidy heap on the carpet.

I filled my own plate with a generous helping of Mrs. Hudson's scrambled eggs, crisp bacon, and buttered toast, and was about to sit down when I heard Holmes's voice coming from behind the newspaper.

"I have ordered a cab for Downing Street. Ten o'clock."

I consulted my watch. The time was half past nine. At eleven, we were due at Downing Street for an appointment with Sir Michael Hicks Beach, Chancellor of the Exchequer. Holmes had been looking forward to the meeting ever since it had been arranged, more than a week ago.

"Then I shall have a half hour to enjoy a leisurely breakfast," I replied.

"I fear not. Inspector Lestrade will be here soon."

"You've heard from him?"

"I have not."

"What makes you think he is coming?"

"An incident reported in *The Morning Post* tells me that his arrival is inevitable." Holmes paused. Then he went on, "It's just as well that Lucy did not notice it."

He was silent as I poured my coffee. There was no point in querying him about the incident. He would tell me what he wanted to tell me in his own time, if he told me anything at all.

Then he said, "I take it congratulations to you are in order, then?"

"Why?"

"Your editor at *The Strand* has engaged you on a new project."

My cheeks flushed hot. "How do you know that?"

"You remarked on receiving his letter when you took it from your mail basket two days ago. You went out for an appointment yesterday afternoon. You returned with a new leather-bound notebook and reservoir pen, which you unwrapped in my presence. And, as I know you would not break our understanding by allowing yourself to become engaged in a retelling of any of our current adventures since I returned from the Reichenbach Falls—"

He paused, lowered his newspaper, and looked at me expectantly. His hawk-like features and keen gray eyes appeared perfectly tranquil.

"That goes without saying, Holmes."

"Therefore, I conclude that you have a new writing project and that it must be one of your own invention."

"I admit that the other links in your chain of reasoning are sound," I said. "But your last conclusion is incorrect."

"You did not invent the new project?"

"I had it thrust upon me, so to speak. My editor has a client— a charity for deserving young women—which needs someone to document the success of the organization in a way that will attract donations. The editor thought that since my name is already known to the public—"

Holmes interrupted in the dismissive, perfunctory way he adopts when he wishes to move the discussion along to other matters. "Then the outcome is satisfactory. You will gratify your natural need for public acclaim, and perhaps your association with the charitable organization will prove congenial. I take it you have already met the lady in charge."

I felt my cheeks go hot once more. "How could you possibly know that?"

For a long moment he regarded me with what I thought was a mixture of fondness and disappointment. It flashed through my mind that I must have betrayed my feelings in some manner that was obvious to him but of which I was unaware.

At that moment, we heard the sound of our bell-pull being rung.

"That will be Lestrade," Holmes said. He folded his newspaper and tossed it aside onto the pile. "We will continue this conversation another time."

* * *

Inspector Lestrade soon was admitted by Mrs. Hudson and appeared on our doorstep, hat in hand, squinting and shivering in his wet mackintosh. He gratefully accepted Holmes's direction to warm himself at the fire and stood for a time on our hearthstones, hands out to absorb the heat as small puddles of rainwater spread from beneath his worn brown boots. His wary, close-set eyes and slumped, furtive posture showed the effects of the grinding frustrations that were his lot as a detective inspector in the great city. Perhaps to compensate, Lestrade had an irritating habit of assuming that his position as a police official made him superior to an amateur such as Holmes—until the opposite was made evident. Yet Lestrade's officious pride never seemed to nettle Holmes, who frequently gave Lestrade credit for successful outcomes in cases that Holmes himself had solved.

Now, Holmes leaned forward. "Inspector, I trust the warmth of the fire has done its work. Will you take coffee? No? Brandy, perhaps? No? Well then. Pray take the chair across from me. I take it you wish to discuss the Mitre Square killing."

Lestrade's pinched features opened up into a cagy, knowing smile. "You have read the papers."

"*The Post*, to be precise. Beyond what I found there, I know nothing. What do you know?"

"Well, Mr. Holmes, I expect that you already have your response prepared to what you think I'm going to tell you. You're going to say what you always say, that every time a dead woman turns up in Whitechapel, the entire Metropolitan police force flies into a panic, thinking the Ripper may have returned. And now that you've read *The Post*, you're going to point out that aside from the location of Mitre Square, where the fifth victim of the Ripper was found, there is no resemblance whatever between this killing and those of nearly a decade ago. You're going to point out that the woman found in Mitre Square last night was strangled and that all the victims of the Ripper were set upon with a knife. Then you're going to wave your hand in an airy gesture of dismissal."

A flicker of interest passed across Holmes's hooded eyes. "So you do know something that is not in *The Post*."

Lestrade fairly beamed. "I know the victim was stabbed, Mr. Holmes. Stabbed in the heart by a narrow blade. And if this really is our man, and we can bring him in—"

"Where is the body?"

"St. Thomas Hospital. We had it moved from Whitechapel to keep away from the press."

Holmes stood. "Is your police coach outside? Yes? Then, Watson, get your coat and umbrella."

"Are we not going to Downing Street?" I asked.

Lestrade's eyes widened.

"We can walk there from the hospital," Holmes replied, "after we have seen what we need to see." To Lestrade, he said, "The Downing Street matter is an unrelated one."

2. AN UNIDENTIFIED BODY

We splashed and clattered through the rain in Lestrade's police carriage, crossing Westminster Bridge to St. Thomas's Hospital, a shadowy presence barely visible through the mist and fog. When we emerged, just outside the hospital entrance, I saw no sign of damage from the bomb that Colonel Moran had detonated nearly two years earlier, but I was hurrying in the rain. Queen Victoria's bronze statue was still intact and regarding us with majesty as we passed through the lobby.

A bespectacled young attendant appeared and, after introducing himself as pathologist's assistant Dawkins, led us, not to the amphitheater for surgical demonstrations, but to a long, dimly-lit basement corridor. Green-lettered signs proclaimed the corridor as the pathology department. Ahead we could see the open doorway to a narrow, white-tiled room, which evidently was our destination. On the right side of the corridor was a row of doors. One of these doors opened as we passed, and I saw the familiar figure of Sir Edward Bradford, Commissioner of the Metropolitan Police.

I was saddened to see that Sir Edward looked more fragile than when we had last seen him in July. White-haired and with a flowing white mustache, he still held himself erect in his old military manner, but he appeared to have lost weight from his already sparse frame and did not move with his usual crisp energy. He nodded at Holmes and stepped aside, out of the way of our little procession. "Go on, Lestrade," he said. "You know the way." His voice trembled as he spoke, and he brought his one hand up to his chin as if to bring the trembling under control.

The commissioner had been a friend to us for a number of years. He had taken up his duties in 1890, after the first Ripper case had, in effect, driven away the previous incumbent. An empty sleeve was pinned against his left side, the missing arm a reminder of his days in India and an unfortunate encounter with an Indian tigress.

The bespectacled attendant led us into the white-tiled room. "I'll leave you to it, gentlemen," he said. "If you need anything, just ring for me."

I noticed there were no chairs. At the center of the room on a marble slab lay the body of a young woman, clad in a torn and dirty skirt and coat. One side of her face had been disfigured. My eyes were drawn to an ugly, dark-red, open wound where her cheekbone had been smashed. The blackening crimson contrasted with the garish red of the lip rouge smeared around her mouth.

Squinting a little at the harsh electric light of the mortuary, Commissioner Bradford made a come-along gesture to the man behind him, a tall, ruddy gentleman whose leather surgeon's apron partially covered a well-tailored suit. When we were all inside, the commissioner asked Lestrade to close the door and then turned to make introductions. The moment was somewhat awkward, because Holmes had gone directly to the lifeless figure at the center of the room. He was leaning down to inspect one of the woman's muddy shoes when the commissioner spoke.

"Gentlemen, this is Doctor Matthew Burleigh. Dr. Watson, you may already be familiar with his very promising work with tubercular patients at the Burleigh Clinic."

"An honor," I said, shaking his meaty hand and looking up to meet the sharp, blue-eyed gaze of this robust, hale-fellow-well-met gentleman. I had no inkling of what research was being conducted at the Burleigh Clinic, but I did not say so.

"An honor for me as well," said the doctor. He gave a nod to the commissioner. "Sir Edward is kind enough to serve on the board of our clinic. So, when he asked me to come round as an independent third party for a discreet examination, I was only too happy to oblige. And, Mr. Holmes," he went on, raising his voice, "it is my pleasure to meet you."

Holmes had been focused on his examination of the dead woman. Now, he looked up, but only briefly. "Likewise for me, of course, Doctor Burleigh. Forgive my haste. We are somewhat pressed for time this morning." He was holding the lapel of the mud-stained coat worn by the dead woman. "Has anything been taken from the body?"

The commissioner said, "Nothing. She had no purse. Her pockets were empty."

"Who discovered the knife wound?"

"The constable on duty. He opened her jacket to see if there were identification papers, and of course there were none, but then he saw the tear in her blouse. He knew that the tear signified a knife wound, so he called in, and the call was directed to me. We had the body brought here, as it is close to the Yard and—"

Holmes, holding up the other lapel of the shabby coat, interrupted. "Here is something else. A paper, pinned to the underside of the lapel."

He pulled out a small hairpin and held it carefully between his index finger and thumb, handing me a small, folded piece of paper with his other hand. "Watson," he said. "Would you please read what is written here?"

The note contained two words, printed in block capitals with black ink. My heart froze as I read aloud these words:

I RETURN

"The constable ought not to have overlooked that," said Lestrade. "I shall have a word with him."

"So the knife wound has the meaning we had feared," said the commissioner.

"Someone appears to want us to believe that," said Holmes.

"You do not think this is the work of the Ripper?"

"It is too soon to say," Holmes replied. He went on, as though musing to himself. "Death was not caused by the knife, judging from the minimal bloodstains around the tear in her jacket and blouse. There are bruises around the neck, which indicate that the throat may have been crushed or the breath shut off for sufficient time to so as to cause suffocation. The stabbing was likely an afterthought. And the note"—his voice trailed off for a moment as he considered—"the note appears to be a clumsy gesture. As if the metropolitan police would not think to connect the location of the body and the type of victim with the Ripper himself and needed to be prodded into the conclusion."

"Why would he hide the note?" asked the commissioner.

"He very likely thought someone would take it as a trophy if he left it in plain view," Lestrade said. "So he concealed it, knowing it would eventually be discovered by the authorities."

The commissioner said, "There may be something in that. After all, the Ripper has shown that he wants to humiliate the authorities just as much as he wants to degrade his victims." He paused and then added, musingly, "Although this poor creature appears to have fallen far indeed, even before she met her murderer."

"She nonetheless deserves justice," I said.

"Don't we all," said Lestrade.

Holmes said nothing.

Burleigh stood alongside Holmes, looking down at the body. "The woman of the streets, done to death in Whitechapel, with a triumphant note. Surely that fits the pattern, Mr. Holmes?"

"The pattern of nine years ago," Holmes replied. "Yet I do not believe those characteristics are all true in this case."

"Which ones do you doubt?"

Holmes appeared to have lost interest in the exchange. He strode over to my umbrella, which lay where I had left it leaning against the radiator. "Now, regrettably, Watson and I must depart for another appointment. I will read the report of the examination as soon as you make it available. Also, Commissioner, later this afternoon I would like to visit the location where the body was found. In the meantime, I would urge you to keep an open mind and to test for the presence of chloroform or some other sedative."

* * *

A few minutes later, we were outside the hospital, beneath my umbrella, walking at a rapid pace in the rain towards Westminster Bridge.

I said what was on my mind and in my heart. "We cannot conceal this matter from Lucy. She will want to help."

"We will tell her this evening, after I have read the laboratory report."

"You do not think the dead woman was a doxy," I said.

"Her shoes, skirt, and coat were badly worn. But they did not fit, and her stockings and petticoats were new. Her palms and fingertips were begrimed with mud, as was her coat. Yet the side of her face that remained intact was clean, and her neck was clean enough to allow the bruises left by the fingers of her assailant to be plainly visible."

"You did not point that out."

He sounded somewhat nettled by my remark. "Doctor Burleigh is no doubt competent, and the hospital has an excellent staff, which the commissioner will not hesitate to employ. And I may learn something useful at Mitre Square."

"You do not wish me to come with you?"

"You have your appointment at the Bethnal Green School," he replied.

"How do you know that?"

"You left the brochure on our table yesterday, and you told Mrs. Hudson you would be out this afternoon." He gave me an appraising look. "You may want to stop at a barber's for a proper shave."

Our walk to Downing Street lasted roughly ten minutes. During that time, Holmes said nothing further.

WATSON

3. A STUDY IN DIAMONDS

I wondered why the two Queen's Guards were standing outside the door to the Residence of Sir Michael Hicks Beach, Chancellor of Her Majesty's Exchequer. Normally the Queen's guards stand outside The Prime Minister's residence at Number 10, immediately adjacent.

The guards stepped aside as Holmes strode briskly towards the unassuming entrance to the residence. A curtain in one of the lower windows moved slightly.

The door opened before we could knock.

Sir Michael himself stood before us, black-bearded, stern, and hatchet-faced, and as tall as Holmes. A frown furrowed his thick black eyebrows. We had seen him several months previously, during the Queen's Jubilee celebrations on the occasion of Holmes's most recent triumph for Her Majesty's government. Today, he seemed preoccupied, as though dreading an unpleasant duty. He held a finger to his lips. "Thank you for coming," he said quietly, stepping aside and motioning us into the hallway. "The staff are upstairs, so we shall not be disturbed. It is as well they do not know of your presence. Mr. Rhodes is in the dining room. We can go straight through my study."

Cecil Rhodes stood up from the table as we entered, gray-faced, gray-haired, overweight, and quite unhealthy, a wan smile on his round, dropsical face. One of the wealthiest men in the empire, he had been prominent in British and South African politics of late. His enemies claimed he had fomented war with the Boers for his own gain and at the expense of British lives. His pleasant, open features had once been cherubic, I thought. Now they had grown misshapen with age and possibly excess. There were dark pouches beneath his eyes, and his cheeks sagged like the edges of a partially-deflated balloon. He gasped for a moment, recovering from the effort of standing, hands on the edge of the table. Yet his hair and mustache were precisely trimmed, his eye was keen, and his voice, when he finally spoke, was steady.

"Mr. Holmes. Doctor Watson. Thank you for coming. I know I look a right mess. I have not had time to change my attire since I arrived from Paris this morning. You no doubt have read all about what a heartless imperialist toad I am. Indeed, I fear I am such a pariah that Sir Michael can't even let his servants see me. Yet I hope you will not judge me too quickly."

"First impressions are false more often than not, in my line of work," said Holmes.

We all sat. Rhodes took us in with a long and appraising glance. Then he nodded to Hicks Beach. "Thank you for arranging the meeting, Mr. Chancellor."

Rhodes took from his waistcoat pocket two small linen sacks, each pulled shut at the top with a yellow drawstring. He set them on the table and worked the top of each open with a fat finger. Then he turned the first sack upside down, spilling the contents onto the polished ebony surface.

Two dozen or so stones, tan and cream-colored like bits of soap, clattered onto the table. Rhodes carefully arranged them into a small pile.

"Rough diamonds, Mr. Holmes," Rhodes said. He tapped the centre of the pile. "A few ounces, and worth perhaps fifty thousand pounds sterling, depending on how successfully they are cut."

Then Rhodes upended the other small linen sack. Onto the polished surface clattered a like number of exquisite diamonds. Even though the door to the room was shut, Rhodes lowered his voice. "You see here, Mr. Holmes, the reason for the guards outside. This little pile has been cut successfully. Its value is more than double that of the others."

"Enough to outfit a small army," said Sir Michael. "And just for the sake of politeness and clarity, Mr. Rhodes, no one in this house would call you a pariah. These sparklers are the real reason why my servants were relegated to the upstairs. We cannot afford prying eyes and wagging tongues."

Holmes barely glanced at the stones. He said, "I take it that diamonds are being stolen from your company."

Rhodes nodded.

Holmes turned to Sir Michael. "And from your reference to an army, you believe the diamonds are being sold to foment rebellion in the empire."

"You have it, Mr. Holmes," said Sir Michael.

An awkward silence ensured.

Finally, Sir Michael asked, "Mr. Holmes. We cannot allow rebellion to go unchecked. We need to cut off the source of funds to these brigands. That is the reason for your presence here today. Will you help us?"

Holmes shook his head. "There are innumerable opportunities for theft at your mines, Mr. Rhodes, and countless more along the routes those diamonds must travel as they make their way to London, where they are cut and polished, and then out of London. This is a job for a large organization, not one detective."

"We have called upon our best men in the army and the navy and the police force to address the problem," said Sir Michael. "To no avail."

"I have even retained the Pinkertons," said Rhodes. "And yet, over the past year, a hundred times the amount of raw diamonds you see before you has gone missing from our mines."

"Once again, Mr. Holmes," said Sir Michael. "Will you help us?"

"We will give you all the information you need," Rhodes said. "I can arrange an appointment with the head of the diamond syndicate in Hatton Garden. I can give you the names of the diamond cutters we employ, show you all the transportation records, and provide the names of the shipping companies—"

Holmes held up a hand. "If I take the case, I shall want no introductions. Indeed, no one in your organization, Mr. Rhodes, should be aware that I am involved in any way."

Sir Michael's look showed puzzlement. "*If*, Mr. Holmes?"

"There are pressing matters that occupy my time at the moment."

It flashed through my mind that Holmes had looked forward to this meeting when the invitation first came. Yet now he was reluctant. Was he being deliberately uncooperative? I wondered if he might have some personal aversion to Rhodes and was being diffident due to the presence of the Chancellor and the Secretary. Yet this was not his manner, nor his character. He would generally speak the bald truth, as baldly as possible, in fact.

What could possibly be more important?

Rhodes leaned forward, face florid, eyes wide open, mouth gasping for a moment as though in disbelief. "I will pay your transport first class to Johannesburg. Or wherever in the empire you choose. I will pay whatever fee you name."

"I will not make the journey. As I said, there are other pressing matters."

I wondered. Was he thinking of the young woman found murdered in Mitre Square? Was he thinking of the note he had discovered beneath her lapel?

Rhodes continued. "Mr. Holmes, there are British lives at stake. There are British citizens who will lose their children. There are British soldiers who will die because of the ordinance purchased with those diamonds."

Sir Michael interposed. "British soldiers will die in India as well. And in Ireland. And in the Suez. And in other places where rebellion lies temporarily dormant."

Holmes sat silent. I could see that he was considering the problem, however, for his hand moved for a moment in the direction of his jacket pocket, where he kept his pipe. But then he folded both his hands on the table.

Rhodes gave Holmes a shrewd look. "Surely you are not one of those milksop do-gooders who think we could do away with theft by paying higher wages."

"Criminals will always be with us," Holmes replied.

"Then what is your objection? Come, man, out with it! I have read Dr. Watson's narratives. You positively revel in a difficult problem. Well, this one will give you difficulties aplenty."

"You need not travel," said Sir Michael. "But we need you now."

"Why now?"

Sir Michael turned to Rhodes. "You must swear not to divulge what I am about to tell Mr. Holmes."

Rhodes said, "I'm surprised you would even say that. But, yes, I will swear."

"Our agents have got wind of a great series of attacks being planned against British forces and British capital throughout the Empire, to show the vulnerability of British rule and to encourage rebellion. The attacks are to be simultaneous. The day the outrages are to be perpetrated is referred to among the rebels as 'the day of reckoning.' "

"The attacks will fail, of course," said Rhodes.

"But they will inspire others," Sir Michael said. "And those, in turn, will inspire more attacks. And those will inspire still more, so that more and more lives will be lost and more and more suffering will ensue, until one day—"

He looked at me, as though willing me to use my influence to persuade my friend, and I saw what he was driving at. I said, "Until one day the British people will grow weary of the struggle."

"You have it, Dr. Watson."

"Do you know when the attacks are planned?" Holmes asked.

"Early in the Spring of next year," Sir Michael replied. "According to our reports. When that time comes, there will be hundreds, even thousands, of families who will be mourning unless we can prevent it."

Holmes's eyes flickered, first to Rhodes, and then to Sir Michael.

"My methods will be unorthodox, and I shall work alone," he said. "If I need the assistance of the government, I shall communicate through my brother. Or through Dr. Watson."

Sir Michael looked relieved. "You shall have whatever assistance you require."

Holmes's long forefinger tapped the table, pointing in the direction of the two small piles of precious stones. "I shall also need those diamonds, Mr. Rhodes."

WATSON

4. ᗩNOTHER PLᗩ₵E,
ᗩ LESSER ₵RIME

Minutes later we were outside, in a London four-wheeler cab, on the way to Mitre Square. Holmes seemed not the least concerned that he was carrying on his person diamonds worth more than I could imagine, likely enough to buy every house and furnishing on Baker Street and even beyond, or to build another Buckingham Palace.

I waited for him to speak, but he merely stared out the window, his thoughts goodness knew where.

Finally, I could stand it no longer. "You had been looking forward to that meeting for a week," I said. "Yet, for a while, I thought you were going to refuse to help."

He said, "I told Lucy this morning that I have made the arrangements for her wedding. In St. Paul's chapel. December the 18th."

"You might ask her and Jack to postpone—"

Holmes continued to stare out the window, but he did speak. He said, "Until?"

I saw. There would always be a case. He would always fill his mind with work.

I nodded.

I do not think he noticed, but he went on. "It is the only choice I can make that does not ensure disappointment. Lucy would, I have no doubt, give up the public wedding if she were asked to do so. But her mother—"

Holmes paused, and it occurred to me how rarely he called Zoe Rosario, Lucy's mother, by name. With some men, that might have signaled indifference. With Holmes, I suspected that the exact reverse was true.

Holmes's voice was even as he went on, and yet his tone had altered in some indefinable way. "Lucy's mother was forced to miss witnessing every significant milestone in Lucy's life: her first infant words, her first steps ... her first entrance into school, her graduation, and her first performance on stage. Now she has the chance to see her daughter married—to be fully present for this milestone, at least. I can do no less than give her this moment, for it will be in her memory for her lifetime."

I nodded. Holmes had not said as much, but I knew that he bore the guilt of never having known of Lucy's existence until two years ago and of not having sought Zoe out after their brief affair. Because Holmes had remained apart, focused on the pursuit of his career as the world's first consulting detective, Zoe had been left alone and vulnerable to the Moriarty gang, who had forced her to give up her baby and endure the grief of twenty years' separation from her child.

Holmes pursed his lips and went on. "Yet, the dangers associated with a public ceremony are troubling."

"Your enemies will notice."

He drew a long breath. "I urge you not to speak to Lucy of my fears. I cannot have her think I am reluctant to give her the wedding she deserves. I grumble about all the bothersome preparations, naturally, but I do not wish her to think that I worry about the danger."

"Doubtless she already knows, Holmes," I said.

He was silent until we reached Mitre Square. Then he said, "You go on to your appointment, Watson."

Clutching his umbrella, he fairly leaped out of the cab.

As we drove away, I saw him putting up the umbrella and motioning to get the attention of a uniformed constable and Lestrade. Both men stood nearby, out of the rain, waiting in the shelter of a shadowy brick archway.

* * *

I felt a surge of excitement as the cab pulled over alongside The Bethnal Green School for Orphaned Girls. The dingy brick façade of the building itself was far from inspiring, particularly in the rain, which streaked the soot along the dirty, cracked glass of the large window at the entrance. Judging from the shops on either side—one a jumble store and the other a rundown pawnshop, the school had once been, like its companions, a store on its ground level and tenement flats on its upper floors. But I took inspiration in the dreariness of my surroundings. I resolved to seek out the gold within the dross so that I could in turn inspire donations to improve the building and the lives of those within it.

As Holmes had suspected, the previous day I had indeed met "the lady in charge" of the school when I met with my editor at *The Strand*. By coincidence, she had known my late wife, Mary, when the two were young ladies at a finishing school together.

It was that association, she said, which caused her to visit my editor and to hope that I would consent to help her. Also, she said, she appreciated the way I wrote of women in my accounts of Holmes's and my adventures.

I had accepted without hesitation. Indeed, I had tucked the school brochure she had given me into my overcoat pocket and then stopped at a stationer's where I purchased a new notebook. Moreover, I had to admit to myself, my anticipation of the impending meeting was what had kept me from sleep in the hours before dawn.

I opened the door with some effort, noticing that the paint was worn and the wood had warped and swollen. The lobby—if that was what term I might use to describe what had once been the ground floor store area—was deserted and had a musty odour. Before me was a once-varnished counter behind which a store clerk had once sat. Behind the counter, the wall was festooned with rows of yellowing pages of paper, on which slogans and hand-colored pictures had been emblazoned in alternating columns. The papers had been nailed to the edges of empty shelves, all the way up to the ceiling.

One of the pictures showed a little girl in a school uniform reaching up to take the hand of a white-robed young woman. The slogan beside the picture read, "We'll wiser grow with every day." Glancing at the other pictures, I saw they were all similarly composed, each with a little girl being assisted in some manner by a white-robed young woman.

Behind the counter there was a mirror from which my reflection stared blankly back at me. I hardly ever notice myself in mirrors, but today I did. My mustache was tidy enough. My posture was beginning to stoop a little. I drew myself more upright. My cheeks, I noticed, had begun so sag a bit with age. I smiled to bring them up and erase my jowls. The effect was an unnatural grimace.

You are a grinning fool, Watson.

I walked around the counter and looked beneath, finding only darkness. The musty odour was stronger behind me. The wood frame of the large shop window was also peeling and warped. Puddles of rainwater glistened intermittently around the edge of the room that faced the street.

I called out, "Is anyone there?"

Then, from above me, at the back of the darkened room, I heard a familiar woman's voice. "Just a moment, Doctor Watson!"

Moments later, Lady Amelia Scott, the major benefactor of the school and the woman who had invited me here, appeared, descending the long staircase. She seemed to float, her hand barely touching the rail. Her auburn tresses seemed like an aura surrounding her welcoming face, like the red and gold clouds that sometimes accompany a sunrise. I had a glimpse of her mid-calf patent leather boots. "Oh dear," she said. "You are fifteen minutes early, I believe. We are quite alone."

In a moment, she was at my side. She wore a bright blue crinoline dress with puffed sleeves, and I had the brief impression of a jasmine scent. The boots she wore made her slightly taller than me. She looked down to meet my gaze with a whimsical smile, giving me a brief, firm handshake.

"You must be drenched from the rain. Let me take your hat!" So saying, she lifted it from my head. Then, with the same whimsical smile, she placed it atop her head and turned to examine her reflection in the mirror behind the counter. Beside her, I appeared gray, worn and bedraggled. I resisted the urge to draw myself more upright once again. She was meeting my gaze in the mirror.

"I fear it does not quite suit my outfit," she said. "And it makes me taller still, which is not an advantage beside a handsome gentleman of your height." She put my hat on the countertop and spun around to face me. I noticed that her eyes were a bright blue, very nearly a match for her electric blue dress. She seemed to be regarding me with a mixture of amusement and compassion. For some reason, I was reminded of Holmes.

I said, "The young ladies will be here soon?"

"They should have been here five minutes ago. Returning from the museum, with their instructor. It is a fabulous resource for their instruction. But while I have the opportunity, I have a small favor to ask of you. First, of course, I do want to express my deepest appreciation for your agreeing to take on this project and to lend your talents to our small cause. As you can see"—her eyes turned back to the damp and dinginess that surrounded us—"we are indeed in desperate need of funds."

"Only too pleased. It will be a new challenge."

Her blue eyes held mine. "I'm so glad. Now, as I mentioned, I also do have that small favor."

"Please name it."

"I hope to employ your detective skills in a small but extremely sensitive matter at my town home in Grosvenor Square. A small theft has been committed, and I need someone with wit, intelligence, and utmost discretion to identify the thief."

LUCY

5. AT GROSVENOR SQUARE

"And you are engaged to be married." The Right Honorable Lady Violet Haggerston looked from me to Jack, raising her voice to be heard above the chatter of voices all around. "Good heavens, can you actually *keep* a wife on a police sergeant's salary?"

Lady Violet was a thin, horse-faced woman of somewhere around forty, with straw-colored hair and slightly prominent blue eyes.

"Not that I have ever spoken to a policeman personally." Lady Violet paused, allowing us to imagine the absurdity of such a thing. "But I thought they paid public servants practically *nothing.*"

Jack smiled pleasantly. "Luckily the job's glamorous enough to make up for it."

I snorted, then coughed trying to cover up a laugh. I happened to know that Jack had spent the majority of the day before with the dozen police constables under his command, hunting through refuse heaps in a dirty back alley for the knife dropped by a murder suspect.

Lady Violet gave Jack a puzzled frown. She—thankfully— wasn't our hostess for the afternoon, but had latched onto us soon after our arrival at the tea party and had instantly devoted her full attention to being poisonous.

To give her credit, if she had sat up the night before transcribing a list of the rudest, most condescending remarks she could possibly make, she couldn't be doing a better job.

Although she had, by now, to be growing frustrated. I had been silently grinding my teeth from somewhere around the two-minute mark of our conversation, but nothing she said seemed to bother Jack in the slightest.

Now she laughed, rather uncertainly, raising her voice to be heard above the noise of the other guests.

The room had been decorated in the Palladian style, with high ceilings and plasterwork frescoes on the walls. For the party, the doors between the saloon and the drawing room had been thrown open, creating a space large enough to hold the fifty-odd guests who were in attendance.

"How very … ah, amusing. But do tell me." Lady Violet leaned forward. "As a member of our police force, how much do you value civil liberty as opposed to the authority of the law?"

Jack's calmly pleasant expression didn't alter. "Twelve."

Lady Violet blinked. "I beg your pardon?"

"On whatever scale you use to measure how much you care about civil liberties and the law."

Lady Violet stared at him a moment, her mouth slightly open and her eyes darting sideways towards the refreshments table— clearly struggling between the urge to make an excuse about finding another cup of tea and the determination never to admit defeat.

Before she could make up her mind, a slim, auburn-haired woman sailed over to join us, taking Lady Violet by the arm.

"Violet, my dear." Mrs. Amelia Scott was the founder and

champion of the Bethnal Green School for Orphaned Girls and the organizer of today's charity tea.

Her voice was an attractive contralto, pleasant but extremely firm. "Would you be an angel and go keep the peace between Margaret Selfridge and Joyce Bains? You know they have not been speaking to one another ever since Joyce deliberately copied the design of Margaret's gown for her New Year's ball."

Lady Violet, faced with a will even stronger than hers—or maybe the possibility of a more interesting scandal—moved off into the crowd, and Mrs. Scott turned to Jack with an apologetic smile.

"Sergeant Kelly, I am terribly sorry to ask this of you—particularly when we have only just met. But Lord Haggerston appears to have smuggled in a flask of whiskey and seems currently to be trying to drink himself under the table before the speeches have even begun. I'm unlikely to be able to persuade him to stop, and unfortunately he has a tendency to be … unpleasant, while under the influence. But if another gentleman were to approach him and take charge of the flask … or at least drag him out of here if he shows any sign of being about to make a scene …"

She gestured towards a heavyset man with a ruddy face and pugnacious jaw, who was slouched on a brocade-upholstered bench near the back of the room and scowling as though he were contemplating the violent murder of everyone in the room.

Jack wasn't the only other man here, but I could understand why Mrs. Scott had gravitated towards him.

He was broad-shouldered and lean, strong and capable, with very dark brown hair and chiseled features. Whether in uniform or out, he projected a kind of calm, hard-edged competence that was either reassuring or unnerving, depending on which side of law and order you were on.

He still walked with a limp from the bullet he had taken in the leg last July—but all the same, even a titled scion of the nobility would probably think twice about deliberately defying him.

"I'll see what I can do," Jack said. He squeezed my hand briefly.

I frowned a little as I watched him walk over towards the drunken man. But then, it probably couldn't be any worse than talking to Lady Violet.

"Lord Haggerston is ..."

"Violet's husband, yes," Mrs. Scott said. "And, as such, possibly has some excuse for resorting to drink."

I pressed my lips together but didn't quite manage to suppress a laugh.

I had never met Amelia Scott before today, but from what I had seen, I liked her. She was somewhere around forty, but still lovely, tall and slender, with pale skin and faint lines of laughter only just beginning to gather at the corners of her hazel-colored eyes.

She wore a yellow tea gown with a belt of deeper yellow satin, her russet hair parted in the middle and drawn smoothly back into a low bun.

Now worry replaced the momentary wry humor in her gaze. "You've seen nothing ..." she trailed off.

I shook my head. "Not so far. I promise I'll let you know if I do, though."

Amelia Scott had been a friend of Watson's late wife, Mary. Mrs. Scott had approached Uncle John with a request for help. Uncle John had carried the request on to Holmes, and my father had asked Jack and me to attend the afternoon gathering here, at Mrs. Scott's London town home in Grosvenor Square.

Mrs. Scott exhaled a sigh of relief. "Thank you. Some of the board members have been agitating to go to the police with the matter. And of course, I realize that police involvement may become necessary. But if it's at all possible, I'm hoping to resolve the issue ourselves." She glanced over the room, worry clouding her gaze. "Depending on exactly who is involved, the scandal could do irreparable damage to our cause."

I nodded. Mrs. Scott was probably right. If the organization became tainted with wrongdoing, the same charitably-minded people assembled here today would start running for the hills for fear of guilt by association.

Back in Baker Street, I had pointed out that Holmes could have found the time to attend, to which he had—somewhat justifiably—replied that no one with half a brain would ever imagine he had voluntarily agreed to attend a tea party gathering of ladies from London's most exclusive and upper-class families.

We had been here for only half an hour, but already I was wondering whether Holmes had had another reason for sending us besides his own wish to avoid conversations with women such as Lady Violet Haggerston. Holmes had probably realized—as I was beginning to—that the assembled ladies would be so distracted by the borderline scandal of Jack's and my engagement that no one would stop to wonder whether we had any hidden agenda in being here.

I frowned again, glancing over to where Jack had joined Lord Haggerston on the bench.

Amelia Scott turned, following my gaze. "Now that is quite remarkable," she murmured.

She was right. Lord Haggerston had stopped scowling and was even looking marginally friendly—if blearily so—in response to whatever Jack had said to him.

"I like your young man very much," Mrs. Scott said. "So strong and capable-looking. *And* quite handsome, too. If I were twenty years younger—" She gave me a conspiratorial smile. "Well, I'm sure I would still stand no chance, because it's perfectly clear that he has eyes for no one but you. But I do thank you both for coming. And now I'm afraid that it's time for me to give the opening speech."

"Of course."

Mrs. Scott moved off, and I let my gaze travel over the crowd.

Amelia Scott had founded the Bethnal Green Benevolent Aid Society and the school for orphaned girls it funded, and she had drawn to it the members of upper-echelon London society who were present today.

At the past few meetings of the society, though, items of some considerable value had mysteriously gone missing: A diamond brooch, a necklace, and pair of antique silver candlesticks dating to the reign of King Charles I.

In most cases like this one, suspicion would inevitably have fallen on a servant. But the monthly Benevolent Aid Society meetings were held at different homes across London, attended by different servants each time, according to whoever was playing host. The only continuity was in the society members themselves.

Given that solidly three quarters of the society members bore titles of nobility, it probably wasn't surprising that Mrs. Scott wanted the investigation carried out quietly and with an eye to minimizing possible scandal.

Lord Haggerston appeared to have passed from bad tempered and into the maudlin stage of drunkenness; he was speaking, blinking rapidly, and looking as though he were on the verge of bursting into tears.

Jack was clearly listening to Lord Haggerston with only half his attention. Following the direction of his look, I saw he was watching a tall, gray-haired man with wide, mutton-chop whiskers and a monocle screwed into one eye. The fellow's skin was bronzed from the sun, and he was going on about how his university team owed their victory to hard exercise, good diet, and proper rest. His long arms moved as he spoke, first in a rowing motion, and then raised in triumph. "We carried the day!" he said in a stage whisper.

Mrs. Scott had introduced me to him when we'd first arrived. I searched my memory and came up with the name Lord Burleigh.

Something about Lord Burleigh had clearly caught Jack's attention, but for the moment, I couldn't see what.

I let my gaze travel on to a ginger-haired man with a round, pink face and a clerical collar.

Mrs. Scott had introduced him, too; he was the Reverend Jacob Albright, who saw to the day-to-day running of the school for orphaned girls. At the moment, he was standing in the small alcove formed by a bay window, his gaze fixed on a leather-bound copy of the Bible.

Mrs. Scott stepped up to the podium that had been set up at the front of the room, flanked by two potted palm trees.

"Ladies and gentlemen, thank you all so much for coming today. Together, we are truly changing the lives of the girls in one of the most desperate and poverty-stricken neighborhoods of London, allowing them a chance at an education, an escape from a life of degradation and despair."

LUCY

6. AN ODD ARREST

"Holmes had better be eternally grateful to us for looking into this matter for him," I said. I took the pins out of my hat, tossed it onto the seat opposite, and let my head tip back against the leather carriage seat cushions behind me.

After Mrs. Scott's speech, I had spent the rest of our time at the party circulating among the guests, letting Mrs. Scott introduce me to the other ladies in attendance and listening to their so-called polite conversation—which, for the most part, was nothing of the sort.

Now Jack and I were in a cab, driving away from Grosvenor Square. Yellow fog drifted past the carriage windows, parting here and there to allow a glimpse of another grand town-home ... a coal delivery wagon ... a chimney sweep lugging his buckets and brushes home.

And if I never heard another observation on the damp autumn weather we were having, or a catty remark about another woman's choice of clothing, it would be too soon.

"What did you say to Lord Haggerston to make him stop looking so murderous?" I asked.

Jack shrugged. "Just said I could see he was having a rough day."

I blinked. "That's all?"

"He's not exactly the first drunk I've had to keep from starting a fight," Jack said. "That usually works. Nine times in ten they just want someone to listen to all the grievances they've got against the world."

"So you were stuck listening to Lord Haggerston's list of grievances the whole time? And I thought I had cause for complaint."

"It wasn't that bad." Jack smiled, leaned close, and kissed me, his mouth lingering on mine. "I just thought about being able to do that when it was over."

The carriage went over a bump, jolting, and I caught at Jack's arm to keep my balance. I smiled back at him.

A year ago, I might have offered to investigate a case like this one for Holmes. But I would have had no one to ride home with afterwards, ready to listen to whatever I said.

Not that in all likelihood I needed to say anything, because Jack would have observed the same things I had and usually knew exactly what I was thinking. So far, the investigation didn't show any signs of turning violent. But if it did, he would do anything to protect me, and I would do the same for him.

"I don't suppose Lord Haggerston confessed to being a thief while he was airing his list of complaints?" I said. "Or told you that his wife has an unfortunate habit of stealing jewelry and silver candlesticks?"

"No such luck," Jack said. "He was mostly talking about some sort of dispute over fishing rights on his estate somewhere north of here."

"How unobliging of him. I would *love* to find out that Lady Violet is the guilty party. Why were you watching Lord Burleigh, by the way?" I asked. "I saw you looking at him."

"He had a hole in his coat pocket," Jack said. "He put his cigarette case in, and it wound up on the floor." He shrugged. "Could be nothing; could be that he doesn't have money to get his clothes mended."

I'd missed seeing that. "He's been living abroad, somewhere sunny, to judge by the color of his skin. And he's traveled to Paris recently."

Jack nodded. "French cigarettes. And he had a copy of a Paris newspaper folded up inside his coat pocket."

I made a face at him. "One of these days, I'm going to notice *something* that you overlook. Did you see Reverend Albright?"

"Had a yellow-backed novel hidden inside his Bible?"

I nodded. I hadn't had the chance to speak with Reverend Albright, but I had some sympathy for anyone else bored to distraction by the afternoon's proceedings.

I hesitated, then asked, "What did you think of the aid society—what they're trying to accomplish, I mean?"

Unlike the majority of the aid society members—most of whom, I suspected, viewed slumming as a fashionable form of tourism—Jack had actually grown up homeless and alone on streets just as bleak and poor as those in Bethnal Green.

"It's a good cause."

It undoubtedly was. Mrs. Scott, during one of the few *non-*dull parts of the afternoon, had told stories of some of the girls who had been rescued from the neighborhood slums and brothels. The school provided them with both training and help finding respectable jobs.

"But …"

We were passing close by the embankment and through patches of fog, I could see the river Thames, the boats of all sizes bobbing on the dark water.

Jack was quiet for a second, looking out the carriage window. Darkness fell early in London in late autumn, and the gathering shadows outside sharpened the lean, strong lines of his face.

"I remember once when I was—I don't even know how old," he finally said. "Younger than ten, probably. It was the middle of winter, and a woman in a fur coat stopped me on the street outside a charity soup kitchen and gave me a printed paper. She had a whole box full of them, and she was handing them out to everyone who passed by. She told me it was a tract all about the evils of stealing and drink and that I should read it for the salvation of my immortal soul. I remember thinking if the good of my soul depended on a pamphlet that might as well have been written in Chinese for all I could read of it, I was pretty well doomed. Not that I cared a lot. Salvation was low on my list of things to worry about, compared to finding something to eat."

I slipped my hand into his. "What did you do?"

Jack smiled briefly. "Stole a box of matches and used the paper to help start a fire with some broken crates I'd found in a back alley. Kept me from freezing to death that night, so I suppose it was helpful." He glanced at me. "I'm not saying that the aid society's the same way, or that the school doesn't do some good, I'm just—"

"Not sure that people like Lord and Lady Haggerston can be made to see past the ends of their own aristocratic noses?"

"Something like that. Although maybe that's not fair."

"You were brilliant at dealing with Lady Violet, by the way. I wanted to upend an entire teapot over her head, but you were perfect."

Jack shrugged again. "It's not that different from questioning a criminal suspect. Just remember not to trust anything they say and know they wouldn't spit on you if you were on fire, and you're fine."

I laughed. "I would love to see Lady Violet's face if she could hear you say that." My smile faded. "I'm so sorry." I leaned my head against Jack's shoulder. "I hate it that you have to put up with that sort of thing."

"Hey." Jack put his arm around me. "People like Lady Violet can say what they want to; I don't mind. You're the one I'm marrying, not her."

"Luckily for me."

Jack's arm tightened around me. "Pretty sure I'm the lucky one."

The cab drew to a halt with a rattle and creak of carriage springs. Looking out, I realized that we'd arrived at Commercial Street Police Station, where Jack had been posted since his promotion to the rank of sergeant.

"What time do you have to be at the Savoy?" Jack asked.

"Not until seven; why?" I was still performing nightly in the D'Oyly Carte Opera Company's production of *The Yeomen of the Guard*.

"You can speak Italian, can't you?" Jack said.

"I'm better at singing arias than carrying on an actual conversation, but some."

I'd had the chance to practice while visiting my mother in Rome.

"There was a woman brought in last night," Jack said. "Arrested for smashing a pawn shop window and stealing a gold watch. She doesn't speak a word of English that we can tell. I was wondering if you could talk to her."

"Of course, if you want me to. But why? Do you not think she committed the robbery after all?"

"No, she did it. That's what's strange. PC Giles—he's the one who arrested her—said she did it in full view of not only a dozen other witnesses, but in front of him, too. He saw the whole thing."

That made her possibly slow-witted—or crazed—but I still didn't see what was strange. "Maybe she didn't notice Constable Giles was there?"

Jack shook his head. "No, she did. Giles said she was standing in front of the pawn shop looking up and down the street, almost like she was waiting for him to appear. Then, as soon as she saw him, she looked right at him, smashed the window, and grabbed the watch. As if she were hoping to be seen and caught. She didn't even try to run."

"That is odd."

Beat constables patrolled the same circuit of streets on a regular schedule—which could sometimes be a weakness, because criminals knew exactly when they would appear at a particular spot. Usually, the criminals were hoping to *avoid* being caught in the middle of a crime, though.

"All right," I said. "I'll come in and speak with her."

LUCY

7. LOST IN TRANSLATION

Commercial Street ran through the district of Spitalfields, in East London—one of the most overcrowded and crime-ridden neighborhoods in the city. For my own peace of mind, I was trying to ignore what that meant in terms of Jack's risk of running into danger on the job.

As a section sergeant, at least he no longer had to patrol a beat alone, but he was still responsible for inspection patrols, making sure that the constables in his section were alert, sober, and safely carrying out their assigned duties.

The Commercial Street Police Station itself was a long, three-story brick building with the motto of the British monarchy—*Dieu et mon droit*—carved over the lintel of the main entrance.

The cell blocks were at the back of the station house, behind the outer lobby, and the charge room where suspects would be questioned and—if deemed guilty—formally charged with a crime.

Jack nodded to the blue-uniformed constable on duty outside the block of cells. "Prisoner in number three's still here?"

The constable was in his early twenties, with blue eyes, fair skin, and a scattering of blond hair on his upper lip that it would be optimistic to call a mustache. I'd seen him at the station house once or twice, but never spoken with him.

He grimaced in answer to Jack. "Still here and sweet-tempered as ever. Tried to kick and bite me when I went in with her dinner tray an hour ago."

I raised an eyebrow at Jack. "And this is the woman you want me to talk to? Are you sure this isn't revenge for making you suffer through the Haggerstons?"

Jack grinned, then turned, alert, as a second police constable ran up to us, panting for breath.

"PC ... Dickon." The constable spoke between gasps for air. "He was ... attacked on duty ... near Whitechapel Market. They're bringing him in now."

Jack was instantly serious, the line of his mouth turning grim. "How bad?"

The constable shook his head, still wheezing. "Don't know yet."

Also for my own peace of mind, I didn't know the exact statistics of how many police officers were attacked while on duty—but it had to be approaching half. In neighborhoods like Spitalfields and Whitechapel, the police weren't regarded as protectors so much as the enemy.

Jack glanced at me.

"Go," I told him. "I'll be fine."

Jack nodded. "Thomas will stay with you."

The fair-haired constable squared his shoulders in response. "Yes, sir."

* * *

"You really don't have to come in with me," I told Constable Thomas, as he reached to unlock the door of cell number three.

Constable Thomas looked at me sideways. "No offense,

miss." His voice was polite, but firm. "But I was hoping to keep my job past tonight."

He peered through the spy-hole that was fitted into the center of the door, then slid one of a jangling bunch of keys into the cell lock. "Not that I'm saying anything against Sergeant Kelly. Everyone knows he's fair, and he wouldn't ask anything of you he wouldn't do himself. Still, we had a suspect try and break free the other day before he could be locked up in here—huge man, knocked out the two constables who were dragging him in and gave another a bloody lip. He was making for the front door when Kelly steps in and lands the man on his back before you could blink." There was unconcealed admiration in Thomas's voice. "So I'd rather not be the one explaining how I let his young lady get hurt, if you don't mind. I'm also hoping to *live* past tonight."

He swung the cell door open, revealing a small, square room, with a narrow, fold-out bed attached by two metal chains to the back wall and no other furniture.

The station must have some way of heating the cells, because the air was warmer than I would have expected. The only light came from skylights, high in the ceiling of the cell block, so that at this hour of the day, the space was dim. But I could see a woman's figure slumped onto a corner of the bed.

Constable Thomas was directly behind me. I stayed in the doorway, stopping him from coming any further into the cell. I didn't want the woman to feel any more threatened than I could help.

"*Buon pomeriggio*," I said. *Good afternoon.*

The woman's head lifted a little, as though with surprise at the Italian greeting. But she didn't move.

I ransacked my memory for conventional Italian phrases.

I knew the words to ask *How are you?* But under the circumstances, that seemed absurd to the point of insulting. She was in a police station holding cell; obviously she'd had better days.

"My name is Lucy James," I finally said, still in Italian. "Will you tell me your name?"

Now that my eyes were adjusting to the dimness, I could make out the woman's face more clearly. She looked to be somewhere around thirty or thirty-five, with a square, strong-boned face and olive-toned skin. Her eyes were dark, set under strongly-marked dark brows, her mouth wide. Her hair was a dark, shoulder-length tangle around her face, matted and clumped together with dirt.

"Dove abiti?" I asked her. *Where do you live?*

The woman looked at me, her face slack, her eyes so disinterested that I wasn't even sure she heard me or understood.

She had a short, stocky frame, but at the moment her skin had a pinched pallor that made me think she had been going hungry lately. Her black skirt and dirty gray blouse had either been made for a larger woman, or else she had lost weight since she had bought them.

She would hardly be the first driven to steal out of desperation or hunger—though that didn't explain why she would apparently want to be caught for the crime.

I tried again. *"Sei sicuro."* *You're safe.*

I thought something might have stirred in the woman's eyes at that—a shadow of something angry or at least uneasy.

She shook her head, though whether she was disagreeing with my assurance or simply trying to end the conversation, I couldn't tell.

"My—" I'd forgotten the Italian word for *fiance*. I substituted *tesoro*. Sweetheart. "—is with the police. He just wants to understand what happened. Why you stole the watch from the shop."

The woman's throat muscles bobbed as she swallowed.

"*Ho rubato.*" She spoke in a hoarse, low voice that sounded almost creaky with disuse, as though these were the first words she'd uttered in a long time. "*Andrò in prigione.*"

I stole. I will go to prison.

"You *want* to go to prison?"

The woman's hands clenched, gathering fistfuls of her skirt. She had large, capable, calloused hands, and at the moment they were tight enough that the knuckles showed white under her skin. But her face remained slack, empty of expression. It was almost eerie.

"*Ho rubato,*" she said again. *I stole.*

As well as rusty, her voice sounded dull, flat.

I took a cautious step closer.

"Do you have any family in London?" I asked her.

She slumped back into the corner formed by the edge of the bed and the wall, unanswering.

"Are you in trouble?" That was also probably a stupid question, but I was coming up against the limitations of what I knew how to ask. "I'd like to help you, if I can."

The woman still didn't speak, but her dark eyes lifted, fixing on my face with a look I couldn't read. Part wariness, part something like … despair?

The sleeve of her blouse had slipped up past her elbow, baring the skin of her inner arm. She had a tattoo design on her inner wrist: a stylized picture of a dove, its wings raised to create the outlined shape of a heart.

I took another half step forward, smiling as I pointed to the inked pattern. *"Che è bello,"* I told her. *That's pretty.*

The woman's head snapped up, fear flashing across her gaze. Then she yanked the sleeve down, covering the tattoo.

"Partire!" Her voice was suddenly harsh and almost shaking. The word meant *go.* She jerked her head at the doorway for emphasis. *"Partire!"*

I spoke gently. "Please, won't you let me help you?"

The woman dropped her head, sinking her chin onto her chest and wrapping her arms around herself.

She muttered something in a hoarse voice, so quietly that I only just caught the word. *"Campana."*

At least, that was what I thought she had said; I couldn't be certain.

"Campana?" I repeated. *"Il tuo nome?"* *Is that your name?*

The woman shook her head vigorously—the first time she had actually responded to one of my questions with a definite answer. She said, *"Casa di morte."*

Casa di Morte. House of death.

"Someone named Campana is in danger?"

The momentary connection—if it had existed at all—was gone, though. I might as well not have spoken. The woman's whole body was hunched forwards, her eyes fixed on the floor—and, as I watched, she started to rock forward and backward, slowly at first, but then with more and more violence until she was banging her head against the cell wall behind her.

"Miss—" Constable Thomas said behind me.

I stood where I was another moment, torn. But I wasn't doing her any good, and she would hurt herself if she grew any more frantic.

There was one last thing I wanted to try. I turned to Constable Thomas and said, sharply, "Look at the ceiling!"

Constable Thomas's head snapped up to look above us, confusion covering his face. But the woman on the bed didn't turn or even cease her rocking.

I stepped back through the cell door. "*Addio*," I said quietly. *Goodbye*.

* * *

"What was on the ceiling, miss?" Constable Thomas asked me, as he swung the cell door closed and relocked it.

"Nothing. I just wanted to see whether she really doesn't understand any English."

"Ah." The constable's face cleared. "Clever, miss."

"Maybe. It doesn't really prove anything, though." The woman hadn't reacted, but she could be just a very good actress—or she could simply not know the word *ceiling*, even if she knew some English.

I would have to think for a moment before I remembered the word in Italian: *soffitto*.

"Did she have any belongings when she was brought in?" I asked Constable Thomas.

"Precious little," Constable Thomas said. "Just a few odds and ends, but you're welcome to have a look."

"Thank you."

The nameless woman's worldly possessions were pitifully scant. Spread out across the small desk at the cell block guard station, they were a meager collection: a shard of a broken mirror, a comb with more than half the teeth missing, and a crumpled roll of fabric that proved to be a gray flannel petticoat.

Apparently it was the kind of thing given to residents of poorhouses and other charity institutions; the words *Lambeth Work House* were stamped on the petticoat's waistband.

The only other article on the table was a threadbare woolen cloak. I picked it up, shaking out the folds and frowning at the white-crusted stains around the hem.

"See something, miss?" Constable Thomas asked.

"No. Not really." The stains were suggestive, maybe, but they didn't really offer any hint as to who the woman was or what had brought her to the moment of smashing a shop window in full view of the police.

A pocket had been sewn into the lining of the cloak. I fingered the material, frowning.

"That's odd."

"What's odd, miss?"

"This pocket. The cloak is obviously old—almost worn out. But the material for the pocket is practically brand new." It was thick, heavy black wool, and had been sewn into the cloak with obvious care, the stitches made with thicker thread than was usual for sewing clothes. I wasn't an expert, but it looked like carpet thread.

I slipped my hand inside. "Empty. No—wait."

Fishing around in the pocket, I drew out a small scrap of a grape stem.

"Must have bought some grapes at the market or a greengrocer's shop," Constable Thomas said.

I nodded absently, frowning. Something was nagging at me, tugging at the back of my mind—though for the moment, I couldn't place what had struck me.

"I wonder how," I said. "She didn't have any money on her when she was arrested, did she?" There wasn't so much as a ha'penny coin amongst the collection on the table.

"Could have spent her last coin on them."

"On *grapes*?" It wouldn't be the most economical choice, but I supposed it was no stranger than anything else about the Italian woman.

I looked over the small collection one more time.

"Something wrong, miss?" Constable Thomas asked.

I realized I was still frowning. "No. It's nothing." Whatever half-placed memory the sight of the nameless woman's things had stirred was gone.

Jack hadn't come back yet, either. He must still be occupied with the constable who'd been assaulted. And I needed to leave for the theater.

"If she shows any sign of wanting to talk, let me know," I told Constable Thomas. "I can come back and translate at any time."

WATSON

8. OBSERVATIONS AT A SMALL CAFE

Seated at a table in a small café in Hatton Garden, I could see two shadowy figures on the fog-clouded street outside. The curtains on the window were open. Around me, the luncheon crowd was busy with steaming bowls of kosher soups and sandwiches. The clientele were mainly middle-aged men, though some were in their twenties and others were older, with gray beards in varying stages of growth and tidiness. Even though we were indoors, nearly all of the men wore hats, out of respect to the deity who looks down upon all of us. Or so I had been told. My own hat was on the otherwise empty chair across from me at my small table.

Two tables over, Holmes sat hunched opposite a gray-bearded older man. The latter, wearing a black fedora hat, also stared down at the tabletop, so that the brim of his cap nearly touched the brim of the brown wool workman's cap worn by Holmes.

Then, the graybeard leaned back in a disinterested way, took out a lens from one pocket, and screwed it, monocle fashion, into one eye.

Mindful of Holmes's admonition not to act unless necessary and not to attract undue attention to him, I turned away, looking around the room, casually, as a harried, perspiring waiter set down before me a steaming plate of corned beef and cabbage. I busied myself with my food, looking up to take in my fellow patrons at this café, and rarely taking another direct glance at Holmes.

The occupants of the other tables were similarly engaged in the jeweler's trade, when they were not eating their lunches. One after another would place his loupe—what jewelers call their magnifying glasses—to examine small stones. From the kitchen behind me, I heard the clatter of dishes and trays and the calls of men in the Yiddish words that were unfamiliar to me but clearly conveyed a sense of urgent business, waiters importuning the cooks to work faster and the cooks protesting in return.

Outside, the two shadowy figures had not moved. They stood, arms folded, leaning against the wall of the building opposite the café.

I risked another glance at Holmes. He was leaning back in his chair, arms tightly folded across his chest. His lunch companion had put away his loupe and was sawing energetically with knife and fork at whatever was on his plate.

I finished my meal and sat back as well, prepared to delay the arrival of the bill for as long as it took not to become conspicuous. I would have tea, I decided. Then I would ask about the choices for dessert. I was there to protect Holmes, if needed, and to help him guard the diamonds he was carrying. The Hatton Garden district of London was considered a safe place to do business, and indeed, most of the business of the day—inspection of diamonds in their both raw and finished state—was done in plain view. The theory, as I understood it, was that everyone knew and trusted one another and that no one of the community would dare to break that trust lest he be set upon by the others who were all in plain view.

Then, a stranger came through the front door of the café and, pausing for only a moment, strode directly to Holmes's table. He bent over and whispered something to Holmes's companion. The man did not alter his expression one iota—the newcomer might have just told him that rain was expected sometime this week, for all his manner indicated. But he gave the newcomer a dismissive nod, whereupon the man turned and walked out of the café the way he had come in.

Then, Holmes's companion pushed back his chair, stood up, bowed formally from the waist, both hands at his sides, and left.

Holmes remained where he was for a moment. Then he too got up. With a brief glance, he indicated I should follow.

I left some coins on my table to cover the bill and did so. Just outside the entrance, Holmes had stopped and was bent over, fumbling with an umbrella. He spoke without looking up.

"Those two men across the street, Watson. I am going to lead them away from here. Follow us, but stay well back."

I watched Holmes cross the street, heading for the two shadowy figures. But there was still the fog. I thought I saw one of the men move away in the opposite direction, while the other followed Holmes. Mindful of Holmes's instructions, I stayed behind this man. We went on for possibly three minutes, and I saw Holmes pass by a newsboy and turn a corner. Then the man followed. By the time I rounded the corner, I saw Holmes standing over his follower. The man had struggled up to a seated position and was rubbing his jaw.

From behind, a hand grasped my shoulder and pulled me around.

I now faced the companion of the man on the ground before Holmes. A day's growth of ginger-colored stubble coated this man's dirty cheeks. His associate by now had clambered unsteadily to his feet.

Holmes said, "Not to worry, Watson." Turning to the ginger-bearded man, he said, "You are with the Pinkertons, I believe?"

Somewhat abashed, both men produced their badges, which Holmes inspected. "You may as well name your employer."

"Mr. Cecil Rhodes. He hired us to protect you."

"Hired you to protect his diamonds would be more accurate. Well, you may report to Mr. Rhodes that I have resigned the case. I shall have the diamonds delivered to him tomorrow."

"Resigned?"

"He has broken faith. I told him I work alone and there was to be no interference."

"We never came near you."

"Your clumsy attempt to emulate London loiterers was noted outside the café. I was blamed, or, rather, my presence was blamed. My meeting, which could have been productive in advancing Mr. Rhodes's interest, was abruptly terminated. I cannot have that happen again. And since I cannot rely on Mr. Rhodes not to repeat the performance, I am resigning."

A cagy look came into the puffy eyes of the red-haired Pinkerton man. "You have the stones on you?"

"Only this little raw specimen." Holmes produced a small brown pebble from his waistcoat pocket.

"I'll take it," said the other. "I'll see it safe to Mr. Rhodes."

Holmes shrugged and handed over the pebble.

A few minutes later we were inside the Grand Street offices of De Beers, Incorporated, where the diamond syndicate has its headquarters.

Mr. Voortrekker, the manager, a sleek, well-fed gentleman whose plump outlines strained the fabric and buttons of his clothing, was telling us about the syndicate.

"No diamonds are traded without our knowledge. Prices can be stabilized when demand is known. We control ninety-five percent of the world supply. No legitimate trade takes place without our knowledge."

As Voortrekker spoke, Holmes wrote briefly on a piece of notepaper and handed it over.

Voortrekker inspected what Holmes had written and looked up with a blank stare.

Holmes prompted, "Those are the names and Pinkerton badge numbers of two men who stopped us in the street. Have you engaged the Pinkertons? No? Might Mr. Rhodes have done so?"

"Mr. Rhodes is on the Cunard steamer heading south to Johannesburg. I do not believe he would stoop to that level of detail. He would have left that to me. May I ask why the Pinkertons might have been engaged?"

I was somewhat surprised to see Holmes produce two small cloth sacks and hand them over.

"Mr. Rhodes entrusted me with these raw and finished diamonds several days ago. The Pinkertons may have been hired as a safeguard. However, I should like to return them. Would you be good enough to furnish a receipt?"

After first glancing briefly inside each, Voortrekker opened the safe and placed the sacks inside. He shut the heavy door and twirled the knob. "I will have your receipt momentarily," he said.

Within ten minutes Holmes and I stood at the entry door to the London office of the Pinkerton Detective Agency. Holmes bade me wait outside. It was not long before he emerged, a grim look on his hawklike features. "It appears my mistrust of Mr. Rhodes was misplaced," he said. "The names and badge numbers were false."

"Then who were those two men?"

Holmes shrugged and said, "It is a good thing that the pebble I handed to the red-haired imposter was only a pebble."

LUCY

9. WEDDING PLANS

Morning sunlight was slanting through the hallway windows
as I climbed the steps from my own rooms in 221A Baker Street
to the door of 221B.

I paused. Lately, entering Holmes's flat was something akin
to stepping blindfolded out onto the London streets: you might
be struck in the face by a gust of freezing rain, or you might—
possibly—catch a ray of autumn sunshine.

Or you might be struck by a runaway carriage and trampled
into the cobblestones.

At the moment, I could hear my father's voice coming from
the sitting room.

"Apparently they wish to be informed as to whether the table-
cloths in the wedding breakfast ought to be white or cream-
colored. What say you, Watson?"

"I?" I could picture Uncle John's eyes widening. "Good Lord,
Holmes, I haven't the faintest idea. Why don't you ask Lucy?"

"Because we both know that she will immediately assume
that vague, dreamy-eyed expression she gets whenever this mar-
riage is mentioned and say that it doesn't matter and all she cares

about is the fact that she is marrying Sergeant Kelly."

"Hmmm." I imagined Uncle John tugging on his mustache. "It is good to see her so happy, though."

"Perhaps. At the moment, however, I am painfully aware that planning a wedding appears to be a more complicated process than negotiating peace between two warring governments."

Growing up an orphan, I hadn't had any particular vision for my wedding day; even now I honestly did only care about the fact that at the end of it, I would be married to Jack.

His Royal Highness The Prince of Wales had offered his congratulations on our engagement, though, and expressed an interest in attending the wedding. So had Lord Lansdowne, the Police Commissioner Sir Edward Bradford, and apparently half the war office, all of whom were in varying degrees acquainted with my father and my Uncle Mycroft.

Somehow, without my entirely being aware how it had happened, the wedding had turned from a small, quiet affair to a grand society occasion, with a service at St. James Church in Hanover Square and a wedding breakfast afterwards at the Albemarle Hotel, all to be held in the last week of December before Christmas, just over a month and a half away.

By most society standards, it was a scandalously short engagement, although it felt about five times longer than I would have liked.

At the moment, though, I was only putting off the inevitable.

I braced myself, then opened the sitting room door. "Good morning."

"Ah, Lucy."

Uncle John was seated at the breakfast table, finishing a plate of toast, sausage, and bacon, but my father was smoking his pipe, slouched in his armchair by the hearth, still wearing a silk dressing gown over his trousers and shirt. He appeared to be engrossed in his morning newspaper, and his breakfast dishes were still empty and untouched.

"You are just in time to help address these wedding invitations." Uncle John gestured to a towering heap of invitation cards and envelopes that were currently—for reasons only known to Holmes himself—piled in his violin case, which was lying open on the hearth rug.

If I hadn't known better, I would have sworn that the stack had grown since yesterday.

"But I was going to—" I began.

"They won't address themselves," Uncle John said. His voice took on a tone of irony. "And your father is otherwise engaged. As you can quite plainly see, *The Times* commands all of his attention at the moment."

I dropped into the chair opposite Holmes, but sighed. "You know, I'd be just as happy being married by a justice of the peace. Or eloping to Gretna Green, the way they do in old-fashioned novels."

Holmes unclamped his teeth from around the stem of his pipe and fixed us both with one of his steeliest gray-eyed stares. "Your mother will enjoy the occasion."

"I know." My mother had been overjoyed when I wrote to tell her of Jack's and my engagement.

She was performing as first chair violin in the orchestra at La Scala opera house in Milan and wouldn't be able to travel to London until just a few days before the wedding. But she had already sent her own mother's antique lace wedding veil by special post so that my gown could be made to match.

Watching my father now, I saw the slight shadow of regret that always crossed his face when my mother was mentioned.

My parents had reached a state of peace between them, my mother not asking for more than my father could give. But I knew he still felt a twinge of guilt that they had never married.

"There is another factor," Holmes said, reaching to tamp more tobacco down into his pipe. "Given the difference in your stations, if you and Sergeant Kelly were to slip away and be married quietly, there are those who might assume that you were somehow ashamed of the match."

"But that's not even the slightest bit true!"

Holmes struck a match and inhaled. "I did not say that *I* believed it, only that others might."

An image of Lady Violet Haggerston's pinched, long-nosed face flashed into my mind.

"Drat it. Uncle John, can you help find me a pen?"

Finding anything in Holmes's sitting room was a gamble at best.

Uncle John set down his knife and fork. "Certainly, my dear."

I had addressed three envelopes when I suddenly looked up at Holmes, narrowing my gaze. "You said that about public opinion because you knew it would make me finally tackle this, didn't you."

"Possibly." My father's thin lips twitched without quite becoming a smile. "Effective, was it not?"

The sitting room door opened, revealing Mrs. Hudson, Holmes's landlady: pink-cheeked, white-haired, with a plump, motherly face.

She wore a snowy white apron over her high-necked brown dress and held an envelope. "Special delivery with an urgent message, so the carrier said. A letter for you, Dr. Watson."

"Thank you, Mrs. Hudson." Uncle John rose to take the letter.

I bent to address another invitation, then startled, almost dropping my pen at Watson's shocked exclamation.

"What is it, Uncle John?"

Uncle John was staring at the unfolded letter in his hands as though unable to believe what it said. "It's from Amelia— Mrs. Scott," he said.

My father turned to me. "You and Sergeant Kelly attended the charity tea, as we discussed?"

I nodded. "We met a number of people there, but we haven't learned much."

Uncle John shook his head. "It appears that the matter is solved." He was still staring at the letter in his hand and cleared his throat. "The rector of the church directly across from the Bethnal Green School has confessed to a series of thefts at the homes of wealthy donors."

"Reverend *Albright*?" I stared, feeling as shocked as Uncle John looked. "And confessed to whom? To Mrs. Scott, do you mean? Or to the police—"

"It appears that this Reverend Albright has taken his own life. He left a letter in which he begged forgiveness for what he had done."

"That's dreadful!"

I hadn't known Reverend Albright or even exchanged more than a formal word of introduction with him the day before. But it was still terrible to think of him ending his life over a few pieces of jewelry and silver.

Uncle John nodded. "Yes. Amelia was actually the one to find him. She and"—Uncle John consulted the letter—"another lady named Lady Violet Haggerston? Amelia sent this message by special delivery from the rectory. She is still there, staying with the reverend's housekeeper, who is understandably most shocked and upset by her employer's death. She begs that I come at once, if I am able."

WATSON

10. AT THE RECTORY

Lucy insisted on accompanying me. We were soon at the rectory, a brick structure adjoining the St. John's Church at Bethnal Green. In the afternoon sun, the neighborhood was brighter than when I had visited before, but with the gloom of the rain and fog having lifted, the harsh details of worn and ill-repaired storefronts, dirt-ridden pavements, and glum-looking vagrants were all too apparent. I kept Lucy close to me as we walked up to the rectory entrance. The door opened, and a blue-uniformed policeman, Constable Clark, greeted us. Moments later we were inside a rather threadbare parlor, joined by Amelia Scott and a red-eyed, gray-haired woman whom Amelia introduced as Mrs. Huggins, the Reverend Albright's housekeeper.

"'E were poorly," Mrs. Huggins said. "Like I told the constable, he didn't eat his supper. Left it all on his plate and went up to his room, poor man. I knocked to wake him this morning, but he didn't answer. The door was locked, so I used my own key. A very sad and sorry business. I shut the door straightaway and called the police, and then Mrs. Scott, here."

Lucy asked, "Why call Mrs. Scott?"

"The Reverend always calls her when the church has trouble."

"Do you attend church here, Mrs. Scott?" Lucy asked.

Amelia shook her head in sorrow. "Such a dreadful event, Miss. James. The poor man will be sorely missed. Now, to answer your question, I attend St. Paul's, but I always do what I can for St. John's. The location is so very convenient for our girls at the school, and it is wise to have them attend on a regular basis. So it is important that the church should continue to operate and function." She shook her head once again, as though determined to rise above her despondency and get on with needful activity. "I shall call the bishop immediately to arrange a replacement."

"Did the reverend seem worried the past few days?" Lucy asked Mrs. Huggins.

"Oh, yes. 'E generally was always hummin' or whistlin' quiet-like to himself and workin' on papers and such. But not lately." She pointed to a straight-back wooden rocking chair nearby. "He would just sit over there and rock."

"Might we see the room where the body was found?" Lucy asked.

Constable Clark nodded. "Nothing's been touched, except the body's been taken to the mortuary. You can see the note he left. But not to touch. It will be taken away and checked for fingermarks."

Then he added, "The note is wrapped around a silver candlestick. Mrs. Huggins says it's in the reverend's handwriting. It says, 'May God forgive me for what I have done.'"

I would have accompanied Lucy, but at that moment the door opened.

A slender girl, extremely tall and somewhat ungainly, came into the room. Her wrists and part of her forearms protruded awkwardly from below the dark blue sleeves of her ill-fitting school uniform jacket.

She came over and stood, hesitant, clutching a small handkerchief in one hand and dabbing it to wipe away tears from her reddened eyes. She spoke softly, in an odd, tight-lipped manner. "Is it true, Mrs. Scott?" The words came out choked with emotion.

Amelia reached out in sympathy. "Oh, dear Clara. Yes, I'm afraid it is. We are all still in shock, of course. From the loss."

Clara buried her face in her hands for a moment. Then she stood up straight. "We just can't understand why." Her small, dark eyes had a guarded look, close set as they were beneath a high forehead and an overhanging brow. "Though I know this isn't the time for me to be asking you. But Proctor said you wanted to see me."

"I hadn't realized you would be here quite so promptly."

"I'll just be going, then. I don't want to interrupt. You have these people to attend to—"

"Oh, dear Clara, please forgive me for not introducing you. This is Dr. Watson and Miss Lucy James and Constable Clark. All of you, this is Clara Sheffield. She is a very promising candidate and has made great strides since joining us. We hope to be able to place her in a new situation very soon."

"I am most pleased to make your acquaintance." Clara spoke with difficulty due to her emotion, and she was taking obvious care to achieve proper elocution and pronunciation.

"I am happy to make your acquaintance as well, Miss Sheffield," Lucy said. "Constable Clark and I were just going upstairs. Why don't the three of you carry on down here, and we will rejoin you presently."

We sat on the worn upholstery of three parlor chairs, and Amelia explained to Clara who I was and how the writing I would be doing would help the school. Clara seemed to recover her poise.

Amelia said, "Clara is quite gifted and highly intelligent. We are certain she has the makings of a wonderful success story within her."

"But I'm far from perfect, I must caution you," Clara said. "As you can see, my face is quite plain, and I am afraid I do not eat as much as I ought. Yet I have grown so tall that my uniform does not fit. I was gangly to begin with, and—"

"No need to dwell on your appearance, dear," said Amelia. "Tell Dr. Watson about your special talent. He has already seen your handiwork."

Clara's hand went to her mouth for a moment, then she asked, "My sketches?"

She gave a modest, tight-lipped smile, and I remembered the yellowing papers tacked up on the storefront shelves, filled with the many images of the little girl and the angelic young woman.

"I shall need to redo them all, I'm afraid," Clara was saying. "The damp has quite ruined the paper. But when the leaks have been repaired, I shall buckle down and produce more."

"You can see why we need your services, John," said Amelia, giving me a fond look. "*The Strand Magazine* has so many potential donors to our cause that I am certain we shall be able to do a great deal more for our girls once your articles begin to appear."

"Well, I hope so," I said. "Your sketches were quite impressive. Will you use the same model when you redo them?"

"Oh, that was Maybelle. She's gone to India now. Or, at least, she's on her way. It takes three months, you know."

"So you will use a new model?" Amelia asked.

"Or I may work from memory," Clara said, musingly.

I spoke without thinking. "Perhaps you could illustrate the articles for *The Strand Magazine*."

"You really think so?" Clara's eager smile came instantaneously, and with such emotion that I felt a pang of fear that I would not be able to live up to the hopes I had unleashed with what had been my casual remark.

"You see, John, just how much good you can do here," said Amelia. "Perhaps you could have a word with your editor."

Moments later, the constable and Mrs. Huggins came downstairs, followed by Lucy. She was carrying a small pasteboard box.

LUCY

11. SOME DOCUMENTS
IN THE CASE

"How did your wife know Mrs. Scott, Uncle John?" I asked.

We were standing in the sheltered doorway of the rectory, waiting for the cab Mrs. Scott had telephoned for to arrive. A light patter of chill autumn rain had begun to fall, drumming on the roof over our heads and turning the cobbled streets outside slippery and wet.

Watson's wife, Mary Morstan, had been the daughter of an army captain—a perfectly respectable background, but not, I would have thought, of the sort to move in the social circles to which Amelia Scott now belonged.

I always hesitated to speak of Uncle John's late wife, for fear of causing him pain. But he smiled reminiscently.

"They were at school together. And got into all sorts of girlish mischief together, or so Mary told me. But then after they left school, Mary was forced to take a position as a governess in order to support herself—while Amelia made a brilliant match by marrying Theodore Scott, the great shipping magnate. He was nearly thirty years her senior. I believe he made his fortune in trade with the Indies."

"A brilliant match indeed," I murmured. Uncle John didn't seem to notice the irony in my voice—nor, to be fair, would the majority of London high society. Girls were supposed to be universally delighted to marry gentlemen old enough to be their fathers, provided the gentlemen were rich enough.

"Mary and Amelia kept in touch by letter," Uncle John went on. "And Amelia attended our wedding. But until I met her in my editor's office, we had not seen each other since … it must be ten years by now."

"And now you have found one another again," I said. "She seemed very grateful to you for coming today."

Uncle John coughed. The rainy sky and the overhang above us made it barely brighter than twilight where we stood, but I thought the tips of his ears might have turned slightly pink.

"I … that is, I assure you, my intentions are strictly honorable. I intended only to render her what assistance I could—as any gentleman would."

I opened my mouth to answer. The back of my neck prickled, the skin between my shoulder blades feeling suddenly tense.

I turned, trying to look around without obviously appearing to stare.

There was no sign of our cab, but a man in a nondescript tweed suit and brown bowler hat had stopped three or four houses up the street from us and was standing motionless.

The brim of his hat was pulled low down over his forehead, and a thick woolen muffler was wrapped around his throat, shielding his mouth and chin. But I was fairly certain that his gaze was fixed on us.

I turned slightly away, but out of the corner of my eye saw him start walking.

Possibly he was just a parishioner who hadn't yet heard of Reverend Albright's death, but something about the way he moved raised the fine hairs on my arms.

There were other pedestrians on the street, and as this man wove his way between them, his gaze flicked back and forth, constantly alert, gauging the distance between himself and the person nearest to him.

I did exactly the same thing in a crowd; it was how I recognized the look in someone else. It was the kind of look that said a man was used to fighting, evaluating threats.

I kept one eye on the man as I said, "You are *never* anything but gentlemanly and honorable, Uncle John. I never supposed otherwise." Then I lowered my voice, adding in an undertone, "Did you bring your revolver with you?"

Watson's eyes widened. He was good in a crisis, but lacked the combat instinct that would lead him to suspect an attack before it actually occurred.

Or, to put it another way, he had a sunnier view of human nature than Holmes's or mine.

I kicked myself as his head whipped around, instantly scanning the street. If he'd held up a painted sign announcing the fact that we were expecting danger, he couldn't have been less subtle.

"No, I don't have a revolver, I never thought we'd need it—"

The man in the brown bowler hat accelerated, pushing roughly past a middle-aged woman with a shopping basket over one arm.

The woman shook her fist and cursed him with a surprising

degree of creativity, but he ignored her, coming to a halt in front of Uncle John.

"Those be Reverend Albright's things." He spoke with what I thought was a west-country accent—seldom heard in London. He jerked his head at the monogrammed box in Uncle John's arms.

Uncle John glanced quickly at me, but kept his expression pleasant. "So they are. You may have heard of the reverend's very sad death last night. We are taking his correspondence to see whether we can find anything to indicate whether he had a family who ought to be notified."

The stranger had so far ignored me completely—which was helpful, since it gave me the chance to study him without his notice.

Between the hat and the scarf, I couldn't see very much of his features apart from a pair of brown eyes set deep under dark brows.

The man spoke almost before Uncle John had uttered the final word. "Give it here."

Uncle John kept firm grip on the box, but gave the man a hearty smile. He wasn't usually very good at dissembling, but this time, his disingenuousness would have made even Holmes proud.

"Am I to understand that you are actually one of the good reverend's relations? That *is* a relief."

The man's eyes narrowed slightly. "Look, just hand it over."

"Or?" I asked.

For the first time, the man's head swiveled in my direction, confusion crossing his gaze. "What?"

Unlike in chess, when it came to violence it was often an

advantage to force your opponent into making the first move. Then you knew exactly what you were dealing with.

"Usually there's an *or* associated with a demand like that," I said. "Hand the box over *or* …"

I couldn't see the lower half of the man's face, but I imagined his jaw hardening behind the scarf. "Or you're not going to like what happens next."

On the final words, he drew a gun from the pocket of his coat. My stomach dropped; something sharp and scrambling came to life in my chest.

I scanned the street behind him, but there was no sign of a conveniently passing policeman or anyone else who might help. Just women shoppers … children … an old man, bent double over a cane, hobbling up the road and muttering to himself as he moved along.

Altogether far too many innocents who might be hurt if bullets started flying.

I swallowed against the dryness in my throat. "Why should you be so anxious to take the Reverend Albright's private correspondence?"

The man's gaze shifted sideways. "Owed me money, didn't he?"

"Possibly, but that doesn't explain why you would be willing to shoot two complete strangers to get your hands on his letters. I assure you, there's no money inside here." I glanced at Watson. "Did you see any money?"

Uncle John looked slightly white about the edges of his mouth, but he shook his head. "No, definitely no money."

He stopped. I widened my eyes at him, silently willing him to keep on going.

If it came down to it, I wasn't willing to let either myself or Uncle John die over a box of old papers. But the very fact that anyone *wanted* Reverend Albright's correspondence enough to shoot or even kill for it made me want to hold onto the box if at all possible.

Uncle John cleared his throat, then kept going, doing a fair imitation of a man whose tongue has been loosened by nervousness.

"I, ah, I haven't had the chance to look through the papers fully, you understand, but I am perfectly certain that I would have noticed any bank notes, gold sovereigns, Spanish doubloons ..."

The gunman looked down at the box then back at Uncle John, as though checking to be sure of what he had just heard.

I watched him, trying to calculate angles of attack. Grab his wrist, aim the gun upwards, at the same time kick his leg out from under him ...

The man's grip was still firm on the revolver, but maybe I should risk it; I might not get a better chance.

I drew in a breath—and the elderly man making his way towards us up the street suddenly collapsed with a hoarse cry, clutching at his chest, his face contorted in agony.

The gunman's head snapped towards the sound of commotion. I stepped forward, grabbed his arm and yanked him towards me while he was still off balance. He stumbled, trying to recover, but I had already struck him hard on the back of the neck.

He grunted, briefly trying to right himself, but Watson's fist caught him under the chin, making him topple backwards. The revolver clattered to the ground. His head struck the cobblestones with a sharp thud, and he lay still, knocked unconscious. Or faking?

Behind us, the front door to the rectory opened, and Amelia Scott appeared.

"I—" she started, then gasped, one hand flying up to cover her mouth at the sight of the unconscious man on the ground. "Good heavens!" She reached to clutch Watson's arm. "John ... Miss James ... are you all right?"

"Quite all right." Gently, Uncle John detached her hand. "But I must go to that gentleman. I fear he may be suffering from a seizure of the heart."

He gestured to the white-haired old man, who was still lying on the ground, wheezing and clutching his chest. The *supposed* white-haired old man.

I took a steadying breath, letting my own pulse settle back into its normal rhythm. The gunman hadn't moved; he really was unconscious. No longer a threat.

"I don't think you need to worry about that, Uncle John."

LUCY

12. An Unconscious Assailant

"Heart failure, eh, Watson?" Holmes's mouth was twitching beneath the edges of the long white beard that formed part of the elderly gentleman's disguise. "Not to mention Spanish doubloons?"

We were standing guard over the gunman, who was still unconscious, while Mrs. Scott telephoned for the police. Holmes had taken the precaution of using his belt to bind the stranger's ankles together, but so far he hadn't even stirred.

Watson scowled. "Be careful, Holmes, or I may get a sudden urge to write up an account of the affair at the Brighton Grand Hotel."

"You wouldn't dare."

"What happened at the Brighton Grand Hotel?" I asked.

"A murder occurred at a convention of ventriloquists being held there," Watson answered. "None of them would speak to us directly, it all had to be through their puppets ... dummies ... whatever the correct term for them is."

I looked at my father, struggling to keep from laughing. "You had to question a hotel full of ventriloquists' dummies?"

Holmes's expression turned grimly reflective. "Let us just say that it was months before I could so much as look at an advertising poster for a vaudeville act without shuddering."

"Thank you for coming today," I told him. "Even though we weren't expecting you. Was there any particular reason you had for being concerned for our safety?"

"I merely thought it might be productive to make a subtle canvass of the neighborhood in a guise other than my own," Holmes said. "To learn what his nearest neighbors thought of Reverend Albright."

"That, and it allowed you to escape filling out wedding invitations?"

Holmes valiantly ignored me. "That I chanced to arrive here at the very moment you were in need of someone to provide a distraction was purely serendipitous."

"Did you learn anything useful about Reverend Albright?"

"Only that he was both well-liked and well-respected by both his neighbors and his parishioners. Which in itself proves very little. I once investigated a case of a man who buried his aging mother and father in his basement—and his neighbors were all fulsome in their praise and adamant in their assertions that he was the very last person they would have suspected could commit such a crime. Nevertheless, there is nothing to indicate that anyone in these parts had the slightest doubts as to the reverend's good character."

I glanced down at the man at our feet, wishing that Uncle John hadn't been quite so effective at knocking him senseless. I would have liked to ask him a few questions.

"Nor anything to suggest why this man would be so anxious to get his hands on Reverend Albright's private papers?"

"Nothing whatsoever." Holmes's gaze shifted focus slightly as he looked down at our gunman, which generally meant that his thoughts were following some complicated track that would make sense only to him.

With the tip of the cane that had been part of his elderly gentleman's disguise, he drew back the folds of the scarf around the man's throat, baring his face.

"Have either of you seen him before?"

I studied the man. Clean-cut, neutral features, neither particularly handsome nor plain. Medium mouth, medium nose. I already knew that his eyes were of medium brown.

"I've never seen him before." I glanced sideways. "Uncle John?"

"No. At least"—a furrow darkened Watson's brow—"I don't think so. Average-looking sort of chap, isn't he?"

It was true. If someone had set out to find a man who could blend perfectly into a crowd, passing unnoticed by ninety-eight percent of the population, they couldn't have found a better match than him.

"Did you have the impression that he was expecting you to be here?" Holmes asked.

"He was clearly expecting trouble of some kind, otherwise why bring the gun? But apart from that—" I frowned, trying to remember my first impressions exactly. "I don't know. The first time I noticed him was when he was standing a little way up the street, just looking at us. But whether that was because he was shocked to see Watson holding the box of Reverend Albright's correspondence—or whether he was waiting for the right moment to confront us? I'm honestly not sure."

"Interesting. Although as to the gun—" Holmes stooped,

bending to retrieve the weapon, which still lay on the pavement. He broke open the cylinder and spun the chamber—which was entirely empty.

My eyebrows went up. "The gun wasn't loaded?"

"It was not." Holmes didn't sound surprised.

"You were expecting that it wouldn't be?"

"The hollow clatter it made when it fell against the ground led me to believe it was empty of ammunition. It does raise several interesting questions, however."

Holmes stopped as the church bell next door chimed. Half past twelve o'clock.

I hadn't realized it had grown so late. "I need to be at the Savoy for the two o'clock performance," I said. "Of course, I can stay to give a statement to the police—"

Holmes shook his head. "Watson and I can remain here and explain matters. It might actually be to our advantage if you were to depart for Baker Street before the constabulary arrive."

"What? Why—" I stopped, realizing what Holmes intended. "Ah. Conveniently happening to take Reverend Albright's correspondence with me?"

"It would avoid any tedious debate about whether the reverend's letters ought to remain in our charge or be taken in and filed as police evidence."

It was in times like these that I was convinced I was going to make an absolutely terrible police sergeant's wife. Bethnal Green was barely even a mile away from Jack's Commercial Street Station. He probably *knew* the officers who would arrive at any moment.

Although maybe that was another reason I should be gone before they got here.

"And you would naturally prefer that the letters remain in our charge," I said to Holmes.

"Until we establish what is so important about them, I would indeed. I suggest that you see them safely back to Baker Street. Meanwhile—" Holmes glanced at Watson. "I wonder whether you would consider putting your medical skills to use in the examination of Reverend Albright's body."

"Certainly, if you wish it, Holmes," Watson said. "But I must tell you, there was absolutely nothing inside Reverend Albright's room to suggest that his death was anything but a suicide. Lucy inspected the room herself."

Holmes started to turn to me, then checked the motion. "You did not?"

"I was otherwise—"

"You were engaged in conversation with Mrs. Scott, no doubt."

Uncle John gave a slightly martyred sigh. "Go ahead and ask Lucy whether she saw anything suspicious or out of place."

"I didn't," I said. "Nothing at all."

"Nevertheless." Holmes put his fingers together, resting them against his upper lip. "I believe, Watson, that two visits—first to the police station and then to the mortuary—are in our immediate future."

LUCY

13. Flowers from an Admirer

"Lucy!" The door to 221 Baker Street burst open before I had even finished paying the cab driver, and a small girl in a blue dress and white pinafore exploded out to greet me.

Even if I hadn't been impossibly in love with Jack, I would *almost* have married him solely for the sake of his little sister, who was nine years old, bright, endlessly energetic, and often terrifyingly brave.

She launched herself down the front steps, her blond braids flying. "Lucy, Jack had to be on duty this morning—something about one of the other officers being hurt. But he said that if it's all right with you, I can stay with you today, and I know you have a matinee performance, and I could come along if you could bring me to the theatre with you, so can you?"

"Can I bring you to the Savoy, or can I say all of that in a single breath, the way you just did?"

Becky giggled. "Bring me to the Savoy, of course."

"Good." I shifted the file box of Reverend Albright's correspondence so that I could hug her. "Because the other might have given me trouble."

"What is that?" Becky asked, pointing to the box. "Is it something to do with a case? Something exciting?"

"It's—" I hesitated.

Becky was far more conversant with criminal affairs and violence than the average nine-year-old girl, but I still didn't especially want to tell her about Reverend Albright having taken his own life.

"It is to do with a case—remember those robberies that Jack and I were looking into yesterday? As for exciting, though, I doubt it."

During the carriage ride back to Baker Street, I had taken a cursory look through all of the papers inside. I hadn't had time to read every letter in detail, but from what I had seen, the Reverend Albright's correspondence had ranged from the *expectedly ordinary* to the *dull in the extreme*. Letters from parishioners, thanking Reverend Albright for his kindness during a time of bereavement, or for officiating at a baptism or a wedding.

The only papers even approaching excitement or scandal were a whole spate of messages from various members of the parish vestry, who seemed to be almost bloodthirsty in their disagreement over the need for a new church roof.

"Just a lot of slightly boring letters."

That didn't explain why our gunman had been so anxious to get his hands on them. But as Holmes would no doubt tell me if he were here, there was no point in trying to form theories before I knew what sort of story the man had told the police—and what the results were of Holmes's and Watson's visit to the morgue.

"Oh." Becky looked disappointed, but then brightened. "I could still help you look through them, though. You never know, maybe some of the letters are written in a secret code!"

I hesitated. Involving Becky in a case—any case—always made my heart clench. But in this case, it was hard to see how going through a pile of letters could prove dangerous. "All right. Let me just put the box up in Holmes's rooms for safekeeping, and we can read through everything together sometime. If there is a secret code, I'm certain we'll find it."

* * *

At the front of the stage, Elsie and Fairfax—played by Ilka Palmay and Charles Cunningham—embraced, then broke into song.

> With happiness my soul is cloyed,
> This is our joy-day unalloyed!

It was the part of the final scene where the chorus was supposed to echo the reunited couple. But glancing sideways, I saw that next to me, Grace Lilley was standing motionless, staring vacantly off into space.

She had been only half-attentive all through this afternoon's performance—which, of course, was always a danger, performing the same show six or seven times in a week for months on end. It was all too easy to sometimes slip into going though the motions almost mindlessly, and nearly every performer in the D'Oyly Carte company had a story of suddenly finding themselves on stage without any idea of what scene was actually being performed or what they were supposed to be doing.

I jogged Grace's elbow lightly. She startled, and then joined in the refrain:

> Yes, yes! With happiness their souls are cloyed, this is their
> joy-day unalloyed!

Point—the unhappy jester who also loved Elsie—collapsed in despair, Elsie and Fairfax embraced again, and the curtain came down to thunderous applause.

"Are you all right?" I asked Grace, as we made our way off the stage after the final curtain calls had been made.

"What?" Grace was a pretty girl, slightly on the plump side, with blue eyes, an upturned nose, and straight blond hair.

She gathered up the skirts of her 16th century maid's costume to keep from catching them on any of the painted wooden scenery that turned the stage into a representation of the Tower of London. "Oh—yes, I'm fine."

She still looked preoccupied, a faint line of worry or annoyance between her brows. I didn't question her, though. Grace and I were friends here at the theatre, but not so close that I felt as though I ought to press on.

Becky had watched the show from backstage in the wings and was already sitting at my dressing table when we reached the women's dressing rooms. Grace had her space beside mine, and Becky was paging through one of the towering stack of ladies' fashion magazines that Grace kept in a basket beside her chair.

"Lucy, could you do my hair *exactly* like this for the wedding?" Becky pointed to an illustration of a lady with her hair done in an arrangement of braids that looked more complicated than the apparatus for one of Holmes's chemistry experiments.

Privately, I thought it would take an act of Parliament and a minor miracle to make Becky sit still long enough, but I said, "Of course, if you like. I'll probably need to practice first, though."

"Look, Lucy, someone's sent you flowers," Grace said. She

gestured to the dozen long-stemmed red roses that sat on my dressing table, smiling and raising her eyebrows. "A certain police sergeant, maybe?"

"They wouldn't be from Jack." Becky turned another page in the magazine. "He knows Lucy better than that. She doesn't really like flowers."

"Flowers themselves are pretty; I'd just rather have a living plant than something that will die in a few days," I said. Which was practically heresy for an actress, but I couldn't help it.

"Besides," Becky added. "Whoever sent the flowers was left-handed. Look at the card."

In addition to lessons in cookery from Mrs. Hudson, Becky also received instruction in handwriting analysis and other points of detection from Holmes every time she visited Baker Street.

I picked up the card that lay next to the flowers. It was plain white and said only, *From an admirer.*

"You're right." The letters were faintly smudged by the edge of the writer's hand having been dragged over them while the ink was still wet, definitely left-handed.

I pushed the flowers aside so that I could sit down at the dressing table and start to take off my stage makeup.

Grace stared at me. "A dozen red roses, and you don't even want them?"

"Not especially." Receiving flowers from anonymous admirers was unfortunately one of the drawbacks of a career in the theater: some men saw us perform onstage and somehow convinced themselves it was the beginning of a romantic acquaintance.

Someone knocked at the dressing room door. Grace checked

to be sure that everyone was decently clothed and then called out, "Come in!"

Mr. Watts, the new doorman of the Savoy theater, appeared in the doorway.

He was a large man of fifty or so and had been a police constable with the London City Police for twenty years until he'd retired. He still had the gruff, almost paternal look with which I imagined he'd patrolled the streets. The look of a man who knew all his charges' worst faults, but had a hidden fondness for them all the same.

"Message for you, Miss James." Mr. Watts held out an envelope to me. "Delivery boy said it was urgent."

"Thank you."

My heart quickened at sight of the writing on the envelope, which was addressed in Uncle John's neat but slightly-cramped hand. I set it down on my dressing table unopened.

My connection to Uncle John and to Holmes still wasn't known to anyone at the theater, which meant that I didn't want to read Watson's message in front of Grace.

"Oh, Mr. Watts?" I asked.

The doorman had turned to go, but halted. "Yes?"

"Do you know who sent these flowers?" I gestured to the roses.

Mr. Watts eyed the arrangement, then shrugged. "Some dirty foreigner," he grunted. "Never seen him before tonight."

We had all quickly discovered that, with Mr. Watts, *dirty foreigner* could cover a great deal of ground. Not that that was unusual; since moving to London, I had discovered that a fairly large portion of the population considered anyone not from England as approximately as trustworthy as a rattlesnake, whether they were from Scotland, France, or Argentina.

I suspected it was only because I was engaged to Jack that Mr. Watts consented to speak politely to me at all; marrying a policeman *almost* canceled out the crime of being American.

"Were the roses from this foreign gentleman, or was he just delivering them?" I asked.

Mr. Watts grunted again. "How do I know? He handed over the roses and a shilling to deliver them." He gave a contemptuous snort. "Foreigners. An Englishman would have made it half a crown."

I scrutinized his craggy features, wondering whether that was a hint that I should make up the difference in delivery fees, or whether he would be offended at me for offering him money.

I finally took out a coin and handed it to him without appearing to notice what I was doing.

"Thank you, Mr. Watts. Good night."

"Good night, Miss James."

"You should give the roses to Grace," Becky said, when the doorman had gone. "Maybe her young man will think she has another admirer, and it will make him finally propose to her."

Grace stopped in the act of changing into her street clothes and stared at Becky, her mouth dropping open.

"You've marked pictures with wedding dresses in all of these magazines," Becky said, gesturing. "But for all different seasons—spring, winter, fall—which means you can't have a definite date when you're getting married, and also—"

She stopped, catching sight of Grace's expression. "I'm sorry. Is that one of those things that grown-ups don't like to have discussed?"

Grace's expression cleared. "It's all right, sweetheart." She stooped and kissed Becky's cheek. "You're not saying anything I haven't thought for myself a dozen times. I will take the roses, though, Lucy, if you really don't want them. Not to make Charlie jealous—even if he deserves it. Just because they shouldn't go to waste."

"Of course, you're welcome to them."

Grace finished pinning on her hat and tucked the bouquet of roses in one arm. As she opened the door to the hallway, I saw a fair-haired young man straighten up from where he'd been leaning against the wall.

"Walk you home, Grace?" he asked.

Grace shook her head. "No, thank you, Will." She spoke politely but firmly.

The young man's face fell slightly, but he didn't give up. "I could carry those flowers for you."

I heard Grace blow out an exasperated-sounding breath. "Believe it or not, Will, I am perfectly capable of carrying a bunch of flowers all the way back to Lambeth by myself."

She swept past him.

Will looked up and grinned crookedly when he saw me watching him through the open doorway. "I think I'm wearing her down."

Will Simpson sang a tenor part in the chorus and always made me think of a bouncing golden retriever puppy. He had the same chocolate brown eyes, the same energy and slightly over-eager manner.

Speaking to him, you kept being tempted to pat him on the head. But he was as *likable* as a puppy, as well—to everyone in the company, apparently, except Grace.

Will had asked whether he could walk Grace home every

night for the last two months, and every time, Grace had refused. You had to credit Will with persistence if nothing else.

"I grow on a girl, you know," Will went on. He saw Becky beside me and winked at her, making a comic face. "Of course, as this young lady is probably about to observe, so does a rash."

"That wasn't Grace's young man, was it?" Becky asked, when Will had gone.

"No." I'd never met Grace's Charlie, but I knew he wasn't a part of the D'Oyly Carte Company.

"That's a shame," Becky said. "He looks as though he'd be nicer to her than this Charlie, whoever he is."

"You could be right."

Becky frowned. "I wouldn't wait and wait for a boy who made me unhappy. If anyone tried to treat *me* that way, I'd punch him right in the nose."

I smiled. "Your brother will be glad to hear it."

Grace had gone, and no one was watching us, so I slit open the envelope from Uncle John.

"What does Dr. Watson say?" Becky asked. Of course she would recognize Uncle John's handwriting.

The message was brief:

All ligature marks on the dead man's neck perfectly consistent with death by self-inflicted hanging. No other bruising or injuries, no signs of a struggle.

Our armed—or perhaps I should say armed-yet-unarmed— assailant claims he was hired in a nearby pub to burgle Reverend Albright's house and steal any and all items of a personal nature. He had planned to go in through a back window, but seeing us leaving the rectory, thought he had better stop us from taking anything away in case it affected how much he was paid for completing the job.

A weak story, but—as Holmes murmured under his breath when he heard it—possibly just weak enough to be believed.

I folded up the paper and slid it back inside the envelope. I wasn't entirely opposed to telling Becky about the incident with the gunman—but not until I'd had the chance to tell Jack first.

"He says it looks as though the culprit to the robberies I was telling you about has been found. Now." I stood up. "The real question is, what are we going to do for the rest of our afternoon?"

Becky jumped to her feet, too. "Can we go to the new house?"

I smiled. "Perfect," I told her. "You must have read my mind."

LUCY

14. AT THE FUTURE HOME

As part of his promotion to sergeant, Jack was assigned a house on Palmer Street, a quiet side street about a ten-minute walk from the police station. The landlord who owned most of the houses on the street had offered number 8 to the police force rent-free, ensuring a police presence—and thus added security—in the midst of his properties.

The London Police force didn't spend its energy making sure the homes offered to officers were palatial estates, so Becky and Jack were still living in their old lodgings in St. Giles while we worked at making the new house more habitable.

My father would undoubtedly have paid for the necessary repairs if I'd asked him. But I liked doing the work. It made the whole place feel more as though it actually belonged to me.

Becky bounced on her toes as I fitted the key into the front door. "I'm going to go upstairs and work on my room, all right, Lucy?"

"Of course."

Becky gave me a stern look—or as stern as her round blue eyes were capable of looking. "Promise you won't peek?"

Becky had chosen one of the upstairs bedrooms as hers and was doing the painting herself, refusing to let either me or Jack come in until it was finished, so it would be a surprise.

Judging by the number of cans of paint she had dragged up the stairs, she either changed her mind about the color every ten minutes or was aiming for a rainbow-hued effect.

I held up one hand, in oath-taking fashion. "I solemnly swear."

We had stopped off in Baker Street to collect Prince, Becky and Jack's huge brown and white mastiff, who had spent the afternoon snoring in Mrs. Hudson's kitchen while Becky and I were at the theater.

Holmes and Watson had both been out. Watson was making the rounds of his patients. Holmes, as Mrs. Hudson had put it, was "the Good Lord only knows where."

Now Becky tugged on Prince's leash, and the big dog trotted up the stairs after her. I could hear them overhead a moment later—Becky's quick pattering footsteps and Prince's nails clicking against the wood floors.

Our new home was a small, narrow brick row house, with a sitting room, dining room, and kitchen downstairs, and three small bedrooms upstairs. The floors tilted at odd angles, the wallpaper was stained and peeling in places, and the kitchen chimney smoked, but I didn't care even a little; I still loved every square foot.

I went into the dining room and lighted the lamp I'd left on the mantle. I was dressed in the boots, plain cotton shirt, and trousers that I wore when I was crossing through an area of the city where I was safer to appear as a boy. My hair was tied back with an old scarf.

I was halfway through my current task—painting the window trim—when a footstep in the doorway made me look up.

I'd expected to see Becky, but it was Jack, still in his blue police uniform.

I smiled at him. "Hello."

I'd seen him just yesterday, but my heart still turned over in my chest at the sight of him in the doorway, broad-shouldered and handsome, his dark hair still slightly damp from the drizzling rain outside.

I had spent my entire life alone, taking care of myself, solving my own problems, relying on no one else. It was almost frightening to care about another person so much. But then, I had also never felt this happy at sight of another person before.

"How did you know we'd be here?"

"I telephoned to Baker Street from the station, and Dr. Watson told me. You're all right?"

I could see worry at the back of his gaze. Uncle John must have also told him about the gunman.

"Fine. Really," I added. "The gun wasn't even loaded, and I barely had to do anything—first, Holmes distracted him by pretending to have a heart attack, and then Uncle John knocked him unconscious."

Jack's eyebrows quirked up. "There's probably something wrong about the fact that that counts as a slow morning for you."

"I'm sorry you had to find out from Uncle John. I was going to tell you; I just wanted to wait until you were off duty."

"That's all right, Beautiful." Jack came over and kissed me on the top of the head, keeping away from the paint. "How's everything else? All right?"

The last time we'd been here, a section of plaster had fallen from the kitchen ceiling. Jack had repaired it, but we were still on the lookout for any other minor disasters.

"Well, Becky has asked for three new colors of paint so far. And *you* may possibly need your eyesight examined if you think this qualifies as beauty. But apart from that, everything is fine."

"I thought smears of paint across your nose were a new fashion."

"Just for that, you can pick up a paintbrush and help me."

"I will if you want me to," Jack said, "but I was thinking I would take a look at the electrical wiring for the lights over the mantle."

"Of course."

In addition to owning properties all through the East End, the landlord of our street had also bought stock in the Edison and Swan Power company—with the result that, unlike the vast majority of houses in the neighborhood, ours and several more on the block had been wired for electricity.

Mice had taken up residence in one of the walls at some point in the not-too-distant past, though, and chewed through the wires. Jack had been working on replacing them.

I listened for a moment to make sure that Becky was still safely upstairs, then asked, "So Uncle John told you about the Reverend Albright?"

"He did."

"And? What do you think?"

Jack shrugged out of his police overtunic. "It's not what I would have expected. But then, I didn't really talk to him. I only saw him the once. You?"

"The same." I went back to my painting, concentrating on not leaving any smudges of paint on the windowpane. "Did Uncle John tell you anything about the gunman's story—the one who tried to steal the reverend's private papers? He sent a note to me at the theater, but he didn't really go into much detail."

"He said that according to his own account, the man's name is Adam Smith."

"*Smith*? Really, that was the best he could do?"

Jack shrugged. "I know, but according to Dr. Watson, he actually had an old Royal Navy pension card in that name."

"All right, I suppose the reason Smith is such a common last name is that some people actually *are* called that. He was in the navy, though?" I thought of the man's wary, athletic movements.

I would have said army was more likely, but I supposed it was possible.

"His story is that he was in a pub down the road when a man came over and offered him five pounds if he'd rob Reverend Albright's house. The man said the reverend had just died—"

I interrupted. "He knew about the reverend's death?"

"Apparently. He told our friend Mr. Smith that the Reverend Albright owed him money, and there was no chance of his getting it back now that the reverend was dead and gone, so he was willing to hire Mr. Smith to get it for him. He said the house ought to be unguarded."

"And Mr. Smith was stupid enough to take him up on this offer?"

"He was stupid enough to try and threaten you and Dr. Watson with an unloaded weapon practically in the middle of a public street."

"True. What did Mr. Smith say that this man who hired him looked like?"

"Medium height, middle-aged, didn't get a good look at his face—the pub they were sitting in was dark."

"In other words, the sort of description that could apply to practically anyone."

"More or less."

"What do you think of the story?" I asked.

Jack shrugged again. "I've heard stranger. I will say, when someone's lying, they usually try to invent too many details— thinking that'll make it sound more believable. I'd have a harder time buying Adam Smith's story if he gave the man who hired him a dragon tattoo or a squint or a cast in one eye. As it is—"

"It's just a weak enough story to be believable?" That was what Holmes had said, too, according to Uncle John. "It's just—" I stopped, shaking my head. "Never mind, I'm probably thinking too much."

"That'd be a change."

I made a face at Jack. "You realize I could just as easily paint you as the walls."

"You could try." Jack looked at me, his brief grin fading. "Is there something bothering you about it all, though? You don't get suspicious for no reason. If you think something's wrong, it probably is."

"That's just it, there doesn't seem to be anything wrong at all—apart from Reverend Albright having committed larceny and then taken his own life, that is. I honestly don't think it can have been anything other than a suicide. The doors and windows were locked, there was no sign of anyone else having gotten in, the suicide note was definitely in the reverend's handwriting—I checked. Uncle John agreed with me, too. He went to the mortuary this afternoon and said nothing about the body suggested anything but death by self-inflicted hanging. Uncle John may sometimes misinterpret clues at a crime scene, but he doesn't make mistakes when it comes to medical evidence. As for Adam Smith's mysterious employer, unless he tries to contact Adam Smith again, there's almost no chance we'll find him."

"Unless he or someone else he's hired tries to rob the reverend's house again." Jack said.

"Is Holmes posting some of the Irregulars to watch the rectory?" Given that Holmes had been out this afternoon, it wouldn't shock me to learn that he was keeping watch himself.

"So Dr. Watson said."

"Well, unless Amelia Scott wants us to keep digging into the matter—which I can't imagine she will, for fear of making a scandal—we don't even have a client, so I'm officially going to stop worrying about it."

Investigating would only serve to tarnish Reverend Albright's reputation more, which, however much he'd stolen from the Aid Society, I couldn't think that he deserved.

I finished the last section of window trim, then asked, "How is the man who was attacked on duty last night. Constable ... Dickon, was that his name?"

"He's got a cracked skull and a stab wound in one arm, so he'll be in the infirmary for a few days, but he was lucky," Jack said. "As lessons go in what happens if you're drunk on duty, that one came cheap."

"He'd been drinking?"

Jack picked up a pair of pliers and used them to twist the end of a copper wire. "It's not that uncommon. A lot of the public house owners leave a free pot of ale out on an open windowsill for whichever beat constable is assigned to walk past. They see it as a trade—free drinks in exchange for the constable putting in a good word when the publican's license is up for renewal."

"Really? Did you used to take them up on the trade back when you were a beat constable?"

"No." Jack shook his head. "Like PC Dickon just found out, getting slow or sloppy when there are people around who'd like nothing better than to see you dead in the gutter? Not a good idea."

I wrapped my paintbrush in turpentine-soaked rags and came over to the other side of the room where Jack was working.

He had the sconce over the mantle unscrewed and taken out from the wall, and as I watched, he deftly twisted two wires together, a slight frown of concentration between his straight dark brows.

I looked from him to the tangle of wire protruding from the wall like a nest of snakes. "Are you certain you know what you're doing?"

"Well, either that or I'll start a fire and burn the house down to the ground. One or the other." Jack looked up and grinned at my expression. "I'm pretty sure about it. It's not that hard."

"Speak for yourself." I picked up the book on electrical circuitry that he had borrowed from Holmes and frowned at one of the diagrams, which, as far as I could see, looked like a jumbled maze of meaningless squiggles and straight lines. "This actually makes sense to you?"

"Let's hope so, anyway." Jack reached for a set of pliers, then paused, smiling at me.

"What?"

"Nothing. Just nice to know there's something you're not

automatically good at. You're frighteningly good at everything else."

"Just wait until you try to eat something I've cooked. Becky has already made me promise to let her do all the cooking and only to help under her strictest supervision."

Jack laughed.

"Is the Italian woman still in the holding cells?" I asked.

Jack nodded. "She's supposed to be transferred to Holloway on Monday, but she's still at the station for the time being. Did you find anything out about her?"

"I doubt I leaned anything that you don't know already. She's newly arrived in this country, and she came via ship."

"Saltwater stains?"

"Exactly—on the hem of the cloak she was wearing, but they're not muddy, the way they'd be if she got them down at the London docks at high tide."

Jack nodded, still focused on the wiring.

"That's slightly odd, though," I went on. "Because she also had a petticoat from Lambeth Work House, and I wouldn't have thought she could have been in the country long enough to have had to resort to a workhouse."

Workhouses were, in theory, a way of taking care of the poor—and, in practice, more of a way of punishing the inmates for the crime of being impoverished. Grim, cheerless, disease-ridden places, they inflicted harsh discipline—up to and including outright abuse—on the residents and gave them barely food and shelter enough to stay alive.

"She doesn't have to have been a workhouse resident herself, though," Jack said. "She could have bought the petticoat from a rag shop. Or stolen it, for that matter."

"You're right." I hadn't really thought of that, but it was true enough. "As far as my speaking with her goes, she wasn't willing to tell me anything, not even her name."

I remembered the woman's hunched shoulders, the way she had rocked herself back and forth, striking the wall as though she were trying to use physical pain as a way to drive off fear.

"What will happen to her?"

"She'll be charged and taken to Holloway until she comes to trial. That part's not up to me, unfortunately." Jack shrugged. "I could see whether I can somehow get her charge sheet shuffled to bottom of the stack of new cases that just came in today, though. Might buy us another day to see whether there's anything else we can find out."

"Thank you. I can come and talk to her again in the morning. I just hate the feeling that there was more I could have done or something else I should have realized about her."

I frowned, suddenly remembering. "She did say one thing—the only words she spoke to me the whole time, except to tell me to leave. A name, or at least I think it was. Though not her name. *Campana.* Then she said *Casa di morte.* That means 'death house.' "

"*Campana?*" Jack repeated. "*Death house?*"

"That's what it sounded like. She had an accent, though, and she wasn't speaking clearly, so I can't be entirely certain. Does it mean anything to you?"

Jack shook his head. "Nothing."

Something crashed over our heads, followed by a dog's protesting yelp.

Becky's voice—muffled by the floor between us—called down, "It's all right. I accidentally spilled some paint on Prince, but his tail looks nice pink, so it's all right!"

I looked at Jack. "Do you think one of us should go up there and assess the damage?"

"It's possible."

Instead of moving, though, Jack stayed where he was, just looking at me. He reached to tuck a stray curl of hair behind my ear, his hand sliding down to the join of my neck and shoulder and lingering.

My breath caught a little. "If you look at me any harder, the ends of my hair are going to catch on fire."

Jack shook his head, smiling crookedly. "Sorry. Sometimes it just seems like I have to be dreaming this, that's all. Seeing you here. Knowing that this—all of this, living in a place like this with Becky and me—is actually what you want."

"Are you joking? I would marry you right this second, if there weren't a strong chance of my father's murdering me for wasting all his efforts at planning the wedding. And as for the house, I *love* it."

I looked around at the small, square-shaped room. Small or no, it would still be cozy with a fire in the grate and rugs covering the floor. "It's the first place in my entire life that I've been able to think of as really home."

221 Baker Street came close, but it was and always would be more Sherlock Holmes's place than mine.

Jack let go of the wires and wrapped an arm around me, gathering me close.

"You're going to get covered in paint, too," I warned him.

"Probably." Instead of letting go, Jack lowered his head and kissed me.

WATSON

15. MIDNIGHT AT BAKER STREET

At my writing desk, I put down my pen and closed my new notebook, having completed a brief article on The Bethnal Green School in which the young and hopeful Clara Sheffield played a leading role. I had been taken with her youthful aspiration, and I had reviewed the materials given to me by Amelia at our first meeting, which listed names and locations of girls who had been successfully placed in the colonies or other far-flung corners of the Empire. The article practically wrote itself. It would fill a column on the magazine page, possibly two if I could persuade my editor to include an illustration. I had in my mind the provisional title of "Youthful Hopes for the Future."

Upon completing my work, I realized that the time was past eleven. Holmes was poking up the fire and adding new coals, an indication that he was still occupied. He returned to his own desk and sat, taking up his magnifying glass and bending over a ponderous volume that filled the writing surface. In my own chair before the fire, I allowed the warmth on my face and the flickering gold and blue flames to lull me into a dreamlike state. Then I realized that the volume Holmes was inspecting so closely was the Rand McNally Atlas.

I sat up. "Holmes, why look at maps of the world at this late hour?"

"Seaports, Watson. Seaports."

"You said you were no longer on the diamond case."

"I did indeed." His words were delivered with that overly-patient undertone that he used whenever he wanted me to make some deduction on my own.

"You said you were no longer on the diamond case, but you have changed your mind. Or—" I tried to read his expression as he bent over his magnifying glass. "Or you did not mean it the first time. No, you were dissembling, Holmes. Laying a false track ... for whoever you suspect has betrayed us ... let word of our involvement get out, resulting in our being accosted in the street by those two thugs."

He did not move. "Go on," he said.

"But I do not understand. You returned the diamonds to De Beers."

"To what end?"

I tried to tease out the sequence of events. "Mr. Voortrekker will notify Mr. Rhodes. The chain of communications that leaked before will leak again, allowing whoever learned of your involvement the first time to now realize that there is no point in accosting us, since the jewels, raw and cut, are now out of the reach of thieves in the De Beers safe."

"Quite so." Still he did not move.

"Yet you said you needed the jewels if you were to investigate."

Now he moved. He sat up and pulled open the drawer to his small desk. Moments later, he deposited two bulging black silk sacks atop the pages of the atlas.

I stared. "Those are the real diamonds?"

"Indeed. The sacks are new and a trifle too small, but the diamonds inside are the originals. Regarding the two sacks in Mr. Voortrekker's safe, the conditions are reversed. If I am to proceed to involve myself with the diamond smugglers, I will need genuine bait. These people will spot a fake immediately. Yet I cannot have us accosted at every turn or have our rooms broken into. What I did was the only logical solution."

"What if the exchange is discovered?"

"That will depend on when the discovery occurs. When the case is concluded successfully, I shall of course make full restoration. Until then, I shall deny any knowledge and claim to De Beers that I did not inspect the jewels closely, having relied on Mr. Rhodes to proffer only the genuine article."

"How will you make time for this, when you have the other case? To say nothing of the impending wedding."

"Which other case?"

"The Ripper, of course."

"Actually, there are three other cases, Watson." He extended his long fingers as he ticked them off. "First, there is the case of the petty valuables, some not so petty, that Mrs. Scott asked you to investigate. Second, there is the suicide of the Reverend Albright. If we are to take the confession as a fact, the two cases would cancel each other out. And yet, why should a man of the cloth steal from his benefactors, when he has no hope of their continuing benevolence if he is caught and every expectation of it continuing if he merely accepts their generosity and carries on? It is highly irrational, a trait which a clergyman may of course exhibit as well as any other man, but one which presents us with a puzzle nonetheless."

"I do not understand why you would wish to involve yourself in affairs of such relative insignificance."

"Consider the timetable, Watson."

"I do not follow."

"You are asked by your publisher and Mrs. Scott to perform an act of professional charity, helping a worthy cause with your writing. But then the puzzle of the stolen silver and jewels emerges, and then the Reverend's death. All hot upon the heels of your first meeting with your editor. You had no time even to write in your new notebook before you were called upon to detect. Do you not find that a puzzle?"

"I see a coincidence, surely, but I do not see anything more than that."

Holmes gave a resigned sigh. For a long moment he was silent, merely leaning back in his chair, the atlas and the two sacks of diamonds before him, his fingertips steepled together in his characteristic fashion.

Then he said, "It is as well that I see puzzles of this sort everywhere. I shall remain here, with my work, while by the end of November Lucy and Jack will be married and in their new home. And, as you have married before, you will eventually marry again, either to Mrs. Scott or to someone else."

My face flushed hot and not from the warmth of the fire. "Holmes—"

He held up his hand, bidding me to silence. Then he resumed. "After the two cases concerning Reverend Albright, case three is that of the dead woman unidentified at present, strangled and mutilated in Whitechapel at the scene of one of the crimes of Jack himself. A corollary of that case, of course, is the discrepancy between her outer clothing and her other garments and the note found in her lapel. So you see, Watson, you need not concern yourself as you get on with your new writing projects. I have more than enough to occupy my time."

He bent once more over his map.

I went upstairs to my sleeping room.

I tossed and turned for several hours and had just fallen asleep when the ring of our telephone awakened me.

I heard Holmes answer. Then his voice hardened. He said, "Of course." Then I heard the click of the receiver on the switch-box as he hung up.

He called out, "Watson!"

PART TWO

LUCY

16. GRIM NEWS

I woke in the darkness and for a disorienting moment lay still, uncertain of what had awakened me. A glance at the trundle bed showed me Becky's small form curled up under the blankets, fast asleep, her blond head resting on the pillow.

Jack was on duty for the night, which was why Becky was sleeping in Baker Street.

Prince was awake. A thorough scrubbing in Mrs. Hudson's largest washtub had removed the pink paint, and now the big dog had lifted his head alertly and was snuffling the air, his head cocked and ears raised.

I listened, too, and heard them: footsteps, mounting the stairs to 221B. Not Holmes or Dr. Watson; these footsteps were heavier than my father's and without the slight limp that marked Uncle John's.

I slipped out of bed and put a soothing hand on Prince's neck. "Shhh, it's all right." I spoke in a whisper so as not to wake Becky. "Down, boy. Stay with Becky."

With a sigh, Prince settled back into his place at the foot of the bed, although he didn't look convinced that everything was as it should be. Or maybe that was my own uneasiness speaking. The clock on my dressing table showed the time to be three-forty-five in the morning. Experience had taught me that visitors never arrived to speak with my father at this hour with *good* news.

I started to reach for my dressing gown, then changed my mind and found a black skirt and white shirtwaist instead.

* * *

"So you see, Holmes—" Inspector Lestrade broke off as I opened the door to 221B.

He sat on the sofa beside a second man, a distinguished-looking, white-haired gentleman whom I recognized as Sir Edward Bradford, the police commissioner.

My father stood beside the mantle, his expression clouded, though he raised a hand in a gesture of greeting at the sight of me.

Uncle John sat in an armchair by the fire, a troubled look on his blunt, square-cut face.

Sir Edward was the first to speak. "Miss James. I have just finished apologizing to your father for disturbing him at this hour, but I fear the matter could not wait. However, I must warn you that it is a grave, terrible business, and perhaps you ought not—"

Holmes cut him off. "You need not bother. Informing my daughter of the gravity of a situation is akin to waving a red flag in front of a bull. Or it would be, if bulls were, in fact, capable of discerning color."

His voice was calm, but there was a hardness to the words that raised a warning prickle across my skin. "What's wrong?"

I divided the question equally amongst all the men in the

room, but it was Sir Edward who answered, his face pinched with a look between worry and distaste. "I must warn you again, Miss James, that the details are quite distressing—"

I could have snapped back that *crime* was distressing; that was the whole point of why my father—and now I, as well—were committed to fighting it.

But Sir Edward was neither the first nor the last man whose misguided chivalry I would face, and he honestly didn't mean any harm.

I studied the cardboard file of papers that lay between Sir Edward and Inspector Lestrade on the sofa.

"Is this to do with the woman who was found strangled in Mitre Square last week? The one who made you suspect a return of the Jack the Ripper killer?"

Both Lestrade and Sir Edward looked at me with expressions of mild astonishment.

Holmes cut in with an impatient wave of his hand. "In addition to her many other talents, Lucy is capable of reading— even at a distance and upside down. She has no doubt by now discerned that the file resting between you contains evidence gathered from the first series of Whitechapel killings."

"There is reason to suspect that the matter may be more serious than you first supposed?" I asked steadily.

Holmes inclined his head. "As you say. Lestrade and Sir Edward have come to inform us that there has been another murder."

* * *

In the past two years since I'd first come to London, I'd grown familiar with police procedure.

Over the course of the next days and weeks, the whole of Whitechapel would be canvassed for witnesses, interviews would be conducted, suspects detained, until as accurate a timeline of the night's events as possible could be formed.

For now, though, the facts—as narrated by Holmes—were scanty at best.

A young couple had been walking along Hanbury Street at somewhere around two o'clock this morning. They could give only vague reasons for having gone into the rear yard of number 29 Hanbury, and Lestrade grunted that they were more likely a prostitute and her paying client than a bone fide couple.

In either case, the pair had ducked into the shadowed privacy of the rear yard—and discovered the body of a woman huddled in the recess between the yard steps and the property's back fence.

"Her throat had been slashed, and there were several further cuts to her lower extremities," Holmes said, "though we will know more about how she died when we have had a chance to personally examine the body."

I frowned. Holmes's cool, detached tone was jarringly at odds with the violence he was describing, but that wasn't what troubled me; I had trained myself to be accustomed to it by now.

"I agree, that sounds similar to one of the Ripper's attacks. But it could equally be a lover's quarrel turned violent, or a revenge killing, couldn't it?"

Holmes studied me for a moment, then sighed as he appeared to make up his mind that there really would be no leaving me out of the affair. "How familiar are you with the details of the original series of murders?"

"Only through what I was able to read in the newspapers

I smuggled into school."

In 1888, I had been thirteen, and the Ripper killings had made all the newspaper headlines, even in America. But the accounts were decidedly *not* the sort of thing considered proper reading for a student at Miss Porter's School for Girls.

Holmes spoke in the same dry, precise tone. "The rear yard of number 29 Hanbury Street was the murder site of Annie Chapman, on the 8th of September, 1888. Just as Mitre Square— the location of last week's killing—was the scene of Catherine Eddows's death, on the night of the 30th of September of the same year."

Holmes went on. "There is more. Following the death of Elizabeth Stride—who was murdered by the Ripper on the same night as Catherine Eddows—a singularly unreliable man named Matthew Packer came forward with a story of having sold grapes to a man and a woman whom he identified as Elizabeth Stride. According to Packer's statement—as reported by the press— the couple came to his shop at around 11pm on the night of the double murders. The man asked the soon-to-be murdered woman whether she would prefer white grapes or black, adding, *You shall have whichever you like best.*"

My father paused. I had never heard him speak of the Jack the Ripper murders before, but apparently he had all of the facts— dates, times, eyewitness accounts—at his fingertips. He couldn't possibly have had time yet to go through the files Lestrade and Sir Edward had brought.

I frowned, though, trying to dredge the half-forgotten details I'd read in the newspapers up from my memory.

"Wasn't there some question as to whether Mr. Packer was actually telling the truth, though? I remember a grape stem was found—"

I broke off, the air going out of my lungs as though I'd just been struck in the chest by a mallet.

I jumped up.

"Lucy?" Uncle John spoke, sounding concerned. "Lucy, what's the matter?"

I saw Sir Edward and Lestrade exchange a look, as though asking one another whether the grisly details really had been too much for me.

I crossed to the telephone. "I can't explain now; there isn't time. I need to telephone to Commercial Street Police Station."

According to the clock on Holmes's mantle, it took less than a minute for the exchange operator to process my request and put me through to the Commercial Street station, then for me to ask the desk sergeant who answered the telephone to find Jack.

According to my own *internal* sense of time, it was an eternity before I finally heard Jack's voice on the other end of the line.

"Lucy? What's wrong?" He sounded worried. Understandably, given that I was calling at nearly four o'clock in the morning.

"The woman in cell three," I said. "The Italian woman. Have you seen her tonight?"

"Not since I came on duty." Jack's voice instantly sharpened, turning alert. "Why?"

"I'll explain after, but for right now you need to go and check on her now, straight away."

Jack didn't argue, didn't ask any other questions. "All right. Do you want me to telephone you back?" he asked.

"Yes. I'm upstairs, at my father's."

I drew a shaky breath as I hung up the receiver, then turned back to face Holmes and the other men.

"Were you going to tell me that someone had come forward after this murder with an identical story to Mathew Packer's, of selling grapes to the murdered woman and a companion?" I asked.

Holmes answered. "It is not yet established whether the grocer in question—not our old friend Mathew Packer, incidentally, this was a street vendor, pushing his cart along Hanbury Street—actually sold grapes to the murdered woman. For that, he will need to be brought to the mortuary, where he can make a positive identification. However, the constables who arrived first at the scene of the crime found a crushed grape stem beside the body, and upon canvassing the neighborhood, encountered the fruit vendor, who recounted a story identical to Mathew Packer's from nine years ago."

"Identical, meaning ..."

"Meaning that he reported the male half of the couple speaking precisely the same words that the supposed killer of Catherine Eddows did on the night of September 30th: an offer of white grapes or black, and a promise that his companion would have whichever she liked best."

Ice slid across my skin, trying to burrow into my veins.

"Your telephone call—" Holmes began.

I forced my gaze away from the telephone cabinet, though I didn't stop silently willing Jack to call back.

"Two days ago, a woman was brought into the Commercial Street station, arrested for smashing a pawn shop window and stealing a watch, all in full view of an on-duty police constable. As though—"

"She wished to be arrested and placed within the secure

confines of a prison cell," my father finished for me. No one could ever call Sherlock Holmes slow to move from the facts to the logical conclusion. "Go on."

"She only spoke Italian, which is how I came to know about her," I said. "Jack asked me to see whether I could get her to talk to me. Which I couldn't, but I did get a look at her belongings. Inside a pocket of her cloak, she had a grape stem."

I saw Inspector Lestrade and Sir Edward exchange another glance and held up a hand. "I know, a single grape stem isn't conclusive evidence. Obviously. But she was a recent arrival in this country. I doubt she can have been here more than a week or two, at the most."

Maybe not even that long. No one could go long in London, in the autumn, without being caught in the rain. And getting soaked in a rainstorm would have washed the saltwater stains on her cloak away.

"But she also had a petticoat in her possession—one stamped with the name Lambeth Workhouse, just like—"

"Mary Ann Nichols, the Ripper's second victim," Holmes finished for me. He really *did* have a complete mental catalogue of the facts of the first round of murders.

I nodded. The newspaper reports had also published a list of the dead woman's pathetic collection of worldly possessions and the marked petticoat that had been instrumental in identifying her as a former inmate of Lambeth Workhouse. The name had stuck in my memory because it had sounded like something out of *Oliver Twist*.

That was the forgotten detail I'd been trying to call back yesterday.

The telephone rang.

"Lucy?" Even through the buzzing interference of the telephone wires, Jack's voice sounded grim. "We just found the Italian woman in her cell. She's dead."

LUCY

17. AT THE STATION HOUSE

"How could this have happened?" Sir Edward barked.

Constable Thomas blanched visibly. He opened his mouth, but no words emerged.

I curled my fingers into my palms, trying to clamp down on my own impatience.

I could hardly blame PC Thomas for being nervous; he had in this moment to be living out any young police constable's worst nightmare: standing before a tribunal consisting of not only his sergeant and a station house inspector, but the commissioner of the London police force himself *and* Sherlock Holmes.

Inspector Lestrade and Uncle John had gone to the Whitechapel mortuary to view the body that had been found at Hanbury Street, while Sir Edward chose to accompany my father and me.

Now we were standing in the station house charge room. The air smelled of the carbolic acid used for cleaning, and the electric lights on the walls were all shaded by wire mesh rather than glass. Glass could too easily be shattered and used as a weapon by any criminal disinclined to be brought in.

And taking PC Thomas by the shoulders and shaking him wouldn't make answers emerge any more quickly.

"I—I don't know how it could have happened, sir," Constable Thomas finally managed to choke out. "On my life, I don't."

"She was shot through the right temple," Holmes snapped. "I think we may take it as reasonably certain that she did not suffer a sudden fainting spell and plunge, head-first, onto a stray bullet that happened to be lying on the floor of her cell. So I repeat Sir Edward's question: What happened?"

Constable Thomas swallowed visibly, making the collar of his uniform bob. He was probably imagining his own future career with the police force suddenly being measured in minutes rather than years.

"I—" He gulped again.

Jack had been standing next to me without speaking, but now he put a hand on the constable's shoulder.

"Look, after we find out what happened tonight, we can all think back and wonder whether there was anything we could have done differently. I could have looked into the cells when I came on duty and checked in with you. I didn't. I don't usually; that's the custody sergeant's territory. But would it have made a difference if I had? Maybe." Jack met PC Thomas's gaze. "Right now, though, we just need to hear exactly what happened tonight. Everything that you can remember."

Constable Thomas straightened up and made a clear effort to pull himself together.

"Yes, Sergeant Kelly. I—" He blew out a breath and frowned, as though trying to order his thoughts, then said, "I came on duty at eleven o'clock. I looked in on the prisoners. Everything was as usual, although numbers one and six were kicking up a devil—" he stopped and cast an apologetic glance at me. "That is, an awful row. Yelling and shouting something fierce."

Sir Edward cast an inquiring glance at the fifth man in the room, Inspector Thomas Hawkes.

"Drunk and disorderly," Inspector Hawkes said. He was a spare, gray-haired man, with a sharp-featured face and the faint scars of some childhood pox on his cheeks. "Two men, brought in earlier tonight."

Constable Thomas nodded. "That's right, sir. I banged on their cell doors and told them to pipe down, but they kept at it."

"The woman in cell number three was alive at that point?" Sir Edward asked.

His expression was tense, set.

If I remembered rightly, the previous police commissioner, Sir Charles Warren, had been forced to resign over the Ripper murders. It wasn't clear whether he could have handled the crimes any differently, but public opinion had still blamed him because the killer had never been caught. Right now, Sir Edward, too, was probably seeing his position hanging by a thread.

"I ... I think so, sir." Constable Thomas's voice faltered again. "That is, I can't really remember. I know I looked in on her through the Judas Hole in the cell door, and I saw her curled up on the bench. I thought she was asleep, but maybe—"

I turned to Jack. "How was she found?"

"On the floor, on her left side."

I pushed down the image that instantly rose in my mind's eye. *Don't think about it now.*

"So she can't have been shot while she was lying on the bed."

Holmes gave the constable another piercing glance. "And then?"

"Then I went back to my station. And then, I, ah ..." Constable Thomas's cheeks reddened. "Then, I ... well ..."

My father interrupted. "Then you had a visitor, I presume. A young, attractive female, who begged to be allowed an interview with one of the inmates of the holding cells?"

PC Thomas's jaw dropped open, astonishment replacing embarrassment in his expression. "How ..."

Sir Edward looked very nearly as amazed. "Holmes, how on earth—"

My father gave an impatient huff. "There are a limited number of options for distracting a man on guard and inducing him to leave his appointed post. I simply chose the most obvious." He fixed Constable Thomas with another hard stare. "What happened then? Did the lady turn faint? Did she ask you to fetch her a glass of water?"

"I—" Constable Thomas's eyes were still wide. "Yes. That is, it was exactly as you said, sir. A young lady came into the station."

"The particulars of her appearance?" Holmes snapped.

"Appearance?" PC Thomas stammered. On an ordinary day, I doubted he was actually a stupid young man, but he also wasn't the first to be thrown off his stride by my father.

"What did she look like?" I asked. "What color was her hair, and how was she dressed? Was she short or tall?"

"Well—" Constable Thomas made a clear effort to remember. "Well, I think she was young—about your height, miss, maybe a bit taller. Blond hair."

"Eye color?" Holmes demanded.

PC Thomas swallowed. "I ... I don't know, sir. She had a handkerchief up to her face most of the time. Very upset she was, crying and all."

Holmes gave a wordless exclamation of disgust, and Constable Thomas flinched.

"She was wearing a black jacket with a bit of fur on the collar, I do know that. And PC Edwards brought her back to the cells; maybe he got a better look at her. She said her father was one of the drunk and disorderlies we'd locked up. Said her father'd never done such a thing before. But then, just as we were starting down towards the cells, she suddenly took faint. I offered to help her back out, but she said she'd be all right if I could just fetch her something to drink."

Holmes was looking at PC Thomas with an expression of mingled resignation and frustration. "And I suppose that when you arrived back with the water, the young woman had vanished?"

Constable Thomas pushed back the brim of his helmet. "That's it, sir. A couple of the fellows in the reserve room said they'd seen her go out again through the front door. I thought she'd gotten scared that her father mightn't thank her for finding him in a prison cell."

A bold plan, but, I had to admit, a solid one. That was more or less what I would have done if I had wanted to gain illegal access to the Commercial Street holding cells.

My father glanced at Jack. "Did you see this female personage?"

Jack was almost as good at Holmes at registering details. He would have noticed her height, weight, eye color and any identifying marks just as a matter of habit. But he shook his head. "I would have been out on the streets, making the rounds of the beat constables on patrol. Speaking of—"

He looked at the clock on the wall.

It must be time for him to check in with the patrolling constables again. Probably it was past time; almost an hour had passed since I had first telephoned.

Inspector Hawkes looked at the clock, then nodded. "Yes, you may be on your way, sergeant. Tell the men on patrol to look out for this blond-haired woman in case she may be still in the neighborhood."

Holmes made another dismissive gesture. "That will almost certainly prove an exercise in futility. The young woman took some pains not to let anyone here get a good look at her face, which leads me to believe that any identifying markers she did possess—such as the blond hair and fur-trimmed jacket—are currently residing in a nearby rubbish bin. However, I suppose it must be done."

Jack glanced at me. I could see him not wanting to leave me. I didn't want to see him go, either. Everything else aside, someone out there on the streets had committed murder twice tonight already.

"Take the reserve constables with you," Inspector Hawkes added. "Have them begin canvassing the streets from here towards Whitechapel. The killer of the woman on Hanbury Street may have fled this way."

"Miller's court, Buck's row, George yard, Berner Street, and the junction of Brick Lane and Osborne Street." Holmes delivered the list of names with the rapid-fire precision of a Maxim gun. He was looking at Sir Edward. "Not all of those locations fall within the jurisdiction of this station. However, I would strongly suggest that an inspection of them be carried out as soon as possible."

Those must be the other sites of murders committed by the Ripper nine years ago. I had recognized one or two of the names, though I couldn't have listed them the way that Holmes had done.

Sir Edward jerked his head in agreement. "Carry on, sergeant. Alert any available men in the station, as well, that they're needed out on the streets."

Jack nodded. "Yes, sir."

Inspector Hawkes didn't look particularly happy to have his authority effectively superseded in his own police station. But he could hardly argue with the police commissioner—or, for that matter, with Sherlock Holmes.

I turned, following Jack as he moved towards the door and back into the hall that led out of the charge room.

"I—" I started to say in an undertone, too quiet for anyone else to overhear.

Jack didn't let me finish. His eyes were dark, intense on mine. "Just be careful, all right? No crazy risks, no reckless chances, no—" he stopped, running a hand across his face. "I have no idea why I'm even bothering. As if you ever see a crazy risk without running to take it."

I was staring at him, my mouth still slightly open. "How did you know—"

"That you're going to go out and find one of your father's underworld connections to talk to about all this?" Jack finished. "Remind me what it is I do for a living?"

"I'm sorry." I looked up at him. "I can't let my father go alone, though. Wherever he's planning to go, it has him slightly worried."

"You can tell that?"

"Well, his eyebrow twitched slightly when he was thinking about it just now, though that may be because he knew I would insist on coming along. I already left a note for Mrs. Hudson before I left Baker Street," I added. "She'll look after Becky just in case I'm not back by the time she's awake in the morning."

From somewhere in the building came the sound of a ringing telephone. Down the hallway, someone was shouting what sounded like slurred curses. Probably another drunk and disorderly being brought in.

Jack looked at me. "So you're going out on some of the worst streets in London in the middle of the night to track down a witness who has even Sherlock Holmes worried. How does that rank as a good idea?"

"It's not the middle of the night anymore; it's almost dawn."

"That makes all the difference."

"I'm sorry," I said again. "I swear I honestly will be careful, this time, and not take any unnecessary risks."

For most of my life, the word *caution* and I hadn't had more than a nodding acquaintance. But now an unexpectedly cold lump of anxiety was forming under my ribcage.

If something happened to me tonight, I would never see Jack or Becky again.

"You have to promise me that you'll be careful out there, as well, though," I told him.

Jack looked at me a long moment, then exhaled a hard breath. "All right, Trouble." He leaned forward, resting his forehead just briefly against mine. "I will if you will."

* * *

When I came back into the room, Holmes was just asking Constable Thomas whether he had heard any sound of a gunshot.

"No, sir." The constable shook his head. "But then, the drunks were still kicking up an almighty row, and I had to go all the way to the kitchen to fetch the water ..."

I glanced at my father. "Do you think the drunks ..."

"Possibly hired on for the purpose." Holmes spoke almost absently. "That will have to be investigated. Though I would estimate with ninety-two percent certainty that at best they will tell a story of being approached by a stranger in a public house who offered to stand them drinks in return for creating as much of a disturbance as possible, both outside the police station and in. However—" he fixed a steely eye on PC Thomas. "Is interviewing them a job with which you may be entrusted, constable?"

Constable Thomas nodded jerkily. "Yes, sir. I'll go right away, sir. That is—" he looked at Sir Edward and Inspector Hawkes, both of whom made gestures of permission.

"Go, Thomas, and report back what you learn," Inspector Hawkes said.

PC Thomas went out.

Inspector Hawkes remained where he was, his sharp-featured face creased in a frown. "I was assigned to this station nine years ago, during the first Ripper murders," he said. "I saw the body of that poor girl, Mary Jane Kelly, the one who was butchered in her own room." The inspector's jaw hardened. "If the fiend who did those murders is back, we need to catch him this time. Hanging's too good for the likes of him, after what he's done. But are we saying he's trying to re-create his first round of killings? If that's true, then God help us all. But in God's name, *why?*"

"The man is mad, clearly," Sir Edward said. His mouth pinched shut beneath the bristling white mustache. "A deranged murderer of the most base and venial disposition. How can we even begin to guess at what twisted reasoning may lie within his mind?"

Holmes cleared his throat. "There appears to me a danger, Sir Edward, in dismissing any facts with the sweeping statement that the acts of a madman cannot be subject to logic or reason. However, the fact remains that we have under the roof of this station house a woman who was apparently sent out with certain markers—the Lambeth Workhouse petticoat, the grape stem. Presumably, she was intended to become another murder victim—possibly, she would have been the one discovered tonight at number 29 Hanbury Street, had she not—"

"Had she not committed a crime in blatant view of an on-duty policeman and gotten herself deliberately arrested," I finished for him.

The words had a bitter taste as I spoke them. "She somehow guessed at the danger that she was in and tried to save herself by getting locked up behind bars."

Holmes watched me a moment.

If he felt any sense of failure for having refused to further investigate the first killing in Mitre Square—and I imagined that he did—it at least didn't show on his face.

This wasn't the first time, and I was certain it wouldn't be the last, that I wished I could be more like Sherlock Holmes.

My father turned to Sir Edward and Inspector Hawkes. "Gentlemen, I believe it is time that we viewed the unfortunate woman's body."

LUCY

18. A TATTOO

My muscles felt tight with dread as we made our way down the block of cells to number 3. Constable Thomas was still speaking with one of the drunken prisoners; I saw that the door to cell number 1 was partly open and caught a low murmur of voices inside.

"How do you think she was shot?" I asked Holmes. "Do you think Constable Thomas's visitor somehow opened the lock on the cell door?"

"Possibly." Holmes's brows were knitted together, his thoughts clearly far away.

He moved to the door of cell number 3—which was closed. I had a few seconds longer to put off the inevitable.

"Although my attention is immediately drawn to these ventilation holes, here."

Holmes rested one long finger against the holes—about a half inch in diameter—that had been drilled into the metal cell doors.

"I believe one could place the muzzle of a small-caliber revolver against one, fire, and be reasonably assured of hitting the target inside. Especially if one used the fish-eye lens attached to the Judas-hole in order to ascertain the precise location of one's victim."

He tapped the glass-covered lens set at eye level into the door. I followed his gaze, frowning. "It would still be an incredibly lucky shot, though. Your victim might not be in a vulnerable position. What if the angle was wrong—or good only for a wounding shot, not a killing one? The killer—if it was PC Thomas's blond-haired woman—took a terrible risk."

Holmes twitched one shoulder. "I am not so sure the risk was so very extreme. What did she have to lose if the angle proved disadvantageous, after all? She could simply choose not to fire her gun and walk out of the police station entirely unmolested, having committed no crime. However, your point is a fair one: to have gone to the trouble of killing in such a fashion, our murderer must have been desperate to see the woman eliminated."

"Because she could identify him?" Something—something more than my own sense of failure—was troubling me.

"You're Jack the Ripper," I said.

My father's eyebrows climbed towards his hairline, but I kept on going.

"You want—for reasons possibly plain only to your own diseased mind—to recreate some aspects of the murders you committed in Whitechapel in the Autumn of 1888. So you ... what? Hire a woman off the streets—a recent Italian immigrant, as it turns out, who speaks little to no English. You give her a petticoat marked with the proper stamp from the Lambeth Workhouse, feed her grapes, try to entice her to one of the original sites of the killings. And then when she somehow suspects your murderous intent and runs away, you track her down inside a police station and hire yet *another* woman to come in and shoot her in cold blood?"

"You find that line of reasoning flawed?"

I blew out an exasperated breath. "Is that even a real question? Leaving everything else aside, it presumes that the Whitechapel killer was willing to collude with—or at least hire someone else—to do his killing for him. Nothing that I've ever read or heard about him has suggested that he's anything less than a lone player."

"You are assuming, are you not, that the weeping female who so adroitly distracted Constable Thomas *was*, in fact, a female."

I stared. Maybe I was more tired than I had realized, because that hadn't even occurred to me. "You think it was *him*? That the Ripper dressed himself up as a woman so that he could walk straight into this police station and commit another murder?"

My father twitched one shoulder. "I myself have passed for a female on no less than eighteen separate occasions, the most remarkable of which was a stint twenty-odd years ago in the chorus of a cabaret in Paris. It can be done."

I tried to picture a twenty-year-old Sherlock Holmes in a ruffled skirt, dancing the can-can, and failed completely. Apparently even my imagination had its limits.

Holmes went on. "The facts surrounding the identity of the killer from nine years ago are scanty in the extreme. We have conflicting reports of a man who may, possibly, have been the killer. None mark him as a particularly tall or muscular man. Even the name—Jack the Ripper—comes from a letter that was almost certainly not written by the actual killer's hand. We know that in at least one instance, he killed with what appeared to be a left-handed slash across the dead woman's throat. We know that he was familiar enough with the lanes, back alleys, and byways of East End London to commit murders practically under the noses of patrolling police constables. We may theorize an almost fanatical hatred of women from the frenzied nature of the attacks he carried out. But we have few certainties other than those—and any additional facts that might have been gleaned were obliterated in the all-too-typical hash the police made of the investigation nine years ago."

I scrutinized my father's face. There was absolutely nothing surprising about Holmes criticizing police methods of investigation; actually, it would have been odder still if he *hadn't* had a few choice words to say about the handling of the Ripper murders.

But there was also a strangely hard, bitter note in my father's voice that made me look at him closely.

He took hold of the cell door. "And now I believe the time has come to see what may be gleaned from the scene of *this* crime."

I focused on breathing in and out as the cell door opened and the crumpled figure lying on the floor inside came into view.

I could feel Holmes watching me. "Are you certain—"

I didn't let him finish. "Yes."

I edged my way into the cell and crouched down beside the dead woman.

She lay on her side, just as Jack had said, one arm folded under her. There was a small, round bullet hole in her temple, crusted with blood, but her face was peaceful, all the fear and tension I'd seen in her expression smoothed away.

Maybe it was wrong—dead was dead, after all—but I felt slightly better knowing that she hadn't suffered and almost certainly hadn't even seen death coming or had time to be afraid.

"Dead approximately three hours," Holmes said, feeling the dead woman's neck and hands. "Although Watson would be able to give us a more exact estimate. Still, it tallies with PC

Thomas's account."

"Look here." I wouldn't have lasted long in my father's profession if touching a dead body bothered me.

Or, rather, it *did* bother me, but I had trained myself not to let it show.

I gently pushed back the sleeve of the woman's tattered gray blouse, exposing the tattoo on her wrist.

"I noticed this before, when I spoke to her. Do you think it might help with getting her identified?"

"Hmm." Holmes made an indeterminate sound in his throat as he studied the marks. "Recently done—she can have had this no longer than two months at most, possibly less."

"Do you recognize the artist who did the design?" It wouldn't shock me if he knew and could identify the work of every tattoo artist in London.

"Not offhand," Holmes said. "It was done in this country, however. The blue shading of the doves' underwings is quite distinctive. Have you paper and pencil?"

I nodded; I always carried a small notebook and pen.

"You want a sketch of the tattoo design?" I wasn't a good enough artist to produce a recognizable drawing of the woman's face, but the design of the doves I could probably manage.

"As you say, it might prove helpful in learning her name."

I started to sketch the outline of the first bird's raised wings, watching out of the corner of my eye as Holmes abruptly bent, snapped the fraying lace on her left boot, and slid it off her foot.

Her stockings were black wool and ancient-looking, more holes than actual material. Through one of the fraying gaps, I could see bruising around her ankle.

I drew in a sharp breath. "Is that—"

"Knife?" Holmes interrupted.

I reached for the knife I carried in my own boot top and handed it over. A quick slice with the blade, and Holmes had cut away the remains of the stocking, exposing the ring of angry-looking purple that circled her whole ankle.

My stomach lurched. "She was chained up. Held prisoner somewhere."

"And recently, too." Holmes studied the marks. "These bruises are less than a week old."

I worked at matching Holmes's calm, though I couldn't entirely manage it.

"So the Ripper isn't just killing women now, he's ... what? Keeping them prisoner so that he can release them and then hunt them down? That doesn't line up with what the last round of killings implied about him."

The corners of Holmes's mouth were drawn tight as he continued to study the dead body. "Any new sensation or experience must sooner or later become familiar—and thus lose its novelty. In order to maintain the thrill, the experience must be intensified. An addict, for example, must expose himself to ever-increasing doses of his drug of choice in order to produce the same elevated effect."

Holmes, with his seven-per-cent solution of cocaine, would know that better than anyone.

"So killing women and cutting them open isn't enough anymore; he has to play some sort of twisted game of cat and mouse with them?"

I swallowed, remembering the blind terror in the Italian woman's eyes.

Holmes was past master of the vague, open-handed gesture.

The one he made now didn't quite mean *perhaps*, I didn't think; it was less definite than that. Closer to *perhaps, but also perhaps not.*

"Perhaps everything we thought we knew about how The Ripper operates has always been wrong."

He handed the knife back to me, then straightened.

"I'm coming with you." I spoke before Holmes could say anything.

His gray eyes regarded me steadily for a long moment, probably gauging whether he could find a way to covertly slip away from the police station without my following.

"Jack already knows," I added. "He hates it, but he understands."

Holmes rarely did anything as human-sounding as sigh, but now he braced a hand against the bridge of his nose, exhaling a slow breath.

"I could wish that Sergeant Kelly were not quite so accommodating. However, if that were the case, you undoubtedly would not be marrying him. Very well. I had never planned to take my daughter to the Old Nichol. But it would be a first for the Ripper affair if anything proceeded according to plan. Let us go, before either Sir Edward or Inspector Hawkes thinks to inquire about our plans."

LUCY

19. HELP FROM A STREET BOY

Dawn was breaking over the city, but the streets were still barely light. Outside our carriage window, thick yellow fog crawled along the muddied cobblestones.

"What exactly is the Old Nichol?" I asked Holmes.

"Nine years ago, it was considered the worst of the East End London slums—which, as you know, is a not-inconsiderable distinction, given the competition," Holmes said.

I had seen London in all moods these past two years I had lived here: jolly and bustling with life ... shadowy and mysterious ... This November morning, though, I thought the streets we rolled past had a wary, hostile edge, the people walking hunched over and hurrying, darting nervous glances to left and right, seldom pausing or stopping to talk.

"They know," I said. "They already know that there's something to be frightened of out there."

"News in East End London spreads with the rapidity of an overland telegraph wire," Holmes said. "I have no doubt that they will have already heard of last night's murder."

He looked out the window. "Although whether they most

fear a return of the Whitechapel killer, or the police attention the subsequent investigation will bring down on them, is open to debate."

I dragged my thoughts forcibly away from what could be happening to Jack out there on similar streets, right this moment. He trusted me to stay safe; I ought to be able to do the same for him.

"This is what happened to the Old Nichol," Holmes went on. "It was originally composed of twenty narrow streets, containing some seven hundred houses in deplorable condition, which in turn provided housing for approximately six thousand people. In the wake of the Ripper killings, however, the London County Council decided that the slums ought to be cleared and have in the past nine years been engaged in pulling down the worst of the buildings and putting up new, county-funded housing in its place."

Our carriage drove over a rut in the road, making the wheels bounce and the springs creak in protest. I braced myself against the edge of the leather seat, watching the scene unroll outside our window as we drove by.

The fog shrouded the dilapidated houses and store fronts we passed by, so that I caught only fragmentary glimpses on the other side of the pane of glass: a man, drunk, asleep, or possibly even dead, huddled inside a doorway. A pair of women combing their hair on the front steps of a common lodgings house. Dirty, barefoot, ragged children, watching our cab go by with dull, hopeless eyes.

Our cab driver slowed at an intersection to let a passing wagon go by, then drew to a halt outside a dismal-looking public house.

"We will have to walk from here," Holmes said. "The streets grow too narrow to accommodate a carriage, besides which, we will likely have to conduct a search for the individual we are seeking."

As we climbed down from the cab and Holmes paid the driver, a boy limped over to me.

"Spare a penny, pretty miss?" He had a pair of makeshift crutches fashioned from scraps of wood propped up under his arms.

His voice was high-pitched, with a practiced beggar's whine, his face thin, dirty, and sharp with perpetual hunger—and he appeared to have only one leg; on the right side, the leg of his ragged and much-too-large trousers was empty from the knee down.

He was also, though, eyeing the coin that Holmes was handing over to our cab driver, with a look that reminded me of a fox confronted by an unexpected feast of young chickens.

I studied him more closely. "If you're hoping to try robbing us, you'll be able to run away much faster if you stop tucking up your leg inside your trousers to appear as though you're crippled."

The boy gaped at me.

"It probably helps with getting charitable coinage," I went on. "But if you make a grab for my father's wallet, I'll trip you and take the money back before you can get five steps."

The boy eyed me, apparently deciding that I meant it, because his other leg—spindly and filthy as the rest of him, but perfectly whole—dropped down, and he made a quick, eel-like movement, about to dart away.

"Wait a moment." Holmes's hand landed on the boy's shoulder. "We may possibly be able to find work for a bright lad such as yourself."

The boy gave us a look of deep suspicion. "What kind of work?"

"We have need of a guide. Someone who may help us to find

an old friend of mine."

The boy snorted at that, his lips curling in derision. "A toff like you have a friend around these parts? Don't make me laugh."

Holmes's voice remained perfectly pleasant. "Ah, you see, that is precisely the sort of perception and intelligence we have need of."

The boy still looked ready to bolt at any second.

Holmes took out a half crown coin and held it up. "Yours, if you help us to find the individual we seek."

The boy gave him a look, one part wariness, three parts shrewd calculation. "If it's worth one bull to you, it'll be worth two."

Bull must be the street term for a half crown. I filed that away in my increasing vocabulary of East End London slang.

Holmes took out another coin without hesitation. "One now, one when you tell us what we wish to know."

The boy considered, then jerked his chin in a nod. "Fine. Who're you looking for?"

"Thomas Newman."

The boy's thin face blanched under the coating of grime. "Oh, no." He held up his hands. "Keep yer money. I'm not tangling with Newman."

"All you need do is tell us where and how to find him. You needn't bring us to him," Holmes said.

With studied casualness, he took a third half-crown piece from his pocket.

The boy licked his lips. "Not coppers, are you?"

"No."

There was another moment's silence, in which the street traffic surged around us on either side. Then, finally, the boy gave another jerky nod.

"Round the corner. Three streets up, turn left, then right, then left again onto Nelson Street. You want The Victory pub. Newman's usually outside."

He almost snatched the coins from Holmes's hands and raced away.

I bent, picking up the wooden crutches he'd dropped and propping them against the soot-stained brick wall beside us. "I suppose he can always come back for these later. Who exactly is this Thomas Newman?"

"A member of the so-called Old Nichol gang, a criminal organization that nine years ago specialized in preying on the prostitutes who worked the streets in this neighborhood and in Whitechapel. They would accost a woman immediately after she had been paid by one of her clientele and demand that she hand over either part or the whole of her dubiously-gotten money. They were known to administer beatings if refused. Indeed, one of the first women to die by violence in the autumn of 1888 is thought to have been a victim of the Old Nichol gang. Emma Elizabeth Smith, who was brutally assaulted by a gang of men on the night of April third, but dragged herself back to her lodging house and was rushed to London Hospital. She lived long enough to describe the attack, but lapsed into unconsciousness and died four days later."

Holmes's voice was as coldly clinical as ever, but I still looked at him sharply. "There is no possible way that you can have acquainted yourself with all of these dates and details in the time since Lestrade and Sir Edward came to Baker Street last night. You were already familiar with the details of the Ripper killings."

Holmes made another of his vague, one-handed gestures;

this one I took to mean, *Of course.*

"So this Newman was one of the men who assaulted Emma Smith?"

"That I do not know. If not guilty himself, however, he almost certainly is well acquainted with the men who did carry out the attack."

"An entirely charming character, then."

Holmes looked at me. "Nothing would give me greater pleasure than to leave you to wait in the cab."

He had—thanks to paying three times the going rate for a ride of the length we had taken—secured the cabbie's promise to wait.

I shook my head. "No." It wasn't that I didn't think that Thomas Newman and whatever confederates of his we might encounter were a genuine threat. That would mean that I was too stupid to be walking the streets of Old Nichol in the first place.

I bent over, sliding the knife out of my boot top and tucking it into my sleeve, ready to drop into my hand at a moment's notice.

"No, I'm looking forward to making Thomas Newman's acquaintance."

"In that case, I commend your attention to the second-hand clothing store just across the street."

Holmes gestured to where a narrow, dingy-looking storefront sat sandwiched between a glasscutter's place and a shop advertising furniture caning.

"I suggest we avail ourselves of what changes of costume it may offer."

LUCY

20. AN OLD OPPONENT

The clothing shop proved to be little more than a space the size of a small kitchen pantry, with a jumbled heap of ragged trousers, shirts, skirts, shawls, and dresses of all sizes and all varieties on a single central table.

But at least the shopkeeper was profoundly incurious—or else profoundly drunk. He was somewhere around sixty, balding, and sat slumped on a three-legged stool behind a bare wooden counter, staring vacantly off into space.

"Are we trying to keep the gentleman we're visiting from learning who we really are?" I asked.

The shopkeeper didn't appear to be paying us any attention, but to judge by the boy's reaction, it was probably safest not to use Newman's name.

"Not necessarily. However, it would probably be as well if he *thinks* that we are attempting to dissemble."

I sorted quickly through the heap, searching for clothes that looked least likely to give the wearer fleas or other wildlife.

"Because a man who's seen through an obvious trick will be less likely to look for a less obvious one?"

"Precisely. Overconfidence in one's opponent is a trait that should be cultivated whenever possible."

I picked up a dark knitted shawl that was stained without actually being too filthy.

"Opponent? I take it our informant isn't likely to welcome us with open arms, then?"

"I should estimate that there is an eighty-three-percent chance of his trying to murder me on sight. Here." Holmes handed me a battered-looking black straw hat, with half its artificial flowers gone. "It looks appropriately disreputable, but is in fact quite clean inside."

I opened my mouth, then closed it again. "And the other seventeen percent?"

"I would give perhaps a ten percent likelihood of his simply sending some of his thugs out to deliver a beating. Which leaves a seven percent chance that he will actually speak with us of his own accord—while of course still trying to leverage the meeting to his advantage. There is a mirror over there."

Holmes gestured to a cracked and greenish-tinted mirror that hung on the back wall of the shop.

I turned, sliding the pins out of my own hat, and pinned on the black straw one in its place.

"Do I want to know why he has such a grudge against you?" I asked.

Holmes was bent over, rifling again through the pile of clothes. "We were opponents a little more than ten years ago in a bare-knuckled boxing match at Alison's rooms."

"And you won?"

"Worse than that, I had an opportunity to kill him and failed to take it."

"*Kill* him?" I knew of my father's more than passing acquaintance with prize-fighting. But I hadn't known that the sport was quite so vicious as that.

"This was not during the official match, you understand. It was afterwards, when Newman and some of his cronies ambushed me on the street, thinking to teach me a lesson for having bested him. I believe I am sufficiently ready, if you are?" Holmes asked.

I wrapped the shawl around my shoulders, then turned away from the mirror. "Yes, I—"

I stopped, my voice dying as I caught sight of Holmes.

He had swathed himself in a rusty black dress in a style popular thirty years ago, with puffed sleeves and a full, sweeping skirt. He also wore a matching black bonnet, trimmed with so many dyed black feathers that it looked as though an upside-down chicken had perched on his head. Strings of jet beads dangled from the brim of the bonnet, brushing my father's forehead.

"As I mentioned, inducing a sense of overconfidence in one's enemies gives one a distinct advantage." Holmes turned, sliding a few coins onto the shopkeeper's counter. "I believe that should cover the cost of our purchases."

The shopkeeper sat up, peered at him, then hiccupped, wiping his mouth with the back of his hand. "Really suits you, that does." He gestured to the bonnet. "Brings out the color of your eyes."

* * *

Unease started crawling across my skin a short while after we had made the second of the turns in the boy's instructions.

I glanced at Holmes. "Are we—"

"Being sent to the public house mentioned via a circuitous route?" Holmes finished for me. "We are indeed. A pity. The lad obviously had intelligence; he might have made a worthwhile addition to the Irregulars."

I supposed I couldn't blame the boy for looking out for himself first and foremost; in neighborhoods like this one, that was the first—often the only—rule of law.

But I noticed something else: the other pedestrians on the street had vanished. Up and down the narrow lane, shopkeepers were closing up their shutters, despite the fact that it was barely midday.

Obviously Holmes and I weren't the only ones anticipating trouble.

I'd tucked my knife up into my sleeve instead of my boot top; I sent out a quick, silent mental apology to Jack as I let it slide down into my hand.

"What should we—"

Before I could finish, Holmes gave me a quick, hard shove that sent me into the mouth of a narrow alleyway that ran between two crumbling brick buildings.

My hearing was usually good, but Holmes's must have been preternatural. I had regained my balance by the time I heard what he must have already registered: the sound of running footsteps coming from further up the road.

Holmes shot me a fierce, scowling look that plainly meant, *Stay where you are.*

Then he turned and stood motionless in the center of the road.

There was a towering stack of empty packing crates near the

mouth of the alley. I pressed myself into the wall behind them, out of sight of anyone standing in the road outside.

The footsteps slowed to walking as they drew closer, then stopped.

Two men, I would guess. Both heavyset, by the sound their boots made on the cobbles, and one of them walked with a slight limp, either from injury or chronic deformity.

Holmes could probably also have told their exact height by calculating the length of their stride from the seconds elapsed between footfalls.

"Well." The voice that spoke was nasal and unpleasantly grating. "You've a nerve, showin' yer face here. Though it was nice of you to dress up fer the occasion. Fetching bonnet, that."

The second man laughed at that, a deep chuckle that I thought was edged with faint nervousness.

Newman would probably be the first speaker, the other an underling.

"Ah, Mr. Newman." Holmes's voice reached me. "I see that you received my message."

"What message?" Newman growled.

"About my wishing to speak with you, of course."

"Funny." Newman rasped out a laugh of his own. "I'd something other than talking in mind when it came to you."

There was a slight gap between the pile of wooden crates and the crumbling brick wall. I leaned in until I could look through it and was rewarded with a view of a narrow slice of the street.

Newman and the other man stood very nearly on a level with my alleyway, with the man I took for Newman nearest to me.

He was somewhere about forty or forty-five, with a coarse-featured face, a heavy jaw, and a nose that jutted out in profile and showed signs of having been broken at least once. Straggly-looking reddish hair was visible beneath a cap that was pulled low on his forehead.

Scars on the backs of his knuckles indicated that he was accustomed to using his fists for fighting. The good quality of his boots and the expensive Turkish cigar tucked into his breast pocket said that he had money—and the overall filthy appearance of the rest of his apparel said that he didn't care to use that money for bathing.

The other man was harder to make out since he stood on the other side of Newman, but I could tell that he was burly, well over six feet tall—and stepping towards my father with one meaty fist raised.

I jerked back, trying to calculate my chances of getting out to the street in time to stop Holmes from being pounded into the ground.

Before I could take more than a half-step towards the mouth of the alley, though, I heard the sound of a heavy thump, followed by a groan, and then my father's voice, sounding both pleasant and calm.

"If you fear a rematch of our fight ten years ago so much, you could simply admit it, Newman, instead of attempting to send another in your place."

Looking back out through the narrow gap, I was in time to see my father toeing the body of Newman's hireling—who now lay, face down and unmoving, on the muddy ground.

Newman growled under his breath and started to speak, but Holmes cut in, drawing himself up.

"Now. Are you ready to conduct a civilized conversation, or must we have more tedious demonstrations that I am still the better fighter?"

I had to credit my father.

Dr. Watson had, in a written account of one of their cases, famously told Holmes, *I never get your limits*. Until this moment, I wouldn't have believed that even Sherlock Holmes could manage to be intimidating in a widow's gown, beaded bonnet and half a chicken's worth of feathers.

But he was. More than intimidating, really.

The steely gaze he directed at Newman made the other man take an instinctive step back, crossing his arms over his chest.

"Heard you were dead," he finally grunted.

"And I am sure you would infinitely prefer it if those reports were accurate," Holmes said. "However, we all must cope with disappointments in this life."

"What d'you want?" Newman shifted position as he spoke, uncrossing his arms and clasping his hands behind his back.

I narrowed my eyes, but Holmes's expression didn't alter.

"You will have heard of the latest killings in Whitechapel?" he asked.

"'Course I have." Newman spat contemptuously on the ground at his side, then reached behind him, appearing to scratch his own back.

In my head, I pictured telling Jack about this later today, when we were both back in Baker Street.

I couldn't have just stayed hiding in the alley, I argued in my imaginary conversation. *It wouldn't have been—*

Safe for Holmes, was what I had been planning to say.

But imaginary-Jack interrupted with, *Crazy enough for you*.

I edged away from the wall, watching where I stepped, being very, very careful not to knock against the stack of crates or kick any of the assorted rubbish that littered the ground.

"I own these streets. Nothing happens in these parts without my hearing about it, one way or t'other." Newman was saying. I could no longer see him, but his voice still reached me. "A fly can't land on a trash heap without my knowing."

I stepped out of the alleyway, grabbed hold of Newman's wrist, and yanked his arm up sharply, twisting it behind him.

The knife he had just drawn from the back waistband of his trousers dropped to the ground.

"Possibly." I raised my own knife, resting the tip of the blade just under Newman's ear. "But you apparently *don't* know enough to watch your own back when you're thinking of committing murder."

Newman jerked, moving as though he were going to make a grab for me.

I pressed the knife in a little harder, just on the verge of breaking the skin. "I really wouldn't try it."

I didn't particularly like hurting people, even men like Thomas Newman. But I also didn't picture myself lying awake tonight, stricken by guilt if this encounter turned violent and I had to defend myself and Holmes.

I was close enough to feel the anger tightening Newman's muscles, simmering under his skin like an electric current.

"I've got others out here looking for you," Newman ground out. "One shout from me, and I could have some of the lads here in five seconds flat."

"And I assure you that my companion could slit your throat in less than one," Holmes said. "Which would be both messy and completely unnecessary, since all we require is information."

For a brief instant, I saw Newman's hands clench. But then,

with a controlled effort, he relaxed first one hand, then the other.

"Fine. Call off yer pet ladybird here, and we'll talk."

Holmes's gaze remained calmly fixed on Newman. "I think not. You will pardon my distrust, but I believe the odds of our gaining an honest answer from you are significantly greater if she remains where she stands. Now."

Holmes's expression didn't alter, exactly, but his face still hardened in some indefinable way, his eyes turning cold as flint. "I have approximately enough patience left to ask politely once more. If I fail to receive an answer, I will resort to impolite means—which, I assure you, you will enjoy far less than I."

I felt the blade of the knife bob as Newman swallowed.

"Ask yer question, then."

"Did you know the identity of the man who committed the Whitechapel murders nine years ago?"

As Holmes spoke, I realized that it was perfectly possible. The police had failed to catch the Ripper, but a man like Newman would be approximately as likely to share his knowledge with the police as he would be to put on pink ballet tights and turn pirouettes up and down the Old Nichol.

Actually, if I remembered rightly, there had even been some suggestions in the newspapers that the killer might be found amongst the members of a street gang.

But Newman shook his head. "Nah. I'd like to shake his hand, though. Givin' those women what they deserve."

I had to hold myself tightly in check to keep the knife steady.

Holmes's expression was impassive, but I could see the icy distaste in his eyes.

"Have you heard of any new high rip gangs trying their luck at stepping into your territory?"

Newman stiffened again at that, his voice dropping to a growl. "What kind of question is that?"

So far I had been letting Holmes do the talking, but I dug the knife just a little harder into the space under Newman's jaw. "What if you just *answer* the question? I promise you, my list of reasons to dislike you is quite long enough without your wasting our time."

Newman shifted, growling under his breath. "Wouldn't be alive if they'd tried to cut in on my turf."

"Do you recognize this?" Holmes asked. He reached into the bodice of the black silk dress and drew out the pencil sketch I'd made of the Italian woman's tattoo.

Newman didn't jolt or seem especially troubled by the sight. "What is it?" He sounded indifferent.

"Have you seen the pattern before?"

"No."

I was focused on Newman, but as he spoke, I thought I caught just a brief flicker of movement in the window of the house opposite us. But it was gone before I could be certain.

Holmes regarded Newman steadily, his eyes half-closed, with the look that meant he was deliberating.

I waited, trying to decide whether my father was more likely to force further answers by producing inescapable proof that Newman was lying, or whether he was about to ask some obscure, seemingly inane and utterly irrelevant question—like whether or not Newman had taken draft beer or ale with his dinner last night—that would somehow prove to be the key to unlocking the whole affair.

Both approaches would be believably Holmes.

My father nodded at me. "You may release him. I believe we

are done here."

I stepped back, letting the knife blade drop away from Newman's neck—though I kept a tight grip on the hilt, just in case.

Holmes stepped forward, and before I even had time to react, delivered a sharp right-hook to Newman's jaw.

The punch caught Newman as completely off guard as it did me. His head snapped back, and then with a faint sigh that wasn't even quite a moan, he slid sideways and landed with a thud on the muddied cobblestones.

I stared at Holmes, open-mouthed.

"I wished to prevent his attempting to follow us." Holmes spoke as though he were ordering tea at a restaurant, his breathing not even elevated. "Also, there is a limit to the amount of time I can spend conversing with a man of his type without wishing to punch him in the face."

LUCY

21. A MISSING WOMAN

Holmes stepped calmly over Newman's unconscious body, stripped off the black gown and bonnet, and with equal calm deposited them in a pile by the side of the road. Then he took out his pocket watch, ostentatiously holding it up to peer at the watch face.

"Would it help to take out a coin and casually flip it in the air a few times?" I murmured.

Since, as far as I knew, we had no particular reason to be worried about the time, I took it that he wished to make it clear to someone that we had money to spare for luxuries like watches.

"I doubt we will need to resort to quite that degree of conspicuousness." Holmes was eyeing a window in the building opposite, the same one where I'd thought I had seen movement before.

"I believe that if we were to make our way down the road—slowly—and pause just around the nearest corner, we might be rewarded with some further information."

I took the arm Holmes offered, and we started down the road.

"What is that building back there?" I had to force myself not to turn and look back over my shoulder.

"A common lodging house, or doss house, where those who are without a home and stand in need of a night's shelter may purchase a bed for a few shillings a night. That one is a particular favorite with the prostitutes who frequent the Old Nichol."

"And you think one of the women inside there will want to talk to us? Why?"

"We offer less risk and greater potential reward than the actual clients such women encounter on the streets, particularly now that the Ripper is suspected to be once more at work."

It was hard to argue with that.

We turned the corner and found the remains of what had probably been a weekly market, set up the day before. The stalls were closed now, the vendors clearly gone elsewhere. All that remained were trampled and wilted flowers, some dried and scattered beans on the ground, and a barrel of fruit that must have been too bruised or rotted to sell.

Three or four barefoot boys were pawing through the squashed apples and oranges, trying to find any morsels that were still edible.

Going over and offering them money would draw not only their attention but the attention of every vagrant and urchin on the street—which would, in turn, frighten off any informant we were hoping to attract.

"It is a cruel part of the city, without question," Holmes said, as though reading my thoughts. He was also watching the children—who had started to shriek and pull each other's hair. "If one had any particular faith in human nature, it would soon be cured by a visit to the Old Nichol."

He stopped, turning around to come face-to-face with the

woman who had just rounded the corner behind us.

She gasped at the sight of Holmes, looking halfway ready to turn around and bolt back the way she had come.

Holmes held up his hands. "You have nothing to fear from us, I assure you."

The woman wore a green skirt and a black velvet jacket, with rows of three jet buttons on the underside of the sleeves, fastening the cuffs. One or two of the buttons were hanging by a thread with the stones missing from their metal settings, and the velvet material had gone threadbare in a few spots. For a moment I wondered whether she'd bought it at the same secondhand clothing shop where Holmes and I had just been.

The woman's gaze darted nervously between me and Holmes, and her tongue came out, flicking over chapped lips.

She looked to be somewhere in her middle thirties, with dirty, straggling brown hair hanging limply over her shoulders. Her face was plump and doughy-looking, with heavy pouches under her eyes that made it look as though she had only just woken up—or perhaps hadn't been to bed last night at all. Her eyes were pale and watery blue, bloodshot with the effects of what I would guess to be several glasses too many of gin.

"We will be more than happy to pay you for the pleasure of your company," Holmes added.

I had seen Holmes coax similarly reluctant witnesses into speech before; he had the technique down to a masterful near-science.

As the woman watched, he drew out a gold sovereign and held it up between his thumb and forefinger, keeping it just out of her reach.

The woman licked her lips again. Drunk enough to be wishing that she had money to pay for another glass of gin—but not so drunk that she would forget to be cautious.

"What d'you want to know?"

Her voice was husky, but not unattractive. She would probably have a pleasant alto voice for singing, though she was unlikely to ever have had the chance.

"You witnessed our conversation with Mr. Newman a few moments ago."

For the first time, the tight, nervous mask of the woman's face cracked, transformed by the flash of a sharp grin.

"Saw you punch him right in his ugly dial, which is something I've been wantin' to do for years."

"We were asking whether Mr. Newman knew of any current threats to the women of your neighborhood," Holmes said.

The woman's expression changed, turning tense and wary once more as she eyed Holmes. "Who wants to know?"

"Someone who wishes only to help you and others like you."

"Help." The woman laughed, a dry, humorless scrape in her throat. Her words were slightly blurred with drink, but her eyes were hard, narrowed. "Heard that from men before. It's never help they give."

She was on the balls of her feet, her whole body poised, ready to run—the gold sovereign coin Holmes held notwithstanding.

I took a half step forward. "You're right, you don't know him. But *I* do." I stopped, meeting the woman's gaze directly. "A woman like you will have learned how to tell when people are lying. You're intelligent and good at reading people. So you'll know that I'm not lying now. I've trusted this man with my life, time and time again, and I'm still here. You can trust him, too."

The woman's puffy, bloodshot eyes stared searchingly into mine for a long moment, then she let out a shuddering breath. "Fine."

She stumbled—perhaps drunkenly. She lurched forwards and might have fallen if I hadn't put out a hand to steady her.

Not unexpectedly, she smelled of gin, smoke, and human body that hadn't been washed in far too long.

"Will you tell us your name?" I asked.

"Jemma. Jemma Howle." The woman straightened, lifting her chin a little as she spoke. Then she lowered her voice. "I'm not saying I know anything, mind." Her eyes darted warily all around us, as though checking to see if we were being watched or overheard. "But Thomas Newman and men like him—maybe 'e's not the Ripper 'imself. But the Ripper's doin' 'im a favor, if 'e really is back. All this killin's good for Newman's dirty business."

Holmes's brows climbed a fraction. "How so?"

Jemma huffed an impatient breath. "Well, last time the Ripper got to work, all the fine ladies and gents came down, all afire to reform the wicked ways of us poor East Enders. Preaching against the evils of drink. Got the brothels and bawdy houses closed down. Lands the women in 'em right out on the streets, right in Newman's territory." Her expression wavered briefly, then hardened. "Like I say, good for Newman and his gang's type of business."

She meant that prostitutes forced to work on the streets, rather than in the comparative safety of a brothel, were easy pickings for extortion and robbery by the high rip gangs.

"Have any women been hurt recently?"

Jemma laughed, the sound a bitter scrape in her throat.

"Women are always hurt around here."

"Have you—have they—reported the attacks to the police?" I asked.

Jemma looked at me as though I'd just asked her if she could swim the English Channel. "The police? What do they care if a dollymop gets a beating?"

Thinking about Jack and the men at his station, I knew that wasn't always true. But, on the other hand, it was true often enough that I could see why Jemma Howle would think so.

Jemma hiccuped.

A knife grinder was pushing his cart up the street towards us. He was an old man, wizened and bent, his shoulders too slumped with fatigue to look as though he would be a threat to anyone. But still, the intrusion seemed to jolt Jemma into awareness that she'd been speaking more freely than she intended.

"I've told you what you wanted. Now I've got to go."

Holmes held up the coin again. "I can offer—"

"I said, I'm leaving." Jemma spun, lurched drunkenly, then set off up the street, almost at a run.

I looked after her, frowning as she vanished out of sight around the next corner.

"Odd that she didn't even want the money."

A deep furrow had appeared between Holmes's brows, as well. "As you say." He pocketed the gold sovereign, then glanced at me sideways. "That was an impressive speech you made."

"About her being able to believe you because I could see that she was good at judging people?" I shrugged. "I don't know where the saying *Flattery will get you nowhere* comes from. In my experience, with most people it will gain you a great deal. Not that I didn't mean what I said about your being trustworthy," I added.

I just doubted that Jemma would have a gauge for trustworthiness beyond who had offered to stand her the latest round of drinks. Which wasn't entirely her fault; she probably hadn't encountered enough decent men in her life to recognize one.

Another man might have been offended; Holmes smiled fleetingly. "Asking her name was a particularly good touch, as well. People of her class are always hungry for some assurance that their existence matters to anyone besides themselves."

"I let her pick my pocket, too—when she pretended to stumble and bump into me? She took my handkerchief. I knew she'd be more inclined to give us information if she felt superior, as though she'd managed to put one over on us."

It was what kept me from feeling too guilty about having manipulated her.

I looked up the gray, cheerless street, towards the point where she'd vanished around the corner.

"Women like her *don't* actually matter, though, do they? I mean, they should. But practically no one cares about them— they, themselves, as individuals. Even reformers who want to sweep in here and shut down all the brothels, root out the dens of iniquity—they all talk about the fallen women and the unfortunates of the East End as a whole. But would most of them actually want to make a woman like Jemma Howle's acquaintance— actually talk to her, hear her story?"

Remembering Amelia Scott's charity tea party, I was fairly sure I already knew the answer.

Holmes didn't answer at once. At last he said, "You are not wrong. The women killed by the Ripper nine years ago—no one outside of Whitechapel would ever have heard their names or cared about them in the slightest if they hadn't been murdered in such dramatic fashion."

"Is this why you usually take Uncle John with you when you're investigating a case like this?"

"Watson's unfailing faith in goodness and human virtue does frequently serve as an effective antidote." Holmes was still frowning down the street in the direction that Jemma Howle had gone, his gaze abstracted, as though something were puzzling or troubling him. But then he shook his head as though to clear it. "I believe we have gleaned as much information as we are likely to here." He offered me his arm. "Shall we depart?"

LUCY

22. AN INTERVIEW WITH HOLMES

I studied my father's profile.

"May I ask you a question?"

We were back in the hansom cab, driving west on Exeter Street, and the difference between the view out the window and the alleys of the Old Nichol that we had just left behind was so pronounced it was almost physically jarring.

In just a mile or two, the filth, the poverty, the crowding and the reek of desperation and despair were gone. The streets here were broader, straighter. The shops that lined the road were prosperous-looking. To our left, I could see the famous dome of St. Paul's cathedral rising over the skyline.

Holmes's look now wasn't precisely encouraging, but he twitched a finger in a way that usually meant *go ahead*.

If I had to guess from the glance he shot me, he had already deduced the substance of the question I had for him.

"Why didn't you investigate the Ripper murders nine years ago?"

The news of last night's murder was already in today's edition of the morning papers. So far, we had passed no fewer than eight newsboys standing on street corners and calling out headlines about last night's murder and the Ripper's return.

Holmes rested his hands on the top of his walking stick, his gaze still on the street rolling past outside. "What makes you so certain that I did not?"

"Because, if you had investigated, you would have caught the killer in 1888, and we wouldn't be having this conversation now."

Holmes's mouth twitched in a smile that was somehow even grimmer than his usual faint, wry quirk of the lips. "Your confidence is reassuring—though in this case, greatly unwarranted."

He was silent a long moment, then exhaled. He seemed to drag his gaze back to mine, but when he spoke, his voice was dispassionate, the words filtered through the sieve of his will so that they sounded detached, almost casual.

"The year of 1888 was one of the busiest of my career to that date. My fame as a consulting detective had spread to a degree that ensured there was a steady stream of applicants begging me to lend my services and police asking for my assistance with a particularly trying case. As you know, when I am preoccupied with a case, I occasionally ... lack balance in other areas of life."

Considering that Holmes's standard practice was to entirely refuse both rest and food until a case was solved, that was a little like saying that the Hatfield and the McCoy families back in America suffered from minor differences of opinion.

But I let it go.

"Despite Watson's increasingly pointed remonstrations, I persisted in taking on case after case, with scarcely more than a day's interlude between," Holmes went on.

"Uncle John didn't approve?"

"I believe his exact words were, *It's as though you're sending me a formal, written invitation to utter the words 'I told you so'.*"

Despite myself, I smiled a little; that sounded like Uncle John. "And did he?"

"He did not, as a matter of fact. When I came to the inevitable resounding crash, Watson was a model of steady friendship and solid medical advice."

That also sounded exactly like Uncle John.

Holmes went on. "The fact remains, however, that he was in the right. I spent the majority of the autumn of 1888 fatigued by over work and with my natural faculties both clouded and over-stimulated by cocaine—a fact which Watson, ever-loyal, was at pains to conceal when he published his accounts of the cases we had investigated. I heard of the Ripper killings in the newspaper accounts, but they scarcely penetrated my consciousness, so lost was I. By the end of November, I had made an effort to drag myself out of the cocaine-filled pit into which I had fallen. But at that point—"

"The killings had stopped," I finished for him. "So that's why you know all the dates and details of the Ripper murders so thoroughly."

Holmes didn't fail often—nor had he outright said that he felt responsible for not having caught the Ripper nine years ago. But I knew him well enough to be sure that his conscience wouldn't allow him to rest easy on that score.

If Sherlock Holmes had exacting standards for the rest of the world, he was hardest of all on himself.

Now he didn't wince, but I saw the line of his jaw tighten just briefly.

"I'm sorry," I said quickly. "I didn't mean—"

"Your statement is entirely accurate," Holmes said. "I might have stopped the Whitechapel killer nine years ago, but did not. I have since then made it my business to know every detail of those earlier cases, in anticipation of precisely this sort of occurrence: that the killings would begin again."

Holmes wouldn't want me to tell him that it wasn't his fault, that he was only human and couldn't be expected to save everyone. He wouldn't believe me if I said that the number of murderers he had caught in his lifetime outweighed the balance of one who had slipped through his grasp.

He *especially* wouldn't want me to ask whether he still dosed himself with a seven-per-cent solution of cocaine. Even if I couldn't help wondering.

"You expected that the Ripper would return?" I asked instead.

Holmes gave an impatient twitch of one shoulder. "A killer of that ilk—one who murders not for gain or revenge or even personal hate but for the sheer lust for blood—does not suddenly reform. He stops only when he is forced to, either by death or imprisonment."

"And you never believed that the killer was dead?"

"There were two other cases—both of them inconclusive, but hinting at the possibility that the killer still walked the streets of London. Alice McKenzie, murdered in July of 1889. And Frances Coles, whose body was found beneath a railway arch in Swallow Garden on 13th February, 1891. Both victims' injuries bore striking resemblance to those of the original Ripper victims."

"But nothing between 1891 and now?" I asked.

"As you say." Holmes's brows edged together. "Which inevitably brings to mind the question of *why* the six-year gap?"

"What do you think of the fruit vendor's account of the couple last night buying grapes?" I asked.

"I think it is quite possibly the most remarkable detail in this affair."

"Because it shows that the killer wishes to recreate details from the murders nine years ago?"

"On the contrary." Holmes shook his head. "Because until this morning, when the fruit vendor's account came in, I had dismissed Mathew Packer's nine-year-old account of having sold grapes to Elizabeth Stride and her supposed killer as the purest fabrication. You may not have read of it in the American papers, but Packer changed his account of that evening with the frequency of a weathervane changing direction in a hurricane. He first claimed to have seen nothing whatever unusual that night and to have had no customers due to the pouring rain, causing him to close up shop. Then, when he learned that the newspapers would pay handsomely for anyone providing an eyewitness account of either the victim or the murderer, he promptly and conveniently recollected that he had sold grapes to a woman answering the description of Elizabeth Stride."

I could see Holmes's point, but I offered, "He could honestly have just forgotten. I imagine most shopkeepers don't pay particular attention to their customers in the ordinary way. He might only have put two and two together after the murder."

"Possible. If barely. However, he came forward later that autumn with an account of having received a visit from the Ripper's cousin."

I felt my eyebrows climbing. "The Ripper's ... cousin?"

"Indeed. Mr. Packer gave a statement to a newspaper reporter that he had been visited at his shop by two men who purchased 12 shillings' worth of rabbits from him. The men then asked if Mr. Packer could give them a description of the man to whom he had sold the grapes—the man supposed to have committed the Berner Street and Mitre Square murders. Apparently, one of the men believed that the killer was his cousin who had moved to America, but had returned to London seven or eight months ago and had confessed to a wish to cut prostitutes' throats and, I quote, 'rip them up.'"

"And the Ripper's cousin just happened to confide all of this to Mr. Packer, a greengrocer whom he'd never met before?"

"That and more, according to the statement Mr. Packer gave to the newspapers. The story went on to provide several more corroborating details that would appear to link this mysterious gentleman's cousin with the Whitechapel killer—including a habit of addressing his acquaintances as 'boss'. Which, of course, echoes the famous *Dear Boss* letter supposedly sent by the Ripper to Central News Agency."

I shook my head. "Anyone who can't tell better lies than that ought to give up trying."

"So I should have said. I had dismissed Mr. Packer out of hand as an attention monger, nothing more."

Holmes eyes unfocused as he stared out the window, plainly lost in thought.

"All of this was in the newspapers at the time, though," I said. "Anyone could have read it; it doesn't mean that it actually is the same man doing the killing. And where does the Italian woman fit in? She was shot—and the Ripper never used a gun on his victims before."

"That we know of."

I gave Holmes a questioning look, and he let out a quick, impatient puff of breath. "We know practically nothing of the killer, beyond the facts surrounding the victims he left on the streets nine years ago. He could have made a habit of exterminating others in more subtle ways. He could, in his spare time, have been a circus performer, an inventor, a doctor—I have even heard it suggested that he had royal blood in his veins. Regardless, we would not know of it."

I could see Holmes's point. It would be a mistake to make too many assumptions about the killer's identity—to try to confine him to any particular box—when everything about him was a hazy, shapeless unknown.

I had been doing my best not to think of the nameless Italian woman, but now the memory of her face rose before me—her face and the ring of bruises we'd found on her ankle.

She had come to this country *from* somewhere—somewhere she belonged, maybe somewhere she was even now being missed by a family or friends. And she'd wound up first a prisoner, then shot down and killed when she tried to escape.

"Whoever it is doing the killing, we need to find him and stop him," I said—speaking before Holmes could raise any of his usual objections to my being involved in a dangerous case. "I mean we *personally* need to. This isn't vanity speaking; I'm just stating facts. We've succeeded in the past where ordinary police investigations have failed. Doesn't that make it our responsibility now to do everything we can to see that the killer is caught—whether it's actually the Ripper or some other deranged lunatic at large?"

Holmes's brows drew together, but he said nothing.

"Are you going to tell me that I'm wrong?" I finally asked.

Holmes finally spoke, his gaze fixed out the window. "That would be hypocritical in the extreme, considering that those are precisely the same arguments I employed against Watson nine years ago when I persisted in accepting every case that presented itself to me."

Holmes didn't need to say any more or spell out the fact that the approach obviously hadn't ended well.

He drew out his watch. "I believe that you are due at the Savoy Theater in a short while, are you not?"

"That's right." There were times when my work with Holmes and my life at the theater felt so disparate from each other that they couldn't even be made to fit as parts of the same whole, and this was one.

I had nearly forgotten, but I had a rehearsal this afternoon for the new show, *The Grand Duchess of Gerolstein*, that would be opening at the beginning of December. Then there was the *Yeomen of the Guard* performance tonight.

I would have to set aside all thoughts of women being chained up and groomed like lambs for slaughter and instead sing about true lovers' hearts and songs of a merry maid.

"It matters." Holmes's voice cut in on my thoughts, making me look up.

"What?"

"The work you do, the operas you perform at the Savoy. They bring people happiness—a chance to forget their own cares, the vicissitudes of their own lives. It matters," Holmes said again. His voice was quiet, but weighted with emphasis.

I looked at him, startled—not that he should have deduced the lines along which my thoughts were going; that was so entirely typical as to barely even register as remarkable anymore. But I'd never heard him speak of the theater that way.

"Thank you."

I looked at Holmes's watch. There wasn't time enough for me to go back to Baker Street and ask whether Becky wanted to come with me again. Jack might be off duty by now, although given last night's murder and the exhaustive manhunt that had to be even now underway, he might have been asked to stay.

With luck, he might have been able to catch a few hours' sleep in the police station dormitory, where some of the unmarried constables slept.

"What are you planning to do now?" I asked Holmes, as the cab driver drew to a halt outside the stage door entrance.

"I shall seek out Watson, to hear what he has uncovered in his visit to the mortuary." Holmes looked at me, seeming to struggle with something a moment, then said, "You will be sure to take a cab if you are returning to Baker Street after dark?"

The Savoy was absolutely nowhere near Whitechapel, but I nodded. "I promise."

I climbed down to the pavement, then turned back to look up at Holmes, still seated in the carriage.

"The answer is no," Holmes said.

I frowned. "The answer—"

"You were wondering whether I continue to indulge in the cocaine habit," Holmes said. "The answer is no. I have not done in some time."

I felt my jaw drop slightly. Holmes never volunteered personal confessions. Never. At best, he would allow either myself or Watson to drag information out of him, but I always had the distinct impression that he would rather undergo surgery without anesthesia.

"In some time, meaning—"

"Two years, to be precise." Holmes's mouth curved in one of his quick, wry smiles, gone so quickly you might almost have imagined the expression was there at all. "Not since November 1895."

November 1895, was the month when I had first met Holmes and soon after discovered that he was my father.

I had always thought of it as something of a cosmic irony. His friendship with Watson aside, Holmes existed so entirely in and of himself, as though his entire personality and temper were designed to prove John Donne's line about *no man is an island* wrong.

And then fate had deposited me into his life, the family he had almost certainly never thought to desire for himself and never known he had.

Holmes smiled fleetingly again at my expression of astonishment. "I will see you back at Baker Street."

He tapped with the handle of his cane on the side of the carriage, signaling the cabbie to drive on.

The cab had rolled away and been swallowed by the London traffic before I realized two things: first, that I hadn't had the chance of asking what Holmes intended to do *after* he caught up with Uncle John.

And second, that if my father intended to carry out some dangerous plan and wished to distract me from asking about it, then he had—between his unexpected speech about the value of the theater and his revelation about giving up cocaine—effectively done just that.

A reminder that Thomas Newman wasn't the only one who should never, ever underestimate Sherlock Holmes.

23. HOLMES ENLISTS MY AID

It was midmorning when I next saw Holmes. I had put on my overcoat and was on my way out of our sitting room when I heard the sound of his footsteps coming up our staircase. He opened the door and stood for a moment.

"Ah, Watson. You are on your way to meet with Mrs. Scott, I see. Your freshly-shaved cheeks with perfectly trimmed mustache, your clean shirt collar, and your perfectly knotted necktie proclaim as much."

Feeling oddly truculent, I merely said, "And?"

"Have you a moment to enlighten me as to the Hanbury Street murder victim?"

I had had a difficult time of it and felt the need to unburden myself. "I can certainly report that the Whitechapel mortuary is as vile a location as one might imagine, with an appalling lack of both hygiene and security. The place was simply chaos. It is a wonder that the body made it to the examiner's table at all. I could find no confirmation that it was indeed the body that had been found. No one was present to identify it. No one had appeared to claim it. Police left it in the line in the corridor among others. A pad of paper on the clipboard piled onto the slab showed the name of the officer who had found the body. But he was going off duty. I waited for nearly an hour, because the examining physician was late in arriving. I kept myself awake by pacing the corridor—"

"Please describe what happened after the examining physician arrived."

"Undraped, the body proved to be that of an elderly, gray-bearded beggar man."

"And then?"

"I took the examiner with me into the corridor. We looked under the shrouds until finally we found a body whose description tallied with what the commissioner had told us. But, as I said, it took me—"

"Yes, yes, Watson. You did indeed examine the correct body?"

"It was after dawn. The next examiner was to come on duty. The other went home. I had to wait more. I was with the examiner until just half past nine this morning. Whereupon I came here, performed my morning ablutions, and dressed as you see me."

"What was the cause of death?"

"Her throat had been cut, and she had lost a great deal of blood."

"The commissioner mentioned cuts on her lower extremities?"

"They were an odd pattern. I found it quite ominous, Holmes."

"Writing? Symbols?"

"A series of ten small cuts, all in a row. Then there were two cuts that had been crossed, so to speak. Cut over to form an 'x' pattern."

I had thought Holmes would react to this macabre touch, which to me suggested that the killer was sending a message that this woman was his second victim and that he intended to kill eight more times.

But Holmes merely said, "You are positive the throat was the only cut—other than the markings on the legs?"

"The cuts were on the shins, to be precise."

"Fine. Now I may release you to your urgent appointment. Where are you going, may I ask?"

"To Madame Tussaud's. The young ladies are having a history lesson of sorts." At his raised eyebrow, I continued, "The idea is to give the young ladies experiences that will make for interesting conversation when they are governesses, in their places of employment."

"I understand. Everyone has heard of Tussaud's, but only those who have been to London have seen it."

He paused. Then he said, "I wonder if I might ask a favor of you, Watson."

WATSON

24. AT MADAME TUSSAUD'S

I had intended to arrive early at Tussaud's so as to reconnoiter the rooms undisturbed. My purpose was to select a place from which I could watch Holmes meet with a potential diamond smuggler on the following day, assuming that both parties agreed that the museum was a suitably safe place. If the meeting went wrong, as had the one in the Hatton Garden café, I could intervene if necessary.

Holmes had suggested the upstairs Chamber of Horrors as a possible meeting location within Tussaud's. "It is always busy, so your presence will not be seen as unusual," he said. "I can meet with my quarry at the center of the room, between the effigy of the French revolutionist Marat and those of Milsom and Fowler, the Muswell Hill murderers. I suggest you locate yourself to the immediate right of the entry, between the effigy of Lee, the Romford murderer, and Rush, the Stanfield Hall killer who dispatched his victims with a blunderbuss."

"If you are so certain," I said, feeling somewhat nettled, "why do you need to take time away from my interviews with the young ladies?"

"Because it has been more than five years since I have visited Tussaud's. The exhibits may well have been rearranged in the interim."

Now, having entered and paid for my ticket, I saw immediately what appeared to be a setting that would provide better cover and allow me to stay with the young ladies. The entry hall had been devoted to the depiction of a tiger hunt.

The nine-foot replica of a huge war elephant, shown in the act of trampling an attacking Bengal tiger, offered a wonderfully massive bulk behind which I could conceal myself. I walked around the great gray beast, checking my lines of sight.

Then the Bethnal Green School girls swept in behind their governess, a small, tidy, black-haired woman of perhaps thirty years of age, with alert dark eyes and a tight-lipped, stern expression. She caught sight of me immediately.

"Doctor Watson," she said. "I am Agnes Peebles of the Bethnal Green School. You will forgive me for not lingering, I hope. I am responsible for keeping order among this ... gaggle of youthful chatter that fills this room at present. But I wanted to thank you personally for your assistance. Mrs. Scott has told me of your generous promises to utilize your writing reputation and talents to help us. We are most grateful."

Then, with a tight little nod, she turned back to her charges.

I realized that the location would not serve, after all. Had Holmes and his quarry been standing in the area, they would have been surrounded and unable to discuss business. Also, Holmes would be carrying diamonds, and I would have to intervene if Holmes's quarry turned aggressor. A more private spot would be required.

I was about to go upstairs to reconnoiter the Chamber of

Horrors as instructed, but then the tall, thin student named Clara also recognized me.

She hurried to my side and gave me a metallic smile. "I'm allowed to show you more of my sketches. Have you spoken with your editor at *The Strand*?"

"Not yet."

Her face fell. Then she brightened. "You have patients, of course, and they need you when they need you."

"I will most definitely speak with him as soon as I can."

"Of course. Don't worry, I believe you. But please don't say anything about it to Lady Scott. We're not supposed to be thinking of jobs other than the governess positions we're being trained for. She's coming in right now, with Lord Burleigh, that tall gentleman at her side. I've seen him at the school before. He's taller than me!"

Clad in bright blue taffeta, Amelia was indeed entering the museum. She hung on the arm of a ruddy, sunburned gentleman who appeared to be in excellent health and had a masterful air about him. He strode confidently through the ticketing area. There was something familiar about his features.

Then I made the connection. This man resembled the doctor we had seen at the morgue, the man who had been introduced as Dr. Burleigh. The two men were alike in the face, though less so in the body. Since the names were the same, I thought that this man here with Amelia must be a family member.

Amelia saw me and said something to her tall companion. Then she flew to my side.

"John! How good of you to come. I'm afraid I have another favor to ask of you. For the good of the school."

"Only too pleased to do what I can," I said.

"Oh, thank you. I shrink from appearing brazenly single-minded in pursuit of my charitable cause, but needs must, as you well know. Nothing ventured, nothing gained, and the poor girls are so much in need."

"Please, do not hesitate. How can I help?"

"Well, it concerns that gentleman over there." She indicated the man Clara had named as Lord Burleigh. "He is a patron of the school, and in the past year he has been our most generous benefactor. He is recently returned from the Transvaal, where he raises Afrikaners cattle on the family ranch."

"He spends a great deal of time in the outdoors," I said.

"Oh, he is something of a health fanatic, you see. He's lived on his family's ranch for years, the rugged simple life. His family has land holdings all over the world. He also has property here in London. You no doubt have heard of Burleigh House. Anyway, I mentioned what you were doing—those articles in *The Strand Magazine*—and he told me he will be meeting with some friends—highly-placed friends—two days from now. He wondered if he could have a copy of your article printed up to show them."

"My text is not complete yet—"

"His friends could make a great deal of difference. For example, four of our girls are graduating and on their way to the colonies, traveling to Canada, Bermuda, Bangalore, and Perth. We *so* hope to have new wardrobes ready for them. They sail Monday. We need the funds to buy their new outfits by this Friday. Lord Burleigh and his friends could easily provide those funds, and far, far more."

"But to have printed copies, only two days from now—"

Amelia was holding my arm, looking imploringly into my eyes. "Please, John. One gift from him could be far greater than all the funds we could hope to raise through *The Strand Magazine*. He has it in his power even to allow us to occupy Burleigh House. No more leaky roof and windows, no more mildew and mold—"

I pictured Clara's beautiful sketches, now yellowed and drooping from their pins along the wall shelves. If funds were available, she could create new sketches and know that they would be suitably framed and displayed to those who could provide patronage and future work.

I nodded.

Her face lit up with a wonderful smile of gratitude. "Oh, a thousand thanks! I must tell him you will do it. Then you can be introduced, the two of you. Just wait here one moment, and don't mention that you are accelerating your writing schedule on his behalf. It would embarrass him dreadfully."

She returned to Lord Burleigh, and I saw her whisper something into his ear. His eyes widened in pleasure. Moments later, the two had come over to me, and Lord Burleigh was clasping my hand in a warm, firm grip. "So glad you're helping the cause, Doctor," he said. "These girls—these young ladies—will have their influence for good in the world. Good for the Empire. Good for us all."

I said only, "Happy to do what I can."

"Now I must be off. I'm sure you have plenty to occupy you. Amelia, I really must dash. Thank you again, Doctor."

Amelia gave me a winning smile, "Yes, John. Thank you." I was about to ask her where to deliver the manuscript, but she had already turned to follow Lord Burleigh.

I looked for Clara, but she was gone, and the other young ladies also had dispersed.

Alone, I made my way upstairs, to examine the Chamber of Horrors.

LUCY

25. MORE FLOWERS FOR GRACE

Gladly we'll celebrate this happy wedding day,
We'll make the merry cannons roar,
We'll wave the banners—

"Halt!" Mr. Harris's shout and upraised hands cut off the singing in mid-word. He turned to Mr. Henry Lytton, who in the role of Prince Paul was about to be wedded to the titular Grand Duchess of Gerolstein.

"Mr. Litton, you are supposed to convey to the audience that you are passionately in love with this woman." Mr. Harris gestured to Florence St. John, who played the Duchess. "*Not* that you are a cow in the last stages of consumption."

There were a few laughs from the company on stage, and Mr. Harris clapped his hands. "Again!"

As we sang through the final number of the third act, I glanced at Grace, who was once again standing beside me. She had been more attentive for this rehearsal than yesterday's performance, but her eyes now had a fixed, glassy look, and the line of her mouth was rigid, as though she were trying not to cry.

Finally, Mr. Harris declared himself satisfied, and we made our way off stage.

"Is something wrong?" I asked her.

I was afraid all the songs about weddings and brides and bridegrooms had upset her, but Grace blinked fiercely, shaking her head and glowering at the Tower of London scenery that was being dragged into place for tonight's performance.

"I can't wait until we're on to performing the Duchess. I *hate The Yeomen of the Guard*."

"What? Why?"

"Because not everyone winds up happy at the end." Grace scrubbed an impatient hand across her eyes. "Haven't you ever noticed? Practically every other opera from Mr. Gilbert and Mr. Sullivan ends up with everyone happily paired off, two by two, like … like Noah's Ark animals. Even if it never happens in real life like that, at least you can be happy for all the characters in the play. But in *Yeomen*, poor Point winds up all alone—still in love with Elsie, but knowing that he can never have her."

We stepped out from the stage wings and into the hallway that led towards the changing areas.

"Miss James!"

I turned at the sound of a woman's voice calling to me and found Mrs. Amelia Scott walking rapidly towards us down the passage.

"Is that Mrs. Scott?" Grace asked.

I looked at her, startled. "Do you know her?"

Grace fished in her sleeve for a handkerchief, wiped her eyes, and nodded. "A cousin of mine was taken in by that school she runs in Bethnal Green."

Mrs. Scott was wearing an afternoon walking suit of a deep,

rich teal, trimmed with black braid on the sleeves and hem and with a matching spray of feathers on the crown of her hat.

She smiled as she approached us. "Miss James, and—" her eyes widened a little as she looked more closely at Grace. "Why, it's Miss Lilley, isn't it? You are—"

"Maybelle's cousin, that's right." Grace made a clear effort to arrange her face in an answering smile. "How is Maybelle getting on? I haven't heard from her in ages."

Mrs. Scott frowned. "Did you not hear? I made sure to tell her to write to her family. Maybelle was offered a post as governess to a family in India. She sailed last month."

"I haven't visited with my aunt in ages; I'm sure I'll hear all about it next time we have tea," Grace said. Then she looked past Mrs. Scott, to where Will Simpson was just hurrying down the hall. "I'd better go. It was nice to see you, Mrs. Scott."

Amelia Scott watched her go, then turned to me. "Miss James, I was hoping for the chance to speak with you."

"Of course. Is it something to do with Reverend Albright's death?"

Mrs. Scott looked startled, and then a shadow crossed her face. "Oh—oh, no. I have been helping to make arrangements for the funeral, of course. So unfortunate, and of course a great embarrassment to the church, their views on suicide being what they are. We are hoping, of course, that the inquest returns a verdict of suicide while of unsound mind, so that poor Reverend Albright may be buried on church grounds."

"But there's been no other trouble at the rectory?" I asked. "No one trying to break in again?"

"No. The place is quite empty, of course, save for his housekeeper. But she says that there has been nothing of that sort."

Was Adam Smith still in police custody? I realized that with the Ripper murder scare coming up, I hadn't even thought to ask Holmes.

"What I wished to speak with you about today was quite another matter entirely," Mrs. Scott went on. "John"—I thought a faint tinge of color stained her cheeks as she hurried on—"that is, Doctor Watson and I were trying to think what might be done in the wake of these terrible murders."

I set aside my moment's surprise that she had apparently seen Uncle John today.

"Done?" I asked.

"For the women of Whitechapel, of course. I had thoughts of establishing some sort of shelter for those without homes— a place where they might go to be safe."

"You mean for the—" I searched for a term that wouldn't cause offense to a woman of Mrs. Scott's social standing.

Ordinarily, I mightn't have bothered. But if she was thinking of setting up a safe haven in Whitechapel that would keep vulnerable women off the streets, I didn't want to do or say anything that might discourage her.

"Prostitutes," Mrs. Scott finished for me. "I have no patience for euphemisms, I'm afraid."

I smiled. "I haven't either, actually."

"Excellent. Then you may be willing to lend aid to the scheme I have in mind. I'd like to put on a charity concert, to raise funds for such a shelter to be established. It would be similar to the work we are already doing in Bethnal Green, but targeted specifically to the women who ply their trade on the streets of Whitechapel. I had hoped that I might speak to your stage manager?"

I wanted to get back to Baker Street, both to make sure that Holmes had survived whatever rash scheme he had been plotting and to see Jack and Becky.

But I nodded.

"Of course. Mr. Harris is his name. I can bring you to speak with him now, if you'd like."

* * *

"So if you could perhaps see your way to assembling a group of fifteen or twenty singers, Mr. Harris?" Mrs. Scott finished. "I will, of course, be willing to pay for the performers' time."

"Yes, yes." Mr. Harris was perched on a stool in the right wings of the stage. He waved an impatient hand in answer to Mrs. Scott and continued to bend over the libretto for *The Grand Duchess of Gerolstein* that he was currently making notes on in bright blue pencil.

Mrs. Scott gave me a bemused look. Having never spoken with our stage manager before, she wasn't familiar with his habit of never focusing on one task at a time when he could do two or three things at once instead.

"You are ... agreeing to participate in a charitable concert?"

Mr. Harris finally dragged his attention away from the script he was marking. "Certainly. It should be easy to accommodate you. I've just gotten word that nightly performances are to be canceled, thanks to this Ripper business."

"Canceled?" I repeated, startled.

"Yes, it's very inconvenient." Mr. Harris's slightly rotund face pulled in a scowl. "Ticket sales for tonight's performance are abysmal; no one is willing to risk setting foot outside their doors at night unless they absolutely have to. I was just about to make an announcement, but you can tell anyone you see, Miss James, that they may as well go home. We'll rehearse *The Grand Duchess* tomorrow afternoon, but all evening performances are canceled for the week as of now, until either the killer is caught or else the public gets bored with the story and stops being afraid."

Mrs. Scott opened her mouth and closed it again. "That is very ... good of you. Shall I let you know what night will best suit?"

Mr. Harris had returned to jotting down indecipherable notes in his script margins, but waved one hand again. "Certainly, certainly."

We were clearly being dismissed. Mrs. Scott and I turned away.

"A rather singular man, your Mr. Harris," Mrs. Scott murmured as we made our way offstage.

"Not so unusual as stage managers go, I don't think. He's not unfeeling, really. It's just that for him, all of this—" I gestured to the stage lights and painted scenery all around—"is a little more real than the world outside the Savoy."

Amelia Scott smiled a little wryly. "In that sense, not terribly different from people like Lord and Lady Haggerston, for whom nothing is quite real outside the bubble of their own pampered existence."

"And yet you manage to make them care about supporting the Bethnal Green Aide society."

"Yes, well." Mrs. Scott's wry expression deepened. "The secret, Miss James, is that everyone wants to feel virtuous— even essentially selfish people. I simply provide them with that opportunity, at a minimal inconvenience to themselves."

She sighed, looking momentarily a little tired, but then

straightened her shoulders. "Ah, well. If it allows us to help—or at least gain justice for—women who come to this country without any kin or any connection to their homes save for a tattooed mark on their arm, I suppose I shouldn't quibble. One has to begin somewhere."

I glanced at her quickly. "Uncle John told you about the Italian woman who was killed last night?"

"Yes, poor soul." Amelia Scott seemed to hesitate, then said, "You call John—that is, Dr. Watson—*Uncle*. You must be very fond of him."

"I am. Very."

Mrs. Scott opened her mouth, but then seemed to change her mind about whatever she had been about to say.

"And he of you, I'm sure." She smiled. "And now, Miss James, I will thank you for your help with Mr. Harris and wish you good day. I'm sure you must be wanting to see that handsome young policeman of yours."

* * *

As I was making my way towards the Savoy's rear entrance, I almost bumped into Grace, who was just coming out of the dressing rooms.

"Oh. Hello again." Grace looked a little brighter than before, I thought, her arms filled with a bouquet of pink roses. "Look—these were addressed to me this time. At least, Mr. Watts said they were."

She held up the roses, which had a card attached, just like the one yesterday. *From an admirer.*

"Maybe they were for you all along, and Mr. Watts made a mistake with the names?"

The words were definitely in the same neat but distinctly left-handed writing.

Grace wrinkled her nose. "Grace Lilley and Lucy James? They're not very much alike."

"They are if they're spoken to Mr. Watts by anyone who he thinks might be of foreign birth. I think he makes it a point of pride not to understand anyone without an English accent."

Grace laughed, gathering the flowers closer. "Well, whoever they're from, I'll take them and enjoy them." Her smile faded, the corners of her mouth quivering before tucking tight.

"Has something happened?"

Grace didn't answer right away. "You remember your little friend Becky's idea about the roses yesterday?" she finally asked.

"It didn't work?"

"Oh, it did." Grace's mouth twisted. "Too well, actually—and without my even trying. Charlie took one look at the flowers and accused me of keeping company with someone else. He wouldn't listen to a word I said otherwise, just said that I was lying, trying to make a fool of him."

"I'm so sorry, Grace."

We had reached the end of the hallway that led to the theater's rear exit. Grace pushed open the door, gulping another shaky breath.

"It's fine. I'm not going to cry for him anymore; he's not worth it."

The sun set early in London in November—and that was when it could be seen at all. Stepping onto the street, Grace and I were surrounded almost at once by curls of patchy fog that leant an eerie, almost spectral aura to the horses and carriages and other pedestrians all around.

An elderly woman thrust a basket of oranges towards us—then vanished into the fog a moment later when we both shook our heads.

"That's what Becky said about Charlie, too," I told Grace.

Grace hiccupped an uneven laugh. "I knew I liked her."

"Grace!" The voice behind us made us both turn around to see Will Simpson just coming out of the stage door. His fair hair was rumpled-looking, and he was breathing as though he'd run to catch up. "I was just wondering—"

"No!" Grace interrupted. "No, I would *not* like you to walk me home, no I would *not* like your help in carrying these flowers." Her voice climbed as she dashed at her eyes again. "As I have been saying for the past two months at least, I have no interest whatsoever in associating with you outside of the theater. How you are finding any of that confusing is beyond me."

Will's expression changed, turning from eager to resembling a puppy who's just been kicked. I couldn't help wincing inwardly, even though I sympathized with Grace.

"I just—"

"Is there a problem here?" A deep bass voice interrupted.

I almost jumped at the sight of Mr. Watts, stepping out of a patch of fog to the right of the stage door. He gave Will the sort of look he'd probably used on vagrants and suspected thieves during his time with the police.

Will flinched nervously. "No. I was just—I'll be going now. I'm ... sorry, Grace. I'm just ... sorry." He flushed, ducked his head and turned, striding away.

Mr. Watts transferred the stern look to Grace and me. "You should be getting along, too. This isn't a good day for young ladies to be out on the streets alone."

"Thank you, Mr. Watts."

Grace swallowed, shivering a little as we turned away from the theater. "Do you think there really is any danger?"

Glancing at her, I suspected that what she wanted me to say was that since we weren't Whitechapel prostitutes, of course there was no danger at all.

"I don't think anywhere in London is ever *completely* safe."

I actually liked that about the city, on an ordinary day. Not the danger, exactly, but the feeling of possibilities—as though anything could happen at any time.

The Strand was one of the busiest thoroughfares in London and was never quiet—not even this afternoon. The foot traffic was perhaps a little less than usual. But even if the theaters were canceling their performances, there was still Charing Cross Station, the Law Courts, and innumerable shops and newspaper offices and hotels to draw people in.

"I don't think we're in any danger now, though."

Grace and I started down the road, walking towards Trafalgar Square.

"I suppose I should have been kinder to Will," Grace said after a moment's silence. She looked at me, her mouth tightening a little. "Do you think I ought to take the Grand Duchess's advice? All that about 'if you can't have those you could love, you must try to love those you can have'?"

That was a direct quotation from the Duchess of Gerolstein in the show.

I shook my head. "I think you should be with someone who makes you happy. But just because Will Simpson admires you doesn't mean that you owe him anything. I *did* wonder whether he could be the one who sent the roses, though."

I nodded to the flowers in her arms.

"Ugh. I hadn't thought of that." Grace pressed her eyes briefly shut. "I'm not sure whether the idea makes me want to pitch them into the nearest trash bin—or feel guilty for yelling at him."

An omnibus rattled past us towards the stop up the road.

"That's the 'bus to Lambeth," Grace said. "I'd better hurry and catch it. My landlady, Mrs. Rudge, is the nervous type. I wouldn't put it past her to lock the boarding house doors as soon as the sun goes down."

WATSON

26. A MEETING ENDS BADLY

I was in the Chamber of Horrors, stationed at my agreed-on vantage point behind the replica of the guillotine and alongside the actual wax cast made from the severed head of Marie Antoinette. I saw Holmes arrive. He wore a flat cap and black corduroy overalls with a seaman's jacket of black wool. Silent, he took the place we had agreed upon a few hour earlier, to the left of Marat's effigy, his gray eyes on the entry corridor and the staircase beyond. I knew better than to try to signal him from my place of concealment. Doubtless, I thought, he had already taken a circuitous route and confirmed my presence.

Then, emerging from the crowd gathered around the head of Robespierre, came a florid-faced, portly man advancing towards Holmes. He was dressed in business attire, and not at all distinguished, as though dressed to blend into a crowd at any moment. His thinning black hair was slicked down and brushed straight back. Coming up on Holmes's right, he said something that I could not hear. Holmes nodded and said something in return. He waited for the stout man to reply, which, after a moment, the latter did. Holmes nodded. Clearly a password or code created for the purpose of mutual identification had been exchanged, and the exchange had been satisfactory.

I fingered the handle of the Webley revolver in my coat pocket, hoping that the remainder of the meeting would also proceed smoothly.

The stout man waited expectantly. Holmes reached into his waistcoat pocket and brought out two stones, which he placed in the palm of his other hand. Then, he closed his fist and waited.

The stout man produced a monocle from his own tight-fitting waistcoat pocket and pressed it into his eye.

Holmes handed over one of the two stones. I could not tell whether it was the raw diamond or the cut one. I knew the purpose of the meeting was to strike a deal to cut a quantity of raw diamonds and smuggle out of the country a quantity of gems already cut, followed by the smuggling of the rough gems once they had been processed and cut. I wondered: did Holmes have the other diamonds with him? He had still refused to take me into his confidence on that point.

The stout man had just finished his inspection of the first stone and was nodding, apparently in satisfaction. He handed it back, whereupon Holmes gave him the second. The process was repeated. The stout man gave a final nod, straightened up with his hands at his sides in a soldierly posture, then bowed formally. He took Holmes's arm, and the two set off into the crowd at the Victoria exhibit.

It was my turn to take action now. I needed to keep Holmes in my sight at all times in case he was endangered. One hand gripping my Webley, I pushed through the crowd on tiptoe to try to keep Holmes's flat cap in my field of vision. His stout companion, fully a head shorter than Holmes, was obscured by the crowd. We moved along the edge of the Bastille exhibit and then to the staircase that led to the tiger hunt exhibit and the entrance. I saw both Holmes and the stout man go down the stairs. I followed, one hand on the rail, the other on my revolver. The two men were at the bottom of the staircase, then past the elephant and the tiger, then in the lobby, then at the outside entry door.

From behind me, I heard a voice, a harsh whisper, which made it impossible for me to identify the speaker.

"Best laid plans, eh, Doctor Watson?"

I turned and saw a tall figure in a top hat, face hidden behind a muffler. I had only the fleeting impression of sharp eyes above the gray wool fabric. A brass-handled cane flashed into my view, and I felt it hook over my right wrist, pulling my hand away from the support of the rail. At the same time, the man kicked my right leg just behind my knee, so that my leg buckled beneath me. Simultaneously, a firm hand shoved me at the center of my back.

Launched forward, I fell out and down and landed hard on my side, tumbling over and over down the stairs. I pinwheeled my arms, trying to stop my fall, but only succeeded in knocking my elbows and wrists against the hard marble stair treads.

Finally, I came to rest, lying on my side at the foot of the staircase, breathless, with the wind knocked out of me.

I pulled myself up on hands and knees and turned back, craning my neck, hoping to identify my attacker. But there was no sign of him on the staircase.

Staggering, I stumbled towards the door and past the astonished ticket man. I had no time to spend asking him what he had seen or where my attacker had gone. I needed to find Holmes. I patted my coat pocket and was grateful to feel the heft of my

Webley. Then I bolted through the door and out into the cold October afternoon air. I stood on the pavement. Then, seeing a cab in the street, I clambered up on top of the driver's chair in order to see further around me.

I saw Holmes in his flat cap and seaman's jacket, still walking side by side with the portly man. The two were heading for The Regent's Park.

I leaped down from the cab, pressed a shilling into the hand of the astonished cabman, and staggered on. The two were still in my sights when I passed through the gated archway into the park. As I hurried past, I had the vague impression of a shadowy figure detaching itself from the column beside me to my right.

Then, a great light and a harsh, blinding flash of pain burst from the back of my skull. The impact radiated through my entire frame as though a bolt of lightning had struck me.

And then there was only darkness.

LUCY

27. A MESSAGE FROM LESTRADE

Jack and Becky were seated on the couch when I opened the door to the 221A sitting room. Jack looked tired, though he smiled at the sight of me. Becky jumped up and came to hug me. I thought her small arms clung more tightly than usual, and for once, she didn't say anything.

Before I could ask whether anything was wrong, though, Mrs. Hudson put her head in through the door.

"Come along, Miss Becky, there's work for us in the kitchen." She spoke gently but firmly. "I've a lemon cream cake that's not going to ice itself *and* an entire plate full of cream puffs that need filling."

Becky still looked more than usually subdued, and she gave me a last, fierce hug before following Mrs. Hudson out.

"I told her what's been happening," Jack said, when the door had closed behind them.

"About the killings?" That explained Becky's frightened look.

"I didn't tell her the ugliest parts. But I knew she'd find out about it sooner or later, and I wanted her to hear it from me."

That was a given, knowing what I did of Becky's intelligence and determination to root out the truth behind any mystery.

I sat down beside him, and he put his arm around my shoulders.

"You did the right thing," I said. "Most people go through life thinking that the world is safe, that bad things can't possibly happen to them. Then they're caught completely off guard when danger or tragedy does find them. I wish Becky didn't have to hear about women being murdered in Whitechapel, *ever*. But I don't think you'd do Becky any favors if you let her grow up to be one of those people who think the world is all sunshine and roses until they find out that it's not. I don't think Becky would let *you* let her grow up that way."

"I'm not sure if that's reassuring or depressing, but thanks."

"Is my father home?" I asked. "Or Uncle John?"

"Not that I've seen."

I tried to ignore the uneasiness that crawled down the base of my spine.

"I suppose I should be grateful Holmes at least took Uncle John with him. That way he'll have someone to defend him in case any of the informants he's talking to get rough—or, for that matter, try to make amorous advances before they see past his disguise."

Jack gave me a confused look. "Would that make sense to me if I hadn't been awake all night?"

"I doubt it. My father almost never makes sense to me, no matter how well-rested I am." I twisted my head to look up at him. "Did you get any sleep at all?"

Jack shrugged. "An hour or two, maybe. I'm all right."

"Are you too tired for me to kiss you?"

"I said I'd been up all night, not that I was dead." Jack bent his head and kissed me, but then drew back. "You wouldn't be distracting me from asking what happened after you went off with your father, would you?"

"I wasn't, actually. Although now that you mention it, maybe distraction isn't a terrible idea."

"What happened?"

I sighed. "I'll tell you about it, but I have to warn you that when I imagined having this conversation, you weren't especially happy."

"Oh good. Well, you obviously survived, so it can't be that bad."

"Do you know of a man called Thomas Newman?"

Jack rubbed his eyes. "I was wrong. Maybe it is that bad."

"I was never in danger, not really." I filled Jack in on Holmes's and my visit to the Old Nichol. When I finished, Jack was staring at me, disbelief etched across his face.

"You held Thomas Newman at knifepoint? Are you out of your mind?"

"That's more or less what you said in my imaginary version of this, too."

"At least I'm consistent." Jack frowned. "So to sum up what this Jemma Howle told you, Newman wouldn't mind if the Ripper came back, but he himself doesn't admit to knowing anything."

"That sounds accurate." I was watching Jack.

He raised an eyebrow. "What?"

"You're not going to be angry with me for breaking my promise about not taking risks? Although actually I *was* careful."

"You assaulted and threatened a notorious gang leader very

carefully." Jack shook his head, but then a faint smile started to tug at the edges of his mouth. "I think I'm just going to be happy you're back safe."

I relaxed back against him. "In that case, can you stay awake long enough to think about some of the questions we still don't have answers to?"

"Just some? I didn't think a question existed that you didn't want answers to."

I made a face at him, and Jack smiled. "Go ahead. You can pinch me if I fall asleep."

"It's a bargain."

I stopped, listening for any sign that Becky was coming back. I could hear the distant clink of pots and pans in the kitchen and then the murmur of her voice with Mrs. Hudson's.

"First of all, I made a drawing of the Italian woman's tattoo," I said. "If I make copies, could you give them to your constables and have them show them around on the streets? It could help us put a name to her."

"I'll make sure it happens when I go back on duty." Jack was silent, then pulled me a little closer, his cheek brushing against my temple. "You should know that if we find whoever did this to her, it will be because of you." His voice was quiet, serious. "I know you wish you'd made the connection to the Ripper killings sooner, but you're the only one who made that connection at all. I wouldn't have seen it."

I leaned my head against his shoulder. "Can I have that in writing?"

The guilt was still there, but maybe a shade less heavy. Lighter enough, at least, that I could focus on the unsolved mystery of the woman's death instead of my own sense of having failed her.

"Thank you," I added. I hesitated, then asked, "I hate to say it, but could Constable Thomas have been somehow involved?"

Jack let his head tip back against the couch cushions. "Do you want strict facts or what I actually think?"

I considered. "Strict facts first."

"It's possible. He's the one who left our mystery visitor with the blond hair alone in the cell block. We only have his word for it that she took faint. She could have bribed him to leave her alone. Or she could have been completely innocent, but he used her coming in as cover to commit the murder himself. Any other time, and he would have been the first one suspected if one of the cell inmates was shot while he'd been on guard duty."

"And what you actually think?"

Jack shook his head. "Possible but not likely. I've only been at Commercial Street a month, so maybe I don't know him that well. But from what I've seen, he's a rule follower. I don't see him taking a risk as big as letting someone murder one of the prisoners in his charge."

Jack stopped, shrugging. "I know that's not proof, though. You can keep him on the suspect list if you want."

"No, it's all right, I'll take your word for it. You're a good judge of character."

Jack gave me a questioning look.

"You're marrying me, aren't you?"

The telephone in the corner of the sitting room rang, making me jump. Jack sat up, instantly alert. I crossed to lift the receiver.

"Hello?"

I was hoping that it might be Holmes, calling to tell me what he had been doing all afternoon, or at least letting me know that he was all right. But instead the exchange operator's voice said,

"Hold for Scotland Yard, please."

Inspector Lestrade's voice came on the line. "Miss James? I can't reach your father; do you know where he is?"

"I don't. Is something wrong?" Even through the crackling static of the telephone connection, I could hear the tension vibrating in Lestrade's tone.

He didn't answer at once. Probably he was trying to come up with a way to avoid telling me.

Whether he thought that a woman's place should be in the home—or simply didn't like me in particular—Inspector Lestrade more often than not leaked disapproval over my getting involved in my father's cases.

Finally, though, I heard him blow out a breath. "I suppose you'd better know so that you can pass the message on to your father if you see him first. There's been a message sent to the Central News Agency."

"A message?"

I pictured Lestrade's narrow, sharp-featured face turning grim on the other end of the line. "Like the *Dear Boss* letter from the Ripper Killings. Says there's going to be another murder—tonight."

LUCY

28. DEAR BOSS

"Is that what was written in the letter?" Jack gestured to the sheet of paper in my hand.

I'd caught up both it and a pencil and scribbled down the words that Lestrade had read to me over the telephone.

"Yes." I handed the paper over to him. I already felt as though I could recite the words by heart anyway.

Dear Boss,

By now you'll have heard of me getting to work again, and grand work, too. Look out for a double event tonight. I'll rip up a copper as well as a whore, just for a jolly, and send you the bloody knife. Ha ha.

Jack took the paper from me and read through it, his brows drawing together.

"The handwriting?" Jack asked after a moment.

"Similar, according to Lestrade. Although I don't know how expert the Scotland Yard handwriting specialists are." They almost certainly weren't as good at handwriting analysis as Holmes. "He did say that the letter is being photographed now and that he'll have copies sent over by special messenger as soon as the plates are developed. But I'm not sure what it means—what any of this means. My father—and not just him, but most people who investigated the original murders—think the *Dear Boss* letter was just a fake, written by some attention-grabber."

"If we're right that this is all just designed to stir up panic, that doesn't matter, though," Jack said. "The whole city will be in an uproar when word of this gets out."

That was patently true.

"Do you think that the threat of committing another murder tonight is a fake, too? It seems like an insane strategy—alerting the press to a murder *before* it's committed."

Jack's brows drew together, but he shook his head slowly. "Maybe, but I don't think we can afford not to take it seriously. Whoever's behind this has already proved they're willing to kill."

A cold knot tightened under my ribs. "You're going to have to go back to the station house."

There was no possible chance that every available police officer in London wasn't being called in to duty right now. I was actually surprised that the telephone hadn't already rung again, with orders for Jack to report in.

In my mind's eye, I could picture the words I'd written down: *maybe I'll rip up a copper this time.*

As though he'd read the thought—which he probably had—Jack said, "Nothing's going to happen to me."

"You do realize I was *just* at the station house when a constable was brought in who'd been beaten and—" I forced myself to stop, letting out an unsteady breath. "I'm sorry. I'm being the world's worst hypocrite."

"It's all right." Jack stood up and came to take my hand. "Lucy—"

"Wait." A thought had just struck me, with the sharp chill of a razor blade pressed against my skin. "I promise I'm not going to do this to you every time you have to go out and do your job. But Constable Dickon—where exactly was he when he was attacked?"

From the look on Jack's face, not only was I right, but he'd also already made the same connection I had just done. "He was outside the Ten Bells pub."

I looked up at Jack. "That's where at least two of the Ripper victims went to drink."

I remembered reading about it in the case files. Both Annie Chapman and Mary Kelly had been customers there—Annie Chapman just hours before her death.

I swallowed. "Of course, hundreds of people probably drink at the Ten Bells. It could just be coincidence that Constable Dickon happened to be hurt near there. Or—"

"Or not," Jack finished for me. "I know." He looked down at me. "As long as we're talking about being hypocritical, I know I can't ask you not to—"

"It's all right." I leaned up so that I could kiss him lightly. "I'll stay here with Becky tonight. Barring any unforeseen disasters, I swear I won't even set foot outside the front door."

I could probably count on the fingers of one hand the number of times I'd ever seen Jack caught off guard. Now, despite the cold press of worry, I almost smiled at the look of complete, blank astonishment that crossed his face.

"Well, it's nice to know that I can still surprise you. Did you think I was going to try dressing up as a lady of the evening in hopes of entrapping the killer?"

In fairness, it wouldn't have ranked as the most reckless thing I'd ever done.

"It had crossed my mind." Jack was still staring at me. "You're actually offering to stay here? Out of danger?"

"I doubt I can do more than the entire London and City police forces combined. And Becky's going to be frightened enough with just you out there on the streets tonight. I can't give her one more reason to be afraid."

Jack didn't need to be distracted by worry for me, either.

I gave Jack a small, crooked smile. "Besides, much as I hate to admit this—of the two of us, you're more likely to pose a threat to the killer if you do come across him."

Jack stepped close to pull me against him, his arms closing tight around me. I could feel the steady beat of his heart under my cheek. "Can I get that in writing?"

PART THREE

WATSON

29. CARRY ON

I awoke to the coarse feel of wet gravel and the smell of grass. Opening my eyes, I saw before me a stone column. My head ached. My hand went instinctively to the place on my skull where I had been struck. I drew a deep breath of relief and gratitude that my exploring fingertips could find no blood or fracture. As I moved, short little aches all over my body reminded me of my encounter with the unknown attacker and my headlong tumble down the stairs at Tussaud's.

Where was Holmes?

I peered into the gloom of the park. My body sagged against the stone column as I realized how completely I had failed in my task to guard Holmes and that now I had no idea whatsoever where he had gone. All I could remember was Holmes and his stout companion, walking far ahead of me into the shadows.

The park was huge and growing darker in the evening. Worse, I had no assurance that Holmes had even remained nearby. I looked at my watch. Nearly half an hour had passed since Holmes's meeting at the museum. By now he might be anywhere in London.

I shook my head and was rewarded with a flash of pain. But the moment passed. I forced myself to concentrate. I could walk, but I needed help if I were to have any chance to locate Holmes. I would need to summon Lestrade and all his forces.

Within my fuddled mind emerged the image of our telephone at Baker Street.

I groped at my coat pocket and felt the weight and outlines of my Webley.

Before me, carriages and trams clattered along the Outer Circle drive that surrounded the park.

Shaking my head once more and attempting to sort out my thoughts as to what I should tell Lestrade, I staggered along, trying to keep my boot toes straight in front of me. Baker Street would be only a few minutes' walk.

LUCY

30. AN UNWELCOME VISITOR

"Anything?" I asked.

Becky shook her head, dropping the letter she'd been reading onto the growing pile on the coffee table. "No. Just a note about new uniforms for the girls at the Bethnal Green School. Have you found anything?"

We were sitting together on the couch, with a blanket tucked over us, and Prince sprawled out and snoring on the hearth rug.

The death of Reverend Albright was, to all intents and purposes, a closed affair. But after Jack had left for the station house, I had dragged out the box of the reverend's correspondence, more in hopes that it would serve as a distraction than because I thought we would find anything useful.

Jack was gone, and my father and Uncle John hadn't returned yet, either.

Now Becky and I had been reading for more than an hour, though, and I felt as though I was going to go cross-eyed if I had to wade through one more letter about church vestments or the schedule for bell ringers' practice.

"No, nothing."

Becky started to reach for another paper from the box, but then stopped, looking up at me. "Lucy?" Her voice was small. "You do think Jack will be all right, don't you?"

In deference to the fact that it was past midnight, we were both wearing night clothes and dressing gowns. But we hadn't even bothered trying to go to bed.

I put my arm around Becky. "Of course he'll be—" I stopped myself, changing my mind about what I'd been about to say.

It wasn't even six months ago that Becky and I had sat together in the waiting room outside of Uncle John's surgery, waiting to hear whether Jack would live after being shot.

Becky wouldn't believe easy, glib reassurances any more than I would have done.

"I'm worried, too," I said. "But I honestly think that it's more than likely he'll be fine. He's strong and fast, and he knows how to fight—and he'll be on his guard."

I set the box of Reverend Albright's letters aside and pushed back the blanket.

"I think this situation calls for hot cocoa."

Becky gave me a dubious look. "Can you make hot cocoa?"

"I can, actually." I smiled at her. "I learned to make it at school, on a gas burner that I secretly borrowed from the chemistry laboratory. And it's probably my one useful domestic accomplishment, so I expect you to be suitably complimentary."

Becky finally gave me a small, answering smile. "All right."

A knock sounded outside on the street-level front door.

Prince sat up with a short, sharp bark, the ruff of fur on his neck bristling. Becky gasped, and my heart jolted against my ribcage.

Too late for an ordinary caller.

My father or Uncle John wouldn't have to resort to knocking.

It could be Lestrade's messenger, delivering the promised photographs of the purported killer's letter. Or someone from the police, coming with the news that Jack had been hurt on duty or—

I snapped off that thought before it could take root and turned to Becky. "You can leave the sitting room door open and stand just inside so that you can hear, but stay out of sight. And keep Prince in here with you. Promise?"

Becky swallowed and gave a shaky nod, hopping up to take firm hold of Prince's collar.

I pulled my dressing gown more tightly around me and went down the hall to the front door.

Ever since I had moved into 221A, Holmes had seen that the Baker Street house's entrances and exits were roughly as well protected as a bank vault. There were three bolts on the front door alone, besides a key-turning lock and a security chain.

I drew back the bolts and turned the key, but left the chain in place as I opened the door.

"Yes?"

Through the three-inch wide gap the security chain allowed, I could see a man standing on the front step. Not a policeman; he wore a shabby tweed coat and a soft cloth cap that largely shaded his face. But I caught a glimpse of a ginger-colored beard, topped by craggy, rugged features.

"Got an urgent message 'ere for Mr. Sherlock 'Olmes." His voice was a deep bass rumble. "Is he in?"

"He's not available at the moment. You could give the message to me, and I'll see that he gets it, though."

The man looked me up and down in a manner that just skirted

the line between appraising and insulting.

"Sorry, miss, can't do that. My orders were to give it straight into the 'ands of Mr. Sherlock 'Olmes. Maybe I could come in and wait for him?"

He smiled—probably trying to appear harmless and ingratiating, but the effect was somewhat like putting a baby's bonnet on a rabid dog.

I smiled back, keeping my tone light, friendly and ingenuous. The kind of voice that would make it easy for my caller to underestimate me.

Being young and female came with disadvantages like corsets, being forbidden to vote, and being labeled less than respectable if you dared to ride in a hansom cab without a chaperone.

The *advantage* was that, until proven otherwise, men hardly ever thought I had the wits to outthink them.

"I'm not sure whether Mr. Holmes will be back at all tonight, so I don't think that there's any point in your waiting."

As I spoke, I looked out, past the stranger's shoulder.

Baker Street was entirely empty, silent and still. Ordinarily at this hour, there might be theater-goers coming home, or guests at a neighbors' dinner party departing in their carriages. But just as Mr. Harris had said, no one was going to be going abroad at night in London unless they absolutely had to now.

The quiet emptiness made it childishly easy to spot the other two men, standing in the shadows on the other side of the street. Both of them were large, burly, and dressed similarly to the man in front of me—and they were watching us. I could feel the weight of their stares, like being caught in the cross hairs of a loaded shotgun.

I returned the stranger's smile with a bland one of my own. "Can you tell me who the message is from, maybe I can—"

I didn't for a moment think that he would tell me anything useful, or not willingly so, at any rate. But I *was* going to try to prolong the conversation, just to see what information I could gather.

Turning my head just a little, though, I caught a brief glimmer of movement at the far end of Baker Street, away from the men lurking across the road. Someone else was there, close to the intersection of Crawford Street.

He was being careful to keep out of the glow of the street lamps, but I could just make out a shadowed figure, leaning against the low garden wall of the house on the corner.

I stepped back, refocusing on the man in front of me. "You could try coming back in the morning if it's really urgent. I imagine Mr. Holmes will be home by then."

I shut the door before the man outside could answer, flipping all the bolts shut and turning the key. Then I turned and ran back to the sitting room.

LUCY

31. ON BAKER STREET

I picked up the telephone receiver, listening for the voice of the operator. But there was nothing. Not a buzz, not a click, nothing but the rapid, painful thud of my own heart in my ears.

"You can't get through?" Becky asked. Her eyes were frightened.

"No." I suppressed several words I wouldn't want Becky to learn and set the receiver down. "The line must have been cut from outside."

I stomped hard on the fear that welled up and ordered myself to think.

Somewhere, the universe had to be laughing at me. The one time I had actually tried to do the sensible thing, to stay out of danger—and fate had delivered a threat quite literally straight to our front door.

Prince was pacing back and forth in front of the sitting room door, his teeth partly bared and a low growl rumbling in his throat. He knew something was wrong.

"All right. We need to get dressed—quickly," I told Becky.

Becky's eyes widened, but she followed me into the bedroom and tugged on the pink and white gingham dress she'd worn today.

I turned to my own wardrobe, quickly rifling through the contents and yanking out garments. Skirt, shirtwaist, stockings, shoes.

"Lucy, what's happening?" Becky asked.

"There are men outside in the street, watching the front door. I imagine that there are more of them guarding the back door, as well, because I just saw Uncle John out there—and he's not approaching, which means that he can't find a safe way inside."

Becky's eyes went wide again. "Dr. Watson? Are you sure?"

"Almost certain."

I'd had only a glimpse of the standing figure in the shadows at the end of the road, but everything about the man's stance, the set of his shoulders, had telegraphed Uncle John.

"Either he's been separated from Holmes," I said, "or Holmes is hurt, and Uncle John has had to leave him somewhere close by." I pulled on my boots, forcing my fingers not to shake as I did up the laces. "Or it's possible that Uncle John is injured."

Becky was already dressed. She bent over, starting to lace on her own boots. "So we need to draw them away—distract them, so that Dr. Watson can get inside safely and we can find Mr. Holmes."

Becky was almost as quick as Jack to pick up my exact line of thought in situations like this. It was equal parts helpful and terrifying.

"That was my plan." I hesitated, looking down at Becky's small blond head. But now came the part of the plan that was making me feel most sick to my stomach—not the threat of the men outside, but the question of whether or not I should bring Becky out there with me.

I could leave her here, inside the house. But that might actually be more dangerous. There were locks on all the doors, but the windows could still be broken. The men might see me leave and decide to break in and see for themselves whether my father was, in fact, at home. If that happened, they'd find Becky here, alone.

There were three men out in the front of the house and an unknown number behind. I needed a way to neutralize at least the three out front—and, at the moment, the best and most likely chance of success that I could see also required Becky's help. I couldn't see any other way.

Becky, at least, seemed to take it as a given that she would be accompanying me. "Should we wake up Mrs. Hudson?"

I hesitated, then nodded. "Yes. Run and wake her, but tell her to stay in her room and lock her door."

Mrs. Hudson slept in a small set of rooms that opened off the kitchen—which, I had to imagine, would be the last places any intruders would look for Holmes. Besides, if we succeeded, there wouldn't *be* any intruders.

My gaze landed on Prince, who was still at the sitting room door, alternately growling and whining to be let out.

"Leave Prince with her," I told Becky. "He should be able to protect her, even if someone does break in."

Prince, at nearly the size of a young Shetland pony, was an excellent deterrent to violent attack.

"Can I run upstairs and get something from Mr. Holmes's rooms, too?" Becky asked.

I unlocked my dresser drawer, where I kept the Ladysmith pistol that Holmes had given me, and started to load bullets quickly into the chamber.

"Will it help?"

Becky bobbed her head. "Yes."

There wasn't time enough for me to ask her to explain. Depending on what condition Uncle John was in—and how impatient the men outside were—we actually might not have a minute to spare.

"Then go ahead," I told her. "Just be very quick."

LUCY

32. ATTACKED

Becky and I stood inside our front door. "Remember what I told you," I said. "Don't look behind us, and when I tell you, run straight up the street to Mr. Warbrick's and ask to use the telephone."

Mr. Warbrick, who lived at number 203, was an elderly bachelor and an amateur antiquarian. He kept late hours, sitting up in his library and poring over ancient Greek and Latin texts.

Becky nodded. She was still a little pale, but she actually looked less frightened now than when we were just sitting together reading Reverend Albright's letters.

I wasn't the only one who hated being forced to do nothing but sit and wait.

I unlocked and opened the door. At first glance, the street looked entirely empty, deserted. But I could just make out the dark figures across the road. They had moved into a patch of deeper shadow and been joined by a third man—doubtless the same one who'd knocked on the door.

I forced myself not to turn or look in their direction again, instead locking the front door behind us and dropping the key into my bag.

Then I took Becky's hand. "Mr. Holmes said that we're to go straight to the Savoy Hotel."

A useful part of theatrical training was learning to project your voice without shouting. I was fairly certain that the men across the street could hear my every word.

"We'll flag down the first cab we see."

Becky hopped down off the front step, two-footed. "And Mr. Holmes will meet us at the hotel? Do you think he'll let us get something to eat? I'm hungry."

She'd practiced the line inside so as to get it exactly right.

"I imagine so. He's booked a suite of rooms under a fake name, though."

If any of the three men got away from me, I was hoping to make them—or whoever they worked for—spend the rest of the night trying to find a supposedly-anonymous guest at the Savoy Hotel. Where we could send the police to find them.

"All right," Becky said.

We started down the sidewalk, walking towards Crawford Street.

The back of my neck prickled, my muscles all tightening with the need to look behind us. But for this to work, the men had to believe we were completely oblivious to the fact that we were being watched.

Becky skipped along beside me. She was gripping my hand very tightly, but otherwise was putting on an incredibly good performance of appearing to be without a care.

She turned to look up at me, her whisper almost inaudible, even on the quiet street. "Lucy, are they—"

I nodded.

I could make out the sound of stealthy footfalls from behind us. Only one set of footsteps. They must have decided to let one man tail after us, while two remained on guard at the house.

Perfect. I just hoped we didn't have to pay for that small stroke of luck later.

"Get ready," I whispered to Becky.

She ducked her head in a nod, and I slipped my hand into the pocket of my coat.

Our follower had been keeping his distance at first, but he was coming closer.

I waited until I estimated that the footsteps were about fifteen feet behind us, then gave Becky's hand a quick squeeze. "Go!" I whispered.

Becky ran, racing towards the lighted windows of number 203. She was very fast. I'd barely counted off six beats of my heart before she vanished down the narrow tradesman's alley that ran along the side of the house and led to the servant's entrance.

I heard the footsteps behind me pause for a split second, no doubt in shock, then quicken to a run. I spun around and found myself face to face with the same craggy-faced man who had knocked on the door earlier—although this time, he wasn't making even a token effort at looking disarming.

He bared his teeth at me, his hand gripping the hilt of a knife. "Don't move."

I held the bearded man's gaze. Inside my pocket, my hand was already curled around the grip of the Ladysmith.

I wouldn't shoot to kill unless he threatened my life or Becky's. But I could shoot him in the arm, kick his legs out from under him while he was still off balance, then take the knife when it fell from his hand.

I could see the maneuver play out in my mind's eye, the whole thing over in under three seconds.

The sound of gunfire, though, would summon the other two men, and I wasn't sure that I could win a confrontation against all three at once.

At the very least, I wanted to give Becky more time to get safely inside Mr. Warbrick's house.

I took a half step back so that I was well out of his arm's reach, adjusting my stance just in case the man decided to lunge at me.

I cleared my throat. "You usually use a smaller knife than that, don't you."

The man blinked. "Wha—"

"You're gripping the knife with your thumb along the spine of the blade." I gestured to his hand. "Which is all right for a smaller knife, but it's not a good idea with a knife of that size."

The weapon he was gripping had a blade that was solidly six inches long; it shone dully in the yellow glow of the street light.

"You're hyper-extending the thumb, which means that your thumb itself and its tendons are vulnerable to injury. What happens if someone aims a heavy strike at the cutting edge of your knife? Your thumb is going to be forced back towards your wrist—which is going to cause a strain at best, damage to the ligaments at worst. Not to mention, that grip is restricting your rotational movement."

I could have added that I would guess him to have been a sailor at some point in his life and to have sailed in the South Pacific, since that particular style of knife fighting was common in the Philippines.

But he was already shifting his weight from foot to foot,

twitching with impatience. I doubted I could hold his attention for much longer if I simply kept talking.

The man stared at me for another second, squinting as though he were trying to pinpoint the exact moment when control of this encounter had slid away from him.

Then he bared his teeth, taking a menacing step towards me. "You should be worryin' yourself about what I can do with the knife, not 'ow I'm 'olding it."

I could see him trying to work out why I *wasn't* more frightened. The slowly-turning wheels were almost visible behind his eyes.

I didn't want him to come to the conclusion that he ought to be more on his guard.

"Maybe." I gave him another friendly smile. "But then, this sort of thing happens to me more often than you might think."

I was right about the impatience. I had barely spoken the final words when he made a dive towards me—although *not* trying to strike with the knife. He held the blade loosely, down at his side, instead making a grab for me with his free hand.

I ducked out of the way, spinning and delivering a hard kick to his kneecap.

I heard him grunt in pain, but he didn't go down. *Drat.* The chances of this encounter remaining silent had just shrunk to infinitesimal.

He lashed out, this time slashing with his knife hand. I drew the Ladysmith and fired two shots in quick succession into the upper arm on his right hand, then followed with two more quick shots to his left.

We hadn't quite crossed the line where I was willing to live with his death on my conscience.

The bearded man screamed, the knife clattering uselessly to the pavement.

I stepped closer, hitting him across the face with the butt of the gun, and this time he collapsed, moaning, onto the ground.

The sound of running footsteps echoed from further up the street.

A window opened up in the house to my right, and a woman's startled face looked out, surrounded by the white-ruffled frame of her nightcap. Mrs. Rutledge, who lived at number 207.

"Stay inside—and call the police!" I barely had time to give her the warning before the other two men loomed up out of the darkness.

They were big and burly, their faces pale slashes in between peaked cloth caps and heavy mufflers wound round their throats and covering their chins.

The pair of them were also both armed with knives—and, given that their fellow assailant was currently lying bleeding on the ground behind me, they weren't likely to make the same mistake of assuming that I posed no real threat.

The Ladysmith's chamber held six rounds, and I'd used four of them on the bearded man.

Two shots left, and two opponents.

I aimed, sighting at the man on the right. But before I could make the shot, another figure loomed up out of the darkness and swirling fog behind them.

"Stop!"

It was Uncle John's voice.

His command came in what I thought of as his army voice: iron hard and brooking no opposition.

The two men spun, took in the revolver he was leveling at

them—and then ran, veering into the road and bolting towards the intersection of Crawford Street.

Interesting. I narrowed my eyes at their fleeing backs.

Uncle John took a half step after them, but I stopped him. "No, let them go. Even if we caught them, we couldn't stop them. You're out of ammunition, and I nearly am."

We were lucky that the two men had bought Uncle John's bluff with the revolver.

He stared at me. "How did you—"

"If the revolver were still loaded, you wouldn't have been skulking in the shadows before."

Now that I could look at him more closely, I could see Watson's coat was dirty and torn, and he had an angry, swelling bruise on the side of his head, near his temple.

"What happened, Uncle John? Where is—"

I cut off speaking at the sound of running footsteps from somewhere up the road, amplified and yet weirdly distorted by the fog.

"There were men at the back door, too?" I asked quickly.

Uncle John's lips tightened. "They must have heard the shooting."

And now they were coming towards us.

"How many?"

"Two, that I saw."

I gripped the revolver more tightly, blood beating in hard bursts, all the way to the tips of my fingers. Two bullets, two opponents. We were back to exactly the same far-from-ideal odds as before.

The two figures came at us from out of the mist. The first of them had a pistol in one hand. I couldn't see the other man clearly, but he was reaching one hand into his pocket in a way that made me think he might be armed as well.

Bluffing them into running away had just become a far harder proposition.

I fired the Ladysmith, catching the first man in the shoulder. The second man lunged for me—

And a small, blond-haired figure came darting out of the shadows and flung something in his face.

A sharp, astringent scent filled the air, stinging the back of my throat and making my eyes prickle.

The man screamed, staggering backwards and clawing at his eyes.

I spun, kicked the legs out from the man I'd shot, and clubbed him over the back of the head as he fell forwards.

Then I turned, staring at Becky and trying to catch my breath. "I thought I told you to stay safely inside Mr. Warbrick's."

"I know." Becky looked uncertain of whether she was going to get a scolding. "I thought you might need help, though."

I stepped close and hugged her tightly. "Thank you."

The man she'd hit was on his knees, now, choking and gasping. His eyes and nose were streaming, and his skin—what I could see of it—looked angry and mottled red.

"What on earth did you throw at him?"

"Pure oil of menthol," Becky said. "I helped Mr. Holmes to extract it from peppermint oil with his chemistry things the other day, and he warned me not to get any of it on my hands or in my eyes, because it's very strong."

"It was perfect." I hugged her again, then turned to Uncle John.

"Can you stay here and guard these three? Stop the two I shot from bleeding to death, if at all possible."

Dead men couldn't give up the name of whoever had hired them.

Uncle John exhaled hard, then nodded.

"Where is Holmes?" I asked. "Is he hurt? Did you have to leave him hidden somewhere?"

Between Becky, Mrs. Rutledge, and any other neighbors who would have reported hearing gunfire, I couldn't imagine that there would be much delay before the police wagons came. But I still wanted Holmes inside the comparative safety of the house as quickly as possible.

Whoever had sent at least five hired thugs to go after Holmes could easily have more men out here now, searching the neighborhood.

At his despairing look, my stomach dropped.

"I've been trying to tell you, Lucy," he replied. "I don't know."

LUCY

33. FOUND

"He's not here," Becky whispered.

There was a street lamp positioned close to the alley entrance, allowing us to see the full length. Beyond two houses silhouetted the end, across Allsop Place, was only the deep darkness of Regent's Park.

A few broken scraps of wooden barrels and packing crates littered the ground up ahead—and to our right was a heaped-up rubbish pile, the stench of which was enough to make me take an instinctive step backwards.

Otherwise, the alley was empty. No Sherlock Holmes.

I took a breath, trying to steady my racing pulse. We were making a circuit of all the likely places around the neighborhood where Holmes might have concealed himself, but really I had no guarantee that Holmes was anywhere close by. I was only hoping that, like Uncle John, he would have escaped his attackers and returned to Baker Street.

"All right. We just need to keep looking."

I cut off speaking as I saw, far in the distance at the end of the alley, a shadowy, staggering figure emerging from between the two houses. It was Holmes.

I knew.

I ran.

Moments later, I was at the end of the alley and at his side, with Becky coming up behind me.

He was holding himself stiffly, as though trying to stop from curling forwards in pain. One hand clutched a wadded-up woolen scarf to his side, which I could see was stained and rusty with what looked like dried blood. His trousers and coat were thick with mud.

"How badly are you hurt?" I asked. "Can you walk?"

"Certainly." Holmes took a breath and then winced visibly, steadying himself with one hand against the wall at his back. "Although I may perhaps require a slight degree of assistance."

I turned to Becky. "Can you run back and tell Mrs. Hudson that we're going to need brandy and Dr. Watson's medical supplies?"

"And hot water for a bath," Holmes added. He grimaced, leaning back against the wall and shutting his eyes. "Long acquaintance with Mrs. Hudson leads me to suspect that she will insist on it. I am far too begrimed with the mud of Regents Park pond."

Becky nodded, although before she could turn to go, Holmes opened one eye to look at her.

"You found a use for our menthol extraction experiment, I am happy to see. The results were satisfactory?"

Holmes must have smelled the menthol, which was distinguishable even above the stench of pond muck.

Becky smiled a little. "Yes, Mr. Holmes."

Holmes gave her an approving nod. "Excellent."

Becky set off at a run. She had less than a block to go, and I could already hear the voices of the police who had by now joined Uncle John down the street. She would be safe.

I stepped to Holmes's side, offering him my arm to lean on. He accepted the help—which I took as a mark of just how awful he must actually be feeling.

We walked in silence. When we reached Baker Street, he paused, taking in the scene. Two policemen were frog-marching two wounded thugs into the police wagon. Uncle John held his pistol trained on the third, who still lay inert where he had fallen after I had clubbed him down.

Holmes spoke between shallow breaths. "You did not … attempt to follow me today."

"Are you surprised?"

"Somewhat. I kept looking over my shoulder, expecting to see you had tracked me down."

It was flattering that Holmes thought I would have been *able* to find him if I'd chosen to.

"If you had wanted my help, you would have asked for it."

Holmes gave me a sideways look, his expression one I couldn't interpret. "And yet here you stand, having just shot two of Watson's and my assailants."

I turned towards the entrance to 221B, supporting my father's weight. "You may not have asked for my help. But that doesn't mean that you don't need it."

LUCY

34. A MISTAKE

"Those men outside," Becky said. "What's going to happen to them?"

The two of us were back inside the house, curled up on the couch of 221A. Upstairs, I could hear the sounds of movement as Uncle John tended to Holmes's assorted injuries, but I hadn't offered to help. I knew without even asking that my father would vastly prefer I sat out that process.

"They'll be brought to the hospital wing of Holloway Prison, I assume," I told Becky.

"Do you know who they were?" Becky was starting to look tired, her eyes heavy-lidded, her head nodding a bit.

Prince had forgiven us for making him stay inside with Mrs. Hudson. Now the big dog flopped protectively at Becky's feet, his nose resting on his massive paws.

"I don't. I'm fairly certain they were just hired on for the purpose of the attack, though, and that they didn't have any personal grudge against my father or Uncle John. The ones who were only armed with knives took one look at Dr. Watson's and my weapons and ran—meaning they decided that they weren't getting paid enough to risk getting shot."

Becky nodded, yawning.

It was also the reason I hadn't insisted on questioning them personally; I doubted whether hired thugs would have anything to say that would be worth the risk of my leaving Becky and Holmes alone tonight.

"Did you telephone to Commercial Street Station?" I asked her.

Jack's station house wouldn't have been the one alerted to what had just happened here. Commercial Street was H division, and Baker Street was D division, under the jurisdiction of an entirely different set of police officers.

Still, on the chance that Jack tried to telephone us and couldn't get through, I didn't want him to have to wonder what had happened.

Becky nodded. "Jack wasn't there, but I left a message with the desk sergeant on duty. I said that our phone wasn't working, but that he shouldn't worry and we were fine."

I knew there was absolutely no version of tonight in which Jack heard that message and didn't conclude that *something* untoward had happened. But there wasn't very much I could do about that now.

Becky yawned again, then instantly sat bolt upright. "I'm not tired!"

"Of course not." I stood up and kissed her forehead. "I'm just going to go and fetch another blanket so that we don't get cold."

By the time I came back with the blanket, Becky was fast asleep, her head pillowed on the arm of the couch and her lashes resting like fans against her cheeks.

I covered her with the blanket, turned off the lamp, and then tiptoed upstairs.

Even before I opened the sitting room door, I heard Watson's voice, raised in exasperation.

"You must take something for the pain, Holmes. I have laudanum, or I could give you an injection of morphine—"

"Brandy will suffice." My father's voice sounded clipped.

"But Holmes—"

"Brandy." I couldn't see Holmes's face, but his tone indicated that if Uncle John chose to argue, he would be wasting his breath. "I prefer not to have my wits dulled tonight."

I opened the door to find Holmes sitting up in his armchair beside the fire, wearing a dressing gown over shirt and trousers.

There was a pile of bloodied bandages on the floor, as well as gauze, sticking plaster, and surgical needles and thread. The stab wound must have been bad enough to need stitches.

"How do you feel?" I asked. I sat down, perching on the edge of the couch.

Holmes ignored the implied request for information about his injuries—if he registered it at all.

"As though I would like some answers. As, I have no doubt, would you." Holmes looked at me "Before I give you my account, however, will you tell me what happened here tonight?"

"Becky and I were sitting up together. You've heard about the killer's letter to the Central News Agency?"

Holmes nodded. "It was being cried aloud by every newsboy on every street corner as I approached Madame Tussaud's a few hours ago."

Watson, looking resigned, had crossed to the sideboard and poured out a measure of brandy. Now he carried it back, handing the glass over to Holmes.

"Well, we were waiting up for Jack to come home," I went on. "And then someone knocked at the door, asking for you."

Holmes took a swallow of brandy, downing half the glass in a single draught. "A right-handed man of six-feet-one inches in height, wielding a borrowed knife, and with a background as a seaman, possibly in the South Pacific?"

My eyebrows went up, and Holmes made a brief, impatient gesture that obviously jarred his injuries, because his breath hissed in slightly. "I encountered him earlier. It was his unaccustomedly large knife that left me with the souvenir to which Watson has just finished tending."

And Holmes had deduced all of that while fighting off an attempt to end his life.

"Our possible sailor made an effort to talk his way into the house, saying that he had an important message for you and you alone," I went on. "I was going to try to question him, to see whether I could find out where he came from, but then I saw Uncle John down the street. The rest you know. Now can you tell me what you've done to irritate someone so much that they send a mob of hired thugs to try and kill you?"

Holmes looked at me. "I don't know."

"What?"

Holmes's lips pressed together. "The words are subject to only the one interpretation of which I am aware."

I could forgive him the shortness of his tone. He had never openly admitted as much, but I suspected that *I don't know* was his most-disliked phrase in the entire lexicon.

"But you obviously had something dangerous to do today— some errand that you didn't want me to know about."

"In fact, I was engaged on another case."

At my astonished look, he continued, "As Watson can tell you, there is a ring of diamond smugglers that Her Majesty's Government has asked me to help apprehend. I was impersonating a potential customer with a small cache of diamonds to smuggle. However, what I had thought was a clandestine interview was actually an attempted robbery. When the robbers had determined that only two small diamonds were on my person, one of them stabbed me, and the other pitched me into the Regents Park Lake, leaving me to drown. They returned here, I suspect intending to break in and search my rooms for the diamonds."

"But Lucy was here, and she stopped them. Another of their number had already taken me from behind, leaving me unconscious." Watson said.

I looked quickly at Watson, who had settled with a heavy sigh into his own chair on the opposite side of the hearth. No wonder he looked rumpled and bruised.

"Are you all right, Uncle John?"

"Perfectly, my dear, perfectly. Apart from this"—he touched the swollen bruise on the side of his head, wincing—"they left me unharmed."

"But you think there is no connection with the Whitechapel murders?" I asked.

Holmes jerked an impatient shoulder. "Impossible to say. However, there has been another development along that front, as Watson has learned from the policemen outside. The body of the Hanbury Street murder victim was examined and found to be that of a known Whitechapel prostitute of French nationality who calls herself Marie DuBois."

"So her characteristics bear a remarkable resemblance to those of the Ripper's victims." I met my father's gaze, fairly certain that his mind was moving along the same lines as mine. "This can't possibly be the work of the original Ripper, though," I said slowly. "Not unless he's developed a sudden taste for conspiracy. This is all far too much for one lone madman to be behind it all."

"As you say."

"Do you think the men who attacked you in the park and came here tonight could have been from Newman?"

Holmes pursed his lips, appearing to consider. "Possible, but I deem it unlikely. As loathsome a specimen of humanity as he undoubtedly is, Newman is at heart a businessman. He does not move unless the action will be directly profitable to him, and unless he was hired for the purpose, there is no profit in merely attacking Watson and myself. The reverse, in fact. He is intelligent enough to know that such an attack would provoke a police inquiry, which would, in turn, draw the unwelcome attention of the law on himself and his affairs."

Then Holmes turned up a palm. "On the other hand, if he had been hired, or if he believed that I had a sufficient quantity of diamonds on my person to offset the risk, Newman may very well have provided the muscle to make the attack. It is quite impossible to be certain, one way or the other."

That—unfortunately—was true.

"So, to summarize, we have a complete lack of evidence, suspects, witnesses, or leads."

Holmes's expression looked pinched, but he couldn't argue.

Uncle John sighed and stood up. "More brandy, Holmes?"

My father accepted the tumblerful that Watson splashed into his glass and downed it as he had the first. I saw with a prick of worry that his hand shook slightly. He badly needed rest, even if he wouldn't admit it. I glanced at Uncle John, but he was sitting forward, a perplexed expression on his face.

"I'm sorry, Holmes," he said. "I only just remembered. One of the police officers outside had an envelope that Lestrade had sent over from the Yard. He said it was some photographs of the message sent to the news agency."

He started to drag himself to his feet again, but I stopped him. Watson looked as though he needed rest almost as badly as Holmes.

"Let me, Uncle John."

"Thank you, Lucy. They're in the pocket of my overcoat, there." He gestured to the coat rack near the entrance to the sitting room.

I crossed and drew out the envelope. There were only three photographs inside: one, an image of the original letter, sent nine years ago and signed, *Jack the Ripper*—the first time that name had been used to identify the Whitechapel killer.

The second photograph showed an image of the more recent letter, while the third was an exposure taken from close-up of the final lines.

I'll rip up a copper as well as a whore, just for a jolly, and send you the bloody knife. Ha Ha.

And then the signature: *Jack the Ripper*.

I read through the letter once, then twice, trying to force myself to pay attention to the handwriting and syntax and not what the words actually said.

Not that it worked. When I had finished, I still found myself staring at the clock over the mantle, trying to calculate how long it would be before I could expect Jack to be off duty and back here.

"What is your opinion?" Holmes asked.

I shook my head, trying to clear it. "I don't know; it could be written by the same hand that wrote the original *Dear Boss* letter. I'm obviously not an expert."

I held up the two letters side by side, the one written in 1888 and the one just received by the Central News agency today.

Something flickered through the back of my mind as I read through the words on each one last time: a vague sense of … familiarity? It was gone, though, before I could even fully identify what the impression had been.

Maybe it was just that today's letter did resemble the original. The writing was similar—the same neatly-rounded, well-formed letters.

I handed the photographed letters to Holmes, who took them and stared at the images side by side, just as I had done.

"Similar, as you say," he said slowly. His eyes had unfocused again, his lids half-shut.

I thought he was simply lost in thought again, until he went on, "I believe—"

The words sounded slightly blurred.

Holmes cut off speaking abruptly, his head snapping up. "The brandy!" He was staring at Watson. "What did you put in the brandy?"

"Veronal." Watson's expression was entirely calm.

Holmes made a violent movement, as though struggling to rise from his chair. His face was already going slack with the effects of the drug, but there was enough outrage in his gaze to make strong men run for cover.

"I expressly forbid—"

Watson planted a hand on my father's shoulder, holding him in place. His expression was still calmly implacable.

"If I want to deduce the color of a man's eyes and his mother's maiden name from the size of his footprint, I promise that I shall turn to you, Holmes. However, unless and until you obtain a degree as a qualified physician, I shall continue to consult my own opinion when I am in need of medical advice."

Watson leaned forward slightly, lowering his voice for emphasis. "You need rest, Holmes. Your body requires it, so that you may begin to heal. That is my considered medical opinion, and as your physician, I have no compunction whatever in ensuring that you get the rest you need, even if I have to drug you to do it."

Holmes struggled a moment more against Watson's grip, but he was fighting a losing battle. His long fingers relaxed, the two photographs fluttering to the ground. He slumped back in his chair, his eyes sliding shut—although the deep furrow remained between his brows, and the edges of his mouth were turned down.

I watched him a moment. "He looks as though he's dreaming about strangling you, Uncle John."

"It wouldn't be the first time." Watson gave a quick, wry smile, beginning to pack up his medical supplies. "Left to himself, he would have spent the entire night sitting cross-legged in the middle of the floor here, smoking his pipe."

"I know. You did the right thing. And I'm sure he'll forgive you."

"Eventually."

I picked the photographs up, then straightened, frowning. "There was one other thing I forgot to tell Holmes. The man with the knife—the one who also knocked on the front door. He wasn't trying to hurt or kill me. At least, not at first. He was armed with the knife, but he only tried to grab me, at first, as though he wanted to take me prisoner or hostage. But why?"

Watson frowned. "That doesn't seem to be a very difficult question. As Holmes said, he was likely going to search the house for the diamonds. On the chance that you knew their location, he would keep you alive."

"Thank you, Uncle John." I leaned over and squeezed his hand. "Now, you should take your own medical advice and get some rest, too. That bump on your head looks like it's going to turn into a nasty bruise. I can finish clearing up here. Only, should we let Holmes sleep where he is or try to move him to the couch?"

Watson considered. "I believe he will do best where he is. I don't want to risk jarring the wound." He spoke almost absently, a worried frown between his brows. "Do you think the danger is over for tonight?"

I knew from experience that Watson would sit up all through the rest of the night—or try to—with his army revolver on his knee if he thought the threat hadn't passed.

"I do. Did you ask Lestrade to leave some men on guard?"

Uncle John nodded. "Two of them. With the hunt of the Ripper on, he didn't want to spare any more. But there's a constable at both the front door and the back. And he's sent over a special unit to repair our telephone line. They should be at work now."

"That was good of him."

Uncle John snorted with uncharacteristic cynicism. "I doubt that goodness had as much to do with it as a profound desire not to see his career go up in smoke. Lestrade and the entire rest of Scotland Yard have to be shaking in their shoes at the thought of what will happen to their positions if they fail to catch the killer this time."

"Do you know whether Holmes has a particular theory about the killings?"

"When has Sherlock Holmes ever shared his theory about a developing case?" Watson sighed, his eyes on Holmes's sleeping face. "He was very serious today, however. He looked … grim every time the murders were mentioned."

"As opposed to how he usually looks."

Watson looked up, exhaling a brief half-laugh. "You have a valid point, my dear." He was silent a moment, then said, in a different tone, "Nine years ago, it nearly killed him to have let the first Whitechapel murderer go uncaught and unpunished." He glanced at me. "Has he spoken of it to you?"

"Some."

"What he may not have told you is that after the murders ceased—after it became clear, even to his drug-hazed mind that the killer's identity was a mystery that would remain unsolved— he seemed to descend even further into the throes of addiction. For nearly a month, he scarcely moved, save to reach for that red morocco case where he kept his cocaine."

Uncle John's eyes darkened with the memory.

"He was lucky to have you to stand by him through it all," I told him. "He's *still* lucky to have you for a friend. And we will make sure—whether this is the same killer or not—that these murders don't go unsolved."

LUCY

35. Another Surprise

I jolted awake, and for a confused moment, couldn't remember
where I was, or why I had a tense, crawling feeling of fear—like
a headache that had spread to the entire rest of my body.

Then I remembered: I was lying on the couch in my downstairs sitting room because I hadn't wanted to risk actually going
to bed unless I was absolutely certain that there were to be no
more attacks.

The pale gray light filtering in through a chink in the sitting
room curtains said that it was almost morning.

And there were footsteps coming down the hallway from the
front door.

I sat up, reaching automatically for the gun I'd put under my
pillow—just as Jack appeared in the doorway.

Relief swept through me, so intense I felt almost dizzy. Before I could even stand up, though, Becky had come out of the
bedroom and seen her brother, too.

"Jack!" She launched herself at him, hugging him tightly.
"You're all right!"

"Of course I am."

I thought there was a shadow about Jack's eyes, but he picked Becky up and spun her around, making her giggle.

"You didn't think you were going to get rid of me that easily, did you?"

He set her down, and Becky leaned against him, yawning. Jack rumpled her blond braids. "Go back to sleep, Beck, everything's fine."

Becky didn't argue, which had to mean that she really was exhausted. She rubbed her eyes. "All right." She looked up at Jack. "Do you have to be back on duty?"

Jack shook his head. "Not until tonight, unless something happens."

I studied his expression, then held out a hand to Becky. "Come along, I'll tuck you in."

Jack was on the sofa when I came back to the sitting room, his police uniform tunic already off and draped over the back of a chair. I dropped down next to him, tucking my feet up under me and leaning against his side.

"I'm so glad you're back."

"Glad to be."

"You can sleep here if you like. If you're worried about my father, he's ... not exactly in any condition to wake up himself for quite awhile. Much less come down here."

Jack put his arm around me. "Would that have something to do with the reason the telephone's not working and Becky smells like cough medicine Not to mention the fact that you're sleeping with a gun?"

I took a breath.

"A man knocked on the door just after midnight, looking for Holmes. He was obviously up to no good, and Uncle John was trapped outside. When I tried to telephone for help, I found out the line had been cut. So Becky and I went outside to create a diversion. I swear I told her to do absolutely nothing but run to the neighbors and call the police. But she came back and threw a vial of menthol into the faces of the men who were trying to attack me. Which I suppose was lucky. I'd shot one of them, but I was running out of ammunition."

When I finished, there was a moment's silence, in which I could hear the faint rumble of the milk wagon coming down the street outside, the clink and clatter of a chimney sweep pushing his cart of mops and brooms down the sidewalk. The night was over; the great city's morning bustle had begun.

"That's all?" Jack finally asked.

"I think that more or less covers everything."

Jack's shoulders shook. He was laughing.

I rested my forehead against the join of his neck and shoulder, letting my eyes close as I soaked in the feeling of him being here, beside me. The solid strength of his arm around me, the warmth of his skin.

"I think I should at least get credit for *trying* to stay out of trouble."

Jack touched my cheek, tilting my head up so that he could kiss me. "You scare me to death, Lucy James, and I love you."

"Good. Because I love you too." I drew back enough that I could look up at him. "At any rate, that was our night here. What about yours? Was there another murder?"

I knew that *something* had happened. I could tell from Jack's expression.

He let out a breath. "Another attack. Although, actually, this one wasn't as bad as it could have been. The woman's still alive, or she was last I heard. A constable on patrol heard her scream and came running in time to stop her being killed. The word was that she'd been taken to St. Thomas Hospital, beaten and cut, but expected to live."

That was good news—or, at least, far better than I'd been expecting. But I still shivered.

"Where did it happen? One of the other murder sites from nine years ago?"

Jack shook his head. "That's what's odd; it wasn't even in Whitechapel. There was even talk that it was just a coincidence—not even the work of the same killer. It happened in Lambeth, near Blackfriar's bridge."

"That is strange. Although, maybe not so outside the realm of possibility. The killer by this point has to know that the sites of the original killings are crawling with police at all hours of the night and day. Unless he has a death wish, he would know that trying to commit a murder there would be just asking for—"

I broke off, sudden realization cascading though me like a bucket of scalding hot water. My breath caught as though I'd been kicked squarely in the chest.

"What is it?" Jack was looking at me.

"The woman who was attacked tonight—who was she? Do you have her name?"

Jack shook his head again. "The Scotland Yard officials haven't released her name yet. They wouldn't, not when she's still alive and could be in danger."

That made sense, but I jumped up and crossed to the telephone, holding my breath.

There was a click, a buzz, and then the operator's bored-sounding voice came on the line.

"What number, please?"

Apparently Lestrade and Commissioner Bradford must be every bit as desperate to be within easy reach of Holmes as Watson had thought; the telephone line had already been repaired.

I swallowed. "Scotland Yard. Police Commissioner Bradford's line, tell him it's Lucy James calling."

"Hold, please."

The receiver filled with the buzzing clicks of the connection being made.

"Lucy?" Jack asked. "What's wrong?"

My heart was pounding, sickness crawling through me as I turned to look at him, still holding the receiver in one hand. "The other day at the theater, there was a bouquet of flowers sent to me—roses. I didn't think anything of it, not really. People send us flowers all of the time. I didn't even want them, so I gave them to another girl in the company. Then, yesterday, the same person had sent *her* flowers, as well. A dozen roses, and the card with them said *From an admirer.* Just like mine. Which made us both think that there'd been a mistake, and the first round of flowers were for her, too. Not that that's really what's important right now."

I drew in a shaky breath, though whatever filled my lungs felt too hot and gluey to qualify as air. "The point is that the handwriting on the cards—I'm almost certain it was written by the same person who sent the letter to the Central News Agency today. I didn't recognize it at first, although I did think there was something familiar about the letter."

Jack didn't startle or tense or gasp; he just went very still. "How sure are you?"

I shut my eyes, trying to call up a memory of the cards Grace's and my flowers. I should have saved mine—even if at the time, I'd had no reason to think it important.

"Ninety percent? Maybe a little lower, say, eighty-nine." Or maybe I only *wanted* to be less sure.

There was a final click from the telephone receiver, and then Sir Edward's voice, dry and harried-sounding, came on the line. "Yes?"

I didn't bother with greetings. "What was the name of the woman who was attacked tonight?"

There was a pause, and then Sir Edward, sounding now slightly wary and more than a little tired, said, "Miss James, you must understand that despite who your father is, that information is confidential—"

I didn't doubt that if it had actually been my father asking, the information would have been forthcoming quickly enough. But at the moment, I didn't even have room for frustration; cold dread was a heavy lump in my chest.

"Just tell me this: was her name Grace Lilley?"

There was a beat of silence, and I could picture Sir Edward's square, soldierly face tightening with shock, his hand gripping the receiver a little harder.

I had been bracing myself, but my heart still squeezed.

Finally Sir Edward said, "Miss James, I think you had better tell me what you know."

LUCY

36. LOST

"You must understand, Miss James, that if you are correct in your identification of the killer's handwriting, then you and Grace Lilley are our only tangible leads to the killer who is currently terrorizing all of London."

Commissioner Bradford had recovered from his shock and now spoke in a quiet, steady voice, firm but somehow also reassuring, even though accompanied by the electrical hiss of the telephone wires.

He was a former army man, and in the days when he had served in India, had probably spoken to his subordinate officers just this way.

"I do understand that."

I had finished telling Sir Edward everything I knew about the anonymous admirer who had sent flowers to the Savoy—which was frustratingly close to nothing.

"I want to see Grace," I said.

I had already demanded that Sir Edward tell me everything that was known about Grace's condition—which likewise was maddeningly little.

Sir Edward confirmed what Jack had said about word from the hospital being that Grace was expected to live. But I wasn't entirely sure that I believed him.

"Certainly." Sir Edward's voice took on a slightly more re-assuring, even fatherly tone. "Quite understandable, I'm sure. I believe the doctors have given her something to assist her sleep, at present. But perhaps in the morning ..."

I took a breath, interrupting. "Sir Edward, what aren't you telling me?"

"I'm not sure what you mean." If we'd been sitting face to face, I could imagine that the police commissioner's eyes would have avoided mine, though that didn't matter. Even over the phone, he wasn't very convincing.

"You haven't once questioned my opinion that the letter and the notes Grace and I received were sent by the same person. You didn't even ask whether I was sure. If my father made that claim, you might—possibly—believe it straightaway. But I'm not my father. Which means that you must have some evidence you're not telling me about—something that would lead you to believe that I'm right."

There was another long moment's pause, and then I heard Sir Edward exhale heavily on the other end of the line.

"Very well. I had hoped to keep this particular detail from you—at least until we spoke in person—since I know it is in nature quite—" he paused, as though searching for a word. "Distressing," he finally finished. "I am not sure whether you are aware or not, but nine years ago, there was some writing scrawled in chalk on a wall nearby the scene of one of the Ripper murders."

"I do remember." Vaguely. Reports were conflicting as to

what the writing had actually said and whether the message had really come from the killer.

The Jews are the men who will not be blamed for nothing. That was the message the constable who had examined the crime scene had reported—though that didn't even make a great deal of sense.

The mention of Jews, though, had sent authorities into a panic. Already the Jewish immigrant populations were being blamed for the killings; authorities feared an anti-Semitic pogrom would erupt if news of the wall writing spread.

Panicked, the former Police Commissioner had ordered the chalked message to be washed away before it could even be photographed or properly examined. It was one of the reasons he had been forced to resign.

Sir Edward sighed heavily again. "There was a similar message, written in chalk, at the scene of tonight's attack."

"And that message said ..."

I could feel Sir Edward's reluctance, even across the telephone lines. But finally he cleared his throat. "Second best."

For a split second, the entire world flashed white, and the sound of whatever else Sir Edward was saying was drowned out by a ringing buzz in my ears. I clenched my fingers more tightly around the receiver, willing my head to clear.

Jack was watching me, worry in his eyes.

"You think it means that Grace was the killer's second choice after me?"

I was working so hard to speak steadily that the words sounded almost expressionless. But at least my voice didn't waver.

"When we initially examined the crime scene, we had no idea

what the words meant. However, combined with what you have since told me ..." Sir Edward's voice trailed off, and then he asked, "Mr. Holmes is still incapacitated?"

"Yes."

I almost shut my eyes again at the thought of telling all of this to Holmes. Broken ribs, stab wound, or no, he would drag himself up and refuse to eat or sleep until the killer was found.

"That is unfortunate," Sir Edward said. "We will, of course, wait until he is recovered before forming definite plans. But you must understand, Miss James—"

I already knew what Sir Edward was going to say. I couldn't even disagree.

"You want me to act as bait for the murderer."

Sir Edward gave a distressed-sounding murmur. "I would not like to use that term ... that is—" I heard him exhale heavily, as though reminding himself of his military training, and when he spoke, his voice was firm once more. "The choice must be entirely yours, once we come up with an actual plan, Miss James. But the devil of these murders is that they present the proverbial problem of searching for a needle in ... not a haystack, say, rather, an entire city's worth full of other needles. We have until now had no clues to the killer's identity, no real reason to suspect one man over thousands of others in London—no idea where or when the killer may strike next. I realize how unpleasant this must be for you—"

"Unpleasant." I had a flicker of wondering whether Sir Edward's army training had included a course in understatement.

"—but your assistance might give us exactly the kind of information and advantage we need in order to capture him and prevent him slaughtering any other defenseless women."

I bit my tongue before I could say that sounded a great deal more like a goal than even the makings of a plan.

"I understand."

Sir Edward kept speaking, making reassuring statements about my safety of course being their first priority, and suggesting that I might wait for police officers dressed in plain clothes to follow me any time I went out.

I said, "I understand," again, told him that I would speak to Holmes, and cut the connection.

Jack was sitting motionless when I turned around from hanging up the receiver, his head in his hands.

I swallowed hard. "Are you going to forbid me to do this?"

He had to know just from hearing my side of the conversation what Sir Edward wanted.

Jack raised his head to look at me. He didn't look angry, exactly, just grim, his eyes dark. "I can't forbid you to do anything. I wouldn't even try."

A kind of frozen numbness had settled over me in the moment I heard Sir Edward confirm Grace as the victim of tonight's attack. Now, though, it was starting to melt away.

I swallowed again. "Actually, I almost wish you could—or would. I'm ... scared."

I couldn't remember ever having actually admitted that out loud before, but the words seemed to come out on their own.

Jack's expression changed, softening as he held out an arm to me. I came back to the couch and let him pull me close.

"What exactly does Sir Edward want?" he asked after a moment.

"They are going to sort out more details but essentially they want me to go visit Grace in the hospital tomorrow, alone, on foot, and close to dark. He's hoping to lure the killer out and capture him."

I could feel the tension in Jack's muscles. "That's a goal, not a plan."

I gave a shaky half-laugh. "That's exactly what I said—or thought, at least."

"You don't have to do this," Jack said.

"I know. But what would you do? This man—or group of men, if there's more than one—whoever they are, they've murdered at least three women and maybe held who knows how many more captive. I don't *want* to do this. But if it were you, and you had a chance of whoever is behind all of this—wouldn't you take it?"

Jack didn't say anything, but then, he didn't have to; He was a police officer. He dedicated his entire life to protecting the innocent.

My gaze landed on the closed bedroom door across from the sofa. Becky hadn't woken up, not even at the sound of my using the telephone, but she would, sooner or later. We would have to tell her some part of the truth; if we didn't, she was bright enough to work it out for herself.

I took a breath. This was doing nothing but confirm my father's opinion that emotion accomplished nothing.

My heart cramped at the thought of Grace, lying injured and alone in her hospital bed now, although thinking about what she must have suffered last night was worse.

"I do want to go and see her," I said. "I have to." I tensed, trying not to shiver. "I just wish I knew whether going to the hospital was playing directly into the hands of whoever's behind all of this."

Jack's hand framed my face, brushing my cheek with his thumb. "I would die before I let anyone hurt you."

His eyes were dark; his voice was laced with so much intensity I almost shivered.

I shut my eyes. "I don't want you to die. Maybe when all of this is over, you and Becky and I should go off and live out in the middle of nowhere somewhere—someplace where our closest neighbors are five miles away and no one has ever heard of a crime worse than sheep stealing."

"That's what you want?" I could hear the surprise in Jack's voice.

I rested my head against his shoulder. "I know, it doesn't sound very much like me, does it? I just ... I don't think complete and utter boredom has ever sounded quite as appealing as it does right now." I glanced at Jack as something else occurred to me. "Do you remember the original Ripper killings? I was at school in America, but you were in London then."

Nine years ago, Jack would have been fourteen, still fending for himself on the streets.

He shook his head. "Not much. I mean, I heard what had happened, of course. Probably all of London did. But I was living in Cheapside. I almost never set foot in Whitechapel."

I nodded. Whitechapel and Cheapside were only about a mile and a half apart. But to a good portion of their respective residents, they might as well have been in other countries.

"Mostly what I remember is how many more police patrols were out on the streets," Jack said. "That and the panic. People being afraid to set foot outside at night."

"Which will happen this time, as well. If the killer wants to create a mass panic, he's going about it in the right way.

I didn't have the chance to tell you before, but even the Savoy is canceling evening performances until either the killings stop or the murderer is caught. Mr. Harris made the announcement yesterday afternoon."

"Wait a second." Jack held up one hand. "Say that again."

I looked at him, puzzled. "Mr. Harris made the announcement yesterday afternoon?"

"No, what you said before that—that made sense."

"Haven't we established by now that *everything* I say makes sense? Which part?"

"What you just said about—"

Jack broke off as the doorbell rang. I jumped, starting to get up off the couch, but Jack was already on his feet, putting a hand lightly on my shoulder to stop me.

"Not a chance. Whoever that is, I'll go. You can stay here and practice being boring and safe. Start with five minutes now; maybe in a year or two you'll be able to go a whole hour without any disasters."

I made a face at him, but sat back. "Fine."

I curled up on the couch again and heard Jack saying something to Mrs. Hudson in the hall outside, probably telling her that he would answer the door. Then his footsteps, going further down the hall towards the front door—

The window shattered behind me, exploding inwards in a shower of broken glass and splintered wood.

I jumped, reaching for the revolver, but before my fingers could close on it—before I could even get up off the couch— strong, rough hands gripped my from behind, dragging me backwards.

I kicked and felt my foot connect with a solid body behind

me. A man's voice grunted, as though in pain. But then a pad of something wet and sickly sweet-smelling was clamped over my nose and mouth.

Chloroform, a distant part of my mind registered. *That means you have less than five seconds—*

I was struggling not to inhale, but I'd already gasped reflexively when the pad was first pressed against my face.

I didn't even get to finish the thought.

My lungs burned, my vision swam, shivering and darkening at the edges—and my muscles refused to fight anymore.

From somewhere far, far off, I thought I heard Becky's terrified voice, screaming my name.

But then darkness swallowed me.

37. COUNCIL OF WAR

Holmes was awake, sitting cross-legged on the floor, pipe in hand, his third cup of Mrs. Hudson's coffee on the carpet beside him. Lestrade's men, called by Jack, had come, and some of them had gone, leaving four behind to guard our front and back entrances. Jack had returned after a half hour's search of the neighborhood, seeking in vain for a clue to Lucy's abductors. He and I, and Holmes himself, had all examined Lucy's room and had found no evidence of bloodshed or protracted struggle amid the fragments of broken glass and window frame. The child Becky sat curled up beside Mrs. Hudson, biting her lip and holding her breath to control her tears. I had nailed up a blanket over the shattered window. Tomorrow morning the repair carpenter would come.

Tonight our task was to form a plan.

It was hard for me to look at Holmes, knowing that my surreptitious introduction of the barbiturate Veronal into his brandy was responsible, at least in part, for his slow reaction when the crash came from Lucy's room below us. I myself had heard the unmistakable sound of breaking glass from my sleeping room, but by the time I had come down the two flights and realized where the noise had come from, it was too late. Had Holmes been awake, there might have been a different outcome. I had been torturing myself with the thought, though I knew Holmes might have been injured or worse had he confronted the attackers in his wounded condition. I was thankful that I had made the dose of the sedative only a light one and that Holmes seemed to be recovering his faculties.

Holmes was speaking.

"We will assume that Lucy is alive and being held prisoner. Our task will be to discover the location. To that end, we will use whatever resources we possess. Lestrade and his men will canvass the neighborhood to learn what they can about the means of abduction. Someone may have seen something unusual— a coach being loaded, a moving van, some other activity that might have seemed out of place for that time of night. With the Commissioner's assistance, we will widen the search to the train stations and to the seaports if necessary."

He paused and then continued. "Detective Constable Kelly and I will seek out Mr. Newman and attempt to extract whatever information he may possess. Failing a lead from that quarter, we will move on to several of the prospective diamond smugglers that I have spoken with. It may be that one or more of them saw through my disguise."

"You think they are after the diamonds?" Jack asked. "Holding Lucy hostage and demanding you surrender the diamonds in exchange for her life?"

"There may be another motive." He turned to me. "Watson, I would beg your indulgence and ask that you take up a different line of inquiry."

"You have but to name it," I replied.

"I shall, in due course. First, however, I should like you to go to the Bethnal Green School and inform them that a particularly vexing case has come up and you will be unable to devote any more time to their project until that case has resolved itself. Do not elaborate on the nature of that case. Feel free to gather more information from the young ladies while you are there. Talk with anyone you like. You are saying goodbye, but only for a time, and you simply wish to let them know the circumstances so that they will understand and not lose hope in you or the value that the school hopes to receive from your project."

"A very gentlemanly thing to do," I said, "And I shall do it, but would a note or a telegram not suffice?"

He shook his head. "It would not. Please keep your wits about you and let me know the reaction of the girls and the proctor and Mrs. Scott, if she happens to be present. Do not speak of my involvement under any circumstances."

I nodded assent.

"And take Becky with you," he said.

LUCY

38. THE UNANSWERABLE QUESTION

Fear washed through me in a cold, slimy wave before I even opened my eyes. My head was throbbing, my whole body hurt, and a part of me wanted to just sink back into unconsciousness. That way, I wouldn't have to face whatever was going to confront me when I came fully awake and remembered—

Sometimes memories trickled back slowly. This one, though, hit me with the sharp precision of a knife sliding between my ribs.

Baker Street ... the window breaking ... chloroform ... Becky's scream ...

My eyes flew open, and I sat bolt upright—which made my head spin and my stomach twist, bile rising in my throat. I had to press my fingertips against my eyes to stop the world from tilting sideways.

Which was when I discovered the manacle and chain around my right wrist.

My heart thudded hard enough to blur my already shivering vision as I felt the thick metal cuff and the chain that didn't so much as budge when I yanked on it.

I wound the chain around my hand and yanked again, harder. Nothing. The metal links cut into my palm, but the chain didn't come loose at all.

I gave up, breathing, forcing myself to look around.

I was in a dark, windowless room—a cellar, to judge by the dirt floor and the raw, damp feeling in the air. It was also freezing cold. Now that I was coming fully awake, I realized that I was shivering and that my fingers felt almost painfully numb.

A single oil lamp had been left burning maybe ten feet away, casting a feeble pool of light, showing the bare earthen floor and one bare stone wall but leaving the rest of the cellar in darkness.

I dragged myself upright and walked forward, following the chain, until I bumped into another stone wall. The lamplight only barely reached here, but my fingers found a thick metal loop attached to the chain, affixed to the wall with bolts as thick as a man's thumb.

No wonder I hadn't been able to budge it just by pulling.

I swallowed hard, turned, and started to walk in the opposite direction, picking up the lamp as I went past.

The space was huge—far bigger than I had originally thought. I reached the limit of the chain, and a long, low-ceilinged space still stretched in front of me. Even when I held up the lamp, I still couldn't make out the furthest wall.

Whatever building stood over my head had to be vast. A factory, maybe? Or a warehouse?

The metal shackle was cold against my wrist, and the resistant tug of the chain when I tried to take another half-step forward brought a flare of instinctive, heart-tightening panic. I *hated* the feeling of being helpless, imprisoned.

At least I could still move around some.

I had about twenty feet of chain, I would estimate, and I still hadn't fully explored the limits of what I could reach. Holding the lamp up, I turned and walked in the opposite direction, keeping my gaze fixed on a something big and bulky that loomed up in the shadows to my left.

For a second, I thought it was a cage or a prison cell—thick metal bars formed a square enclosure from the ceiling to the dirt floor. But when I had come as close to it as my chain would allow, I saw that what was inside was a machine of some kind.

I couldn't quite step near enough to touch the bars of the cage, but peering inside I could make out two huge metal wheels that flanked twin metal cylinders. It was unmoving, now, but I assumed that the wheels must be able to turn.

A memory stirred in the back of my mind. The book that Jack had about electricity had an illustration that looked something like this.

I pressed my eyelids shut, fighting not to think about the rest of the last evening that Jack, Becky and I had spent at the new house. As much as I wanted to hold onto the memory, remembering right now wouldn't accomplish anything except to make me feel sick with the wish that I could magically transport myself backwards in time.

And I needed to think.

I peered through the bars of the cage and the flickering shadows cast by the lamplight.

A dynamo? I thought that was the name I'd seen written in the picture's caption. I hadn't paid particular attention, but I did remember reading when I glanced through the book that a dynamo was a machine capable of generating electric current.

What was such a machine doing … wherever I was?

I picked up the chain so that it wouldn't drag on the ground and continued my circuit, working my way back towards the bolt where it attached to the wall.

There was a narrow doorway maybe five feet away from the bolt that I hadn't noticed before.

The door was wooden, with peeling white paint, and hung a little crookedly in its frame. I reached for the doorknob, expecting it to be locked, but instead it turned easily. My heart quickened as I pushed the door open.

Inside was a washroom, lined with white tiles that had turned grimy and chipped with age. There was no bathtub, but a big old copper wash boiler in one corner made me think that this might have been part of a laundry operation at one time.

As discoveries went, it wasn't as helpful as a way of escape. There was a single window, so caked with grime that hardly any light filtered through. But it was set high in the wall and so narrow that there was no possible chance I could have managed to climb through it, even if I had been able to reach it before the length of chain ran out.

Which I couldn't.

I could, though, reach the chipped white sink—and when I turned on the tap, a jet of cold water shot out, rusty, at first, but then turning clear.

Water was better than nothing, although it was so cold that it made my bones ache. Still, I cupped my hands and made myself drink several long swallows, then splashed some on my face, trying to let the icy shock of it clear away the haze of chloroform.

I was alone, unarmed, and chained up in a freezing windowless prison that could be anywhere in London.

Or anywhere *outside* of London?

How long had I been unconscious?

I could feel fear hanging over me, just waiting to strike as soon as I could fully absorb the cold, hard truth of my situation.

But there was a small spark of reassurance, too, in finding myself alone in the cellar.

Remembering how I'd heard Becky scream, I'd had a horrible, heart-stopping moment of being afraid that whoever had taken me had kidnapped her as well.

Unless they *had* taken her, and she was just in another part of whatever building I was in.

I forced myself to breathe. That was possible, but it wasn't likely. Jack would have come running back the second he heard the sitting room window break.

Unless whoever had rung the front doorbell had a gun and had shot and killed him first.

I switched off the cold water tap and then shook out and rebraided my loosened hair—more to give my fingers something to do than anything else.

The air outside the wash room had felt marginally warmer, so I went out, shut the door behind me, and sat down against the wall where my chain ended.

Until I knew otherwise, Jack and Becky were both alive and safe. I needed to concentrate on staying alive and getting myself out of here so that I could be with them again.

A door creaked open somewhere above me and to the right.

A glow of light appeared in the shadows past the door to the wash room, revealing another set of metal bars—these ones enclosing a set of stairs that looked more like a steep, sloping metal ladder.

Footsteps started to descend, the glow of light growing

brighter as they came nearer.

My heart sped up, and I braced myself, wrapping a length of the chain around my hand and making a fist. Not much, as weapons went, but it was better than—

A woman's figure appeared at the foot of the stairs, carrying a tray in both hands. She was short and plump, dressed in a shapeless dress of plain brown material, with an unkempt mop of blond hair partially shielding her face.

A man loomed up behind her. He was the one carrying the lantern. Its glow showed a tall frame, burly and heavily-muscled, with powerful shoulders and a thick neck. He wore a close-fitting black mask that covered his face, leaving only his eyes visible.

I sat up straighter. "Where is this place? Why have you brought me here?"

That sounded slightly like something the brainless heroine of a gothic romance would say when kidnapped by the dark and brooding villain. But it was what I most wanted to know.

The woman shot me a quick, scared look, then ducked her head. The man ignored me completely, reaching past her to unlock what looked like a padlock on the metal bars at the foot of the stairs.

A series of images flashed though my mind.

The dead Italian woman's face.

Every grisly, gruesome mortuary photograph of the original Ripper killer's victims that I'd ever seen.

The man in front of me now might not be the same killer who had cut and mutilated women nine years ago. But that didn't mean he wasn't every bit as dangerous or deranged.

The metal bars swung open, and I had to work not to exhale

a breath of relief as only the woman stepped through. The man stayed where he was, motionless on the second-to-the bottom stair, watching as the blond-haired woman walked towards me.

There was something jerky, nervous and a little awkward about the way she moved, holding the tray tightly in both hands as though she were afraid every moment that she might accidentally drop it.

She only had to cross about fifteen feet of bare earthen floor to reach me—but in that distance, she cast three quick, frightened-looking glances at the man behind her.

She bent, set the tray down on the ground, then stepped rapidly backwards, almost tripping over her own feet in her haste to get away.

Up close, I could see that she was no more than twenty-five or six at a guess, with pale blue eyes. She was also either terrified out of her wits or else an extremely good actress.

"Thank you." I met her gaze directly and smiled as I studied her.

There was something about the cast of her features that made me think she wasn't English. Swedish, maybe? Or possibly German?

The hands that had held the tray were work-roughened, red and painfully chapped-looking, and the shoes she was wearing were of cracked leather and looked at least two sizes too small for her feet.

If she was a willing participant in whatever operation the man had going here, she certainly wasn't the one profiting from it—

My thought snapped off, as cleanly as though it had been cut with scissors. On her wrist, just visible under the cuff of her sleeve was a tattoo: a stylized picture of a dove, its wings raised to create the outlined shape of a heart.

Shock pulsed through me, sending the blood drumming in my ears.

The woman ducked her head, turning quickly away and walking back to the stairs.

The masked man had stepped down, coming to stand just outside the metal gate at the foot of the stairs. The blond woman stopped, staring at him dumbly, and he gave her an impatient jerk of his head.

"You first."

His voice was rough, with tones of East London in the accent—but that wasn't what made me stop, feeling as though I'd just been struck in the solar plexus.

You first. He'd only spoken the two words, and maybe I was wrong—

I was so stunned that, for a second, I'd actually forgotten to be worried about the fact that he had stepped to my side of the metal bars and appeared to be sending the woman away.

With another quick, nervous glance, she edged past him, hugging the wall, as though she were afraid to have even the hem of her skirt accidentally brush against him.

I held very still. I couldn't reach him yet. But if he came about ten steps nearer—

I played out the scenario inside my head.

Jump up, kick one of his legs out from under him, duck behind him and get the chain around his neck—

I could do it.

Probably. As long as I had the element of surprise, I'd give the maneuver maybe a seventy-nine percent chance of success.

Of course, in using the chain to choke him, there was a danger

I would kill him—strangle him or snap his neck—before he stopped fighting. And if the woman ran away or refused to help me get free, I would be trapped down here in the cellar alone, chained up and likely to either freeze or starve to death.

Before I could make up my mind whether to risk it, though, the woman's foot landed on one of the metal stairs, maybe the third or fourth from the bottom; from this angle, I couldn't be sure.

The gate at the bottom suddenly swung shut with a ringing clang of metal on stone. I almost jumped, not from the noise but because the gate had simply swung shut on its own.

The masked man hadn't touched it with so much as a finger, which meant that there had to be a mechanical trigger of some kind on the stairway, somehow embedded into the stair that the blond woman had stepped on.

She jerked back, whirling around and staring at the gate with one hand over her heart.

A second ringing clash sounded from somewhere up above her. Another gate must have just swung shut at the top of the stairs.

The woman's blue eyes were wide and terrified, her mouth a perfect round 'o' of fear as she looked from the bars to the masked man.

I swallowed, willing all trace of unsteadiness from my voice. One terrified female in the cellar was enough.

"What are you doing to her?"

Without answering, the masked man took out something from an inner pocket of his coat. For a split second, seeing the glint of metal, I thought it was a gun.

There was absolutely nothing I could do to save myself if he intended to shoot me from where he stood.

But it was a pocket watch. He flipped it open, holding up the face so that I could see it. No, not a watch. A timer. The sort of thing horse trainers or athletic coaches would use.

He depressed the knob at the top of the timer, starting the second hand ticking its way around the circle.

Five seconds, and a metallic clank and a whir of gears sounded from the opposite side of the room. The dynamo coming to life—it had to be.

The blond woman's face was still pale and frightened, but she also looked as confused as I felt.

She really wasn't in league with the masked man. Fear, anger, joy—all of those could be acted. Members of the D'Oyly Carte Company did it nightly on stage. But quieter emotions like ignorance or puzzlement were actually much harder to fake without overacting—and I had never seen anyone manufacture such a convincing expression of having absolutely no idea what was going on or why.

I bit my lip, wondering whether I should risk asking another question. I had one that—if what I suspected was true—would be an effective distraction.

But that scrap of knowledge was the one advantage I might have, and I didn't want to squander it unless I had to.

The man half turned towards the stairs, throwing the words at her over his shoulder.

"Just stay there." He held up a hand, too, palm-out, as though the woman wouldn't understand an English command without an accompanying gesture.

The woman still didn't speak, but she swallowed and gave a jerky nod of her head.

I held still, my heart drumming in my ears, watching the hand of the timer inch its way around. One minute ... two ...

At two minutes and thirty-three seconds, there was a sudden hissing crackle from the stairway. The blond-haired woman gave a tiny sound—just a squeak, really, nothing more. Her whole body jerked for a moment, rigid, her back arched, the muscles of her throat standing out like cords.

Then she collapsed, tumbling to lie sprawled in an ungainly heap at the foot of the stairs, her neck bent at an odd angle against the metal bars and her eyes wide and staring.

Dead.

I stared at her, struggling to take it in. Though my mind seemed to be pushing back, arguing that this was one too many horrors to be absorbed.

The noise of the machine in the corner had been slowing, and now it came to a halt.

Before I could even force my voice to work, the masked man strode forward, used his key to unlock the hinged metal bars, and then picked up the blond-haired woman's body. He slung her over his shoulder as casually as though he were transporting a sack of potatoes. Or taking out a bag of rubbish.

"Where are the diamonds?" he asked.

I went still, my mind scrambling. The question should have proved that this was about my father's case. Not me. Not my investigation into the Ripper murders. Which meant that the man I was facing wasn't the Whitechapel killer.

Except that the dead woman had the identical tattoo to the Italian woman who'd died in the police station cell.

"Nothing to say?"

If I'd been less shocked, less sick with the chloroform—or, in other words, more like my father—I would have thought of an answer that would draw more information from my captor.

As it was, I was drawing a blank. And one of Holmes's cardinal rules was never to volunteer information without being certain of receiving intelligence in return.

The masked man studied me a moment, his head on one side. I couldn't see his face, but my skin crawled with awareness of how helpless I would be if he decided to try less pleasant interrogation methods.

But he only nodded. "Perhaps you will remember soon."

The masked man glanced in the direction of the dynamo, nodded once as though to himself, and then climbed the stairs, vanishing from my line of sight. I heard the metal clang of what I assumed was an equivalent metal gate upstairs being unlocked, opened, and then closed again.

Then silence. I was alone.

39. A REVELATION

Becky and I were in the cab on the way to Bethnal Green School. From the beginning of our journey, the child had been silent and thoughtful, head downcast, scarcely looking out the cab window as the morning rush of vans and carriages clattered around us. But now as we drew closer, she began to speak, still leaning forward, hands clasped, eyes downcast on the seat beside me.

She said, "Everything feels awful this morning."

"You've had a shock," I replied. "Your feeling is a natural reaction. Soon it will pass, and you will feel more like your old self."

"Not if we don't find Lucy."

"We will find her."

"Why are we going to Bethnal Green?"

"Because Mr. Holmes asked us to."

I did not want to confess to Becky that I also had the same question. I wondered if he was getting me out of the way, for fear that I might observe something in his medical condition and stop him from completing whatever task he had set for himself. But this was not a burden Becky ought to bear.

I added, "You have helped on other cases. You saved us with the oil of mint camphor just yesterday."

"But what is there for me to do at this Bethnal Green School?"

"Mr. Holmes has a reason, even though I do not know it. He may think you will see something that I do not."

"But how would anything at the school help us find Lucy?"

I shook my head. "I do not know. My task is to deliver my notes and tell these young ladies that for now I will not be able to help them any further."

Becky persisted. "The ladies at the school will wonder why you would bring me with you."

I could think of nothing plausible at that moment. The cab had stopped. Outside the window was the now-familiar row of storefronts on the Bethnal Green Road. As the driver opened the door for us and, after we were on the pavement, held out his hand expectantly for the fare, I tried to imagine the circumstances that would cause me to bring a ten-year-old child on my farewell errand of temporary apology and farewell. I paid the driver. We walked the few steps to the school entrance. I had still thought of nothing plausible as I opened the door.

Perched on a stool behind the counter and hunched over a sketchpad was Clara, the tall, slender sketch artist. She looked up, and her face crinkled in a metallic smile.

"Dr. Watson! How wonderful to see you! And who is your young friend?"

I was about to make the introduction when Becky spoke, her words tumbling out in a rush. "I'm Mrs. Hudson's niece. She's Dr. Watson's landlady. I've always wanted to travel, and Dr. Watson told me about the school. So I made him bring me along." She took a breath and continued, "What's that you're drawing?"

"Oh, just a sketch of my friend from school. She's traveling to India right now."

Becky came closer, inspecting the work. "She looks like the ladies on all those sketches up there. Except for her beauty mark."

"She was the model. She wanted to be fashionable, to attract a husband." Clara gestured at the yellowing papers tacked up on the shelves. "But all these ladies on the wall represent spiritual guides. They're about as far away from the world of fashion as one can get." She giggled. "So I couldn't very well give any of them a beauty mark."

"Will you send the sketch to your friend?"

"In a few months, when she arrives and sends me her address."

"So she'll know you haven't forgotten her! That's so very nice!"

From the landing above came Amelia's voice. "Do we have visitors, Clara?"

I called up, "It's John Watson, Amelia."

As Amelia came down the stairs, Clara closed up her sketchpad and tucked it beneath the counter, replacing it with a slim book of arithmetic instructions and then putting a finger quickly to her lips. I gave her a wink in return. A few moments later, Amelia was clasping my hand, and Becky was repeating her explanation.

Amelia surveyed Becky with a kindly sympathetic look. "Are you an orphan, dear?"

"Yes, ma'am. Though I don't like to think of it much. My aunt takes care of me most times, and I have an older brother."

"Well, I hope you will pay attention to your studies, dear.

Education is the most important thing a girl can possess. If I had not taken pains to educate myself after my parents died, I would—well, I don't know what I would have done or what I would have become. It was education that gave me the opportunity to meet Mr. Scott, who became Lord Scott and then married me. God rest his soul. He is the reason I have been able to try to do the same for other young ladies. As Dr. Watson knows. Dr. Watson is helping us so much with our fundraising."

I cleared my throat. "I need to speak with you about that."

"Wonderful!" She brightened. "Clara, while Dr. Watson and I are talking here, why don't you take Becky upstairs and show her some of the rooms and the classrooms."

She turned to Becky. "It's departure day for four of our young graduates, as we like to call them. They'll be packing all their new things, putting away their school uniforms for the new girls and trying on what we call their lady governess attire, what they'll wear on the voyage and when they reach their new places of employment."

"Very exciting, I'm sure," said Becky.

"We won't be long," I felt uncomfortable and hoped to bring the meeting to a quick conclusion.

The two girls went upstairs. Amelia said, "Now, John, there is something troubling you. I can always tell with a person, and you are a wonderfully honest gentleman. What is it? How can I help?"

Her hand rested lightly on my forearm, her wide eyes looked directly into mine, and her hair smelled of jasmine.

I decided that honesty was the best policy.

"Here are my notes for the handbook we spoke of. Also, here are the story drafts for several of your young girls, including

Clara. They are not yet quite in form that you could provide to Lord Burleigh, or to *The Strand*, but I hope they will be useful." I put my notebook into her hands and stepped back. "Now, for the immediate future, I must devote all my energies to a new case. A person has gone missing."

She put her hand on my forearm again, in sympathy. "Someone you care about, I would imagine, from the tone of your voice."

"You have met her, in fact. She came to your fundraising event only a week ago to investigate the matter of the missing jewelry and other household valuables."

I could see the realization dawning on Amelia. She gave a shocked gasp. "Miss Lucy James? Oh, that is most troubling! But she is such a strong, capable young woman! And engaged to that handsome young policeman! Is it possible that she may simply be on her own and occupied with some other activity elsewhere? Perhaps she has not yet had an opportunity to let you know of her whereabouts?"

"Quite impossible, I fear." I did not want to divulge the disturbing circumstances of Lucy's abduction, and I also did not want to create any impression that I would be able to take time to resume any activity on behalf of the school while the matter was unresolved.

"Well, I have every confidence in your ability, John. I will hope that you will come to a speedy and satisfactory conclusion and then return to my little educational enterprise and me. Who knows, by then we may already have brought some new life to these drab quarters. I have every hope that Lord Burleigh and his friends will be generous." She tapped the notebook with her fingertip. "Perhaps one day we will even be able to open a branch of the school at Burleigh House, near the park, where the girls can stroll and take exercise without fear of the dangers that are rife in this neighborhood." She gave a little sigh. "I fear I must detain you no longer."

Lifting her gaze to the staircase she called, "Clara!"

LUCY

40. HOW TO SEND A MESSAGE?

I waited until my hands had stopped shaking, until I was absolutely sure that I wasn't going to be sick or give way to the
shimmering darkness that was flickering at the edges of my vision. Then I made myself move, crouching down to inspect the
tray that the blond woman had set down.

Dead woman, my mind automatically corrected.

I tensed, trying not to shiver.

As far as I could tell, the woman had been killed purely as
a demonstration, a graphic warning of what would happen if
I tried to escape.

Even if I could somehow manage to unlock the shackle from
around my wrist, and *if* I could do the same for the lock on the gate
in front of the stairs ... there must be some sort of pressure sensor
in one of the steps that automatically sealed off the stairway.

The machine over in the corner was still silent.

I wished I knew more about how electricity worked. But
there must be some sort of engine running it ... a steam engine?
Or a battery? ... that took a minute or two to build up enough
electrical charge to kill.

Two minutes and thirty-three seconds, to be exact.

I pressed my hands hard against my eyes, drew in a breath, and smelled ... burning. A faint but sickly-sweet, charred odor that made my stomach churn, but also got me no nearer to any plan for escape.

The woman hadn't *just* been killed as a warning. I was certain her death was also meant to terrify, to intimidate me into sitting here in helpless compliance. And if I let the tactic work that way, then my captor had already won.

The tray held a cup of what looked like milk, a thick slab of crumbling yellow cheese, and half a loaf of bread. Even the thought of food made my stomach clench, but I supposed I could take it as a good sign: food meant that whoever was holding me captive here wanted me alive, at least for the time being.

There was a blanket, too, rolled up and set beside the tray; I'd missed seeing the woman set it down. It was gray wool, thin and scratchy, but better than nothing—and when I shook it out, something tumbled out of the blanket's folds.

A box of matches.

I picked them up, wishing that I could think of a way of somehow using fire either as a weapon or means of escape.

The walls and floor were all stone, though, and there was nothing I could burn.

At least now I had a means of re-lighting the lamp if I blew it out to conserve fuel.

I straightened, picked up the lamp again, and went to see what else I could deduce about my prison and whoever had brought me here.

WATSON

41. A CLUE

That afternoon, Becky and I returned to Baker Street to report. We found Holmes seated cross-legged in his chair, a blanket covering his shoulders, in a meditative posture like an Indian yogi. The firelight shimmered on his face, but it did not obscure what I knew to be fever spots on his cheekbones. He opened his eyes as we entered.

Becky asked, "Where is Jack?"

He sat up a bit straighter beneath his blanket. "Your brother is at Scotland Yard, organizing the reports that have come in from the train stations, seaport docks, hotels, rooming houses, or hospitals. Anything that may be connected to Lucy's abduction is being noted. The results will come here three times daily."

"With so much activity, we are bound to find some connection," I said, hoping to encourage Becky.

"Very possibly," said Holmes, with one of his tight little smiles. "Although I am attempting other lines of inquiry. By the way, Mr. Newman is considerably the worse for an encounter with Jack and me this morning. Regrettably, he did not know or would not tell us anything useful. Watson, do not trouble to protest at my leaving Baker Street. My wound is quite manageable, I assure you. Now, please tell me about your visit to Bethnal Green."

"Mrs. Scott was there. I gave her my notes and delivered my message. She took the news well. She was certain I would be successful and said she would look forward to my resuming my writing tasks for the school after Lucy had been located."

"You told her of Lucy's absence?"

I nodded. "But nothing of the circumstances."

Holmes said, "Satisfactory. Now, Becky, what did you see at the school?"

The child went over to sit in my chair, across from Holmes. "I don't know why you would care what I saw, Mr. Holmes," she said.

He held up a hand. "It was remiss of me. I apologize. Becky, Dr. Watson is working on behalf of the school and will likely resume once we have found Lucy and brought her back safely. When that has been accomplished, I may also wish to provide some financial assistance for those young ladies. But I want to be certain that whatever support I provide will be well used. I hope to get your impressions of the school. Is it a good place? There are so many places of the other kind. Unscrupulous operators attract funds from sympathetic donors and yet misappropriate them for their own selfish reasons. In such cases, the orphans—the young beneficiaries—are generally unhappy, even though they may not be fully aware that something dishonest is going on."

"Oh, I didn't see anything like that," Becky said. "The young ladies were all excited about the four of them who were going off to their new futures around the world."

"Please tell me what you saw and heard. Leave nothing out, not even the smallest detail."

"Well, the four going away all had new clothes. They were packing them away into new suitcases and new trunks, too. So I can tell you for certain that the school was spending money on them."

He smiled again. "Very astute. But can you start at the beginning? When you entered, did people greet you in a welcoming manner? Did they appear to have anything to hide?"

Becky described everything she had seen, starting with our encounter with Clara. When she concluded, she said, "Oh, yes, there was the one other thing—what you said about people hiding something. Only it wasn't that anybody hid anything when we came in. It was when Mrs. Scott was coming down the stairs. Clara tucked away her sketchbook and pulled out the arithmetic lesson she'd been supposed to be working on. But she wasn't hiding the sketchbook from us. She gave us a wink, even."

"Can you describe what Clara was drawing?"

"It was her friend Maybelle, who'd already gone off to her new job. Maybelle was the model for the ladies in lots of the pictures hanging on the wall, only this new sketch was different."

"In what way?"

"It was Maybelle's actual face, not just the face of the lady she was supposed to be in the other sketches."

"Maybelle was the model for a benevolent spirit guide," I put in. "The sketches on the walls each showed a kindly lady dressed in a white robe, holding the hand of a little schoolgirl. There were maxims written beneath each image, urging good behavior and good character."

"Thank you, Watson," he said. "Now, Becky, can you tell me how you knew the difference between the Maybelle in the new sketch and the Maybelle in the other drawings that hung on the wall?"

"Why that's easy," Becky replied. "She wasn't in a white robe. She had a school uniform, just like the one Clara wore. And in Clara's sketch she was wearing a beauty mark, right here." The child reached up to tap her left forefinger against her cheekbone. "Clara said Maybelle wanted to get a husband, though I'm sure I don't see why sticking on a little black spot would help her do that."

"The mysteries of fashion," Holmes said, with another of his tight little smiles. "I do not understand them either." He turned to me. "Now, Watson. Has anything been left out of your morning's visit to Bethnal Green School? Anything at all, no matter how trivial it may seem?"

I considered, staring into the fire. Finally, I gave up. "As nearly as I can recall, Becky has described the entire sequence of events," I said. "Now, Becky, if you would go and ask Mrs. Hudson to give you something for lunch? And, Holmes, I really ought to have a look at that bandage of yours. At a minimum a fresh dressing is required, and it is entirely possible—"

I broke off as Mrs. Hudson came into the room. Our landlady was pale and trembling as she held an envelope in one hand. "Oh, Mr. Holmes, sir. This just arrived by the post. I thought it might be about Miss James—"

Holmes leapt from his chair, fairly snatching the envelope from Mrs. Hudson's hands and ripping it open with a single, quick jerk of the pen knife he kept on the mantle.

He said nothing, but I heard his quick, sharp intake of breath.

"Holmes?" I crossed to his side.

Wordlessly, Holmes held out the missive, which was written on a single sheet of cheap white notepaper. It read:

Deliver the diamonds to Newman. Forget you ever heard of smugglers. Or she dies.

LUCY

42. SURVEILLANCE

The arrangements hadn't just been made for me. No one would go to the trouble of installing a dynamo and an electrified staircase to hold onto a single prisoner.

With the lamp in one hand, I walked as far along the wall as I could go and found ten more metal rings bolted into the wall. And that was only as far as I could reach. Peering into the shadows, I estimated that the wall was long enough to fit at least five more.

Which meant that fifteen or sixteen prisoners could be chained up here at a time.

I shut my eyes, picturing the Italian woman, newly arrived off the ship from her own country, lost and alone ... and then chained up here.

I still didn't even know her name.

The washroom, with its basic sanitation facilities, would be needed in a place housing so many prisoners at a time, otherwise the stench would have grown unbearable.

The electrified staircase meant that a single jailer could keep a large group of prisoners secure and cowed; even if they banded together, somehow, they had practically no chance of escape.

I made another slow, careful circuit of the room, but found nothing else of any help. Examining the window of the washroom, I thought I could detect a very faint, gray light filtering through the dirt-encrusted glass. But that meant precisely nothing, except that it could be early morning, early evening—or any hour in between on a typically gray and rainy English autumn day.

The only article of even mild interest was a small glass bead that had rolled into one corner of the room—the sort of thing that might be found on a woman's bonnet or a shawl or shoe.

I folded my fingers around it, wondering where that woman was now.

I sat down, wrapped the blanket around my shoulders, and forced myself to eat a bite or two of the cheese, then a torn off piece of bread.

I sniffed both, tasting them cautiously at first, and did the same with the milk. But I couldn't detect any aftertaste or hint that they'd been drugged. The unpleasant truth was that whoever was holding me here wouldn't have to drug me; I was already more or less incapable of posing any threat.

I tried to cut off that way of thinking, but now that I'd exhausted the list of everything I might immediately do here, a cold, hollowed-out feeling spread steadily through me.

I'd grown up without any family, without even knowing who I really was. But I couldn't remember ever having felt as absolutely, utterly alone as I did right now.

Jack and Holmes would try to track the route of whatever carriage had driven me away from Baker Street.

My father would send out his army of Irregulars, combing

the streets for anyone who had seen a fast-moving carriage that night.

Unless they thought I was already dead.

No. They wouldn't give up that easily.

The cellar's cold felt as though it were trying to burrow under my skin, though, all the way down to my bones.

Holmes would probably scoff at the superstition, but I still tried to send out a message into the darkness, wishing that it could somehow cross however many miles lay between us.

I'm still alive. You just have to find me.

43. DEFYING AN ULTIMATUM

In the course of our long acquaintanceship and, I dare say, friendship, I could count on one hand the number of times I had seen Holmes's iron composure crack. Now, though, as he sat staring at the note that lay on the breakfast table, his eyes were blank. Frighteningly so. Many had accused Holmes of a lack of caring, but at the moment I knew that it was not that he felt no fear for his daughter's fate. Rather, the depth of his feelings was so overwhelming that he was struggling with all his considerable will to hold them in check.

Jack had returned from Scotland Yard with the bleak news that there were no promising leads as to where Lucy might have been taken. In a city the size of London, she might be anywhere. Now his face was both grim and weary, but he was nevertheless the first to break the silence.

"At least this proves she's still alive."

"For how long?" Holmes' voice had a bitter, almost despairing note I had never heard.

Jack's lips tightened, but his voice remained steady. "Until we find her—or until she fights back against whoever's taken her and gets free on her own, sir. You know Lucy. What would she tell us if she were here?"

For the first time since the note's arrival, the frightening blankness lifted from Holmes's gaze. "She would no doubt say to never, under any circumstances, allow a minor matter such as a death threat to intimidate us into giving up."

Jack nodded, though I saw his eyes go to the note on the table. "She would."

Becky had been sitting on the couch, hugging herself, and had been silent until now. But she suddenly sat up as she, like her brother, peered at the note more closely. "Jack? I recognize the writing!"

Holmes sat up as though galvanized. "The handwriting—" he snatched the message up, but then let it drop, disappointment etching his narrow features.

"I'm afraid that it is not a match to the *Dear Boss* letters of last night, if that is what you were thinking—" he began.

Becky, though, shook her head. "No, Mr. Holmes. Not that. I've seen that writing before, but it was in the papers I was looking through with Lucy last night. All those papers she had from the Reverend Albright's."

Holmes leaned forward, his attitude that of the hunting dog who at last catches a scent. "Which paper?"

Becky frowned. "I'm wrong. It wasn't a paper. Just an empty envelope with Reverend Albright's address on the outside. I thought it was strange, because who would save an empty envelope without a letter inside? But I'm sure—almost sure—that the handwriting was the same."

Jack drew a ragged breath and squeezed his sister's hand. "Well done."

Holmes leapt to his feet, then almost instantly wavered, steadying himself on the back of a chair.

I was alarmed. "Holmes, your wound ... at the very least, you must allow me to change the dressing—"

"No time for that—we must be off!"

"But Holmes—the note—we may be putting Lucy's life in danger if we continue to investigate—"

Holmes's lips tightened into a smile as grim as any I had seen. "We shall not be investigating the case of the smuggled diamonds. However, the message made no demands that we abandon our search for the Whitechapel killer. We will proceed to St. Thomas Hospital at once!"

LUCY

44. TO STAY ALIVE

I woke to groggy half-awareness and the impression that I'd heard a woman's voice speaking ... or crying?

I couldn't be sure that I'd heard anything at all, though, or whether it had just been part of some confused dream.

I sat up, stiff in every limb, and despite the thin blanket's covering, feeling as though I could never get warm again.

I rubbed my hands up and down my arms and then groped for the lamp and the box of matches I'd left right beside me.

Oil lamps only burned half an ounce of oil per hour, which meant that by my calculations I had enough oil to last me roughly one hundred and fifty hours. I didn't want to even think about being trapped here for that long, but the weighted truth sat on my chest that unless I found a way out—or Holmes and Jack came—I very well could be.

My fingers were so stiff and clumsy with cold that it took me three tries to get the lamp lighted.

I stumbled to the washroom and found the grimy window dark—which was marginally more definite. At least I knew it was some hour of the night.

My fingers were so cold that the chilly water actually felt almost tepid. I ran my hands under the tap, splashed some water on my face, too—then froze.

I *had* heard a woman crying before. The sound now came from somewhere above my head, muffled by the floor between us so that I couldn't make out the words, only the tone.

She sounded as though she were sobbing, pleading with someone …

There was a dull thump, followed by silence. The crying had stopped.

I dug my nails hard into my palms as I strained my ears, listening. I thought I could just catch the faint thump of footsteps, but I couldn't tell where in the building they were coming from, much less get an idea of what the layout of the rooms up above me was like.

I went back to the main room and sat down by the tray of food, tearing off another piece of bread.

Food would keep me from freezing to death; it would keep me strong—it would make it fractionally more likely that I could find a way to get myself and the crying woman, whoever she was, away from here.

WATSON
45. ROUGH WEATHER

We were in the women's ward at St. Thomas Hospital, a large room crowded with long rows of beds on either side. Holmes had drawn up a chair beside the bed of Grace Lilley. A sweet-faced blond girl with a bandage covering her left cheek, she had shrunk away the moment we had approached, turning herself onto her side and burying her face in her pillow. Beside me, a nurse whispered, "She won't have any visitors. Doesn't want anyone so see her with those bandages on her face."

I merely nodded. I wanted to hear what Holmes was saying, though the noise in the ward coming from the other patients made that difficult. Holmes was speaking quietly to try to preserve a semblance of privacy. I came closer.

"—has been kidnapped," Holmes was saying.

Miss Lilley sat up in bed, her eyes rounded with distress. "Lucy kidnapped! Oh no! She was always so sweet to me. Who could have done such a dreadful thing?"

Only one who knew him well would have detected the minuscule tightening at the edges of Holmes's mouth.

"We believe whoever attacked you may have also taken her.

That is why we are here. Hoping that, painful though it may be to recount your attack, you may give us some clue—"

But Grace was already shaking her head. "I don't know! I don't remember anything." Her voice was thick with tears. "Just someone pushing me down, and then I hit my head—"

She broke off with a sob, her fingers going to her bandaged cheek.

I could sense Holmes's impatience, but he made a clear effort to keep his voice calm as he asked, "Did anything unusual occur at the theater these past days? Did anything happen that was out of the normal routine? Were there any strangers hanging about?"

"We got flowers. Lucy and me both."

I stepped closer. "We already know of the flowers, Holmes. Jack told us that Lucy recognized the handwriting on the cards as belonging to—"

Holmes held up a hand, ordering me to silence. "Miss Lilley, have you any family you might go to, after your release from here?"

Grace Lilley shook her head. "Not in London. I've only my cousin, and she's gone off to India with some other girls from the Bethnal Green School."

I stared. It was rarely that I saw Holmes surprised, but I was aware that he was doing the same. "You have a cousin at the Bethnal Greene School?" Holmes finally asked.

Grace frowned, puzzled by the intensity of the question. "Yes."

"Did you know a Reverend Albright?" Holmes asked.

Grace shook her head. "No. Why? Should I?"

"What about Lord Burleigh? Are you acquainted with him?"

Grace shook her head. "I don't … I think maybe Maybelle once mentioned him coming to the school? But I'm not sure."

Holmes shook his head and got to his feet. "We have tired you enough with questions. We will leave you to rest and recover."

"Have a care for her," he said quietly to the nurse as we passed out.

"Of course. That is what we do here."

Then something new seemed to occur to him, and he whispered into the nurse's ear.

In response, she quietly bent over the small white-painted cabinet at the side of the bed. She opened the drawer and removed a small box, wrapped in foil paper and tied with a silver satin bow. She handed the box to Holmes.

"Just the one visitor. Big chap. I didn't get his name, and she didn't know him from Adam, she said. She turned away from him, just like she turned away from you. He left these on the table, after. I think they're chocolates."

"We shall have them analyzed," Holmes said. "Until you hear otherwise from me, will you kindly ensure that she has no more packages—"

He broke off at sight of a fair-haired, spaniel-eyed young man just poking his head in at the door to the ward.

"You there!" Holmes strode forward, jabbing a finger in the young man's direction. "I have seen you at the Savoy Theater. What is your name?"

The young man swallowed nervously at the peremptory tone. "It's Will, sir. Will Simpson. Are you with the police, or … you mentioned the theater. Are you two gentlemen on the Savoy board of directors?"

Holmes ignored the question. "You are here to see Miss

Lilley?"

The young man's eyes strayed to the rows of hospital beds behind us. "Yes, sir."

Holmes eyed him keenly, in the manner that always reminded me of a hawk assessing its prey. "You are aware that Miss Lilley has been attacked and may yet be in danger?"

Mr. Simpson had not so far impressed me as being a young man of particular fortitude, but to my surprise, at that, he straightened his slender shoulders. "Yes, sir."

Holmes nodded slowly. "You have already sent Miss Lilley chocolates, I believe."

"Chocolates?" Mr. Simpson sounded astonished. "I haven't sent her anything." A brief, wry smile touched his mouth, then vanished. "I wouldn't dare. The second she knew it was from me, she'd just pitch the box into the rubbish bin."

Holmes was silent another beat, then, with a flourish, he withdrew a pencil and envelope from the inner pocket of his coat. "If you would just oblige me, Mr. Simpson, by signing your name here?"

Mr. Simpson looked bewildered. "Certainly, sir, if you wish it. But why—"

"That will become apparent in due course. Your signature, please."

Still with a perplexed look, Mr. Simpson took the pencil and scrawled, *William A. Simpson, Esq.* across the back of the envelope.

Holmes studied it, then gave another decisive nod. "You may stay with Miss Lilley. I believe that she will be safer with you in attendance."

Mr. Simpson strode into the ward, and a moment later, I heard

Grace Lilley's voice, say, "Will. If you're here for more misguided attempts at courtship—"

The young man interrupted, though, in a tone firmer than any I had yet heard from him. "I'm not here for courting, Grace. But I thought ... I thought that maybe you could use a friend."

As we made our way down the corridor towards the stairwell, I glanced at Holmes, a question on my lips.

But as so often before, my friend correctly interpreted my intent. "Unless I am entirely unable to judge character, Mr. Simpson's denial of having sent the chocolates was genuine. His handwriting does not match in any way either the writing of the Ripper letters or the note that arrived at Baker Street this morning. Therefore, I judge him to be a useful ally in ensuring Miss Lilley's survival."

A few moments later we were out of the ward and descending the stairs to the hospital lobby. Holmes clung to the railing.

"You are fatigued," I said. "There is a coffee shop—"

"No, Watson," he said. "We have more to do here. We must go downstairs."

The wan, greenish light in the mortuary level of Saint Thomas Hospital had not changed, and the corridors were as quiet as when we had last entered more than a week earlier. Dawkins, the same attendant who had greeted us on the morning of October 6, was on duty now.

"You remember us," said Holmes.

"Oh, yes, sir." He had taken off his spectacles and was polishing them on his handkerchief.

"You remember the unfortunate young woman whose body we came to examine? Dr. Burleigh was in attendance. We should like to see her again."

"Won't be possible."

"Perhaps a call to the Commissioner—"

"Oh, no, I didn't mean it that way. I'd bring her out for you right now if I could. But she's gone. Dr. Burleigh took her, along with the report. And the photographs."

"Where was he going?"

"Oh, he didn't say, sir."

"Was anyone with him?"

"Yes, a big fellow. They didn't seem to like each other very much."

"He did not introduce you?"

"Not hardly. No introductions needed for the likes of me, sir. He just said, 'Dawkins, fetch the body for us; there's a good chap.'"

"Did he address the other man?"

Dawkins paused. "Come to think of it, he did. After I had wheeled the body out. He said, 'Trevor, have the van brought 'round.'"

A momentary light shone in Holmes's gray eyes, but he said only, "Thank you, Mr. Dawkins. Now I should like to speak to the examining physician, the man who wrote up the report."

"He gets in after lunchtime, sir."

"Then, if he is not here, I should like to use the telephone in his office to call the Commissioner. I shall need privacy for the call. It is of a confidential and official nature."

We were soon alone in the cramped little office of the attending pathologist.

No sooner had the door shut than Holmes turned to the file cabinets and the battered oak desk. "Quickly, Watson. He may have retained the notes he used to write up the report."

A few moments later, he pulled out a sheaf of papers from the center desk drawer.

"We are in luck, Watson. Here is what we came to see. A photograph. I should like you to examine it closely."

I did so. "It is quite clear," I said. "The wound on the victim's face, the fingermarks on the neck—"

"Look at the undamaged side of the face, Watson. Try to imagine her as once she was, before she was attacked."

"She does look somewhat familiar, Holmes," I said. I tried to cast my mind back to re-imagine the faces of young women her age that I had seen. "In fact, she somewhat resembles Grace Lilley. Though that may be because of the facial disfigurement."

Then I had it.

"I have never seen her before," I said. "But I have seen a number of sketches of her. At the Bethnal Green School."

Holmes nodded. "I believe you said the young woman who modeled for the sketches had a beauty mark on her left cheekbone."

"Which explains why the victim's left cheek was disfigured. The killer did not want to provide a clue to her identity."

Holmes picked up the telephone. "Scotland Yard," he barked into the receiver. There was a pause and a series of crackles as he was connected, and then, into the receiver, he said, "This is Sherlock Holmes. I must speak at once with Inspector Lestrade—"

He broke off, listening to whoever was speaking on the other end of the line. I could not hear what was being said, but I saw the growing rigidity of Holmes's shoulders, the way that his long fingers gripped the speaking piece more tightly.

"Holmes!" Barely had he replaced the telephone receiver back in its cradle before the word burst from my lips. "What has happened? Is there news of Lucy?"

My heart was heavy with dread of what that message might be, but Holmes shook his head. "No. We may be grateful at least for that. But there has been a bombing."

"A *bombing*?"

"At the home of the Egyptian ambassador, here in London." Despite his usual control, anger tightened the corners of Holmes's mouth. "It begins, Watson. This may be a precursor to the day of reckoning that Sir Michael feared."

My mind could scarcely take it in.

He continued, "And if we remain unsuccessful, how many more such attacks will follow? How many lives will be lost?"

I had no answer.

PART FOUR

LUCY

46. WHAT DAY IS IT?

The ache of cold followed me even into sleep, making it impossible to fall into anything deeper than a restless doze.

I'd been here—how long? Part of a day, a night, and most of another day?

I thought that was right, but my thoughts felt sluggish, cloudy and slow. Actually, my whole body felt that way.

It seemed completely unjust to be sick on *top* of being a prisoner, chained up by a madman in a cold, damp cellar. Insult added to injury.

But my throat felt raw and painful when I tried to swallow, my head hurt, and I was certain I had a fever. Right now, I was shivering hard enough to make my muscles ache, but at times I was burning hot and had to force myself not to kick away the thin covering of my blanket.

I'd heard the woman crying upstairs twice more, now. But no one had come back to the cellar to check on me—not the masked man or anyone else. I'd rationed the food that he and the dead woman had delivered. But I had finally finished the last crumbs of stale bread ... I was fairly sure it had been last night, which made it several hours ago.

I wasn't hungry now, and I still had access to water in the washroom. But if my captor intended to simply leave me down here to starve—

I sat up. Too quickly, as it turned out; bright flashes of light exploded behind my eyelids, and I had to steady myself with one hand against the wall. I bent down, groping in the dark until I found the lamp—at least the oil hadn't yet run out—then lighted it, trying to keep my hands from shaking and upsetting the lamp as I touched the match flame to the wick.

Jack would find me. Holmes would work out who had taken me and why.

I just had to hold on.

I spread my hands out over the tiny flame to warm them. Then I jumped, almost knocking off the lamp's glass chimney as the door creaked and metal bars clanged open at the top of the stairs.

I held very still, cold that had nothing to do with the frigid air crawling across my skin.

First the man's feet came into view, then his legs, clad in plain gray wool trousers, then the rest of him. He still wore the mask over his face, but I was certain it was the same man as before: broad-shouldered and tall, built like a wrestler.

I watched closely, blinking the dizziness away as he descended the steps. There must be some way of deactivating the trigger step—a switch of some kind up at the top of the stairs that would stop it from starting the electricity running, because he and the blond-haired woman hadn't purposefully skipped over any of the stairs when they'd first come down.

It was only on the way up that she'd set the trap in motion. If he did something now to keep himself safe, though, I didn't see it. Maybe the safety mechanism was at the top of the stairs. On some kind of a timer, maybe?

The man carried another tray of food: more bread and cheese, and I could see curls of steam rising from whatever was in a bowl.

He set the tray down just within my reach, but didn't come any closer—and he stepped back right away, eliminating even the thought of trying to knock him down.

That left me with only option two.

I swallowed, wishing I felt less dizzy and sore. "Thank you, Mr. Watts."

He froze, standing motionless for a long beat.

"What're you talking about?" he finally grunted.

I sat up straighter, meeting his gaze steadily. "I'm an actress and a singer. I pay attention to voices. I could probably close my eyes and identify every single member of the D'Oyly Carte cast, just from hearing them sing a few lines. I recognized your voice, Mr. Watts. The very first time you spoke. And after that, it was easy to look for other things: the way you walk with a slight limp, probably because of rheumatism in your right knee. The way you hold your shoulders. I know it's you."

His eyes, grayish blue behind the mask, stared at me a long moment. Then he reached up, pulling the covering off his face.

"I suppose I won't be needing this, then."

I had been *almost* certain. But some small part of me must not have quite believed my own conclusions, because a pulse of shock still went through me at the sight of him, looking almost exactly as he did at the Savoy theater: stalwart frame, grizzled hair, a gruff but almost fatherly expression on his weathered features.

"I'm sorry," he said into the silence that filled the cellar. He looked at me, then away, ducking his chin with a stiff, almost awkward motion.

It was so unexpected that it took me a moment to identify his expression. But he was actually embarrassed.

"Want you to know it wasn't my idea, locking you up here like this. It's not right, treating a young lady like you this way."

I stared at him.

His voice, his manner were completely genuine, the apology sincere. He honestly was *sorry* to be keeping me chained up in the cellar here. Although not, apparently, sorry enough to let me go.

"What about the woman you killed?" So much for not purposely antagonizing him, but the words came out before I could stop them. "Were you also sorry that you had to murder her?"

Mr. Watts didn't look angry. It was more puzzlement than anything else that crossed his gaze. "I'm not proud of that either. But it had to be done. You needed to see what'd happen if you tried to escape. I was warned about you—they told me you're clever, like your father. T'any rate." He waved a hand, brushing aside the question of the blond woman's death. "She was just a foreign tart, like the other one. No need to worry about her."

I drew in a breath, wishing that I actually felt anywhere approaching clever at the moment. Mr. Watts's statement raised so many questions and suppositions that my head felt crowded trying to keep track of them all. Chief among them, how he knew that Sherlock Holmes was my father.

But at the moment, it was all I could do to keep my mind focused on this conversation.

"So murder is fine, as long as your victim isn't English?"

Mr. Watts grunted, his craggy face twisting with distaste. "Dirty foreigners. Coming to take our jobs, steal the bread out of our children's mouths. Someone's got to drive 'em out. England's not for them; it belongs to the English, the way it always has."

"No it hasn't."

Mr. Watts looked at me blankly. "What?"

It would probably be safer for me to simply stop talking now. "England hasn't always belonged to the English. It belonged to the Picts and Celts first of all, then to the Saxons when they invaded, then the Normans, and then—"

Just for a second, I thought a hint of doubt, or at least confusion, might have flickered at the back of Mr. Watts's eyes. But then he shook his head, his jaw hardening.

"Doesn't matter what a lot of dirty heathens did years ago. England's for Englishmen *now*; that's what matters. Let the foreigners go back where they belong; we don't want 'em dirtying up our country."

Mr. Watts wasn't crazy—not by normal definitions, at least—and I was certain he didn't see himself as cruel. He would probably pick up a crying child and comfort her or help an elderly lady with her parcels in the street.

"What about the woman I've heard with you upstairs?" I asked. "Where is she from?"

Mr. Watts looked mildly surprised that I knew about that. But he said, the line of his mouth still tight, "Germany? Poland? Somewhere like that. Never asked."

I should have been angry, but I couldn't even manage it.

"What happened to you?" I asked.

"What?" Another frown of confusion edged his brows together.

Without the fever and the headache pounding in my temples, I probably wouldn't have spoken this way. But I had no idea when Mr. Watts would be coming back or how many more chances like this one I would get to question him.

He'd asked about the diamonds, which meant that he knew about Holmes's investigation. But he wasn't the one in charge.

They told me you're clever, Mr. Watts had said, *like your father.*

Someone was giving him orders. Someone who knew about me and about Holmes.

I needed him off balance, angry. Anger loosened people's tongues, made them let slip with more information than they meant to reveal.

"Did your son run away to marry a foreign girl, and you didn't approve?" I asked.

No, that wasn't it. I could see it in Mr. Watts's face. Though his expression tightened fractionally on the word 'son.'

"No, not a son," I said slowly, still watching him. "A daughter. What happened to her? Was she attacked—assaulted—by someone of foreign—"

"Don't speak of her!" Sudden rage shivered across Mr. Watts's face, and before I could move or react, his hand shot out, backhanding me across the face.

My head snapped back, my ears ringing as I fell backwards, fetching up against the cellar wall.

"I'm sorry." Mr. Watts was breathing hard, obviously struggling for control. But he still sounded completely sincere—which somehow struck me more coldly than anything else so far.

I could picture him apologizing just as sincerely if he came down here with orders to kill me.

"I shouldn't have done that to you, Miss James."

"Why not?" I put my hand to my throbbing cheek. "I'm not English."

"Your father is."

"But my mother is Italian." I could taste blood in my mouth, and my head was still swimming, but I pushed myself off from the wall. "Did you burn the other woman's body? How many others have you gotten rid of that way?"

I was hoping that he would let slip something about the layout of the rest of the building or the location of this place. Any crumb of information might be a help.

But Mr. Watts only looked startled, then hunched his broad shoulders, like a bull irritated by a buzzing fly. "That's not your concern."

He started to turn around towards the stairwell, about to leave. I would only get time for one more try. I drew in a breath. "Where did you set the explosive?"

He rounded on me. "What are you talking about?"

"You have burns on your fingers and on the sleeve of your coat. Sulfuric acid burns."

I had seen them often enough on Holmes's hands and clothing to recognize the look of damage by sulfuric acid.

"I can smell the sulfur. And since sulfuric acid is a key component in making nitroglycerine—" I leaned forward as much as my shackles would allow. "Who was the bomb for?"

The fear squeezing my insides into a painful knot was that the bomb had been meant for Baker Street, for Jack and Becky, Uncle John and Holmes. Just because Mr. Watts had some compunction about killing Englishmen didn't mean that his employers shared those same scruples.

Mr. Watts didn't answer. Whatever timer device he'd set upstairs to de-activate the staircase must not have switched off, because, without another word, he swung around and stamped back up the stairs.

WATSON

47. MY ASSIGNMENT

Holmes set down his pipe on the mantle and turned to me. "Now, Watson, you have urgent work to do."

The gray dawn light filtering in through the Baker Street windows picked out the gaunt lines of his face and carved out deeper shadows under his prominent cheekbones and close-set gray eyes.

I wanted to tell Holmes that he ought to retire to bed for a few hours' sleep, but I knew the futility of such a suggestion.

We had been at the home of the Egyptian Ambassador—a handsome townhouse in Grosvenor Square—until close to two o'clock in the morning the night before. The bombing had, thank God, caused no loss of life, either to the ambassador or his staff. But, as Holmes had predicted, the damage to the mutual trust between nations threatened to be severe.

The ambassador was outraged and demanded both a formal apology and an assurance from our government that such attacks would not occur again—an assurance that we were unable to give.

Despite Holmes's thorough examination of the scene and the

remains of the bomb—which appeared to have been a package, left at the back door where tradesmen's deliveries would ordinarily be received—we had no clues and no promising leads. Now it was seven o'clock in the morning. Holmes's voice sounded slightly hoarse with smoke inhalation as he continued, "You are to go at once to the Land Registry at Lincoln's Inn Fields. You are to compile a list of all properties owned by Lord Trevor Burleigh or his brother, all properties owned by Mrs. Scott or by the estate of her late husband."

"Mrs. Scott?" I was astounded. "Holmes, what are you—"

Holmes looked grave and appeared to choose his words with care. "Mrs. Scott is a wealthy woman with philanthropic instincts and as such will inevitably be at risk to those who would seek to take advantage."

I recalled Lord Burleigh's attentiveness during his visit to the school, and uneasiness pricked me. "Do you mean—"

Holmes went on as though I had not spoken. "Now, Lincoln's Inn Fields is a two-mile journey. You must leave at once." He paused and held up a finger. "No, wait. Before you return, go to the Bethnal Green School and fetch the student Clara. Bring her and her sketchbook to Baker Street. Make up whatever pretext you can. I shall explain when you return," he said.

LUCY

48. A DISCOVERY

"Lucy?" Jack's voice filtered through the dizzy pounding in my head, the burning tightness that covered my whole body.

"Lucy?"

I could see him, standing in front of me, holding out one hand. His lean, darkly handsome face was so real.

"Lucy, I'm right here, just take my hand."

"Go away." My voice sounded whispery, weak and hoarse in my own ears. "Go away, you're not real, you're just a dream."

Actually, I would have loved to hold onto the illusion a little bit longer, even if I knew it wasn't true. But the overwhelming ache of disappointment when I inevitably woke up and discovered that Jack wasn't really here wasn't worth it.

The worst had been when I'd first had this dream ... I'd lost track of time, but it might have been a day ago? Then I really *had* thought it was true, that Jack had managed to find me—at least until I woke up and opened my eyes.

Now I wasn't even really asleep, although I wasn't awake, either. Instead I was trapped in some confusing, fevered place in between the two.

A part of my mind registered that if I was starting to hallucinate outside of dreams, it probably wasn't a good sign. But I was so tired. Tired and cold ... or was I hot?

The fever made it hard to tell, but my head pounded and my chest felt too tight when I tried to breathe.

I forced my eyes open, wincing involuntarily when Jack melted away, leaving me alone in the cellar once more.

At least I'd left the lamp burning, so I wasn't alone in the pitch dark.

I dragged myself up to a sitting position, resting my forehead against my raised knees.

Another sound filtered into my consciousness. The woman upstairs, crying again, begging, pleading. I'd heard her enough times that I had lost count—sometimes while I was awake—and then other times, her voice turned my dreams into nightmares of what Mr. Watts was doing to her.

Now, though, something snapped inside me. I might be tired and fevered enough that simply lying back down on the floor and waiting for someone to rescue me had a certain appeal. But if Jack actually were here, he would tell me to fight. So would Holmes and Uncle John and even Becky.

I made myself stand up, dragging the now almost unbearably heavy weight of the chain, and walk into the washroom.

I had no weapons, no leverage over Mr. Watts of any kind, and no plan.

But otherwise, I was in a perfect position to turn the tables and escape from here.

I dragged in a breath, switched on the tap, and splashed cold water on my face. It helped, a little. The room no longer spun quite so dizzyingly around me, and my thoughts stopped slipping quite so freely in and out of my head.

My hair was coming undone, again, hanging into my face. I started mechanically to smooth and then re-braid it, tucking the loosened strands back.

Then I stopped, picturing other prisoners who might have stood here, just like me. The Italian woman. And the blond woman Mr. Watts had killed.

If they or any other women like them had been held in this place, they might have tried to finger-comb out the tangles in their hair, too.

It was possible ...

I was almost afraid to hope in case I was wrong. My hands shook as I reached for the metal stopper and lifted it out, revealing a ring of rust and grime around the porcelain. I held up the lamp so that I could see better ... and caught the metallic glint of a single, bent hairpin, trapped by the bend of the sink's pipe.

My fingers were still shaking so much that I almost dropped the pin back down the drain as soon as I had fished it out.

I stepped back, clutching it tightly. The pin was the heavy, old-fashioned kind, made of thick black wire.

I breathed in, steadying myself, then slid it into the lock of the cuff around my wrist.

49. SEARCHING THE RECORDS

It was four-thirty in the afternoon. At the Land Registry, I sat at a long oak table with several heavy volumes before me, trying to complete my task before closing hour. From what Holmes had said, I knew my task was to identify potential hiding places where Lucy might even now be imprisoned.

As I searched the indexes for the names Holmes had given me, my mind rebelled at the tedium of the task. Even though I knew it was important, I thought of the gullible, redheaded Jabez Wilson, hunched over the encyclopedia in his useless copying exercises for the fraudulent Red-Headed League. My mind also went to what Holmes had said. Amelia might be in danger.

The names I was investigating were all linked to the Bethnal Green School. Amelia was the principal supporter, Lord Trevor Burleigh was a financial benefactor, and Dr. Burleigh, his brother, had been at the autopsy of the young woman found murdered in Whitechapel the past week and whose image was on the sketches adorning the front wall of the school. The two brothers had then taken away the body. But was there a connection to Rhodes and Sir Michael and the ring of diamond smugglers? Holmes had said, "the entire sequence of events" was important. Was that his feverish way of expression, or was it really something about the sequence itself from which he had gleaned his insight? I remembered he had said that it was unusual to have so many cases appear following my meeting with my editor at *The Strand*.

I buckled down to my task, writing furiously, determined to continue until I was turned out. At five o'clock, I would take what I had garnered back to Baker Street, and if there was no help to be found in the addresses I had written, I would just have to return in the morning. Or perhaps Holmes would have another avenue of investigation to pursue.

* * *

The sun had gone down and a half hour cab ride in the gathering twilight took me to Bethnal Green and the school storefront. I bade the driver wait, for I knew there was no time to be lost getting Clara. I hoped to bring her out.

There was a younger girl behind the counter, eager and fresh and with a puzzled expression.

"Why, Doctor Watson! Hello! You don't know me, but I saw you at the wax museum talking with Clara. She's ever so proud to have you take an interest in her."

"Would you call her for me? I would like to speak with her." At the girl's puzzled look, I added, "Would you please tell her that I have found a buyer for some of her sketches?"

The girl continued to stare at me, open-mouthed. "But, that's what your note said, Doctor! She was ever so excited to get it when the cabman came."

I asked, "What did she do?"

"She asked me to take her place here at the desk, of course, and then she went off in the cab with Mrs. Scott, just as your note asked."

It must have been Holmes, I thought. He must have decided that the danger was immediate and that the two of them, Clara and Amelia, would be safer in his protection.

"Of course," I said.

"There isn't anything wrong, is there, sir?"

"My friend must have sent the cab. I'm going there now, and we shall have this all straightened out."

LUCY

50. A FEVER

I set the lamp on the floor, then sat down, positioning myself care-fully to be no more than four feet away. Close enough that I could get to it in a step or two. Not so close that Mr. Watts would see it as being within arm's reach and have his suspicions roused.

I hoped.

The shackle and chain were back around my wrist, though, thanks to the hairpin, the cuff was now unlocked and would fall open easily with a quick tug or a shake of my arm.

Something else I had to hope Mr. Watts wouldn't realize.

Now or never.

I drew in a breath and screamed, long and loud. On my third scream, I heard the door at the top of the stairs creak and then the metal gate being opened with a clank. I made myself stay where I was, huddled on the ground as though I were too weak or too terrified to move.

I watched the steps, though, my heart hammering. *Please, please let this work.*

Mr. Watts's feet, then his legs, came into view. Further and further towards the bottom—

He skipped the third step.

My heart jerked. He hadn't taken the time to deactivate the staircase upstairs. He'd been thrown too off balance by my screaming.

I fought down the wave of hope that flooded through me. I was so, so very far from in the clear yet.

My eyes were wide, staring fixedly at a point on the ceiling, when Mr. Watts came down off the final step and peered at me, his expression a mixture of irritation and alarm.

"What is it?"

He might have been outside recently—or maybe it was as cold upstairs as it was down here, because he was wearing a heavy wool overcoat over his trousers and wrinkled-looking shirt.

He unlocked the metal gate at the foot of the stairs, pushing it aside as he strode towards me. "What's all the row about?"

He was coming nearer. Which was natural, but not good.

I kept my eyes wide and unfocused, pointing over his shoulder. "Snakes!"

Mr. Watts frowned. "What?"

"There." I jabbed the air with my finger, shrinking further back—and using the movement to brace the shackle on my other wrist securely against my side so that it wouldn't fall open. "They're climbing all over the ceiling, can't you see them?"

Mr. Watts spun instinctively, peering at the patch of ceiling I'd indicated, over near the stairs. Then he turned back to me, frowning. "Look, there's nothing there."

"Yes, there are! Sometimes it's snakes, sometimes it's spiders. But they start crawling all up and down the walls whenever I try to sleep. It's only the lamp light that stops them from coming over here and trying to get to me." I let my voice break on a half-sob, then raised my hand, coughing.

Mr. Watts's expression cleared, realization dawning. "You're sick—fevered."

I clamped down the urge to ask him why he'd never risen past the rank of constable during his career on the police force.

Instead I kept my voice small, shaking. "I feel strange. Hot and then cold, and my head keeps spinning around and around."

That part was actually—frighteningly—true.

Mr. Watts peered at me more closely, his brow furrowing in concern.

It probably didn't hurt that I really must look fevered and ill. I didn't have a mirror, but I could feel that my cheeks were flushed, and my eyes were probably glassy.

Still, I didn't want Mr. Watts studying me too carefully.

I raised the hand without the shackle, pointing behind him again. "What's that? In the shadows over there?"

I stopped short of adding, *by the gate to the stairs*. If I risked being too obvious about this, Mr. Watts might start to suspect something.

"There's nothing there," he began. "It's just a fever dream."

"*Please!*" I let my voice waver, resting my gaze trustingly on Mr. Watts's face. "Please, look and tell me there's really nothing there. If you tell me, I'll believe you."

Mr. Watts, like all policemen, had been trained to be considerate of a civilian in need or distress.

He also, if I had to guess, liked the feeling of power. He liked to feel as though he were the strongest and smartest person in the room.

His craggy face took on an expression of tolerant, slightly condescending reassurance. "All right, all right." He strode back towards the stairway, tilting his head to examine the ceiling. "No, not a single snake, nor a spider, either."

I let myself exhale a breath of relief—though not for the reason he supposed.

"Thank you." I rubbed my eyes, then said, trying to sound exhausted, frightened, and, above all, guileless, "You said something about my father, before. Is that what all of this is about? Kidnapping me so that my father is distracted trying to find me and doesn't investigate whoever you're reporting to?"

Mr. Watts hesitated, but then nodded. "That's about the way of it."

"And this way, you have leverage over him, too? A way of forcing him to drop the investigation in exchange for my life?"

Mr. Watts looked away from me, hoisting his shoulders in an uncomfortable shrug.

I didn't ask whether they would eventually let me go as long as Holmes cooperated.

They weren't killing me now, probably just in case Holmes demanded a personal message from me, some proof that I was still living.

But from the way Mr. Watts was avoiding meeting my gaze, he might as well have been holding up a lettered sign: *Whatever happens, you won't be leaving this cellar alive.*

I drew in a breath, trying to steady the hectic thundering of my pulse, then let my shoulders slump, rubbing my eyes again as though I were dazed.

"You know, for most of my life, I could almost always count on being the smartest person in any given gathering. School was never difficult for me. I could write an essay in the morning while walking to class and still get top marks. Or forget to study for a mathematics exam but still find all the correct solutions."

Mr. Watts looked at me, his expression slightly quizzical, but not suspicious.

I went on, ignoring the pounding of my own heart—which sounded loud enough in my ears that I was half afraid Mr. Watts would hear.

"Then I came to London, though, and met Sherlock Holmes. He's ... astonishing. The way he can arrive at the truth from the barest handful of clues. The deductions and inferences he makes. Jack, too." I didn't even have to manufacture the way my voice caught a little as I spoke his name. "He was never even able to go to school, but he's so, so smart."

I stopped, swallowing hard. "But do you know what I still know for certain?"

Mr. Watts was still standing in front of the staircase, giving me a puzzled frown.

I sat up straighter. "There are people I can still outwit. For example, there's *you*."

On the final word, I sprang to my feet, caught up the lamp, and then hurled it at Mr. Watts with all my strength.

His eyes widened in shock as the lamp caught him in the chest and exploded in a shower of burning oil and broken glass.

His shirt caught fire, smoldering ... and he stumbled a few instinctive steps backwards, bellowing in rage and pain, as he beat at the flames with both hands, trying to put them out. The back of his ankles struck up against the edge of the lowest step, and he lost his balance, his arms pinwheeling wildly as he sprawled back onto the stairs, his back and shoulders striking hard against the bottom several steps.

Something clicked.

I saw the precise moment when the realization of what had just happened slapped him.

He'd managed to extinguish most of the fire, smothering the burning fabric with the folds of his overcoat. He stopped screaming and stared at me for a split second that seemed to last an eternity.

Then, the pressure plate on the stairs having been triggered, the gate at the bottom of the steps swung shut with a metallic clang, echoed a moment later by the one above.

"I've known other murderers before, Mr. Watts." My voice sounded a little distant in my ears, but steady. "Do you know what they all have in common? They all have what they consider good reason for doing terrible, contemptible things. Then again, I think *I* have good reason for wanting to stop you from killing me or anyone else. Right or wrong, I'll have to live with that. But either way, you now have two minutes and thirty-three seconds left. Well, probably two minutes and fifteen seconds by now."

Mr. Watts stared at me another long moment, his mouth gaping open and shut again, but no sound emerging.

Then he turned, charging back up the stairs.

My ears were ringing, but I could hear the rhythmic clangs of the dynamo from the other side of the cellar, the sound oddly distant and distorted by the dizziness that came at me in waves.

Mr. Watts was at the top of the stairs, pounding on the metal bars, shouting something unintelligible. As I'd suspected, there must be a secondary mechanism that double-locked the door once the electrification switch was thrown. Something that made escape still impossible, even if the prisoners managed to get possession of the cellar door key.

Now that the chain was off my wrist, I could have walked

over to the gate at the foot of the steps. But he was out of my line of sight at the moment, and I was—maybe cowardly—glad enough of that that I didn't want to move.

Seconds dripped by, turning into one minute, two—

The same sharp crack I remembered from before rent the air, the metal rungs of the staircase flashing with hissing sparks. Something thudded dully against the steps at the top.

A while later—I was not sure how much time had passed—I heard the dynamo's steady chugging slow, then come to a halt.

I swallowed hard against the nausea rising in my throat and walked forward to the metal gate. I didn't want to look upwards, but I forced myself to.

I'd done this.

The cellar was dark, now, without the lamp I'd destroyed. But a wedge of light still came from up above through the open doorway at the top of the stairs.

Mr. Watts lay in a crumpled heap on the uppermost steps, his hands still wrapped around the metal bars of the gate that stood just inside the open door. Clearly, right up until the very last second, he'd been trying to escape.

I pressed my eyes shut for a second and then turned my attention to the lock on the gate. My heart dropped. It was a heavy, solid affair. Too heavy for me to force with a hairpin.

I still tried. I tried until the hairpin was hopelessly bent and mangled and my muscles were all trembling with the effort of keeping my hands steady, but the tumblers of the lock didn't budge.

Of course. I rested my forehead against the hard, cold metal. Of course escaping couldn't be this simple.

I was shivering, the fever sliding into an episode of bone-aching chill. I wrapped the woolen blanket around me, trying not to let my teeth chatter.

I had heard the woman upstairs in different areas of the house—which I hoped meant that she wasn't chained up, as I had been, but was more free to move around. Maybe she would take Mr. Watts's absence as a chance to escape and fetch help.

Or maybe Mr. Watts only ever let her out under supervision, and right now she was locked in somewhere, too, as trapped I was.

I drew a breath that hurt, scraping my already raw throat. I was free of the shackle and chain, which meant that I had more of the cellar, now, to explore—all the areas I couldn't reach before. There might be something that would help me.

There *had* to be something.

I was so tired, though, and so cold. Exhaustion felt like a lead weight, wrapping around my ankles and trying to drag me to the floor. The cellar tilted around me, trying to spin away into darkness.

Still shivering, I curled up on the ground, letting my eyes close.

WATSON

51. THE HOUSE OF DEATH

Rain had begun to fall by the time I left the Bethnal Green School, and the evening clamor of horses and vehicles made for an overlong and frustrating journey back to Baker Street. I mounted the stairs two at a time, notebook in hand.

Inside our sitting room, Holmes and Jack sat across from one another at our table. Before each of them was a large, thick volume that appeared similar to those I had been wrestling with at the Registry offices.

Holmes looked up as I entered.

I handed over my notebook. I had filled up four sheets with addresses and names.

Holmes opened the notebook and tore out the first two pages. He handed them over to Jack.

"Telephone records," Jack said, hefting the bound volume he had been examining. "Mr. Holmes used his influence with the Telephone Company. Had them delivered. There are eighty-one thousand telephone accounts in here."

"Address directories, Watson," Holmes said, hunched over my remaining notes and fumbling at the volume before him.

"Jack's copy is identical to mine."

Then he said, without looking up, "Where is Clara Sheffield?"

I stared in amazement. "Why, I thought you would know. She left the school this afternoon in the cab you sent. With Mrs. Scott."

"I sent no cab."

"But—" Fear closed like a fist around my heart. "Holmes—"

"We must face the conclusion that someone has lured both of them away."

He turned back to my notes. "If we are fortunate, they will be holding young Miss Clara and Mrs. Scott at the same location where they are holding Lucy. We can best serve them by continuing our work."

He opened the heavy telephone directory volume, lifting up more than half of the pages with his fingertips. Then his grip seemed to fail, and the book fell shut. His face was flushed. He was perspiring. If anything, he looked more feverish than when I had left him that morning.

"Watson, would you kindly assist. I shall call out the name of the street. You will find the location in the book. Please sit beside me. I should like to see each location immediately."

I sat. We worked our way through half a dozen street names and addresses.

None produced any reaction from Holmes.

Across from us, young Jack was conducting his own search, examining addresses in the phone book that he had matched to those on my other notes.

"Next, Watson. 176 Trafalgar Street."

I found the entry in the phone directory. I put my finger on it. Holmes peered at it.

"Next, Watson."

We were about half way down my first page, when, across from me, Jack spoke.

"Mr. Holmes. Do you know the Italian word for 'Bell?' "

Holmes sat up. "*Campana*. Why?"

"The Italian woman said, '*Casa morte Campana*.' Lucy translated it as, 'Death house bell.'" Getting to his feet, he shoved his phone directory across to Holmes. "Here is a funeral home on Bell Street. Number 25. Dr. Watson's notes say it is owned by the Burleigh family."

Holmes nodded and stood, bracing himself on the chair arm. Then his legs gave way beneath him.

"Watson," he said. "Give Constable Kelly your revolver."

Then he collapsed.

LUCY

52. AWAKENING

"Lucy?" Jack's voice broke through the darkness, dragging me out of sleep. "Lucy, are you there?"

I was still so tired, and my head still throbbed. I didn't want to wake up fully and find out that this was just another dream— that I was still trapped down here, alone in the freezing dark.

"I thought we agreed that you were going to go away unless and until you're actually real."

"What?"

My eyes snapped open, and I saw Jack on the stairs, holding a lantern.

I sat up, and overwhelming relief flooded his expression as he caught sight of me.

"Lucy, thank God. I thought—"

I missed the rest of what he said as my heart pounded, filling my ears. This couldn't be real; it had to be just another dream, because if I let myself hope—

Realization tore through me a fraction of a second later. If this *wasn't* some fever-induced hallucination and Jack was actually here—

"Stop! Stop, you can't come all the way down, you'll trigger—"

I stumbled forwards, towards the bars at the foot of the stairs. But I was too late.

I was close enough, now, to hear a cold, metallic *click* as Jack's weight came down on the third step from the bottom.

The bottom gate was already shut, but the top one slammed closed with a clang.

Jack froze. He was wearing gray trousers and a white collared shirt that I thought I remembered seeing in the wardrobe of one of my father's boltholes. His dark hair was tousled, and his eyes looked as though he'd hardly slept in the days since I'd been taken.

"What just happened?"

"The staircase is electrified. It's what killed Mr. Watts at the top of the stairs."

I was trying to think, but horror and fear stabbed through me, making it impossible.

Jack had come for me; against all odds, he'd miraculously found me. Maybe this was fate's way of punishing me for causing Mr. Watts's death—forcing me to stand here, helpless, and watch Jack die the same way.

"There's an electric dynamo over there." I gestured to the back of the cellar. "It seems to take awhile to build up a charge— two and a half minutes—but after that, it sends a jolt of electricity onto the stairs."

Jack held up the lantern higher, throwing a dim glow of light on the dynamo, the pistons now moving rhythmically behind the bars of its own metal cage.

Shock widened his eyes for a brief second, and then I saw him pull on calm composure.

"All right." He actually managed to sound calm, too. "I'm going to give you the keys. I got them off the dead man up there. You're going to take them, see whether one of them fits the lock over there, and then disable the electric circuit."

I dragged in a breath, squeezing my eyes shut for a second.

I just had to hope that a similar fail-safe mechanism as the one at the top of the stairs didn't secure the cage around the dynamo when it was running.

Jack held out a jangling bunch of keys. "Can I move?"

"Yes. Once the pressure plate has been triggered, going up and down the steps doesn't seem to make any difference."

Jack came down the last steps, reached through the bars, and set the bunch of keys into my hand.

My breath went out in a shaky rush. Until the moment I felt the solid warmth of his hand against mine, a part of me hadn't been convinced that he wasn't just another dream.

Though I wasn't sure the reality wasn't even more terrifying.

I caught hold of his hand. "I don't know how to disable an electric circuit."

Jack's voice was still steady. "I'll tell you what to do."

We couldn't have more than two minutes left by now. "What if I make a mistake, though? I don't want you to get electrocuted!"

Jack reached out with his other hand, folding his fingers around mine. "Good, that makes two of us."

"I'm being serious!"

"You think I'm not? If I've searched every corner of the city just to get electrocuted when I finally find you, I'm coming back to haunt you."

I took a shaky breath, clutching the ring of keys.

"Tell me what to do. Just—" I stopped, resting my forehead

against the metal bars between us, not wanting to say the words out loud.

"I love you." Jack leaned forward, too, so that he could kiss me through the bars of the gate. "No matter what happens." He straightened. "Now go get us both out of here."

* * *

Jack's voice followed me as I made my way across the cellar. The lantern he carried was too wide for him to pass it to me through the bars, but he held it up so that I could see—dimly, at least.

Or maybe the light only seemed dim because I was still so dizzy, with occasional black dots swimming in front of my eyes.

I blinked hard, focusing on what Jack was saying.

"You're going to see wire, wrapped around an inner core. That's called the armature."

My hands were clammy with cold and unsteady, but I managed to unlock the gate around the dynamo. I held my breath, but it swung open without a hitch.

Finally, something had gone right, although we would probably pay for it later.

"All right, yes." I could see copper wires wrapped around a spinning core at the center of the machine. "Can I just pull out one of the wires?"

More copper coils ran down the outside of the machine and disappeared into the shadows along the wall.

"Not unless you've got an axe or something with a wooden handle to stop the electric shock from killing you."

Of course it couldn't be that simple. I scanned the floor all around me. "No. No convenient wood-handled axes."

"You need to stop the armature from spinning, then," Jack

said. "Is there anything you could use to jam the mechanism?"

How much longer did we have? A minute? Less, by now?

My gaze swept the area again. A few broken scraps of wood, innumerable cobwebs and piles of dust ...

"No, I don't think ... wait." My gaze snagged on something that glinted metallically over in one corner. I crouched, reaching for it, and my fingers closed around a hard metal cylinder. "There's a length of pipe here. Maybe three inches around and ten inches long?"

It looked as though it might be a remnant left here by whoever had installed the plumbing in the washroom.

"Would that work?"

"It should," Jack called back. "Try it. But then get out of there, quickly."

"All right." My heart was hammering all the way to the tips of my fingers.

Don't think about what would happen if I failed and this went wrong.

I leaned forward and jammed the length of pipe as hard as I could past the twin pistons, into the inner core of the generator.

The spinning movement of the armature caught the pipe, almost wrenching it out of my hands, but then the mechanism jammed, coming to a halt with a lurch and a groan of protesting metal. The dynamo trembled, shaking, trying to grind itself back into motion again.

I jumped back, to the other side of the metal cage. *Please, please, please ...*

The dynamo shuddered, creaking and protesting. Then it stopped.

"Jack?" My heart had stopped beating in the sudden silence.

His voice answered me from the darkness. "I'm here."

I shut my eyes, relief so overwhelming it was almost a physical force sweeping through me. I crossed back to the stairs. Now that I had time to look, I could see there was a metal rod that descended from the bottom of the gate into a hole in the floor and would hold it in place when the dynamo was running. But it was raised, now.

The gate swung open. Jack stepped through. Then his strong arms closed around me, and the entire rest of the world disappeared.

53. OUT OF THE DARKNESS

"Lucy, my dear, you really ought to be at home, resting," I said.

Lucy's lovely face bore the traces of her recent ordeal. Her green eyes were fever bright, and she was very pale save for a bruise on her cheek. But she shook her head, her expression set with a determination I had come to know well. "I'm all right, Uncle John. What exactly is this place?"

She leaned heavily against Jack's arm as we stood in the funeral home's entrance hall. Jack, for his part, was holding her as though he meant never to let her go.

"It's a funeral home," he said.

"That explains the furnace for cremating bodies." Lucy's eyes darkened as if with unpleasant memory. "Have you searched the rest of the house, Uncle John?"

Jack and I had separated upon our arrival, I to examine the upper floors, Jack the lower ones. Only now was I learning of the danger he had faced in his rescue of Lucy from her prison.

"I heard a woman up here," Lucy said. "Crying. Mr. Watts was keeping her a prisoner, too, I'm certain. Did you find her, or—" she stopped.

I knew, of course, what she was asking, but did not wish to say aloud: Had I found a body?

My own nerves had been tight with precisely that fear as I had combed through the upstairs rooms, which were spread out over two floors: one containing both bedroom and storage rooms and one an unfurnished garret.

At every turn, I had dreaded to find either Clara or Amelia huddled up behind a half-opened doorway, or lying on a hearthrug, their throats cut in the manner of the other women killed.

I shook my head. On this point, at least, I could offer reassurance. "There is no one else here, Lucy. Alive or otherwise."

"There was a woman here, though." Jack gestured to a single woman's high-button boot that lay half concealed behind the umbrella stand that stood by the front stairs. "We just have to hope she ran away someplace safe."

"I did find something else," I put in. "A means by which the stolen diamonds may have been smuggled into the country."

"Where?" Lucy asked.

"This way, if you feel able to climb a few stairs."

The funeral home was dark, furnished in the overly ornate, and to my mind gloomy, style of the previous decade. The scent of funereal flowers hung thick in the air, and yet their fragrance did not entirely serve to mask the faint odor of burning. I did not envy the police the task of combing through the ashes of the furnace I had glimpsed in the kitchen, seeking to identify the remains of victims who had met their end in this terrible place.

We mounted to the top of the stairs, where I pushed open a door to reveal a room stacked with caskets that had been unpacked from rough wooden shipping containers and were now lying on the scattered straw that had been used for padding during the shipping process.

"According to the labels, they are imported from South Africa," I said.

Lucy leaned forwards, plucking a small scrap of fabric that had caught on one of the crates' rough wooden edges. "This is a piece of a flag—a Union Jack. These caskets—" she swallowed. "They must have actually held bodies—maybe of British soldiers who were killed in the fighting there? They must have promised to return their bodies to their families in England for burial and then—"

We all knew what had happened then. The bodies must have been summarily cremated downstairs. I thought of my own military service, the friends and comrades I had seen fall in their service to Queen and country, and my blood fairly boiled with fury.

I said, "There are hidden compartments built into the caskets, secreted beneath the linings that would serve to smuggle diamonds into England. Although that does not explain how the diamonds are being smuggled *out* of the country. Perhaps Lord Burleigh—"

Lucy startled, her eyes widening. "Lord *Burleigh*?"

She looked at Jack, who nodded confirmation. "That's how we found you. This place belongs to him."

Lucy shook her head, seeming to struggle to take it in. "The same Lord Burleigh who was at Mrs. Scott's charity tea and who had recently been to Paris, and—" She broke off and rubbed her forehead. "I should have told you straight away. The woman whom Mr. Watts killed down in the basement. She had a tattoo identical to the one the Italian woman had, the woman who was shot in the Commercial Street station. It's not two cases at all. It's been *one* case—one all along. The diamond smuggling and the Ripper killings and the suicide … they're all connected. And that means—" She stopped short, her eyes widening. "Uncle John, you must warn Mrs. Scott; it's possible that she's in danger!"

I winced involuntarily. I had not yet wished to burden Lucy with that news, but there was no escaping it now. "Amelia has disappeared," I said. "She was lured away from the school under false pretenses, along with Clara, one of the girls from the Bethnal Green School. The police and Holmes's Irregulars are making every effort to find them, but I had hoped that they might be held prisoner here …"

My voice trailed off as the gravity of our failure to find them sunk in. With each hour that passed, it was surely less and less likely that they might be found alive.

"And Lord Burleigh?" Lucy asked. "Has he been questioned? Is that where Holmes is now?"

Jack and I exchanged a glance, and I saw Jack open his mouth, about to speak. But I felt it my duty to spare him the delivery of that further terrible blow.

"Lucy, my dear." I endeavored to speak as gently as I was able. "I am afraid that you must prepare yourself for some grave news."

LUCY
54. BAKER STREET

I woke with my heart pounding, expecting for a disorienting moment to open my eyes and see iron shackles and dark basement walls. But I was warm. For the first time in what seemed like eternity, I was warm all the way through, lying on something soft, with blankets over me.

I finally opened my eyes and exhaled as I saw Becky's small, golden-blond head resting against my shoulder.

She had been already asleep in the trundle bed when Jack, Uncle John, and I had finally reached Baker Street the night before, but she must have woken in the night and crawled into bed beside me.

I carefully eased my way out from under the blankets without waking her and then tucked the blanket more tightly around her shoulders. I picked up my dressing gown from the back of a chair and wrapped it around me. Out in the sitting room, the lights were turned out, but a fire still burned in the grate, the flickering light showing Jack stretched out on the sofa, asleep.

My heart tightened almost painfully as I tiptoed over to look down at him. I'd never been especially good at drawing, but for that moment, I wished that I were, just so that I could capture him the way he looked right now—the tousled dark hair that fell over his forehead, the sweep his dark lashes made against the hard planes of his cheekbones.

I hadn't meant to wake him, but his eyes opened, blinked, and then he smiled up at me. "Hello." His voice was still a little raspy with sleep.

"Hello."

Jack sat up, reaching to feel my forehead. "You're a bit cooler. How do you feel?"

"Better." I did. The fever wasn't quite gone, but the pounding headache had receded. "Is there any news about Holmes?"

Last night, Holmes, too, had been in bed when we arrived in Baker Street, sunk deep in the fever from his too-long neglected knife wound. I had gone in with Uncle John to see him, but his cheeks had been hectically flushed, his lips parched and cracked, and even when he'd opened his eyes briefly, he seemed scarcely to see me.

Now it was nearly five o'clock in the morning by the clock on the mantle, and when I listened, everything upstairs in 221B was ominously silent and still.

Jack shook his head. "I haven't seen Dr. Watson since last night. I know he's worried, though."

I nodded, curling up on the couch next to him. Jack wrapped his arms around me and pulled me closer, and I felt him breathe in and then out, relief so plain in the way he held me.

"I forgot to say thank you last night," I told him.

"For what?"

"For coming for me. I still can't believe that you found me."

Jack pulled back just enough that he could look down at me.

"I would never have stopped looking. I wish I could have gotten to you sooner."

He touched my cheek lightly, where Mr. Watts's blow had left a bruise.

I shook my head. "It's all right. I made him angry, and he hit me. But for the most part, I was just English enough that I qualified for humane treatment. Although I knew he would have killed me in the end. That's why—" I stopped.

Jack's arms tightened around me. "You did what you had to do. If I could bring him back and kill him a second time, I'd do it in a second."

I couldn't remember ever seeing his expression quite so grim or dark. I shut my eyes for a second. "I wish it was over. But it's not, is it? It won't be, not until we find Clara and Mrs. Scott. And Lord Burleigh—" I shook my head. "I still can't believe—"

The ring of the front door bell made me break off, my heart skipping painfully. This was how it had all begun. Jack and I sitting on the sofa, and then the ringing doorbell, and shattering glass—

Jack's strong fingers laced with mine, tugging me out of the memory. "We'll go together. All right?"

I nodded. "All right."

At the end of the hall, Jack opened the door to reveal Inspector Lestrade and a second man standing on the doorstep.

"Is your father here?" Lestrade asked. He gestured to the stranger, who was tall and broad-shouldered, with keen blue eyes and a ruddy, square-jawed face. "This is Dr. Burleigh. He wishes to speak to us all urgently, regarding his brother."

55. A DOCTOR'S CONFESSION

"I have since childhood always been on some level … afraid of my brother." Dr. Burleigh's voice was low and miserable. He sat hunched in the armchair beside the fire, twisting his hat in his hands, with his gaze trained on the floor.

"I remember, as a boy, he was fascinated by anatomy. Or that was what he called it." His mouth twisted. "In reality, it served as a mere excuse to dismember the corpses of mice and rabbits and any other poor, unfortunate creatures who happened to be caught in his traps. Sometimes while they were dead, other times while they were yet alive. He said he was conducting experiments on the nervous system's response to the systematic infliction of pain."

The big man's body shook with a brief shudder of remembrance, but he pulled himself together with a visible effort and went on. "As he grew to adulthood, I was aware of his predilection for doing things to women of—" he cast an apologetic glance at Lucy. "Of a certain class. Although to my great shame, I endeavored to turn a blind eye until nine years ago."

I felt the shock of the words ripple through me. Shock, and

the cold grip of renewed fear. Was he describing the monster who even now held Amelia and Clara at his mercy?

"Nine years ago? Whitechapel?"

Dr. Burleigh's blue eyes met mine. "I have no proof, you understand. But I visited my brother at his home one morning during that terrible autumn. His manservant had become concerned because of my brother's habit of wandering the London streets at night, alone. He was concerned for my brother's safety." The doctor swallowed. "I, however, was plagued with an entirely different fear. The more so when I examined my brother's bedroom and found in the grate of his fireplace the charred buttons of several pairs of men's gloves and a few scraps of burned leather. As though they had been worn and then—"

"Burned," I finished for him.

Inspector Lestrade was standing by the mantle, his narrow face pinched in a scowl. "And yet you did not report these facts to the police?"

Dr. Burleigh spread his hands in silent appeal. "I had no proof," he said again. "And he was my brother. To my eternal shame, I did what I deemed best, and made arrangements for him to travel to South Africa to supervise our family's cattle farming operations in that country."

"Where he set aside his murderous predilections and made the acquaintance of Cecil Rhodes."

Holmes's voice, coming from the bedroom doorway, made me startle and look round.

"Holmes, you ought not to be—" I began.

Holmes looked dreadful, his face a sickly yellow and beaded with perspiration. He swayed as he stood with one hand braced against the doorframe, but he waved aside my exclamation of alarm.

"I will see this case through to its conclusion, Watson." He focused on Dr. Burleigh. "You believe your brother to have channeled his violent tendencies into a scheme for stealing and smuggling diamonds from Mr. Rhodes's operations. A scheme which put the women he used as carriers for the diamonds completely at his mercy."

Lucy's eyes were wide, fixed on her father's face, and I saw her hand tighten on Jack's as they sat together on the sofa.

Dr. Burleigh, for his part, shook his head, confusion marring his brows. "I know nothing of diamonds. Only that these terrible recent killings commenced soon after my brother's return to London, and I feared—" He shook his head, then straightened, some of the misery in his expression lifting as he looked at Holmes. "Mr. Holmes. You will pardon my interference, but I believe you are experiencing the fever associated with a suppurating wound."

Holmes swayed again, seemingly unable to answer. I cleared my throat. "A knife wound. We have been treating it, but it is not healing as it ought."

"Have you tried the application of silver nitrate?" Dr. Burleigh asked. "It is a new treatment, still in the experimental stages, but it has shown promising results in eliminating sepsis. I have a small supply in my laboratory and could have some delivered—"

I had not heard of the treatment and was about to accept Dr. Burleigh's offer with grateful thanks when there came another ring at the front door. A moment later, Mrs. Hudson, her face pale with horror, carried a small, brown-paper wrapped box into the room. Something brown and sticky had dripped from within, staining the corner of the wrapping.

"It's addressed to you, sir," she said, her eyes on Holmes.

Holmes started to step forward, but nearly collapsed with the effort and fetched up with his back against the wall, breathing heavily. "Lucy—" he gestured.

Lucy sprang up to take the parcel from Mrs. Hudson's hands. I moved to support Holmes, and this time he did not refuse, allowing me to help him into an armchair.

Lucy untied the string, the stained wrappings fell away, and she lifted the lid on a small, cardboard box.

I drew in a sharp breath at the sight of what lay within, on a bed of stained and dirtied cotton. A human finger, a woman's, severed at the base of the third metacarpal and still smeared with dried blood.

"There's a note." Lucy lifted the accompanying scrap of paper out, swallowed, and read aloud.

"Dear Mr. Sherlock Holmes. I'm getting tired of these games, but I want one last grand hunt. Tell Miss Lucy James she's to come to Whitechapel tonight and walk the streets alone. Do it, and I'll let the other two go, without even chopping off any more fingers. If I get her, I'll have paid you back for the trouble you've brought me. If you get me—and I know you'll be trying—I'll earn my reward for all I've done in Hell."

LUCY

56. A PROMISE

"What if we're wrong?"

Jack and I were downstairs again in 221B, waiting for Uncle John to finish attending to Holmes upstairs.

We were alone in the house, Mrs. Hudson having taken Becky to stay at the new house in Palmer Street.

Becky had cried and clung to me when it was time for them to go.

"I'll be safe, Becky, I *promise*," I'd told her. "Jack and I will keep each other safe. But we can't do that if we're worrying about you. Just this once, please, stay safe with Mrs. Hudson, and let us take care of the danger."

My last sight of Becky had been her tear-streaked face looking back at me from the carriage window as she and Mrs. Hudson rolled away. And in the hour or so that had passed since, I had had time to grow sick to my stomach at the thought that I might have made her a promise I couldn't keep.

"We're not wrong." Jack sounded far calmer and more confident than I felt. "Martha Tabram was the victim with the petticoat from the Lambeth Workhouse. Elizabeth Stride was the one who may or may not have had grapes purchased for her by the killer. Two different women, and they were killed almost two months apart. But the Italian woman killed at Commercial Street had both, the petticoat and the grape stems."

"And the first woman, the one whose murder started all of this," I said. "Poor Grace's cousin. She was found in Mitre Square."

"Which was where the *fifth* murder victim was found nine years ago," Jack finished for me.

"And rehashing the entire Mathew Packer story ..." I drew in a breath. "We're not wrong," I echoed. But I still leaned against him, feeling almost as chilled as I had back in the funeral home cellar. "I feel as though you ought to get some sort of medal for putting up with all this. For letting me do this tonight."

"I thought we'd decided I didn't let you do anything." Jack was silent for a second, and then he said, in a different tone, "There is one thing, maybe."

I twisted so that I could look up at him. "What is it?"

Jack took my hand. "Marry me."

"Didn't I already say yes to that? I don't think you can get engaged twice."

"I mean marry me straight away. No waiting for December, no grand ceremony in St. James Church. Just the two of us, right away—or as soon as your mother can get here."

My eyes misted, and I leaned forward to kiss him fiercely, a promise of another kind. "Yes. No more waiting."

WATSON

57. CONFRONTATION IN WHITECHAPEL

There was a fog that night. I left Holmes in his bed with a heavy heart, for I feared for his health. Indeed, I feared for his life. His fever had not yet broken. His wound had turned septic, and the infection was spreading throughout his system, with ugly red tendrils of inflammation spreading from beneath the bandages that I had frequently applied and regularly changed.

Holmes had made no objections to being ordered to remain in bed tonight, which alarmed me still more. Although, sick as he was, he had nonetheless insisted on overseeing the plans for the evening. We had enlisted the aid of Lestrade, who had assembled a dozen brave and fit constables to make the journey into Whitechapel. Jack Kelly, of course, was in their number. These men had gone ahead, clearing a pathway, so to speak, for Lucy and me to arrive unnoticed and undisturbed by the regular denizens of the vile neighborhood.

She and I rode through the fog-bound streets in a growler cab driven by Mycroft Holmes. The curtains of the cab were tightly drawn. Inside the cab, a small kerosene lantern cast flickering yellow light upon the heavy black scarf that covered Lucy's hair and on the heavy black wool shawl that covered the red taffeta dress she had chosen for the occasion.

"If I am to be bait," she had said, "I must be as gaudy and noticeable as possible." She held no purse or reticule. On her lap, however, was a Bible bound in black leather, the interior of which had been modified to hold Lucy's Ladysmith revolver. Throughout the four-mile journey neither of us spoke, until the cab stopped and two heavy raps from Mycroft's stick above us gave the signal that we had reached our destination. I opened my watch. The time was five minutes before midnight. We were on schedule for our meeting with the man who had called himself Jack the Ripper.

I opened the door, for the plan was for me to take cover in a certain brick archway and for Lucy to position herself fairly closely nearby on the walkway, close enough so that I could both see and hear her.

When I had stepped onto the pavement and closed the door, Mycroft flicked the reins and the cab moved on, up the narrow way that was barely more than an alley, until it was lost in the fog. A minute or two later, I heard the slow clip-clop of hoofs and the rattle of iron-sheathed wheels on the cobblestones. From the fog up the hill, Mycroft's silhouette emerged. He was still seated atop the cab. I stepped out from my hiding place and touched the brim of my hat to give the signal that it was safe for Lucy to dismount.

I returned to my post. Lucy stepped nimbly down from the cab. She shut the door. She turned and took a few steps away from me, up the hill. Mycroft flicked the reins once more, and the cab left us, traveling down the hill, this time not to return.

The sounds of hoof beats and wheels grew fainter. I heard the muffled cry from one of those unfortunate souls who occupied the surrounding tenements above us. Lestrade's men were in position, I told myself. Behind partially opened windows on the ground floor, they would hear and could bear witness to any incriminating statements made by the man we were there to trap.

Lucy whispered, "He's coming."

I crouched down and risked a glance up the hill. I saw fog and darkness, but I could hear footfalls. Boots. Hard leather soles make a particular sound on cobblestones, a sound I recognized.

Then the shadowy figure of a tall, powerful man emerged. He strode confidently, his cape swaying beneath his top hat. He carried a walking stick, and his movements appeared as comfortable as if he had been walking up to the Lyceum Theatre to enjoy an evening's performance.

Lucy said, "I know you, Trevor Burleigh. Did you bring a knife?"

The figure jerked to a halt. From my place of concealment, it was just barely possible for me to see.

The man was Lord Burleigh, just as we had suspected. But for an instant, in the hazy light of the nearby streetlamp, I should have sworn that a momentary flash of shock crossed his face before it hardened into a sneer.

"Oh, I am prepared. You may rely on that."

"No doubt." Lucy's voice was steady. "A man of your sort needs the advantage of weaponry when faced with a small woman."

"And you have brought your Bible, I see. Were you hoping—"

I had been instructed to hang back, not to sound any alarm.

Lestrade and Police Commissioner Bradford were hoping that Lucy could elicit a confession and have it overheard by the police witnesses who were present; otherwise, the case against a man of Lord Burleigh's stature—even with the testimony of his brother—would not stand.

Lucy interrupted him. She was keeping her distance, her eyes constantly on Burleigh in anticipation of some attack, her concealed revolver at the ready. "A bargain is a bargain. I'm here. Where are Clara and Mrs. Scott?"

My heart beat harder in anticipation of Burleigh's answer, but before he could speak, a shot rang out, the impact of the bullet sending up a spray of brick and plaster dust from the wall just behind them. I jumped, and even Lucy, steady though her nerves were, startled, her head whipping round to seek out the location from whence the shot had come.

Had one of the waiting police constables suddenly lost his head and accidentally discharged his weapon?

Lord Burleigh, too, jolted with shock and then let out a half-animal snarl. In the second when Lucy was distracted, he lunged towards her, his knife raised.

He slammed into her, sending the bible flying to the muddy cobblestones. Lucy lashed out, slamming the heel of her hand hard into Burleigh's nose, but he remained standing.

What I saw at that moment I hope never to see again. Lord Burleigh's whole visage changed, his shoulders hunched, his face twisted, and a monster crawled out of his eyes.

I had no trouble at all believing that he had massacred many unfortunate women.

"By the devil." His voice was low, animal. "I shall enjoy this."

I had no choice. Even before I took out my police whistle

and blew a shrill, piercing blast, the sound that would bring Lestrade's men out of their hiding places, I was firing my revolver. My two shots hit Lord Burleigh directly in the chest and brought him down.

Figures were running towards us from up the street.

But not the police constables I was expecting. These were rougher men, dressed in tattered jackets and cloth caps and armed with weapons ranging from axes to hammers to clubs made from nails pounded into a wooden board.

The police, too, were coming, pouring out of their hiding places, but the new attackers would reach us first.

Lucy snatched up her Ladysmith revolver from where it had fallen and fired into the crowd, sending them momentarily scattering and scrambling backwards. She seized hold of my arm.

"Come, Uncle John! Hurry!"

From behind us came the sound of angry shouts and blows as the line of police clashed with the band of thugs. I raced with Lucy down the side street towards our waiting carriage and pulled myself, gasping for breath, up onto the seats. We were safe, but my mind was still struggling to catch up with what had occurred. I had never known Lucy to run from a fight.

"Ought we not to be lending aid to the fight," I began. "Or at the very least ensure that Jack—"

Lucy shook her head. Her face was very pale in the carriage lights. "Jack isn't here. He's back in Baker Street. With Holmes. But I wasn't expecting—" she broke off, pressing her lips tightly together and shaking her head. "We must get back there now—at once! I'm afraid we're going to be too late."

LUCY

58. CONFRONTATION
IN MARYLEBONE

"I feel as though I am still almost completely in the dark," Watson said.

His tone of voice wasn't accusing, but I felt a prick of guilt all the same. "I'm sorry, Uncle John. If I could have told you, I would have. But I was afraid—"

"You were afraid that if I knew the full truth I would somehow slip up and give the game away," Watson finished for me. He held up a hand before I could say anything more, his expression resigned. "No, don't apologize."

We were on Euston Road, just rolling past the lovely spired brick building of St. Pancras hotel. The roads were almost deserted tonight, by London standards—for which, in a way, I supposed we had to thank the man we had left lying in the road back in Whitechapel. Our carriage was rolling along swiftly, but I still found myself leaning forwards, gripping the edge of the seat more tightly as though that would help us go faster still.

I forced myself to take a breath, but it did nothing to dispel the hard knot of fear inside me. "I can explain if you like—" I began.

Watson shook his head. "You are clearly in no fit state to be burdened with a full explanation, nor am I capable of absorbing one at present." His jaw tightened just briefly. "Just tell me this much: do you believe Amelia Scott and Clara to be safe?"

That distracted me momentarily from my own worry. "I don't know, Uncle John." I couldn't lie to him, not now. "I'm sorry. Do you—" I stopped, wondering whether I should even ask the question, when I wasn't sure it would matter now.

Now that I was out of the funeral home cellar, something else had come back to me: a single, spoken sentence that made my heart cramp.

"Do you care for her?" I finally asked.

He was about to answer when the sound of a gunshot suddenly cut across the rattling of our carriage wheels and the clatter of the horses' hooves.

"Driver! Halt!" Watson called out.

We were on Marylebone Road, and up ahead I could see through the drifting tatters of yellow fog the looming shape of a long, three-story brick building, crowned at one end by a small dome.

Realization twisted through me with the force of a physical blow. "Uncle John—hurry!"

I was already scrambling out of the carriage, yanking the skirt of my gown free when it caught on a loose nail on the door.

Together we ran towards the building's entrance.

"But this is Madame Tussaud's, Lucy," Uncle John panted beside me. "What—" his voice cut off as we reached the museum's front entryway and caught sight of a man's figure, lying slumped on the floor just inside the half-open door. My heart tried to leap up into my throat, but it wasn't my father or Jack.

This was an elderly, gray-haired man wearing the uniform of a night watchman.

I crouched down, feeling for a pulse in his neck, and found it, sluggish but steady. "He's still alive," I whispered to Watson.

Watson, too, bent down, conducting a rapid examination. "He's been struck over the head," he murmured.

"Is it safe to leave him for now?"

Watson straightened. "If you have need of me, certainly."

My eyes were adjusting to the dim light further inside, making out the shapes of the booth where tickets for the exhibits could be purchased, the curtained entrances to the nearest gallery, where the waxwork human figures of the wives of Henry VIII stood at eerie attention.

Together, we dragged the night watchman into concealment behind the ticket counter, where he would—I hoped—be safe from any more attacks. Then I stood, straining my ears to listen. I was positive that the single gunshot we'd heard outside had come from this building. But now everything was ominously still, save for the occasional clatter of a carriage in the road outside.

"Where did Holmes go when you and he were here the other day?" I whispered.

Watson checked once more to make sure that the unconscious night watchman was as comfortably placed as possible and that his breathing was unobstructed, then straightened. "The Chamber of Horrors, primarily."

"Of course. Because clearly this night hasn't been unpleasant enough already."

Together, Watson and I crept up the staircase where he had fallen the other day. The back of my neck prickled, and I kept fighting the urge to whip my head around and scan the darkness for watching eyes or some sign that one of the waxen figures was an enemy in disguise, poised to spring at us when our backs were turned.

A man's figure stood just inside the entrance to the Chamber of Horrors, training the narrow beam of an electric torch at the base of the pedestal supporting the statue of Robespierre.

"Don't move!" Watson barked. His gun was already in his hand, and raised—though he jerked back with a gasp and an exclamation of astonishment as the man straightened up and turned. This room was lit from above by a skylight. That pale glow and the light from his torch showed the man's face.

"I pray you, Watson, do not shoot," my father said.

"Holmes!" Watson gaped at him. "But you were deathly ill …"

My father's face was still almost as pale as one of the waxen statues that surrounded us, but his lips quirked in a genuinely amused smile. "It is good to know that even after the Culverton Smith affair I can still surprise you, Watson."

Watson passed a hand over his eyes. "I suppose you have been warming your thermometer on the hot water bottle, applying turmeric to your skin, beeswax to your lips—"

"I regret the distress and worry I have caused you, but I assure you that it was necessary," Holmes said. He focused on me. "You knew?"

"Suspected, rather. You put on a very convincing performance of being practically at death's door. But you agreed to remain at home in Baker Street tonight a little too readily."

"And I presume that Jack is here, as well?" Holmes asked.

"He was supposed to be. He promised me that he would stay

behind in Baker Street and follow you if you went out." Cold gripped me a little tighter as I said it. "But I haven't yet seen him."

Holmes pursed his lips. He raised his hand for silence, listening, then switched off the electric torch.

"I believe we have company," he said.

A man's voice came from a few feet away. It held a note of menace. "You are correct, Mr. Holmes."

The man stepped out of the shadows behind the Marie Antoinette effigy. I had been sure—almost sure—but I still felt a lurch in the pit of my stomach at the sight of his eyes, cold as a winter sky above the barrel of the revolver he was leveling at us.

My father's face was calm, without even a flicker of surprise. "Ah, Dr. Burleigh. We have been expecting you."

LUCY

59. DIAMONDS AND GLASS

Apart from his eyes, Dr. Burleigh looked exactly as he had done this afternoon in Baker Street: just as hearty, just as cheerful. If I had bumped into him on the street, I would have smiled, said, *I beg your pardon,* and never thought about him a second time.

Watson brought his own revolver up and was holding it trained on Dr. Burleigh. I had already flicked the safety catch off the Ladysmith.

"Drop your weapon!" Watson ordered.

The doctor's mouth stretched in a smile. "I give the same command to you, Doctor Watson." His gaze flicked to me. "Miss James, you can lower your weapon, as well."

Holmes was still watching Dr. Burleigh calmly. "Can you explain why either Watson or Miss James should comply with that request?"

The doctor's smile didn't falter. "Because, if you shoot me, you will never learn where Amelia Scott is being held. That lady is locked up with the young girl, Clara, from the Bethnal Green School. Both of them are where no one will find them, and no one will hear them scream." His broad shoulders twitched in a slight shrug. "An unpleasant way to die, perishing slowly of hunger and thirst in the dark, but it is, of course, your choice."

Uncle John's face twisted in anger, but he bent, apparently starting to set his revolver down.

"Watson, no!" Holmes shouted.

His call was too late. The instant that Watson leaned forward, Dr. Burleigh sprang. He seized Uncle John by the wrist, twisting his arm up tightly behind him and forcing him to drop the revolver. It hit the floor with a clatter.

Dr. Burleigh set the barrel of his own weapon against Watson's temple. "Your turn, Miss James."

I shot a quick glance at my father, but his jaw was tight. He didn't see any way out of this, either. If I tried to fire on Dr. Burleigh, Watson died.

"All right!" I held up the Ladysmith in one hand, crouching so that I could set it on the floor.

"Kick it over to me," Dr. Burleigh snapped.

Not good. I didn't know Dr. Burleigh, but he was proving himself to be far from stupid, the kind of enemy who wouldn't be caught off guard. I did as he asked, and Dr. Burleigh scooped the Ladysmith up, dropping it into the pocket of his coat.

"Now, Mr. Holmes." His gun still pressed tight against the side of Watson's head, Dr. Burleigh turned to my father. "You will tell me where you have hidden the diamonds."

My father's lips clamped more tightly together, but he moved slowly towards the display at the back of the room of Burke and Hare, the infamous murderers who had sold the bodies of their victims for doctors to dissect.

Holmes reached into a pocket of the coat that formed the costume for the wax statue of Burke.

He drew out a small, black silk bag.

Dr. Burleigh's eyes were sharp, fixed on him. "Bring it over here."

Holmes started to turn slowly, the bag in one hand.

"Be quick about it!" Dr. Burleigh's voice was sounding more on edge now.

Holmes spun, and I saw the other item he must have concealed in the pocket of the waxwork figure's costume: a small, pearl-handled revolver, almost identical to mine. He fired, and my heart froze. Holmes wasn't entirely faking being ill. He might not be at death's door, but he was still weakened, off-balance, and I knew from the instant I saw him falter, stumbling just a little as he squeezed the trigger, that the shot would go wide.

Plaster cracked as the bullet buried itself in the wall behind Dr. Burleigh, but he remained unharmed. His face twisted in fury. "I ought to spatter Dr. Watson's brains all over the museum floor for that little trick. Drop it! That's right," he added, as Holmes let the gun fall to the floor.

Dr. Burleigh raised his voice and called out, "Now!"

Men appeared in the doorway to the gallery. Four ... five ... six of them, dressed in the same dark, rough clothing as the men we had seen in Whitechapel. The air went out of my lungs as I realized that I knew the man in the front of the group.

Thomas Newman, his jaw still purple with the mark of Holmes's fist.

My heart beat in short, quick bursts that echoed to the tips of my fingers as Dr. Burleigh dragged Watson around to face Newman and the others. "Do as you like with them," he growled. "My only requirement is that all three of them must be dead by the time you've finished."

Newman's teeth flashed in a grin as he looked from Holmes and then to me. "Oh, we'll have our fun first, I promise you that."

"I'll take those, Mr. Holmes." Dr. Burleigh gave Watson a hard shove that sent him sprawling to the ground, then moved to take the black silk bag from my father's hands.

Holmes didn't move.

My mind scrambled as Dr. Burleigh strode out of the gallery, vanishing into the darkened museum beyond.

No plan was foolproof. Experience with my father had taught me that no planned strategy ever survived a dangerous confrontation unscathed. We had now arrived squarely at the point where all plans hit the ground and exploded like mortar shells.

I needed to think of something, some way of fighting back, but my mind was blank.

Newman stepped forward, his teeth still bared as he leered at me.

And the skylight over our heads suddenly caved in with a shower of broken glass.

A man in a blue police uniform dropped down, directly onto Newman, carrying him to the ground.

"Jack!" I felt my lips shape the word, but for the life of me, I couldn't make any sound come out.

The struggle lasted barely even a moment. Newman must have struck his head and been dazed in the fall. Jack rolled him over and punched him, and Newman collapsed with a faint groan, unconscious. In the same moment, Holmes acted, snatching up the weapon that Dr. Burleigh had forced him to drop.

He fired at Newman's men. "I strongly suggest that you

reconsider your next move." His voice was only slightly out of breath.

The men glanced at their leader on the ground, then at Holmes. Then at Watson, who had struggled upright and managed to recover his own revolver, as well. Then, almost as one, they turned and scattered, running away down the museum's long hall.

Jack turned to me. He had a few shards of broken glass stuck to the wool of his uniform, but he seemed unharmed. "Sorry I'm late. It took me awhile to find a way up onto the roof."

I finally managed to draw air back into my lungs. "You just jumped through a *skylight*. Are you out of your mind?"

Jack grinned, wrapped his arms around me, and kissed my forehead. "You must be rubbing off on me, Trouble."

WATSON

60. AT BURLEIGH HOUSE

Lucy and Jack left the museum to alert Lestrade. Holmes's stride was firm as he took a few steps towards one of the exhibits and removed one of the dividing ropes from its metal stands. He brought the rope to where I stood guarding the unconscious Newman and handed it over for me to cut into sections using my pocketknife.

Newman's breath came in gurgling rasps. His limbs offered some resistance as we lashed the ropes around his wrists and ankles and then tied them together behind his back. The crime overlord of London now lay prone on his fat belly. He had broken some teeth in his struggle with Jack, and a dark puddle was forming on the floorboards below his mouth. I judged that he would survive to stand trial.

"What of Rhodes's diamonds?" I asked.

"When Dr. Burleigh examines the contents of the small velvet sack, he will find the jewels inside are made of glass. They are worthless imitations."

Lestrade joined us a few moments later, accompanied by two strong constables. From his dejected expression it was plain that the plan had not gone as anticipated.

"Two of my best men went after Dr. Burleigh when he left the museum. He was proceeding east on Marylebone Road. But then a big black carriage came rocketing out of The Regent's Park, and he got himself on board. The carriage had four horses. My lads couldn't keep up."

"Which direction did the carriage go?"

"Why, it kept on east. On Marylebone."

"Then things may not be as bleak as they appear. We shall leave your two constables here to attend to Mr. Newman. Lestrade, you will mobilize the remainder of your men outside. Watson and I will accompany you. The others can follow in the police coaches."

"Where are we going?"

"To Burleigh House. It is just north of the Inner Circle, in Regent's Park."

We had less than half a mile to walk through the darkened pathways of the park before the massive Burleigh House loomed up out of the shadows.

"Lestrade, take your men into the main building," Holmes said. "Watson, you and I will enter the carriage house."

The doors to the carriage house were wide open. We found Clara as soon as Holmes switched on the electric light. She was in her school uniform, gagged and lying on her back at the far end of the concrete floor, wrists tied to the base of a hitching post. Her eyes lit up when she saw me. Her fingers were all intact.

Quickly I removed the gag and cut through the ropes that bound her. Clara sat up, shivering. I found a blanket and covered her.

I tried to keep the urgency out of my voice. "Where is Mrs. Scott? Is she all right? Have you seen her?"

Clara looked at me for a long moment. "Mrs. Scott tied me up and left me here. I saw her only about an hour ago, when she drove the carriage away."

I sat down, hard, on the cold concrete.

"She said I wasn't to tell anyone what had happened. She said if I did the school would have to shut down and bad men would find me and cut off my hands. Why would she say such a thing, Dr. Watson? What has happened?"

I got to my feet. "We will find out."

"I want to go home to my friends. May I go now?"

I led her to where the police were waiting. Lestrade agreed that the next day to interview her would be soon enough. I put her into one of the police coaches. She waved at me from the window as the coach pulled away.

Then I heard Holmes's voice, coming from what seemed a long distance. But he was standing beside me.

"An envelope on the workbench," he said. "It is addressed to you."

The envelope contained a letter, on blue paper, in Amelia's characteristic flowery hand. I reproduce the text of the letter here:

John. If you are reading this it will mean that I have gone from England, never to return. I have left this, my farewell to you, because I genuinely like and admire you and sincerely hope you will not think too ill of me. I underestimated you. That was my first mistake A shipment of diamonds was lost when one of the ships carrying caskets from South Africa sank. Our buyers are not the sort of people whom it is wise to disappoint, and

Matthew grew desperate—desperate enough to steal from the Bethnal Green Aide Society members as a means of replacing the funds that had been lost. It was that disaster that led us to search for an alternate way of bringing diamonds into the country. Although the foreign women we employed proved to be even more unreliable and fraught with complications than the ships.

Members of the Bethnal Green Aide Society were threatening to go to the police over the thefts, which would, I feared, aim the spotlight of investigation directly at Matthew and at me. I offered an alternative: Dr. Watson, the famed chronicler of the great Sherlock Holmes. I was certain that it would be a simple matter to ensure that you saw only those truths which I cared to put before you.

Then the Reverend Albright learned the truth behind the school. Matthew would have killed him, but that turned out to be unnecessary. The good Reverend was unable to live with the horror of what he had unwittingly been a party to.

It was a simple matter to confiscate most of his suicide note, in which he set down a detailed account of what he knew of our crimes, and to leave only the last page of his letter, where he begged forgiveness for what he had done.

His poor housekeeper was in no condition to notice what I was doing when the body was found.

I though that you would attribute the thefts to the Reverend, and there would be an end to the matter. That Mathew and I would be safe to continue on our business as planned.

That I am now writing this epistle proves how wrong I was in my assumptions about your intellect.

However, I seem to have distracted both you and Mr. Holmes by my disappearance, along with Clara's, at least sufficiently for Matthew and me to make our escape with enough diamonds to pay our buyers what we owe them, courtesy of Mr. Rhodes and Mr. Holmes.

The loss may well cause you some inconvenience, but I cannot help that.

However, I have spared Clara's life and prevented her from being maimed, which ought to count for something in my favor.

The world is a fine and large place, John, and I hope to lose myself in it. I regret many things, chief among them that I let desperation over take my sense of fairness when it came to the survival of the Bethnal Green School. I would have done anything to preserve the opportunities for those girls and for more like them. I saw myself in them. I had achieved what position I had only through the opportunity to elevate myself. I could not deprive those girls. I expect that soon after you read this the connection to many crimes will be made. I needed the money. Matthew needed the money as well, for his own research. Which is very important and valuable, as I am sure you will appreciate. We got by for a while. Now we will just have to leave those worthy causes—our only children, literally, that we have—to carry on without us. It grieves Matthew as well, I know. We are taking with us enough to make a start somewhere else, and perhaps we will be able to begin new projects and find new worthy causes of a similar nature, wherever it is that fortune and our uncertain funds manage to take us.

I feel particularly guilty of having deceived you, John. I know you loved Mary, and I preyed upon your sense of loss. I should qualify that, though, for after meeting you twice and then after reading the wonderful narratives you had set down for the school,

I felt the presence of a strong and decent and admirable soul. A spirit that I hope to emulate, if I can bring myself to the point of self-sacrifice enough to forego the luxuries that are a part of me and are so essential to my work. Had been so essential, I should say, but will be essential again at some future date, if I can attain a high position in one of the colonies and create a new cause to help those who are as unfortunate as I once was. I know the Bethnal Green School must fail and close its doors when word gets out, as it inevitably will, that I have fled and taken my stolen riches with me. For that I am ashamed, but not sufficiently to change. I do regret, though, that your good work in creating supportive material for our great cause will have been in vain.

I must make my escape now. Do not trouble yourself to look for clues in this letter as to my destination, for there are none. You will never see me again. But I will have your memory, or, I should say, my memory of you. And that will be vivid.

Yours most sincerely,
Amelia.

Holmes folded the letter and put it into his pocket. "It is rambling and self-centered, and patently the writer is incapable of sincere attachment. She writes only to make herself feel better and appease whatever poor excuse for a conscience that she may possess. You have done well to avoid an entanglement. I feel certain that eventually you will find someone more worthy. We must hand the document over to Lestrade as evidence, although I agree it contains no clues to Mrs. Scott's present whereabouts. However, the carriage she drove may be identifiable, and remembered, and the Metropolitan Police will do everything in their power to find witnesses."

WATSON

61. REPARATIONS ON DOWNING STREET

Two days later, we appeared once more at the entrance to Number 11 Downing Street. This time, there were no Palace Guards there, only the usual two stationed next door at Number 10, standing tall and seemingly taking no notice of either Holmes and me or of the chill wind that howled in around us from the Thames. Holmes stepped ahead of me to knock.

I was worried about him coming. If he had been feigning the severity of his illness before, it now seemed to me that he was genuinely touched by fever, and his pulse that morning had been more rapid than I had hoped. But Holmes had insisted on keeping the appointment, and I had at least won the concession of his being heavily cloaked and mufflered against the cold.

Chancellor Sir Michael Hicks-Beach himself opened the door. He gave Holmes a most respectful nod and held a finger to his lips, glancing upstairs to indicate that the servants, once more, had been sequestered to avoid the possibility of anyone eavesdropping on the meeting. Holmes was already removing his coat and muffler as Sir Michael led us to his conference room and opened the door.

Inside, the fireplace coals glowed brightly. At the long table sat Police Commissioner Bradford, and, beside him, Cecil Rhodes.

Rhodes looked up as Holmes and I sat across from him. Light from an electric chandelier shone on his plump cheeks and puffy lips.

"Ah. Holmes," he said. "Now perhaps you'll tell me what I am doing here. Your telegram reached me in Paris yesterday. I dropped everything. What have you to report?"

Wordlessly, Holmes removed two small black silken sacks from his waistcoat pocket. He slid them across the table. "These diamonds are the ones you gave me two weeks ago. There are two other sacks in the office safe of the local De Beers manager. Those are imitations."

Rhodes's pudgy fingers closed around both sacks. He stuffed them into his inside jacket pocket. "You've found the thieves?"

Commissioner Bradford said, "We are in position to eliminate the smuggling ring. Our sources indicate that two of the three principals boarded the *SS Montrose* at Avonmouth yesterday, bound for Montreal. We will keep them under observation after they arrive. It is a voyage of three weeks."

"Why not arrest them?"

Chancellor Hicks Beach explained. "The young ladies who act as couriers have not yet made port. We need to watch them and then wait for those who come to collect the diamonds. Likely those intermediaries will lead us to their local principals, those enemies of the Crown who are so intent on creating havoc throughout the Empire. We have every expectation of accomplishing this before the 'day of reckoning.' But in order to prevent still more attempts, we want the whole ring under arrest."

"With the exception of the couriers," Holmes added. "Those young ladies have committed no crime. They have no idea what is contained inside their suitcases."

"You said two of the principals are sailing to Montreal. What of the third?"

"He is dead. His name was Trevor Burleigh."

Rhodes stared, open-mouthed, heavy gray eyebrows raised.

"Your friend and colleague and investor," Holmes continued.

Rhodes's cigar came up, held at an angle, like a small flag.

Holmes went on. "At first, when he first arrived in the Transvaal eight years ago, the funds he invested with you came from his ranch and his family. His contributions to your campaign for prime minister were likewise legitimate. But his gambling losses and his mismanagement of the Transvaal ranch caused the Burleigh estate to become nearly insolvent. His brother, Dr. Matthew Burleigh, fared no better financially. So the two of them turned to crime."

"But Burleigh gave me investments and political contributions all along. As recently as last month, in fact."

"Funds from the sale of diamonds they stole from you."

"I cannot believe it."

"Only a small fraction went to you, of course. Most of the diamonds went to England's political adversaries to fund those rebellious activities with which we are all too familiar. The small remaining amount has up till now gone to maintaining a fashionable lifestyle, the Doctor's medical crusade, and a humanitarian school for young girls championed by the mistress of the Doctor."

Hicks Beach added, "Both those enterprises are perfectly legitimate, and in London they are even quite fashionable. They received many donations from persons in high positions."

"Burleigh deceived me," said Rhodes.

Holmes went on, "He also deceived the British Army. Coffins containing the bodies of British soldiers killed in South Africa came to London with raw diamonds built into their woodwork. Trevor Burleigh managed the process, along with his South African associates. The coffins were shipped to a funeral home owned by him and his brother. But with a recent lull in the war there were no longer enough coffins, so they turned to the use of foreign women to smuggle in the raw diamonds."

Commissioner Bradford added, "The foreign women brought the diamonds to the funeral home. The operators had recently invested in an electric crematorium. This was the fate of most of the foreign women. One—an Italian woman—escaped. Regrettably, her escape was only temporary."

"They also offered their crematorium services to others who wished to make people disappear off the face of the earth," added Holmes. "A London gang led by a rogue named Newman was one of their major clients. You did not know Newman, of course, but he came to the aid of Burleigh's brother when he was on the point of being captured only two days ago."

"You are certain of the connection?"

"We found his records in Burleigh House," said Commissioner Bradford "We also found other evidence."

"Of an entirely different sort," said Hicks Beach. "And highly distasteful."

Rhodes waited, expectantly.

The two government officials looked at one another, and then at Holmes.

Holmes nodded. "Mr. Rhodes, would you kindly cast your memory back to when you arranged the appointment with me ten days ago. You were in Paris."

"So I was."

"The appointment was to be conducted in secret, you said. Chancellor Hicks Beach even posted a guard and had his servants sequestered. As he has today."

"What of it?"

"Yet you yourself did not keep the appointment a secret. You told Trevor Burleigh that you were planning to meet with me in London in a week's time to stop the company's diamond losses."

"It was my duty to keep him informed. He was a shareholder of the company and my trusted associate. And I was quite pleased with myself for taking the initiative and demanding that you be brought into the case." He drew on his cigar. "But now I see that I was warning him. Unintentionally. But you got him anyway, so that's an end of that. All's well that ends well."

Holmes shook his head. "It did not end well for everyone. Having been warned by your unintended notice, the Burleighs took action. Their plan was to create a diversion, to occupy my attentions and those of the Metropolitan police until their couriers and their diamonds could be safely out of London. You have been away in Paris, so it is likely that you have been unaware of the diversion they chose."

Holmes reached into his briefcase and drew out four newspapers. He slid them one by one across the table to Rhodes. Each bore a heavy black grease-pencil mark, encircling the article that Holmes wanted to accentuate.

"Four young ladies were murdered. Their bodies were left in locations and circumstances intended to evoke the killings of the man who called himself Jack the Ripper, eight years ago."

"How do you know that Burleigh—"

"The first victim was from a school supported by Dr. Burleigh's mistress."

Holmes's words came as if from a distance, and I willed my emotions to stay silent. They did.

Holmes continued, "The school provided training and placement to young ladies who wished to find a position as a governess in a good colonial family. The first victim was about to sail to her new position in India. Unbeknownst to her, Dr. Burleigh and Mrs. Scott had been using the girls' international travel to smuggle diamonds back out of the country. Diamonds worth a large fortune were concealed in her suitcase. Regrettably for her, she found the diamonds as she was packing. Her discovery was itself discovered. She had to be silenced. Her face was disfigured to hide her identity and her clothing exchanged with that of a London streetwalker. Dr. Burleigh himself arranged to supervise the examination of the body, enabling him to insert a message purportedly from the Ripper."

"Was Dr. Burleigh her killer?"

"He may well have been. At least one of the murders, though, was carried out by another man, a rogue former policeman named Watts, who was hired for the task. Likely he also detonated the bomb at the Egyptian Embassy. A weak-minded fellow. Burleigh filled his head with promises and political claptrap to justify the act. Burleigh also, as I previously mentioned, made alliance with a notorious East End gang leader, Thomas Newman. As someone who preyed on the fallen women of the East End, Newman had a vested interest in perpetuating the myth of the Ripper's return, inasmuch as it would lead to the closing of houses where such women find refuge and also keep the women of the East End terrified, desperate to attach themselves to any ostensible protector, however undeserving of the role he might be. Burleigh hired Newman's thugs for attacks on Dr. Watson and myself." Holmes's jaw hardened as he continued, "And for kidnapping one of my close associates."

Rhodes sat stock still, but his wide blue eyes darted back and forth. "So I am responsible for five deaths."

"Not directly, of course."

"But people could talk. Would talk. And the connection with Burleigh—known to be my friend and investor, after all—and this Ripper business—" Rhodes shook his head. "I am shocked. And now I see why I am here. If this story were to get out, the effect on my company—indeed, on the whole market for diamonds—would be disastrous." He shuddered.

Commissioner Bradford said, "Yet we have a great interest in allaying the fears of the British public, informing them that the Ripper has been caught."

"However," said Hicks Beach, "we agree with you that any association of the notorious Ripper murders with diamonds would taint the market and cause a disastrous drop in revenues both for the company and for the Crown."

Rhodes took a deep breath, and then exhaled, his relief evident. "So you will hush it up."

The two officials nodded, their faces solemn.

"But I will owe you."

Again, the two men nodded.

"And that is why I am here."

No one moved. Rhodes sat silent for a long moment.

Then he removed the two sacks of diamonds from his jacket pocket. "These will be sold, and I shall use the proceeds to establish a fund at Oxford College for the furtherance of the British Empire. I shall add to the fund as much as may be required to perpetually enable the higher education of men who possess moral force of character and the instincts to lead."

He paused and gestured across the table where I sat with Holmes.

He said, "Men like yourselves."

For some reason I recalled the face of Clara Sheffield, shivering and huddled and bewildered, under that blanket in the Burleigh carriage house. A red mist seemed to fill my vision. I realized Holmes was looking at me.

Holmes said, "That is not enough."

Rhodes said, "Then what is?"

Holmes turned to me. "Dr. Watson will tell you."

My emotions came to the surface, bringing with them a bold idea.

"You will use those diamonds and whatever additional capital you need to purchase Burleigh House," I said. "And you will donate the building to the Bethnal Green School, along with an endowment that is sufficient to keep it in good repair." I placed both my fists on the table and leaned forward, and added, "In perpetuity."

Rhodes said nothing for a long moment.

Hicks Beach said, "Well, Mr. Rhodes?"

Rhodes squeezed the two sacks of diamonds in one hand. Then he let them fall onto the surface of the table.

"Done," he said.

WATSON

62. NẼWS FROM ĆANĄDĄ

Late afternoon sunlight streamed through our bow window. The day was Monday, November 8, nearly three weeks from when we had last met with Rhodes on Downing Street. I could hear faint piano music coming from the rooms below us, along with intermittent notes on the violin. Zoe Rosario had arrived the day before and would stay until, as she put it, she was quite certain that Holmes's health was no longer a cause for her concern.

I was at my writing desk. Holmes was at our bow window, standing sideways in his usual manner, apparently contemplating the ongoing rush of life outside on Baker Street. But though he had placed his body between his left hand and me, I could tell that he was holding onto the window frame for support. I knew that though he was on the mend, he was not fully recovered, and I agreed with Zoe's intuitive opinion that too great a strain would put his system at risk of relapse. Yet there was no point in remonstrations now.

I was working up another article about The Bethnal Green School, to appear in *The Strand Magazine*. The article would contain illustrations by Clara Sheffield. The illustrations would include Clara's sketch of the school's new home in Regent's Park. There had been some talk about changing the name of the school to reflect the new location, and I was considering whether or not this was a good idea and whether I ought to mention the possibility of a new name in the article.

Then I heard our outside bell pull being rung.

And rung again.

Holmes shifted his weight from the window frame and took a few quick steps to rest on our breakfast table top, supporting himself as he shuffled slowly towards our fireplace. He sank into his usual chair.

"Lestrade," he said.

Soon there were footsteps on our stairs, and then the little inspector was at our door.

His ferret-like features were even more pinched and drawn than usual, and he did not meet my gaze as he removed his hat and overcoat. He sat where Holmes bade him to, in the fireplace chair opposite Holmes.

"We had a wire at the Yard," Lestrade said. "From the Montreal Police Service. Office of the Chief, no less."

Holmes's long fingers drummed impatiently on the armrest of his chair.

"It's not good news."

"Out with it then, Lestrade," Holmes said.

"The SS Montrose made port yesterday. A man and a woman matching the descriptions of Dr. Burleigh and Lady Scott debarked without incident. As per the arrangements made with Commissioner Bradford, Montreal Police Service constables followed the man and woman to a hotel, the Windsor, at Dominion Square. The Windsor is a highly fashionable and reputable establishment, according to the Police Service. The two persons in question registered under the names of Mr. and Mrs. John Watson."

"A touch of cruelty," Holmes said.

"I have no comment," I said.

"Well, they paid for it," said Lestrade. "This morning the maid on duty noticed that the door to their room had been left open. Both the occupants of the room were found dead. The man had been shot in the forehead, and the woman had been shot in the back of her skull. No gun was found in the room. A pillow from the sofa was found between the bodies, with two burns and holes in the fabric. The Police Service detective believes the pillow was employed to suppress the sound of the gunfire. No one on the floor heard any disturbance."

"Or would admit to hearing any," Holmes said.

Lestrade gave Holmes a sharp look. "I think I take your meaning, Mr. Holmes. Several known members of a Montreal criminal gang were seen entering and leaving the Windsor Hotel at a late hour last night by the constables assigned to observe the movements of the two persons involved. Of course, there was no way for the constables to know what was about to transpire. Or had transpired. Their duty was merely to watch for Dr. Burleigh and Mrs. Scott, not to protect them. The wire from Montreal made that point very clear."

Holmes said nothing.

"Come on, Mr. Holmes," Lestrade said. "You look as though you know exactly what happened."

Holmes gave one of his tight-lipped momentary smiles. "One may make a hypothesis, based on facts. Mr. Newman and his men saw Dr. Burleigh place the black silk sack into his pocket that night at Tussaud's. Both he and Dr. Burleigh believed the sack to contain genuine diamonds. A share of those diamonds would have been Newman's payment for his presence that night and for the attack and abduction services previously performed. When Dr. Burleigh fled without making payment, Mr. Newman would understandably have felt betrayed. Though imprisoned, he would have still have had the ability to order his seaport associates to track down the doctor and call upon his counterparts in Montreal to demand payment."

"But the diamonds you gave to Dr. Burleigh were glass," I said.

"Indeed. So Dr. Burleigh was unable to make the required payment when demand was made in Montreal. So the penalty was exacted. Mrs. Scott would have been a witness. She had to be eliminated."

Lestrade gave Holmes another sharp look. "Did you foresee this?" he asked.

Holmes shrugged. "What I foresaw or did not foresee is immaterial. To complete the record of the case, however, I should appreciate having photographs of the dead man and woman. Would you please arrange to have them sent from Montreal to London."

* * *

We heard from Lestrade again that night. He had personally interviewed Newman in the Newgate Prison hospital. The East End gang leader denied having any associates, or even any acquaintances, in Montreal.

LUCY

63. WEDDING BELLS

"You look perfect." My mother's face appeared in the looking glass next to mine.

It was always a slight shock to see myself with her this way, to trace out the resemblance between us when I had spent so much of my life not knowing who my mother was, much less that we looked so much alike. Seeing how the shape of her eyes, the curve of her cheekbones, echoed mine still came as a surprise, but in a warm, happy way.

Today my mother looked lovelier than ever in a deep green gown with touches of lace on the neckline and sleeves. Her eyes misted a little as she adjusted one of the pearl hairpins that held my veil in place, and then she stepped back and nodded her satisfaction. "Absolutely perfect."

"Thank you." I squeezed her hand. "I'm so glad you were able to come."

There was a tap at the door of 221A.

"That will be your father." My mother stepped back and turned to Becky. "Come along, Becky. That's our cue to be upstairs."

Becky and my mother had spent the past three days practicing playing the music for the wedding, my mother on her violin and Becky on the piano that had been carried upstairs from my room.

Becky hopped to her feet. She was wearing a rose pink taffeta dress with a full skirt and a wreath of pink roses in her hair. She looked up at me, her small face unusually solemn. "You look like a princess, Lucy. I'd like to hug you, but I'm afraid I'll step on your dress or wrinkle your veil."

"I'll take my chances." I crouched down so that I could hug her tightly. "You're the best sister I could have asked for."

Becky took my mother's hand and skipped off to open the door of the sitting room, letting Holmes come in. I saw him smile at my mother, and then she and Becky went out.

Uncle John, as best man, was already upstairs along with Jack. Although my mother hadn't let me see him, since, as she insisted, it was bad luck for the groom to see the bride before the wedding.

My father came into my room to meet me. After the close of the case, his fever had climbed to dangerous heights, and he had lain in bed for two days—which for Holmes was practically unheard of. Now he still looked slightly tired, his already sharp features drawn. But he was up and walking, dressed in an immaculately tailored morning suit, with a white gardenia in his buttonhole.

He stood a moment in the center of the sitting room, looking at me with the oddest expression on his face. If he had been anyone else, I would have said that there were tears in his eyes. Then he nodded, twice, without speaking, and cleared his throat.

"Shall we?"

He offered me his arm, and I took it.

"I'm sorry that we're wasting all your efforts and plans for a grand society wedding," I told him.

In the past two years of our acquaintance, I had learned that it was rare for Holmes to smile and still rarer for him to laugh. At that, though, he threw his head back and let out a burst of laughter that echoed through the sitting room.

"Do you know, Lucy, that may be the most amusing thing you have ever said to me."

Upstairs, I could hear Becky and my mother playing, although it was a piece by Chopin that they had also worked on, not yet the music that would signal that it was time for my father and me to walk upstairs.

"Is Uncle John all right, do you think?" Between my mother's arrival and making the arrangements for the ceremony to be performed here, we hadn't had the chance to speak about the end of the case. And I'd barely had the chance to see Watson these past few days.

"He will recover."

"I knew Mrs. Scott was guilty," I said. "Before Watson even found the letter that she'd left. She came to see me at the Savoy, and she slipped—she mentioned something about foreign women who came into the country with only tattoos to identify them. But she shouldn't have known anything about the marks on the murdered women at that point. I couldn't make myself tell Uncle John, though."

My father's expression didn't exactly alter, but it still softened in some indefinable way. "Watson is a rare soul, who has come through uglier experiences than this unmarred and with his faith in human goodness intact." He glanced at me. "You need not worry that he blames you or that his heart is broken."

"Do you think there's any chance that what Dr. Burleigh told us about his brother was true?" I asked. "About his genuinely *being* Jack the Ripper?"

My father raised one shoulder. "On the one side of the ledger, there is the matter of timing. The killings occurred when Trevor Burleigh was in London and stopped when he was sent away to the Transvaal. On the other hand, the details of these latest killings were sloppy in the extreme in their efforts to match the details of the first. The mind of a madman is in many ways, of course, a mystery, but one might presume that the actual killer would wish the recreations to be more exact."

"So it is possible that the Ripper may yet return?"

I hesitated to ask, knowing what it had cost him nine years ago to let the Ripper remain uncaught.

My father's face was serene, though, his gray eyes clear. "If he does, he will not slip through my grasp a second time. Tracking him will be an entirely different matter than it was nine years ago."

"Different? How so?"

I thought perhaps Holmes would say something about the cocaine habit he had given up. But instead he briefly covered my hand with his. "Because you will be with me. Your husband-to-be and Becky will also, no doubt, lend a hand." A quick smile touched the edges of my father's mouth. "It will be quite a family affair. If the Ripper does return, we shall track him together, and he will not escape."

I smiled, as above our heads, the strains of the wedding march on piano and violin began to play.

"Together," I agreed.

WATSON

64. A MOMENT TO REMEMBER

We had cleared the area in front of our fireplace, moving our hearthrug and two fireside chairs to the space just beneath our bow window. I stood with Jack where Holmes's chair had been, close to the mantel, my face and right side feeling the heat from the glowing coals.

Jack wore his black police sergeant's dress uniform. The wool fabric, with three embroidered gold chevrons on each sleeve, now had a pronounced sheen to it, evidence of the furiously intense bout of ironing the uniform had received that morning at the hands of little Becky.

That young lady herself, dressed in pink, now sat on Holmes's laboratory stool beside our entry door, working the upright piano that had been brought upstairs from Lucy's room and now blocked our view of Holmes's acid-charred bench of chemicals and scientific charts. Becky's little fingers roamed over the piano keys. She had completed an air of Chopin's that had been agreed on as the first of the introductory melodies and was now determinedly eliciting the familiar strains of "Jesu, Joy of Man's Desiring." Beside Becky, Zoe sat in front of Holmes's desk, her violin tucked beneath her chin, playing the accompaniment with professional assurance.

The three other guests for the wedding waited on our settee, closer to where Jack and I stood. Mycroft Holmes, in his morning coat, hands clasped comfortably across his capacious waistcoat, occupied nearly half the available space. Lestrade, also in a morning coat, perched uncomfortably at the other end. He had jammed himself in, twisting his body around in an attempt to leave room for Mrs. Hudson, who sat primly between the two men. Our landlady had dressed herself in a yellow taffeta affair for the occasion. As the music continued, her fingertips kept straying to the fabric of her billowing skirt to keep it from overflowing Mycroft's striped trousers.

The date was Sunday, November 14. Not Advent Sunday as originally planned, but nonetheless a joyous day.

We were waiting for the return of Frederick Temple, Archbishop of Canterbury. A robust, genial fellow in his fifties, Temple had arrived only moments earlier and had rushed upstairs in my sleeping room to don his ceremonial robes. He had cautioned us that on no account were the musicians to begin the wedding march until specifically directed. He had an important matter to attend to before the bride and her father could enter.

Mrs. Hudson kept turning towards our entry doorway in anticipation, trying to see around Mycroft. I believe I was the most nervous person in the room. I kept reaching into my pocket to be sure that the rings for both Lucy and Jack were still there, hefting them again and again for reassurance.

Then we heard Temple's footsteps coming down my stairs, and moments later he was among us, his black stole draped over his flowing white robe. He held something in his hand.

"Ladies, would you please continue to play," he said, softly. "Detective Sergeant John Kelly, would you please step forward." Jack did so and came to attention.

"Mr. Kelly, as Mr. Mycroft Holmes here will confirm, I am authorized and directed by Her Majesty's Government to present you with an honor that is long overdue." The Archbishop's friendly face, framed by luxuriant brown and gray side-whiskers, crinkled in a smile as he revealed the medal that he had been holding. He lifted it up so that we all could see. All of us, that is, except little Becky, who, leaning forward and paying strict attention to her music, still kept on playing, her back to those of us who were clustered around her older brother.

The medal was a bronze cross, attached to a crimson ribbon.

The Archbishop's voice, though still subdued, took on a more formal tone. "Detective Sergeant Kelly, I am here because nearly six months ago you saved my life and the lives of many others at the Queen's Jubilee Celebration of Thanksgiving at St. Paul's Cathedral. You were seriously wounded. And yet, three weeks ago you risked your own life once again. You saved more lives that night, and you were instrumental in the capture of a dangerous criminal. This medal is awarded to recognize your conspicuous gallantry in the face of the enemy. It is the Victoria Cross."

The piano music faltered.

I saw Zoe squeeze her eyes shut, but she kept on with her violin, not missing a note.

A moment later Becky resumed play, striking the keys even more firmly than before. Beneath her pink dress, her narrow little back was now ramrod-straight.

The Archbishop continued, "I am honored and grateful to

present this medal to you."

"No more than my duty," Jack replied.

Mycroft, Mrs. Hudson, and Lestrade each nodded in satisfaction.

The medal was soon pinned to Jack's uniform. The Archbishop motioned to Jack to return to his place at my side.

"Now let us all stand and face the entrance," he said, gesturing towards our open entry door and to our hallway and the stairs beyond. "Will the musicians kindly begin the wedding march."

My heartbeat thundered in my ears, but above the sound of the music I heard and counted seventeen footfalls upon each of our seventeen steps, coming upward and ever nearer, and keeping perfect time to Mendelssohn's melody.

Then Holmes and Lucy appeared, framed in our doorway. Father and bride paused for only a moment, her hand resting lightly on his forearm.

His gray eyes flashed as he surveyed the room and caught his breath.

Her green eyes, even behind her thin white veil, shone wide and radiant with joy.

THE END

HISTORICAL NOTES

This is a work of fiction, and the authors make no claim that any of the historical locations or historical figures appearing in this story had even the remotest connection with the adventures recounted herein.

However ...

1. The Bethnal Green School was inspired by a full-page advertisement that appears in *An Almanack for the Year of Our Lord 1897 by Joseph Whitaker*. The advertisement, for "Dr. Barnardo's Homes," states: "All the Girls are brought up in Cottages on the family system, and carefully instructed in the various branches of Domestic Service. 8,725 trained and tested children have already been placed out in the Colonies. Of these, 98 per cent have been successful. FUNDS ARE URGENTLY NEEDED FOR FOOD AND MAINTENANCE."

2. The descriptions of waxwork exhibits in this story are taken from the 1897 *Madame Tussaud's Exhibition Catalogue* written by George Augustus Sala. Madame Tussaud's Museum continues to be located in London on Marylebone Road, near Baker Street, a five-minute walk from The Sherlock Holmes Museum.

3. Cecil Rhodes famously established the Rhodes Scholarship program at Oxford, where he attended classes between 1876 and 1878. He frequently created a distraction during lectures by allowing other students to examine a small box of diamonds that he habitually carried in his waistcoat pocket. However, the idea of Rhodes's funding the purchase of a London estate house to support a school for women is entirely fictional, as are the characters of the two Burleigh brothers and Lady Scott. Additional details regarding the diamond trade have been taken from Rachel Lichtenstein's *Diamond Street: the Hidden World of Hatton Garden*.

4. An abundance of material is available on the Whitechapel murders of 1889, with many theories concerning the historical identity of the person or persons referred to as Jack the Ripper. We humbly and gratefully leave it to others to solve that unsolved mystery.

A NOTE OF THANKS
TO OUR READERS

Thank you for reading this latest book in the *Sherlock Holmes and Lucy James Mystery Series*.

If you've enjoyed the story, we would very much appreciate you going to the page where you bought the book and uploading a quick review. As you probably know, reviews make a big difference!

The other six adventures in the series are currently available in e-book, paperback and audiobook formats. The audiobook version of *The Return of the Ripper* will be available sometime in mid 2018. We hope you'll enjoy it – and that you'll tell your friends!

To keep up with our latest escapades, please visit our website: www.SherlockandLucy.com

ABOUT THE AUTHORS

Anna Elliott is the author of the *Twilight of Avalon* trilogy, and *The Pride and Prejudice Chronicles*. She was delighted to lend a hand in giving the character of Lucy James her own voice, firstly because she loves Sherlock Holmes as much as her father, Charles Veley, and second because it almost never happens that someone with a dilemma shouts, "Quick, we need an author of historical fiction!" She lives in Maryland with her husband and three children.

Charles Veley is the author of the first two books in this series of fresh Sherlock Holmes adventures. He is thrilled to be contributing Dr. Watson's chapters for this and future books in the series, and delighted beyond words to be collaborating with Anna Elliott.

CONTENTS

PREFACE 1

PART ONE

1. A HARBINGER 5

2. AN UNIDENTIFIED BODY 11

3. A STUDY IN DIAMONDS 17

4. ANOTHER PLACE, A LESSER CRIME 25

5. AT GROSVENOR SQUARE 31

6. AN ODD ARREST 39

7. LOST IN TRANSLATION 45

8. OBSERVATIONS AT A SMALL CAFE 55

9. WEDDING PLANS 61

10. AT THE RECTORY 67

11. SOME DOCUMENTS IN THE CASE 73

12. AN UNCONSCIOUS ASSAILANT 81

13. FLOWERS FROM AN ADMIRER 87

14. AT THE FUTURE HOME 97

15. MIDNIGHT AT BAKER STREET 109

PART TWO

16. GRIM NEWS 117

17. AT THE STATION HOUSE 127

18. A TATTOO 137

19. HELP FROM A STREET BOY 145

20. AN OLD OPPONENT 151

21. A MISSING WOMAN 163

22. AN INTERVIEW WITH HOLMES 171

23. HOLMES ENLISTS MY AID 181

24. AT MADAME TUSSAUD'S 185

25. MORE FLOWERS FOR GRACE 191

26. A MEETING ENDS BADLY 203

27. A MESSAGE FROM LESTRADE 207

28. DEAR BOSS 213

PART THREE

29. CARRY ON 219

30. AN UNWELCOME VISITOR 221

31. ON BAKER STREET 227

32. ATTACKED 231

33. FOUND 241

34. A MISTAKE 245

35. ANOTHER SURPRISE 257

36. LOST 263

37. COUNCIL OF WAR 273

38. THE UNANSWERABLE QUESTION 277

39. A REVELATION 289

40. HOW TO SEND A MESSAGE? 295

41. A CLUE 297

42. SURVEILLANCE 303

43. DEFYING AN ULTIMATUM 307

44. TO STAY ALIVE 311

45. ROUGH WEATHER 313

PART FOUR

46. WHAT DAY IS IT? 323

47. MY ASSIGNMENT 331

48. A DISCOVERY 333

49. SEARCHING THE RECORDS 337

50. A FEVER 341

51. THE HOUSE OF DEATH 349

52. AWAKENING 353

53. OUT OF THE DARKNESS 359

54. BAKER STREET 363

55. A DOCTOR'S CONFESSION 367

56. A PROMISE 371

57. CONFRONTATION IN WHITECHAPEL 373

58. CONFRONTATION IN MARYLEBONE 379

59. DIAMONDS AND GLASS 385

60. AT BURLEIGH HOUSE 391

61. REPARATIONS ON DOWNING STREET 397

62. NEWS FROM CANADA 405

63. WEDDING BELLS 409

64. A MOMENT TO REMEMBER 413

HISTORICAL NOTES 417

A NOTE OF THANKS TO OUR READERS 419

ABOUT THE AUTHORS 421